Praise for *The Empty Throne*

'*Those Above* is a clever book, shot through with clever ideas, dry humour and steady world building . . . those looking for well-created and beautifully created fantasy, which also happens to be both darkly comic and devastatingly grim, will find themselves swiftly addicted'   *Starburst*

'At times bleak, never dull and always entertaining, this is the work of a first-class worldbuilder'   *Sci Fi Bulletin*

'Gripping . . . Polansky has pulled off a polished fantasy thriller that's very much in the George RR Martin/Joe Abercrombie vein, but has still given the book its own distinctive style and voice, alongside plenty of evocative world-building. The *Empty Throne* (series) looks set to be fascinating and provocative'   *SFX*

'Prepare yourself to be blown away'
                                        The Bibliophile Chronicles

'A cracking good adventure . . . *Those Above* is *I, Claudius* by way of Tolkien and filtered through Chandler. That is to say, really damn good'   *Pornokitsch*

'The conflict between the privileged and the impoverished comes to a hell of a head in the concluding volume of Daniel Polansky's deterministic duology'   *Tor.com*

'*Those Above* is an excellent new series from an author that has gone from strength to strength. Dark, epic and a eloquent, *Those Above* is a delight to read'

I

Two men came walking past first, porters or one-time porters, thick legs and bent backs and mean eyes. They spent a long moment silently scrutinising Seed and Dray and Quail. They didn't make any threats, except in so far as their presence was a threat; their very existence was a threat.

Seed made sure to look straight back at them, without blinking or bowing his head. They were looking for moles, agents of the Those Above, and Seed was most certainly not that – just your average Fifth Rung slum kid, about at that age when it was time to get marked as a porter, or to get work on the plantations outside of the city. No different from ten thousand others on the lowest levels of the Roost, strutting about in worn pants during the late afternoon, faces dirty, looking to get forget-yourself drunk. He was big and he was tough, but there were plenty boys bigger and plenty men tougher; the Fifth Rung was the sort of place that bred rowdies and brutes and straight-up killers in great profusion. The only thing that made him noteworthy – and this might have been stretching the point – was his busted eye, the lid drooping, the iris lazy and unresponsive. He had never been a handsome man but there was a difference between being homely and being deformed, a difference he had had a long time to ponder in the two and a half years since a Barrow boy had beaten the scars into his face.

Dray and Quail couldn't even claim that distinction, if being made ugly enough that you couldn't get a woman to look at you without a couple of tertarum in your hand was a distinction. Seed did not think it was; in fact he thought it was quite the opposite. Seed thought what had been done to his face was the sort of thing worth holding a grudge about, and he thought also that there was no point in holding on to a grudge when you could even it up. This was the reason that he was standing against the wall of a run-down building a few minutes' walk from the docks, getting eyeballed by a pair of Dead Pigeons.

One of the soldiers nodded, and then they both headed back upslope, and a moment later Thistle came strutting past, and whatever doubts Seed had about his errand were forgotten at the first sight of that arrogant smile, those eyes that were heavy and cold as a stone unearthed from the bottom of a riverbed. 'Hello, brothers,' he said. Seed couldn't remember if he had ever heard him talk before; Seed didn't think so. Seed didn't like the fact that he liked his voice, which was deep and slow and seemed to emanate from somewhere far within his chest. 'Walk with me.'

Thistle turned and headed east, headed east without looking back, and Seed hated him all over again, hated him as much for his arrogance as for what he had done to Seed's eye.

Of course they'd been hearing rumours about the Five-Fingers for years – you could always find men foolish or mad enough to dream and even speak of retribution and rebellion and revolution, as you could find men foolish or mad enough to speak of climbing up the sky and casting the sun down to earth. The Fifth Rung had no shortage of inebriates and lunatics. But then, you couldn't exactly call them madmen, not this last year, not with half the docks attending their secret rallies, not with all the whispers you heard of bulging coffers and gangs of well-trained hard boys. Rumours are like smoke of course, but still, you smell enough of it and you'd be wise to start looking for fire. And amidst the many other stories that spread swift across the lower Rungs, there was one of Pyre, the First of His Line, leader of the militant wing of the Five-Fingered.

Dead Pigeons they were called, after their preferred form of intimidation, birds left bleeding on the doorsteps of their opponents. To murder an avian was a capital offence in the Roost, as far as the authorities were concerned one more serious than theft or assault, worse than rape, worse even than carrying a weapon. A man mad enough to do that publicly was a man mad enough to do anything, and moreover a man who knew where you lived.

If this lesson went unheeded, they had other ways of making their point. A Cuckoo on the Fourth Rung renowned for a particularly severe brand of sadism was found butchered one morning in the whorehouse that he had frequented. A notoriously corrupt bureaucrat, famed even by the standards of his kind for avarice, cupidity and licentiousness, went missing on his way upslope one evening. He showed up two days later absent the small fingers on both of his hands and talking of nothing but redemption, of his own evils and what he would do to make up for them, talking of it loudly and frequently in the main thoroughfare running along the docks, having traded wealth and iniquity for the life of a penniless preacher. There were others – men disappeared into the sewers and men made silent from fear of such, and soon the Cuckoos, the Roost's human guard, had come to speak quietly rather than with their characteristic belligerence, and would not go out in the evening except in the company of their fellows, eyes roaming and hands tight about their ferules.

It was to Pyre that this change was attributed, and the first bounty had gone out on his head a year past: five golden eagles, the Eternal currency, used only by those directly in their employ, the seneschals and high servants. Five golden eagles was more money than a man on the Fifth Rung would earn in a grim lifetime of labour, and though it doubled and then doubled and then doubled again, still it was not enough to bring word of Pyre's location to the men who sought him harm. The Fifth did not give up its secrets so casually.

Seed did not care about any of that. The Five-Fingers could hold hands with the Four and jump in the bay so far as he was concerned. Seed had never given a thought to politics, never even given a thought that someone might. Life at the docks was personal, it started with your best friend and it ended with your worst enemy, and the distance between them was a few minutes' walk.

Thistle led them towards one of the pumphouses, part of the vast engine that leeched water out of the bay and sent it, some several cables, some practical infinity, upslope. The pumps were what gave the Fifth its character, if by character you meant an unpleasant smell of wet and an ever-present slurping sound, like a drunken fart. Two men were half-lounging around outside it; not the sort of thing a passing Cuckoo would have flagged but Seed could tell them for what they were: more security for the boy-king of the Fifth Rung. One of them was large and dark and held Seed's eyes unflinchingly, then opened the door swiftly and allowed them entrance.

Inside was a small stone chamber covered with a thick layer of junk and debris, for in years past the pumphouse had been the gathering place of the neighbourhood children, to get drunk and to boast and to try to while away the impoverished hours of their pointless lives. There was a thick pallet in the centre of the room that Thistle was even then removing, revealing a hole leading down into the earth.

'The sewers?' Dray asked, voice wavering, and even Seed, for a moment, looked less than firm. Because despite living surrounded by this great web of piping the men and women of the Fifth had no real idea of how the thing worked, except that sometimes it was filled with water and sometimes it was not, and when it was full then anything inside it would most assuredly be dead. There was a pumphouse near where Seed lived; it was a rite of passage to descend beneath it and swim across the subterranean river below, a journey of no more than five minutes, tip to tail, but even so everyone made sure to do it just after the last heavy flow had subsided, when the risk of flood was minimal. Seed figured that most of the rest of the boys on the Fifth must have a similar sort of ritual, and most of them displayed the same sort of prudence. There were a lot of ways to die, as Seed reckoned, and none of them seemed very good, but there weren't many that seemed worse than being caught below ground once the slurps started going heavy, the rats screaming and trying to escape, you screaming and doing the same and both of you failing.

But Thistle didn't hesitate, not for even a second, and it was this that made Seed capable of doing the same, though Quail and Dray blanched white as chalk and were a long slow time following them down.

Seed descended hand over hand, and after a few rungs the darkness had grown all-consuming. He could not make out Thistle beneath him, nor the leather of his boots, nor the ladder in front of him nor the hands that held it.

'Don't fear, brothers.' Thistle's voice, ringing clearly from the black. 'Our people have laboured beneath the mountain in days beyond memory, and she has not forgotten us. The demons live atop her and think they know her secrets – as if the owner knows more of a house than its tenant!'

Thistle had a lantern lit and hung before Seed made it all the way down, but its dim light failed to reach to the high far corners of the chamber. At either end were heavy floodgates, drop-walls of thickly forged iron. At different points in the day, according to no particular rhythm that anyone on the Fifth ever managed to figure, those gates would close, and the chamber would be flooded. This was not Seed's foremost concern at the moment, however. In the dim light he could see the waters rushing down towards the bay, and the stone walls covered with moss, and also that Thistle was carrying a knife long enough to reasonably be called a sword. It must have been hidden beneath the travelling cloak that hung now next to the lantern, and Seed stared at it so nakedly and for so long that he thought Thistle must now be certain of his purpose, if he hadn't already deduced it.

'I welcome you then to the abode of the Five-Fingers. Perhaps it does not look like much, but it is ours, brothers, yours and mine, and a shack freely owned is better than a mansion entailed.'

There were three of them against Thistle's one, was what Seed was thinking, and all three of them were carrying blades. But they were small things, shivs really, bits of sharpened metal they had found or stolen. The way Thistle rested his hand on his own weapon made Seed think that neither their knives nor their numbers would do them much good.

But it was too late to back out now – probably Thistle wouldn't let him leave, anyway, and there were still those men waiting outside, likely with the same kind of weapon as Thistle was carrying, likely no less skilled. And then the thought of seeing the sun again, of the light shining on Seed and on the shame as yet unanswered, proved enough to spur him onward.

'I guess you don't remember me.' He had said it a thousand times in his mind, a thousand times a thousand, and it had never sounded so foolish or so hollow.

'Of course I remember – did you think that I would lead three strangers into our headquarters, what with half of our besotted species still doing the work of the demons?' Thistle slipped his blade from its sheath so cleanly and so swiftly that Quail and Dray jumped clear back, and there was an instant when Seed felt sure that he would die in the sewers beneath the Rung, that his body would be food for the rats or float listlessly out to sea, his body and the bodies of his friends.

So when Thistle flipped it to him, hilt first, Seed was so startled that he nearly dropped it into the sewer water; and what a shame that would have been, something so beautiful and so deadly lost amidst the dark. He managed to catch it by the very tip of the pommel, found it was heavier than he had imagined, found that he now had no idea what to do with it.

'You wish revenge,' Thistle said. It was a statement but Seed heard it as a question. 'I cannot blame you. It is all we are taught to do, violence, all we believe ourselves capable of. The demons prefer it that way, prefer us weak and broken and foolish, know that if we ever stopped feuding among ourselves we would recall our strength, as in days of old, and be capable of greatness.'

'Stop talking like that,' Seed said.

'Like what?'

'Like you're on stage, like you're giving a speech, like you're so damn special.'

'You'd rather I dip into that downslope chatter, 'ey boy? Rather I grab a few bullyboys so we can get a good scrap going? You'd rather I turned my sword on you, as I would have when I was Thistle, turned it against you and had half a dozen men waiting down here to do the same? I'm afraid I cannot do so. I have been reborn, consecrated in the service of something a thousand times larger than myself, something so vast and so beautiful that before it my life is as a scrap of paper near a flame.'

'This is birdshit,' Seed said, and when he said it his voice cracked, and when his voice cracked he swung the blade upright. 'You might have the rest of the city conned, but I know you, I know you down to your bones. You're a brute, same as me, same as any of us. Two years ago you was part of Rhythm's crew, going to get the Brotherhood's scar on your shoulder, a pimp and a thug.'

'It is true, my ignorance was vast. For a time, before I heard the truth, before my light was kindled, I was everything that you say. I carried a blade in the service of a man, I leeched from my people, I was a thief and a thug. But no longer, brothers, no longer. Now I carry a blade in service of men, to restore their freedom, to lead them, bleary-eyed and blinking, into the dawn to come.'

'You won't be around to see it,' Seed said, the tip of the sword pointing at the tender flesh of Thistle's breast.

'Perhaps. But it will arrive just the same.'

Seed found that his fingers were curled so tight round Pyre's sword, Thistle's sword he meant, this little Barrow cunt could call himself whatever he wanted but it wouldn't put Seed's eye back into place, would it? Wouldn't make him pretty like he'd used to be, wouldn't make the girls in the street stop turning away when he brushed down the boulevard. And fine, it wasn't as if Seed hadn't done things similar; there was that one dust-up with one of the crews to the east where he'd ended up breaking a bottle over some kid's head, and Seed had never seen him again but had heard he didn't talk so well any more – but so what? This wasn't a question of fairness, this wasn't a question of justice, this was a question of revenge, this was a question of clearing a slate, that was the only justice a boy from the Fifth knew anything about, could ever know.

The sword clattered loudly against stone.

'What is your name?'

'Seed.'

'Seed is the name they gave you,' Pyre said, smiling and shaking his head. 'Boy they called Seed – there is someone you should meet.'

2

Eudokia had last seen Protostrator Konstantinos Aurelia, her stepson and the leader of the Aelerian armies in Salucia, eighteen months earlier, marching at the head of his themas down the great trunk road that led north out of the capital, the entirety of the city thronging the streets, shrieking their love of him until it seemed almost a physical thing, a brisk wind, a strong current. He had accepted the adoration with dignity, if not quite enthusiasm, as if this was one more trial to be overcome, and he would prefer to save his strength for those ahead. He had looked marvellous, absolutely marvellous, dressed as a typical hoplitai with chain armour and a standard short sword, but so broad-shouldered and gorgeous that women were said to faint as he passed by, to faint and be crushed beneath the uncaring hooves of the crowd. It had been the crowning achievement of his life to that point, the moment he had been fitted for nearly since birth; if it had been the end of his labours he could have retired knowing that no man had ever performed so skilfully.

Alas then, that there was still the war to be fought.

Six months they had been forced to wait at the borders of the Commonwealth while the Roost gave its consent for two slave nations to wage war – fine, he could not be blamed for that, nor for the long winter that had after been wasted. And the first part of this year's campaign had gone well enough. They had finally met the enemy at Bod's Wake, and if the result was not the signal victory that Eudokia's propaganda machine had proclaimed it, still it had been the Salucians who had found themselves in rapid retreat northward, towards the heartland and the nation's capital.

But that had been nearly four months previous, and the time since had been spent camped in front of Oscan, the themas diminishing daily and a second winter growing close. As the trees had budded and then blossomed and were now shortly to die away again, so had the gallant youth she had waved farewell to diminished. There was grey at his temples, a shade she found difficult to square with the immaturity he had somehow managed to retain from the first moment he had been presented to her, a tow-headed child of fifteen. He had on the same chain armour that he had worn while marching out of the capital, but it looked better used, no longer an affectation but as natural as the sallow skin it covered. His eyes were cramped, and uncertain.

He sat at his desk, as if so engrossed in his work he had failed to notice her arrival. A pretence, and not a particularly good one either, meant to show how hard he was working, how seriously he took his task though his efforts had not yet been crowned with success. By the gods, how she yearned for a man, a true man, and not simply a long-limbed boy!

'Revered Mother,' he said, rising swiftly. At least he had not forgotten that much. He leaned in and kissed her on the cheek. 'How was the journey from the capital?'

'Tedious. As will be the next leg. How fares the child of my beloved Phocas, upon whom the hopes and prayers of Aeleria reside?'

Konstantinos made an attempt at stoicism, but he wasn't very good at it and also he didn't try for very long. 'It is no easy thing, being the leader of men.'

'Do tell.'

'The Salucians have bottled themselves up inside the city, and they have provisions to last out the winter. Every day we lose ten men from disease, and it won't be long until we start losing more from the cold. If they'd only come out and give fair battle, we'd roll right through them, but . . .'

It was almost as if they would prefer not to die, Eudokia thought. A clever people, the Salucians, but then again wit wasn't everything. A well-timed jibe would not get you so much as a swift blow to the jaw, and whatever the poets might say, one doesn't ride to battle holding a pen. 'Heavy are the burdens required of great men. Broad must be their shoulders.'

'It's not like with the sea lords. The truth is they weren't nearly so hard to kill as everyone made out. A ragtag bunch, and they had no walls to hide behind.'

Not for the first time Eudokia wondered if it had been wise to arrange the short series of naval battles that had cleared the southern coast of pirates and established within the minds of the more credulous citizenry – a group that apparently included Konstantinos himself – her stepson's reputation for invincibility. The Gentleman Lion, they had taken to calling him, and it seemed clear he had heard the name.

'The Salucians send peace offerings weekly,' he informed her, as if she had not already known, as if there had ever been anything, down to the contents of his meal and the specificity of his toilet, that Eudokia did not understand better than did her stepson.

'Yes?'

'They have promised to make Oscan a free city, one without official ties to either of our nations. But I think if pressed, they would agree to allow for incorporation within the Commonwealth, provided we give sufficient guarantees that our expansion will cease thereafter.'

'Honeyed words hide false promises. Weakened and tottering

on the precipice, they offer something that is ours by right and soon in fact. In a few years, when they have rebuilt their walls and replenished their stocks, when they have hired mercenary armies from the east, we will see how firm their commitment to amity. We have not come to wound the Salucians, we have come to cripple them. To ensure that never again will the children of Aeleria fear the machinations of the bitch-Queen of Hyrcania.'

'Every peace is temporary,' Konstantinos said, and for a long moment he would not look at her. 'And I sometimes wonder if the children of Aeleria would not be better served if their lives were frittered away less casually. At Bod's Wake there were so many corpses that you could walk from one end of the field to the next without ever taking your boot off flesh. At night I dream of them, and I dream of Enkedri beyond them, and he asks me what was my purpose in leading so many to death, why my gain needed to be bought with their blood, and I have no answer for him, Mother, I have no answer—'

The sharp slap echoed loudly within the tent. 'Revered Mother,' Eudokia hissed, 'and by the gods you seem suddenly so fond of, do not again forget it.'

It had been a calculated provocation, as was virtually everything that Eudokia did. And, like virtually everything Eudokia did, it had the intended effect. Konstantinos blinked twice, and the colour began to return to his face. He looked angry and ashamed, but at least he no longer looked like he was going to vomit on his trousers, or turn his knife against himself.

'Men die,' Eudokia said simply, 'such is the purpose of men – or did you suppose mortality some recent invention of your own? The themas are blessed to expire in service of their beloved Aeleria, in service of her national destiny. To die is their burden. To lead them into battle is yours, as it was your father's, and it shames me to watch you quiver beneath it. The world is filled with men, the world shakes them off, daily, hourly, every moment, unmourned and unconsidered, as a mutt does fleas. Would you be more than just a man? Would you be great? This is the price asked of you, the price demanded. It is no small thing. It is too much for most.' Eudokia laid her hand along the high cheekbones of her nephew, let it rest there a moment, for one does not rule by the lash alone. 'Be at peace, my beloved child. A great task has Aeleria asked of you, and she will offer the tools to complete it. The Senate, in recognition of the importance of your duty, has voted you three more themas.' And what arm-bending had that taken; two of them had come from the Marches and she had been forced to pay a call on every senator with an estate in the hinterlands, offering assurances that the Marchers had been well and truly obliterated. Which of course had been her purpose in provoking them into revolt some years earlier, making certain of her western flank before moving east.

The news of his reinforcements spread across Konstantinos's face like a shot of fine liquor, steadied his eyes and brought fresh bloom to his face. 'Three themas?'

'March-hardened veterans to a man,' she said soothingly. 'We'll show these Salucians what it is to quibble with the might of the Commonwealth. Aelerian boots will echo on the cobblestone streets of Oscan, and you will be first among the throng. Your name will be sung centuries after your death, future generations of children will play beneath the shadow of the great statues they erect in your honour.' Eudokia stretched her arm out, as if pointing to this vision in the distance. 'All that a man would wish to possess, wealth and fame and fortune nation, all of it, yes, all of it, will be yours.' Excepting power, of course – power would remain in the hands of that person most capable of wielding it, and Eudokia did not suppose there to be any question as to where that lay. 'The strain upon you has been a terrible thing, and you have borne it manfully. But what great task was ever accomplished without sacrifice? One must wager to win, and the stakes in this game are not gold nor silver but blood and sinew and the spirit that animates them. The gods have set this task in front of you, and will not fail so long as you answer it.'

Konstantinos was smiling now, not broadly but the hint of it at least, eyes filled with visions of a future in which the world knew him to be everything he had always supposed himself to be.

Such a narrow thing, between arrogance and dejection! Best to bring him back down a notch. 'And finally, you ought not let your guilt trouble you so, for the simple reason that you are not really in charge, and never were. If anyone will have to answer to the gods for this tally, it will be Eudokia.' She smoothed out the folds of her robes. 'Now if there's nothing else, it's been a very long day, and I could quite use a bath.'

Konstantinos was up swiftly, off to speak to an attendant and see to the Revered Mother's demands.

3

Coming through the basalt walls and into the Fifth Rung, Calla's mouth had gone dry and her knees had started shaking like a drunkard's hands. She had imagined that this was as frightened as she was capable of, that she had reached the very apex of her terror; indeed it was this ignorance that had allowed her to continue downslope, certain that she had reached her moment of truth, and that so long as she continued through it, pushed beyond it, she would find strength on the other side.

For a time this was even true. Her steps eased, she enjoyed a growing sense of confidence. The men who gave her passing looks did so out of lust and not because they saw through her disguise, which was identical to that worn downslope, homespun robes and boots that were more comfortable than lovely. She would betray herself when she spoke, she knew, but then there was some fair portion of the Fifth who had once been servants or workers on the higher Rungs and had lost those positions from misfortune or misbehaviour. And anyway she wouldn't need to do much talking, only to listen and to remember.

But when Calla first heard the call of the pipes – like a fat man's belch, mud leaking into boots, other, less pleasant things – and when they came into sight, splitting out from the depths of the sloping mountain on which the Roost was built, weaving through the crumbling tenements and one-room shacks and worn storefronts like the bleached bones of some long-dead giant, the full and unhindered force of her folly descended upon her. Alone, alone entirely, for the first time in her life beyond the reach of the Lord's four-fingered hands, outside of the protection she enjoyed by virtue of who she was and where she lived, by virtue of being born in a portion of the Roost where the Eternal held a strict monopoly on the use of force.

She pulled herself off the main thoroughfare, set her back against an alleyway, watched the shadows gather, wondering at the time. There were no road signs below the Third Rung, at least none that Calla could identify. The landmarks with which she used to navigate upslope, the Perpetual Spire on the easternmost edge of the Rung, the Source rising above that even, the centrepiece and the highest point of the city, were long since lost from view. On the First and the Second the great clocks rang out at regular intervals, but downslope there seemed to be no public timepieces of any kind, and Calla felt as lost temporally as she was geographically, unmoored entirely from her life's ambit.

When he had summoned her late the evening prior, Calla had known that there was something momentous afoot. For thirty-one years she had served the Aubade, Lord of the Red Keep, now the Prime, first among equals if not the outright leader of Those Above, and nearly ten of them had been as his chief seneschal. During none of them had he ever felt it necessary to call her after the end of her working day. At the very top of his vast citadel, illuminated by the fat autumn moon and its attendant stars, he had run through the situation, explaining the matter slowly, persuading rather than commanding.

'I know what I'm asking of you,' he had said, standing still against the evening, his four long fingers bent round themselves, shoulders straight, tendrils of hair like strong hemp twisting down to his ankles. 'And would have you understand the same. It could be – it will be dangerous. But there are currents at work in the Roost that must be investigated, and they stir in corners of the city where no Eternal could be seen. I have put my trust in your line for half a dozen generations – will you give me the same honour?'

Calla would have said yes to anything at that moment, would have said yes out of sheer pride, even if she did not sense as well as the Aubade that her city was angled atop a precipice, even if she did not have, whatever he might think or know, as deep and profound a love for her home as did any Four-Finger.

Calla thought of that passion then, tried to recall some flicker of it, to kindle that flame into a light strong enough to illuminate a path forward. Late afternoon and the porters were making their last run of the day, bent-backed men carrying goods and foodstuffs upslope without complaint – or, anyway, with no complaint they thought worth voicing. The children of the evening were just beginning to shake themselves out from whatever holes they scuttled into during the day, the men dressed better than the porters and standing conscientiously and stiffly upright. Two women who could only be, even to Calla's unpractised eyes, whores, lounged on the steps of a tenement; blank faces and bedroom eyes, not yet covered in the paint they would use to attract their evening coin.

A fat man coming out of a bar noticed her air of uncertainty, lurched over with a rooster's gait. 'Everything all right there, girlie? You lost or something? You need some help, maybe?'

Looking at him, unpleasant smile and chicken fat greasing back stringy hair, Calla was reminded again of who she was. 'You might move downwind, and relieve me of your stench.'

The lounging whores laughed loudly and without kindness. The fat man scowled nastily, lust to cruelty in three snaps of a finger, like most of his sex. Calla ignored him and continued onward.

She could find the docks; anyone could find the docks, one needed only to walk downslope until one could walk downslope no more, until the mud streets gave way to cobblestone, the vast quay that girdled the eastern base of the mountain and stretched into the bay. On a different day, in different circumstances, it would have been something to see. Even early in the evening it bustled, foreigners and Roostborn. Silk-clad Parthans and servile Salucians and unsmiling Aelerians. Here and here alone among the vastness of the Fifth there seemed to be some semblance of order, the occasional custodian dressed in blue robes and carrying heavy ferules. As little interest or control as the Eternal and human authorities of the Roost had for the lower Rungs, the docks were a different story. Most of the Roost's food came from the plantations outside of the city, the only avenue of work for a downslope youth who refused to turn porter, but everything else – ore and raw materials, trade goods, wine and ale – came from the surrounding nations, as tribute or trade, swallowed in the bellies of the towering wooden ships that obscured her view of the sea, transported thousands of cables across the Tullus coast, spat back out again here at the bottom of the Fifth Rung.

The docks, at least, were clearly signed, and Calla walked swiftly east along the wharf, then over a high-arching, white stone bridge, above a canal of water that had begun its journey as a droplet from the Source. Back on solid ground she turned upslope, following along with the portion of the Lord's directions she had memorised. The Aubade had not told her how he had learned the location of the meeting – as the Prime he had access to whatever rudimentary intelligence service the Roost could claim – but however he had acquired it, Calla found it authenticated almost as soon as she had passed out of range of the docks. The Five-Fingered wore rough canvas trousers and colourless wool-spun shirts, and they wore them as if they were badge or armour, caging a potent and terrible force, one that might erupt into brutality at any moment. They stood at even intervals, watching the passer-by with a more than casual interest. About the same time she realised that her movement was no longer entirely self-directed, that without realising she had gotten caught in a current of pedestrians. They were feeding themselves into a vast warehouse a short way upslope, one of the massive standing structures built for holding stock, though this evening it seemed to have been repurposed. The current slowed and then stopped, the guards at the front inspecting each entrant.

With forward motion stilled it became impossible not to notice the innumerable contrasts that marked her out as alien. Not only her costume, which despite its rough make was finer than anything any of the other women in line were wearing, but her demeanour itself. The crowd stood in a fever of anticipation, nervous and enthusiastic, speaking with expectant happiness to the newly discovered friends in front and behind. Meanwhile Calla's fear had again grown so loud in her mind that she felt certain it must draw attention, that at any moment the packed mass would turn as one and stare at her, first revealing and then punishing her deception.

Before she could make up her mind to leave, Calla found herself at the front, two men guarding the entrance and looking at her with serious attention.

'Greetings, sister,' said the smaller of the two. 'You have come for the meeting?'

She nodded and looked aside awkwardly.

'Do you know the word?'

'I did not know I needed one,' she said quietly, trying to appear meek and unsure of herself, a girl far from home, trying and not finding the guise particularly difficult.

The guards looked at each other, wary though not unfriendly. 'May we see your brand, sister?' said the larger of the two, still smiling but forceful, and coming towards her as he spoke, reaching his hand out to take hers.

She pulled it back quickly, turned her head behind her in the same moment, saw the line of people who were now staring at her with wary concern, knew that there could be no escape.

'What seems to be the problem?' a voice asked.

She would have known the speaker was important even if the two guards hadn't snapped to attention, shoulders rising and levelling off, eyes straight ahead. It was the same tone of command that she might have given to a scullery maid or a new assistant at the bestiaries, assertive and self-certain. 'She is ignorant of the password, and has declined to show her brand.'

'This is your first time here, sister?' the boy asked. Not boy, man, younger than Calla and shorter but with wide shoulders and round biceps. His eyes were dark and blunt as an extinguished torch, and they seemed somehow familiar, though she could not recall the circumstances of their last meeting.

'I was told that all humans are welcome at the meeting of the Five-Fingered,' Calla said. 'That there is a man here who would speak something I needed to hear.'

'The second is the truest thing in the world,' he said, 'though the first is sadly outdated. There are some so clouded as to imagine themselves our enemies, and thus precautions must be taken. May I see your brand, sister?'

Calla knew well the tone of voice, one she had often used herself, polite but unyielding. She brought the folds of her robes up from her wrist, displayed the ink that had been applied earlier that morning. It was good work, Calla knew, but not too good, nothing like the elaborate tattoo that ran up her other arm and to the nape of her neck, which she had powdered over with heavy make-up and which was now obscured by a length of scarf.

'This would make you a worker on the cerulean section of the Second Rung, yes?'

Head halfway to a nod, another flicker of warning or terror and she turned it into a head-shake. 'The third, my lord,' she said, looking down as if frightened, no very difficult emotion to fake. 'I am a maid for a family there.'

He did not smile, but there was some indefinable sense of easing. 'I am no lord,' he said. 'Rank, title, these are lies created by the demons, meant to separate and weaken us. You are human, and thus my sibling, and there need be no question of hierarchy between us. I congratulate you on your courage in coming so far from your home,' he continued, nodding to the guards and waving her inside, 'and I welcome you to your first meeting of the Five-Fingers. Your future starts tonight.'

A stage had been erected at the back of the warehouse, though Calla could only make it out through the mad press of bodies, windows shuttering open and closed through the great wall of flesh. Elbowing her way to a clear view took the better part of ten minutes, and was an unseemly and unpleasant task. The crowd were porters and shop-owners and petty craftsmen and outright vagrants, they were small-time thugs and washerwomen, they were cooks and servants, they were human as she was human and as unrecognisable to her as the back of the moon. She ended up standing beside a family of five, a thick-shouldered husband and a homely wife, three young children standing seriously below them. After a while a man appeared on the stage, middle-aged, handsome, shifty-looking. Calla stared hard at his face, willing herself to remember, folding his image into the recesses of her mind.

'Five years ago,' he began, 'I heard the truth, and was reborn Steadfast, the First of His Line.'

A cheer from the crowd.

'Are you ready to hear the same, brothers and sisters? Are you ready to be reborn?'

A louder cheer, and longer, though when Steadfast brought his hands up it quieted with surprising speed, this mob of downslope ruffians, five hundred souls at least, every one staring silently forward with keen intensity, nothing to be heard but the occasional cough. And then Steadfast removed himself, and the man they had all come to see arrived from off stage. At first glance he did not seem like much, this man who had set the lower half of the Roost on fire with his words, who had drawn this crowd like bees to honey or wild dogs to raw meat. Near fifty, if Calla was to take a guess, though you would only say so by his bright white mane. His shoulders were broad and he stood straight and unbowed, and his eyes were clear blue even from a distance. But he was not handsome particularly, and apart from the hair there was nothing noteworthy about him.

But when he spoke – at his first words, which were sonorous and bright, and which she could hear clearly though she was halfway back in the crowd – Calla understood.

'What is your name?'

He allowed the silence to extend out again.

'What is your name?' he repeated.

This time there were scattered shouts of response from the crowd, *Mouse* and *Hinge* and *Burr,* downslope names without beauty or even much sense. On the First Rung and the Second, children were named after flowers and spices, after sweet-smelling plants, after precious minerals and things beautiful or thought to be so. Down here on the Fifth they seemed to title their spawn after anything that caught their fancy, with less thought than Calla might have given to her supper.

He did not ask the question a third time, only looked on disapprovingly, at those who had spoken and those who had remained quiet. 'Those are not your names. Those are the names they have given you, lies that you have supped upon since birth, falsehoods swallowed down with mother's milk. Untruths that have blinded you to your patronym, to your history, to your very future. In a time that has been forgotten, in an age the memory of which was obliterated, we roamed wild and proud across the land, with our own leaders and our own priests, blessed by the gods, free as man was meant to be free. Until the demons came,' – voice dipping an octave into horror and hatred. 'Without law or justice, thinking themselves divine, jealous of our innocence. They slaughtered your ancestors as cattle, and those they did not kill they enslaved, forced to labour for an unknowable eternity beneath the ground, out of sight of the sun, out of sight, they supposed, of the gods themselves. They broke us, and they thought we would remain forever broken. For generations beyond counting, you have laboured beneath that yoke, knowing nothing different, thinking, in your delusion, in your ignorance, that it was justified, that your bounds were ornaments, that your slavery freedom, that you were what they said you were.'

The crowd was not quite silent – there was still the rustle of clothing and heavy drawing of breath, here and there a cough or a mutter – but when Edom clapped his hands together it echoed loud and clear through the vast hallway.

'It is time to wake now from this nightmare, my brothers and sisters. It is time now, finally, finally and long past time, that you free yourself from your delusions, from your bounds. Free yourself from the whoremongers and the child-poisoners, the gamblers with their loaded dice and false tongues, the knife-boys who come to your businesses and your homes and tell you that what little you have scrimped and saved and salvaged is not yours at all, that it is theirs. And above them, faceless and unknowable, three or five or seven cables upslope, the Cuckoos and their masters, Five-Fingered as you and I but made blind by their own self-hatred, by the depths of their loathing, by their desperate and foolish and impossible adoration of the demons. The world was promised you,' Edom said, his voice rising until it filled every nook and cranny of the warehouse, until it extended into the furthest back corners, until it seeped into the mind and the heart and the soul of everyone blessed to hear it. 'And it is to you to redeem that promise. It will be your strength that frees your children of their servitude, that will begin a new chapter in the history of your race. I am Edom, the First of His Line, and if a free heart beats in your chest, if you yearn for a future beyond that which they have promised, then you are already one of us, and must but speak the words.'

When it was finished, every man and woman and child packed into the warehouse, five hundred souls easily, matched the motion of the man on stage, reflected it, hands uplifted, fingers splayed,

Calla making it along with them and not sure in her own mind if it was pretence.

Afterwards she left the gathering swiftly, well-graced with fear.

4

The Salucians could not fight for shit.

This had been Bas's feeling twenty-five years earlier, and thus far he had seen nothing to force him to reconsider the opinion. The three themas he had brought from Aeleria were newly raised and largely unblooded, and he would not have given all of them for half of his beloved Thirteenth, still serving on the Marches far to the east. But they were chariot-bearers of the war god himself compared to the Salucians. Their infantry were all peasants, badly equipped and worse led. The nobles served in the cavalry, and they looked very impressive – their saddles were trimmed with silver and samite, and the pommels of their weapons elaborately crafted – and Bas supposed that it was their wealth as much as their lives that they sought to protect in similarly fleeing each conflict at the first sign of bloodshed. The only part of the Salucian forces that could fight at all were not Salucian, but foreign mercenaries called forth from distant lands by the promise of gold. The Chazar wielded a sort of hooked spear that worked well enough in pulling a man off a horse, and well enough in cutting him up once they'd done so, and had been the only reason that the battle at Bod's Wake had not been a rout. But there weren't many of them, and there were a damn sight fewer after Bod's Wake. During the last war the Salucians had their numbers stiffened by large contingents of plainsmen, light cavalry having crossed half the length of the continent for the promise of steel weapons and men to use them on. But a quarter-century of grinding western expansion had sapped the marchers of their strength, and the Salucians were left in the unfortunate position of having to fight their own war.

No, the Salucians could not fight – but they could build, as the great stone citadel in front of Bas evidenced, and they could hide behind what they had built, and at the moment it seemed those two skills were enough to make up for the lack of the first. Four months they had been stuck outside of Oscan, the Salucians waiting for the weather to do what their blades and spears and arrows could not. The city had been the proximate cause of the war, a vague satellite of Aeleria, annexed by Salucia after the Commonwealth's armies had been slaughtered by the demons during the last war. It was common knowledge within Aeleria, remarked upon often and in passionate tones, that the citizens of Oscan lamented daily the betrayal that had forced them beneath a foreign yoke, that they would with a moment's notice rise up against their hated oppressors.

That there had been no such signs of pro-Aelerian resistance, not a message passed by arrow nor a throat-slit Salucian nor the dark black smoke of burning buildings, was something Bas had noticed but not remarked upon or felt any way about. The wheel was in motion – the wheel had, in fact, never stopped, its rotation a constant in the more than forty years with which Bas Alyates, called Caracal or sometimes the God-Killer, called worse things also, had walked above the ground. No doubt it had been in motion far longer, as ever man felt greed, as ever man felt hate, as ever man had grudge against man and the hands with which to answer said grievance. Bas did not consider the justice of it any more than he might the falling rain, or the kindled light of day that was just now rising over the horizon.

Morning coming but not yet arrived, and Bas made his way through the great Aelerian camp with the aid of a servant and a large torch. By far the larger portion of the army was still asleep, what was to come was still, hopefully and nominally, a secret and only those units who would be taking part in the assault had been alerted. As he grew closer to the walls Bas found the first evidence of the battle to come, men thumbing the edge of their weapons, checking the straps of their armour, sipping swiftly through their double ration of liquor.

Theophilus sat on a small travelling stool, staring at the walls with no great excess of enthusiasm. 'Legatus,' he said, making a vague effort to rise and salute, stopping once he received Bas's expected gesture to remain seated.

Compared to most of the rest of the soldiers under his command Theophilus was a veteran, an old hand, a year on the Marches and nearly two here in the east. And in truth there seemed little enough of the boy Bas had first met, well-formed but soft, and so desperate to make a good impression as to be near worthless. He had blooded his sword and had swords blooded against him. He had worn calluses into his hands with a trench shovel, had shat out his innards with flux, had drunk too much and vomited on his boots, had grown hard, mean little eyes. And if all that wasn't enough, you could tell he was a true soldier by the face he wore, mute and unmovable as a stone, saving all energies, physical and mental, for some great future trial and having none therefore to fritter away on excess feeling or unnecessary speech.

'They're ready?' Bas asked.

'They won't get more ready before the morning.' He waved to his adjutant – squat-shouldered, pug-nosed, a name Bas had never learned – and the man ran over to refill his cup of coffee.

'If their spies haven't told them you're coming, they'll figure it out by the time you mass ranks,' Bas said. 'Subterfuge is out, so don't make an attempt at it – go hard enough at them and they'll bend, go a little harder and they'll break.'

'Then I'll see you inside,' Theophilus answered, taking the mug from his boy.

Nothing else worth saying and Bas did not attempt it. In truth, he had little enough role to play in the day's events. Bas had spent the better part of the last ten years on the Marches as Strategos for the Thirteenth thema, responsible ultimately for everything it did, every bent pike and late patrol, every failed stratagem and dead soldier. As Legatus in the western army, his purpose was less clear. Konstantinos was responsible for overall strategy, the leaders of the individual themas were responsible for executing his commands. Bas got the sense at times he was little more than a mascot, like the donkey the Thirteenth had kept that one summer when he had still been a pentarche, a spotted thing that someone had taught to drink whiskey. What had happened to that mule, Bas tried to remember, staring up at the walls? Yes, they had eaten him when winter came. A man of greater imagination might have supposed that an unprepossessing portent.

'Then you will attack today?' she asked from behind him.

Bas did not smile, though there was a brief second where it looked like he might. She moved with such grace and silence, it still astonished him, even having seen her daily or near daily for the better part of two years. 'You know I can't say.'

'You do not need to. What else would explain the commotion in camp, and your mustering at the front?'

What else indeed? The only time Bas had ever seen another Eternal they had been locked in mortal combat, and so Bas was not entirely sure of how the Sentinel of the Southern Reach compared to the rest of her species. He had the vague sense that they were not as diverse in type as humans, though he couldn't have said for certain if this was true. She resembled humanity in the way that a horse resembles a mule, larger and finer and better formed. He was not sure if other men would call her beautiful; with her eyes that were like slabs of amethyst, with her fingers that would have stretched a fair length of his forearm, with her height and her tiny, beak-like nose. He was not entirely sure if he thought her beautiful either, or at least he did not allow himself certainty on the subject.

The Roost claimed ownership over all the lands of the continent, by right of their ancient presence, predating not only the Aelerians, who had only come to the continent a scant three centuries before, but even the Salucians and the Dycians and the Marchers, who had resided there for millennia prior. In the eyes of the Others the human nations were their vassals, demonstrated this fealty by yearly tithe – as well as, in theory at least, obeying their commands. The Sentinel of the Southern Reach had accompanied the Aelerian army to remit these orders, though in practice she did little more than observe and occasionally comment in a fashion more acerbic than practical. Bas had named her Einnes to facilitate their communication, though as Bas was the only human with whom she spent any time in conversation, he was also the only one who used or even knew of this name.

'And you will lead them, then, Slayer of Gods?'

'I had not thought to do so,' he said, which had been true before she had mentioned it, though now that the thought had been introduced he had to admit that it held a certain interest.

'It is one of the many things that I do not understand about your species – Those Above would be ashamed to demand a thing of another, rather than to accomplish it ourselves.'

'Your slaves would likely dispute that point.'

'My slaves are too well-trained to dispute with me upon anything.'

He could never tell if she was joking. 'Fair point.'

'The gate seems well defended.'

'We'll take it,' Bas said, a pinprick of pride for his army and his men. 'Theophilus knows what he's doing. And the Salucians have no love of war.'

'And you, Legatus? Are you so enamoured of that mistress?'

'She's always been good to me.'

'Let us hope her affection remains undimmed,' Einnes said,

purple eyes still as the surface of a stone. 'Watch yourself, Slayer of Gods. Die today and I will lose the chance to kill you.'

'We wouldn't want that,' he agreed, watching as she slipped back to her tent, then stalking off to the front of the camp.

The great western gate of Oscan, where once long trails of caravans had entered on their way to the market, where pilgrims and travellers had received their first view of the great border city, had long months earlier been closed, garrisoned by men with short bows and curved blades. It was the most obvious point of attack and therefore the most heavily fortified; there would be nothing clever in today's battle, no stratagems or tricks, only muscle against muscle and steel against steel. The hoplitai getting ready to force it had traded in their customary long pikes, were making do with the short stabbing swords that were their secondary weapon. A picked contingent of the largest and strongest had been assigned to shoulder the turtle, a giant aegis of beaten steel and hardened leather, proof, hopefully, against the arrows and stones and heated oil of the Salucians. Chalked up and down its sides were clever blasphemies in Aelerian and vile profanity in gutter Salucian, and at the end was an iron-beaked ram. Driven with sufficient force this might be enough to cause a breach in the gate through which the rest of the force, and the army behind them, might enter. Such, at least, was the hope.

There was no horn to sound their charge, the Aelerians still holding out some distant hope of surprise, only a sudden bellow from Theophilus, deeper and more forceful than Bas would have credited him. And then the turtle – well, it did not surge forward, being large and ungainly and vastly heavy, but it went forward at least, half-giant Aelerian hoplitai churning the mud, the rest of the thema following close behind, drawn swords and half-shields. A howl from the walls in answer, a howl and a rain of arrows; Bas could not see them but he could hear the chorus of bowstrings and then the screams of his countrymen, a steady and odious depletion, but it did not slow the charge.

In the still-black morning and past the mass of hoplitai Bas could not see the gate breaking, but he could hear it, the clatter of the turtle's head, the squeal of metal sounding strangely like the screams of men. And then the screams of men as well, not so loud bur protracted, as the hoplitai and the Salucian garrison met at last, sharp things drawing blood in the dark.

The dawn came slow, and Bas could not will it on faster. Battle was joined but the outcome yet uncertain. A crowd had gathered, neighbouring hoplitai and pentarchs waiting expectantly, cheering occasionally – though at what Bas could not be sure; it was still too dark to have any idea who was winning. Some ways back, a head taller than the rest of the crowd, Bas could make out Einnes, purple eyes taking in the carnage.

War is a sluggard, war is a lumbering, shambling, slow-footed behemoth, war is a thousand men making a thousand small decisions slowly and generally unwisely. Nothing ever begins on time, no one is ever where they are supposed to be when they are supposed to be there. War is an overloaded wagon with a creaking axle, mud-stuck, pulled forward by a beat-up mule. Except every so often when it is not – when it is transformed into a charging stallion, or a downward-streaking hawk. Bas sometimes supposed, amidst the endless drudgery of his day-to-day tasks, turning boys into killers and killers into corpses, that he continued on as the Caracal simply because there was no other alternative; and then one of these single sterling seconds would arrive, and Bas would again recall his purpose.

Up and past the Aelerian defences so swiftly that none had thought to stop him, past an arrow-shot hoplitai, the first of the day's casualties but not the last, and thoughtless he reached down and grabbed the dying man's shield, bellowing as he went, a bronzed battle horn loud enough to be heard above the tumult. His blade whistled from its sheath, Roost-forged steel red as the last moment before sunset, lighter than a switch of willow and stronger than a hand's breadth of cast iron – the stories called it the Caracal's Claw, or sometimes Red Wind, though Bas had never been known to call it anything, or at least not that anyone had ever heard. He pushed past the loose back rank of soldiers, a sudden shower of arrows doing nothing to slow his passage, though one struck the man next to him just above his hauberk, a death swift and sure, and another would have struck Bas's shoulder had he not batted it aside with a movement of his shield, reflexively, without noticing, something that would have been impossible except for one man in a thousand, and for that man would be the most extraordinary deed he might perform in a long lifetime of war. As a pebble dropped in still water or a rumour whispered in a schoolroom Bas's arrival spread its way through the hoplitai, who surged forward in answer to the Caracal's example.

The west gate was broken, the bottom of the portcullis shattered, the top hanging impotent, but behind that the Salucians were staging an admirable last stand behind a line of barricades, though not for long, no, by the gods, not if Bas had anything to say on the matter. He found himself suddenly among the packed front ranks of hoplitai and then past them, to the very lip of the fortifications. A spearhead caught itself in Bas's shield and he roared and pulled his arm backward and ripped the lance out of the hands of its wielder, cast both to the ground, and then he was atop the wall and down it, and his men were coming furiously behind him.

The Salucians preferred their swords single-edged and slightly curved, and carried half-moon shields, and generally were not any good with either of them. But the soldier in front of Bas then proved an exception to the rule, and he didn't seem frightened of Bas either, and this was rather a surprising thing because everyone was afraid of Bas, not just the enemy either, anyone with a set of eyes and two grains of sense and even a fair number of men who could not claim even these meagre distinctions. But this Salucian was not – beneath his conical cap of boiled leather his eyes were dark and grim and unflinching. The Salucian was brave and the Salucian was fast, and the Salucian knew enough of combat to realise he needed to move swiftly against Bas, to swell in tight and negate Bas's superior reach. What the Salucian did not know was that Bas, for all his more than forty-five years, was still as strong as any man alive, and when they locked their blades against each other Bas planted his legs and tensed with his shoulders and he sent the Salucian hurtling back towards the men swarming to reinforce him, sending three of them tumbling and then falling upon them, once on the attack Bas never relented, not for a single instant. It is a fact that no man is invincible or even particularly difficult to kill, that four men or at the very most five, armed with a long length of wood and a bit of sharpened metal at the end of it, are a match for the fiercest warrior who ever lived. It is also a fact that it is not so very difficult to make five men forget this truth, think of nothing but their own flesh and their own future.

Bas's blade arched above his head, the full rays of dawn blinding bright, then dashed in among packed flesh, heedless of wood or chain or steel. One wide sweep of Roost-forged steel tore the arm and shoulder off a pockmarked pikeman and a return stroke severed the top of his comrade's skull from its bottom, leaving blood and brain to spray off onto the tight ranks of men. Two stray bladesmen, experienced enough to work in concert, attempted to do so, the first closing in tight with him, the second hoping to edge off to his side, and both dead in no more time than it would take a chick to peck seed, two swift motions leaving meat on the ground below.

Bas's soldiers, seized with his savagery, surrounded by the force of his presence, swarmed past him as well. It was too close for spears, it was nearly too close for swords, it was flesh against flesh, and the tide of the Aelerians overwhelming, continuing onward because they could do nothing else, the Salucians recognising this and scattering.

Bas roared as he killed, and so he roared a great deal.

The battle won, his men sprinted past him to take care of the few remaining defenders and to take their terrible reward among the beleaguered populace, the traditional seventy-two hours of plunder, rapine, savagery. Riches stolen and churches befouled and women dragged screaming from their homes. It was not the first battle that had been tipped by the appearance of Bas Alyates, the Caracal, the Killer of Gods, the mailed fist of the Empire. Had not he been the first to feel Dycian soil beneath his feet, climbing the siege ladders with two arrows sticking out of his hauberk and his left shoulder puckering from hot grease? Had he not carried the city of Eiben, in those series of grim half-wars against the border countries standing between Aeleria and Salucia, his sword work not yet masterful but his strength and speed without human comparison? Was he not, alone among mankind, the equal of an Eternal, no, not the equal, the proven better? Leaping back atop the barricade, the world, Bas roared at his soldiers and they echoed it back, near to fifty and still tougher than any man living; what he'd lost in speed he made up for in technique, and he had not lost a step in savagery, no he had not, and was she watching? Was she watching? By the gods, was she watching?

5

Hammer had the bottle hidden below the wide sweep of his travelling coat, prepared a few moments beforehand. Pure alcohol or near to it, vile stuff – although Pyre had drunk worse when he had been Thistle. Years since a drop of alcohol had passed his lips, and he did not lament the interim, indeed the stink of the bottle from half a block away was near enough to make him gag. It was strange, how many of Thistle's old pleasures seemed to Pyre not only foolish but lamentable, links in the chains that had bound him.

'He's awful new to be taking point,' said Agate quietly. This was self-evident and verbalising it pointless, but Agate had the tendency to grow nervous in the moments before a job, edgy and irritable. In the moment itself he was very cool, he was a good man to have standing beside you, blade drawn and scowling, but then anticipation is often the worst part of a thing.

'He'll handle it,' Pyre said with some confidence. 'And so will you.'

Agate nodded and smiled and tightened his grip round the hilt of his long knife.

Not that Agate's concerns were altogether misguided. Only a month and a half now since a boy named Seed had become a man named Hammer, barely enough time to hear the truth, let alone become a member of the Dead Pigeons. But it was Pyre's belief – and he did not think this was parochialism, he had moved beyond such petty concerns when he had taken his new name – that the best soldiers came from within the sound of the slurp. Fighting since they were old enough to walk, kids from half a cable to the east or the west, kids that looked the same and spoke the same and thought the same as they did. Years spent sharpening themselves against poverty and misery and violence, all that was needed was to give them something worth fighting for, and Edom had done that. 'Hammer will do fine,' Pyre said again.

He was doing a keen enough job so far, one more stumble-drunk knocking down the wide Third Rung thoroughfare, a bit grimier than they generally got up here but not worth noticing twice. Coming towards the hour of the Woodcock, late afternoon giving way towards evening, and in preparation a pair of locals were kindling the street lanterns, handsome hardwood poles set at even distances along the main drag. Where Pyre had grown up there had been no such similar custom, moonlight falling unassisted between the pipes and the tenement spires onto upturned mud and cracked brick. The Third Rung was not the Second, and neither of them the First, but still it seemed a very far way from the Barrow and the docks.

Hammer wobbled onward, past an unlovely if intimidating edifice of white brick, distinct from the small brownstone houses that surrounded it, noteworthy by virtue of its size and its ugly appearance and by the two Cuckoos standing outside of it, cudgels swinging lazily at their waist. 'Go,' Pyre said, and Agate sprinted down the alley, circling round to find Grim and his men at their second position. With no chance of stopping it, now that he was irrevocably committed, Pyre felt as he always felt before action, clean and hard and certain. He was smiling when the youth slipped out from a caddy-corner alleyway, actually near Pyre's age though he looked younger. He shouted the sort of things that a young man might yell at a Cuckoo here in the waning days of the Roost, here within sight of the coming dawn, and when they turned to look he threw a stone. It went wide, chance or error, Pyre wasn't sure, but they noticed it regardless, self-defence a function of which even the Cuckoos were basically capable, or at least supposed themselves to be. The boy laughed and made a familiar if offensive gesture and the Cuckoos tore away from their posts and sprinted after him.

On the Fifth Rung or even the Fourth, after a solid year of enemy action, of retaliatory assassinations, of bodies bobbing face-up in the canals, the Cuckoos knew better than to run off into the alleyways, knew better than to go anywhere except in the company of six or eight of their fellows. But up on the Third Pyre his organisation were closer to urban myth than brutal reality, and the Cuckoos still imagined themselves supreme, some stutter-step beneath the demons they aped. These two men would learn the opposite, regrettably to Pyre's mind, but there was no other way for it. Two misguided men with slit throats, two families weeping. Even Cuckoos have families, Pyre had come to learn.

Though he didn't concern himself with them just then. As soon as the Cuckoos were out of sight Hammer swung into action, pulled the bottle out from its hiding spot and held the rough band of fabric tied round its neck against one of the street lanterns. It flared to life and he sprinted towards the building the Cuckoos had just run from, shoving it through a barred window. There was no explosion, or at least not one that Pyre could hear, but there were screams, and then smoke, and then the front door flew open and half a dozen men came sprinting out, coughing, spluttering, terrified even before they saw Hammer standing in front of them, short sword drawn and gleaming. They were clerks and pushers of paper, cogs in the vast apparatus by which the demons kept their human slaves in bondage, no less sophisticated than the slurp itself, though perhaps less wondrous. They were men unused to violence; this far up the mountain it was all but unknown, petty criminality rare and swiftly punished, the big thieves taking care to hang the little ones.

'On your knees,' Hammer shouted, louder than necessary but this was his first action, and Pyre could forgive him his excitement. 'On your knees!' he said a second time, and this time the men were not slow to obey, long robes trailing in the dust.

Grim and three of his men came walking swiftly eastward. One of them was Agate, and one of them was the boy who had thrown the stone, and the last had his blade free, and it was slick with the blood of a stranger.

'Any problems?' Pyre asked.

Grim shook his head vigorously, broad-smiling, turned his attention to the lackeys arraigned before him. 'Which one of you is bossman?' Grim asked. Grim was born closer to here than the Fifth, but he liked to affect the downslope slang, and since apart from that he was tough and fearless and utterly reliable, it was the sort of foolishness that could be overlooked.

None answered, knees bent against cobblestone, eyes firmly on the ground.

'Obey and this will go swiftly and without bloodshed,' Pyre said quietly. 'Hinder our objectives in any way and I will set your mothers to weeping. These are the words of Pyre, the First of His Line, and by the Self-Created I will stay true to them.'

It was as much Pyre's name as Pyre's threats that got them to react. Even here, a seeming world away from the Fifth, they knew of the Dead Pigeons and of the savage young man who ruled them. 'I'm the manager,' one of them said, looking much like the rest, a little older perhaps, a little fatter, one of the faceless multitude of the fettered, thinking themselves free because they did not notice their chains.

Hammer pulled him upright and sent him tumbling back into the building. Agate followed along, though Pyre waited a moment before joining them.

'We'll be done before reinforcements arrive,' Pyre said to Grim, who had taken up position by the door.

Grim smiled. 'Take as long as you want. There aren't enough Cuckoos in the city to bring us down.'

A lie – what was true, however, what Pyre knew to be true without consideration or rumination, was that if the Cuckoos managed to amass a sufficient force to break through they would do so over the corpses of Grim and his men. There was not anyone in the Dead Pigeons who he could not count on to perform likewise.

The interior was ugly, banal, no different from a thousand other such offices on the Rung, places that built nothing, forged nothing, created nothing, nodes of finance, leeches draining life from the body politic. The fire was still smouldering, but it didn't seem to be spreading very fast. If the clerks had been braver they might well have been able to put it out themselves, but then again they'd have no reason to suppose themselves the target of an attack. That had been part of the brilliance of it, to strike in a spot where the demons and their servants imagined themselves protected.

Part of the brilliance, but not all of it. Hammer and Agate had corralled the manager between them, and were staring at him in a fashion that would have alarmed his wife or mother. As if to forestall any abuse, he pointed towards a door and said, 'The vaults are that way. But all the silver is in bars – you won't be able to carry it anywhere.'

'We aren't going to the vaults,' Pyre said quietly. 'Your records – where are the records kept?'

He went white-faced then, and for the first time Pyre felt like hurting him, that fierce, oily rage boiling itself up from somewhere around his cock, because there wasn't anything to these upslopers but greed, that was all that mattered to them, not even silver or gold but rows of ciphers on paper, scratches of ink more important than the lives of their fellows and more important than their own even, they'd lose a limb before seeing their ledgers unbalanced.

Pyre shoved it back down. Hatred, anger, these were the feelings of a boy named Thistle, and not the man he had become.

'Make me repeat the question, and I'll make you scream the answer.'

'Down the hall to the right,' the man answered swiftly, 'down the hall to the right.'

'After you,' and Hammer gave him a good hard shove in the direction he had indicated. Pyre tried to figure how long had elapsed since they'd set the fire, but time was a tricky thing in moments like these. They came to a locked door and this time the manager did not need to be threatened, reached into his pocket and pulled out a long key.

It was a large room. It needed to be, containing records for half the transactions on the Fifth Rung, debts owed by store-keepers and shop-owners, bartenders and porters, managers of small restaurants, mothers pawning their beds and their clothes and their bodies and the bodies of their offspring and anything else that might find value upslope. Ignorant, unlettered, capable of counting to twenty if they took off their shoes and if they hadn't suffered an accident, setting their mark down on a piece of paper that promised they'd spend their lives trying to repay some modest sum.

Hammer smiled wide, knew what needed to be done without Pyre saying so. He had two more bottles hooked against his belt and he hooted loudly and tossed one over to Agate, who caught it one-handed and tore off the cap, opened one of the larger drawers and started to dump it over the parchment inside.

'What are you doing?' the manager asked, though he must have known by then.

'I am filing the bars of a cage,' Pyre said. 'It is the primary occupation of the Five-Fingered.'

'But . . . but . . . these are the records for the entire Fifth Rung! Every loan and financial transaction, tens of thousands of debts!'

'Do you think we came here by coincidence?' Agate asked, laughing, upending one of the drawers against another, the crescendo of wood against the stone floor, paper scattering across the room. 'The Five-Fingered will free their brethren of the yoke of credit, and shove a nice finger into the eye of all of you upslope trash.'

'These are legitimate transactions!' the manager protested, and Pyre was surprised as he always was at the willingness of the bound to fight in service of their own subordination. It was a peculiar kind of courage, preferring to risk injury or death rather than face bluntly the facts of their own slavery. A potent thing, the truth, and there were men who would rather die than hear it. 'You have no right to do this!'

'You gave an eagle to a man fifty years ago, and you have his children's children still paying interest.' Hammer had finished preparing the inferno, faced up against the manager, breathing heavy and with one hand on his blade. 'We ought to clip him right now, let everyone know he's a traitor to the species.'

'He's ignorant,' Pyre said, making a swift motion with his hand to forestall any violence. 'As you were, as I was. Perhaps this will be the moment when the truth reaches him. If not,' Pyre turned suddenly on the man, 'we will meet him again on the morning of the new age.'

'We doing this?' Agate asked. Most of the bureaus were knocked on the ground, their financial secrets spilled across the floor and wetted down with alcohol.

'Hammer, do the honours,' Pyre said.

Hammer turned his snarl from the manager, grabbed a lantern off the walls and dashed it against the far corner of the room. The fire started swiftly and burned fast, dry parchment as good an accelerant as coal oil. They left immediately after, and already the smoke was black and billowy. Back towards the front entrance and the second blaze was hot and high, intended as a distraction though it had gained its own momentum, as fires and causes often do. They would feel this, men on the Second and their demonic masters on the First; it was one thing to kill a Cuckoo in some distant corner of the Roost, to throw graffiti on walls, to hold rallies and demonstrations. To strike at the purse, though, was to take aim at the very essence of the city.

'Any trouble?' Pyre asked Grim once they were all back outside, breathing deep of the early evening air, free finally from the smoke.

'No, but you can hear it coming.'

And indeed you could, rattling downslope, the loud droning of ratchets. The Cuckoos had been alerted and were coming in force, the shock troops of Those Above, ill-trained and worse-armed but there would be plenty of them, there would be enough. Pyre turned swiftly to the functionaries and petty bureaucrats kneeling in the dust, the smoke from their business growing thicker even from the outside. They refused to look back at him, eyes bent and neck bowed, a position with which they had long familiarity.

Though Pyre preferred to see them free of it. 'You are blind, each and every one of you. You suppose yourself free by virtue of the small luxuries afforded you, but this is a lie, and now is the moment of your deliverance. The demons parcel out your birthright, and you are so pathetic as to feel grateful. But a reckoning is coming, brothers, for the demons and for you as well. What was stolen will be returned, what was taken will be replaced. The scales will be righted.'

'By the will of the Self-Created,' Grim said.

'Until the dawn of the new age,' Hammer echoed.

'Leave, or stay, as is your want,' Pyre said, though between the fire and the smoke and the coming certainty of violence they were not slow to make their escape, on their feet and hurrying off as fast as they were able.

'You'd best do the same,' Pyre said to Grim.

'I will see you downslope, or at the foot of Enkedri's throne,' Grim said, smiling.

'You'll see me downslope,' Pyre corrected. 'I haven't given you permission to die.'

Grim slapped his hand against his chest and extended it with each finger unfolded. Then he and Agate and the rest of his men went roaring off west, to follow the Sterling Canal towards the Fifth. Pyre and Hammer headed in the opposite direction, eastward for a few long moments and then downslope towards freedom and home.

The hum of the ratchets followed them through the dimming evening light, but this was an old game to Pyre, fleeing from the Cuckoos, this was an activity at which Pyre was well-practised, and Hammer too. There was a moment when Pyre looked at Hammer and Hammer looked at Pyre and they nearly burst out laughing, the noisemakers echoing louder and still nothing more than a spur to merriment.

They turned out of an alleyway and onto a main thoroughfare and suddenly there were four of them. Pyre never learned if they had been called from upslope or if this was part of their usual beat and it didn't matter anyway. He did not hesitate; that was perhaps the one quality he still shared with a boy named Thistle, there was no interlude for him between shock and violence, and in that brief instant before the Cuckoos accepted the sudden reality of the situation Pyre's blade had cut a hole in a blue robe and a gash in pale flesh. The wounded man screamed and fell back and Pyre continued onward, knowing distantly that speed alone might prove their salvation, that any halt would mean death. His attack was so rapid and so savage that it embroiled two of the Cuckoos in trying to defend against it, backing away fearfully, but that still left the one, and that one was pulling his truncheon back to shatter Pyre's skull when Hammer intervened, catching the blow near the hilt of his short blade, good Aelerian steel biting deep into the hardwood, and still moving he caught Pyre's assailant by the shoulder and yet moving still he hurled the Cuckoo against the alley wall, bone against indifferent brick, and then the blade upright and entering through the ribcage. Ignorant of his reprieve, Pyre continued forcefully against the two remaining Cuckoos, though after a few seconds one retreated at a run and one expired slowly on the ground. Or perhaps he would survive – Pyre was no doctor – but at least he would not again have a left hand.

They sprinted downslope without celebration, the narrow cloistered streets loud with the Cuckoos' cries of warnings, cacophonous and distracting, Hammer turning for a moment and seeing that they were close behind him and then turning back round and not looking any more, Pyre just in front of him, legs pumping and chest straining. Through a small street market, dodging round a brazier frying onion and pig belly, the Cuckoos following after less agile, upending the grill, the proprietor screaming and the Cuckoos screaming also, Pyre and Hammer plunging through a clothing stand, carrying bright strands of cloth along with them for a dozen steps afterward.

When they turned a corner and came up against a blind stone wall and no hope of escape, Hammer felt a first brief flicker of fear, saw Pyre smile beside him, felt it smother immediately. Death was a certainty but fear was not, fear was foolish, there was no point to fear. For a month and a half Hammer had known the truth, known the certainty of his own worth and purpose, and how many men could claim the same? None that Hammer had ever met, none apart from these, his new-found brothers, and how fine a thing it would be to die beside one of them! How fine a thing to die for a purpose! Perhaps better even than to live for one.

The Cuckoos seemed as surprised to discover themselves in a blind alley as had been Hammer and Pyre, and not a happy surprise either, a half-dozen of them coming in two waves, the fatter ones trickling in late. The breed of Cuckoos that nested on the Third dealt mostly with citizens happy in their subjugation, and had no experience with the sort of casual cruelty that was the chief purpose of their fellows downslope. But violence was what was needed now, there could be no question otherwise, no question to Pyre or to Hammer at least, though looking at the infirm faces of their pursuers it seemed no altogether settled question.

Pyre's blade was free and naked. 'Well, brothers,' Pyre began, smiling a smile that Thistle had sometimes worn, in that distant age when he had wished for nothing more than a skull to bruise a knuckle against. 'This will be a happy death for Pyre, the First of His Line – can any of you say the same?'

'You're . . . you're under arrest,' said the bravest of them, though his voice wavered.

'Pyre will walk out of this alley, or he'll be carried.' The steel like a finger pointing at the lead Cuckoo. 'And not Pyre alone.'

The evening falling fast now, too dark to make out the Cuckoos except by their eyes, which were wide and uncertain. And this would be why they would win, Pyre knew, why he fell asleep every night exhausted but happy, why he woke in the morning without regret and brimming full of energy to spill in the name of the age to come. At bottom, the Cuckoos knew the truth, as Pyre had known even before he had taken his new name, as every human knew.

There was no discussion, no debate. The Cuckoo who had spoken looked round at his fellows, and when none met his gaze he swallowed hard and moved out of the way, and the rest of them soon did the same, ferules flaccid in their hands, Pyre and Hammer shuffling through the sudden aperture swiftly and with blades still drawn.

'You're always welcome at a meeting, brothers,' Pyre said, just before turning to sprint downslope towards freedom, yelling over his shoulder, 'The truth comes to all who are willing to hear it!'

6

The stars peeked through a cloudless autumn evening and into the great open hall that made up some modest, some minor, some negligible portion of the Aubade's estate. Great braziers of scented wood were set out at even intervals, each tended by an immaculately dressed house-slave. Other servants – there were many, many servants, there seemed more servants dedicated to the party itself than there were in the entirety of Eudokia's estate, and each was dressed in finery that would have shamed a noble, shamed them as much for the style and cut as for the expense – carried trays of strange and exotic food from guest to guest. Sweetmeats covered in green pistachio, smoked bacon wrapped round freshly cut melon, and where had they gotten freshly cut melon this time of year, Eudokia wondered? Specific sets of servants carried trays to the Others in attendance, though the food did not seem substantially different, or at least not different in any way that a casual glance could detect. To the north one could gaze out at the bay, and the infinite sea beyond, watch the light sparkle on the turning waves. Or one could go eastward a few hundred steps and stare out over the first Rung of the Roost, the innumerable watchtowers and citadels, the houses that were like cathedrals, perfection writ in stone.

If Eudokia was not Eudokia, she might even have been impressed.

Two days prior the Aelerian deputation had entered the Roost, met at the gates of the city and carried via palanquin to a guest-house on the Second Rung, overlooking a wide canal bereft of boat or vessel, its disuse one of the innumerable small signs reminding passers-by that however many human souls resided within the Roost did so to the benefit of Those Above. Not, it had to be said, that this seemed any great imposition or dishonour to the people of the Second Rung. Quite the opposite, in fact – submission to the Eternal seemed a sign of social status, raised above even the most accomplished of the human establishment, the bureaucrats and high-ranking custodians, the foreign merchant princes, the banking magnates. So far as the Roost was concerned, that human responsible for cleaning the chamber pot of an Eternal was to be envied more than the wealthiest scion of the oldest family on the Second Rung, and both were to be regarded above everyone residing outside of the Roost's borders, though he be Emperor of Chazar.

Having seen the First Rung now, in all its splendour, this was a sentiment that Eudokia could appreciate if not share. The Red Keep, the Prime's ancestral demesne, was quite the most spectacular building that Eudokia had ever seen. In terms of scope, the only thing Eudokia could think to compare it to were some of the castles along the border with Salucia, large enough to hold a small army and the provisions to sustain it for months or long years. But in intricacy and refinement it did not, in Eudokia's estimation, resemble any edifice built by the hands of man; it could more profitably be compared to an engagement ring or a music box, to something tiny and precious and crafted out of love or at least vanity. And it was one of thousands of similar structures clustered about the First Rung, finer than many, perhaps, but essentially similar, a vast catalogue of unique and unfathomable wonders.

Jahan stood a few steps behind her, a silent, brooding presence, squat and tight-muscled and ugly, alert as ever for any hint of danger to his mistress as he had been for the more than twenty years he had been in her service. He nibbled at a bit of finger food, but apart from that the wonders of the Roost held little interest, eyes dull and dispassionate.

Out of the corner of her eye Eudokia watched the Prime sitting silently on a throne reserved for that purpose, still and idealised as a statue or a poem. Nearer, two Eternal conversed in their incomprehensibly beautiful speech, a male and a female though it was difficult to tell the difference, each a near reflection of the other's perfection. Her own species, Eudokia did not scruple to admit, had little to gain by comparison. In one corner Senator Gratian was talking to a Roostborn girl, not one of the household servants. It had taken them two and a half months to traverse the distance between the capital and the Roost, covered wagons on well-made roads, a large escort of hoplitai, and Gratian complaining every single moment of it; Eudokia had forced herself to keep silent despite her annoyance, as Jahan was an obedient servant and an errant word on her part would require a swiftly dug grave and all sorts of frantic manoeuvrings.

Which was not to suggest that the notion of arranging some . . . accident for the senator was one with which she had entirely dispensed. Back in the capital the senator's follies and foolishness were easily covered up, particularly in so far as his was not a caste known for their discretion. Indeed, by the standards of some of the rest of his august fellowship, he was virtually a monk – he had never tried to make his boy lover third consul, for instance, and his nose had not yet rotted off from the pox. Regardless, here in the Roost they had rather thinner room for error. It was Eudokia's understanding that Those Above were utterly amoral in terms of sex, had no notion of it as sin, perhaps had no notion of sin at all – but they certainly had a notion of etiquette, and of style, and by the gods, if that fat-titted little sybarite did something to embarrass her in front of the demons, he would find himself not waking up one morning. It was an eventuality that Eudokia had planned out well before accepting this mission to the Roost. Half of his staff were hers, a few drops of something in his drink, a few weeks wearing black, of course they would need to send for another senator, though it would be months and months before he arrived, and in the meantime Eudokia would simply have to muddle through as best as she was able, by default becoming Aeleria's sole representative within the Roost.

Eudokia closed her mind around the fantasy of homicide. It was a dangerous thing to start thinking too far in that direction – one began to look around and see all sorts of people that the world did not, strictly speaking, require the continued presence of, began to to count them off one after another, how much simpler the machine would run with a few dozen less souls in it.

Gratian caught her looking and waved, wrist fat wobbling. She smiled and nodded in return.

Eudokia turned her attention to one of those few members of the assemblage whose presence was neither indifference nor burden, indeed, one of those few individuals on the breadth of the planet who could claim this happy distinction. Her nephew Leon leaned against the balcony, enraptured by the beauty of the First Rung – or, perhaps by the long-necked woman who stood next to him. The son of a cousin she scarce recollected, whose death had introduced him to her household when he was still a child. She had brought Leon because she had thought it might be good for his education, and because, and this was a truth that Eudokia could only vaguely bring herself to admit, she actually enjoyed his presence, found his combination of quick wit and boyish innocence to be a pleasant seasoning with which to take the day.

'And what captivating creature have you stolen away this time, dear nephew?' Eudokia asked.

'I have the honour to present Calla, Sensechal of the Red

Manor,' Leon said. 'Calla, this is my aunt, Eudokia Aurelia, Revered Mother.'

'May the moonlight illuminate your path,' the girl added.

No, not girl, woman, Eudokia thought after a moment, recognising metal when she saw it. She was young enough, and she had the bright eyes and high bosom of someone on the kinder side of thirty. But one did not rise higher than sensechal to the Prime, not if one had five fingers on one's hand at least. And also she met Eudokia's eyes coolly, civilly but without any excess of kindness, and no one who could long bear the gaze of the Revered Mother could justly be called a child.

'It was my understanding that the women of Aeleria held no titles, and had no role in the workings of the state,' Calla said.

'We are a modest lot,' Eudokia assured her. 'And my rank is ceremonial in nature. It indicates I am the head priestess of the cult of Enkedri, and entitled to certain . . . exaggerated honorifics on his behalf.'

'You are a long way from the temples of your god, Revered Mother.'

'But the Self-Created does not reside only in the great stone of his cathedrals. He has another citadel, preferred and longer lasting – the righteous heart of his followers.'

'How . . . pious,' Calla said, as if not liking the taste. 'But still I have difficulty in understanding why the servant of your god, however widespread his powers, would be required as part of the peace embassy that Aeleria has sent to the Roost.'

'I admit to a bit of string-pulling on that one. I am an old woman, and it will not be so very long before Enkedri calls me back to his bosom. I had hoped, since I was a young girl, to see the magnificence of the Roost, and took the opportunity of our embassy to do so.'

'Then your presence here is that of a traveller? You have no public role to play?'

'Think of me as but a simple tourist, hoping only to see the wonders of Those Above before I shuffle off into the night. Of course, any assistance I might give in counselling the peoples of our lands towards peace would be a glory almost too much for my aged heart to bear.'

'Let us hope you prove capable of handling the strain,' Calla said smoothly

As engaging a diversion as she was, Eudokia felt, with characteristic grace, that the seneschal's time might more profitably be used flirting with her nephew. She excused herself and found another drink, sipped it and spent some time staring at the Aubade, or the Lord of the Red Manor, or the Prime, as he was now known, trying to determine if there was something that set him apart distinctly from the handful of other Eternal in attendance, or if it was only her knowledge that he had recently been made whatever passed for leader among the Four-Fingered that was giving him such weight. She decided ultimately that it was the former. Of course, all of Those Above were physically ideal, but there was something about the Aubade, some indefinable quality of excellence, notable in the way he sat casually on his seat, and the way he stared off into the darkness, as if there were things there that he alone could properly observe.

Even among the Others, it seemed there were gradations of nobility.

Eudokia had practised the Eternal greeting until she could have performed it with a bottle of liquor inside her, until she could have done it with an arrow sticking out of her chest. Absent either of those handicaps she performed the series of gestures as naturally as if she was sitting down to toilet. 'My Lord Prime, may the moon bathe you in its rays.'

'Revered Mother,' he said, 'may tomorrow's sun find you well.'

'It flatters me to suppose the Prime has had time to familiarise himself with our delegation.'

'The Sentinel of the Southern Reach has written of you,' he said, rolling over her pleasantry as if she had not offered it. 'She indicates that you are the one to speak with from your nation, that this other man you sent is an ignoramus and a lecher, your puppet and nothing more.'

It seemed that, for all their superiority in various other regards, the Eternal had no very keen grasp of subtlety. Of course, no one in the world had so sharp an understanding of that quality as the Revered Mother, but still . . . 'I'm afraid she rather over-states the case. My position is purely a ceremonial one. Senator Gratian, to whom I must politely insist your Sentinel does an injustice, is the only official representative of the Empty Throne. Any concerns or questions you might have would be best raised with him.'

She was coming swiftly to realise that whatever physical tics Those Above used to indicate mood or change of emotion, assuming they had any, were too delicate for her to grasp clearly. For a woman such as Eudokia, who had long been used to reading the minds of her interlocutors from their blinks and intakes of breath and fidgeting fingers, it was like having to navigate blind. It also gave her a swift little jolt of excitement, a rare enough emotion for one so used to easy victory.

'Then the senator is the individual whom I ought to be speaking to, if I wish to understand the cause of Aeleria's recent belliger-ence, bellicosity and intransigence?'

'There is, perhaps, no need to distract him at the moment. I cannot answer you in any sort of official capacity, but perhaps I might be allowed to offer you some insight into the mind of an Aelerian patriot. For twenty-five years, the Salucians have held the city of Oscan, the very heartland of Aeleria, within their palm, held it and mistreated its people. Two and a half years ago we called for a conference to discuss the issue, a conference that was attended by our beloved Senator Andronikos, a man who loved peace above all other things, a man who wished for nothing more than to see the differences between our nations amicably resolved. A man who was as close to me as a brother,' this added with a hiccup of emotion, hinting at a wellspring of despair beneath. 'I am sure my Lord has heard of the . . . atrocity that befell him, his brutal murder at the hands of the Salucian population. Surely the Regent would not ask that Aeleria remain supine before this injustice? What would the Roost do, if their representative, invited freely into a foreign land, were butchered? What vengeance would they pursue, in reckoning for such an evil?'

It was a very fine speech, Eudokia thought. Certainly those in earshot, humans and High-born alike, turned to look at her, and she made sure to take advantage of the moment, displaying a facade that was at once contrite and stern, saddened and stoical.

'We had heard,' the Prime said, 'of this unexpected and unfortunate development, one which the Salucians seem willing and more than willing to make good upon. And yet we have heard also that their pleas for peace find no purchase in the minds of the Aelerian Senate, that they will not consider the recompense offered, nor engage in negotiations of any kind.'

'If you will forgive me, my Lord Prime – there are issues of honour at stake, which cannot be casually ignored, not even in the interests of continued peace.'

'What would a Dayspan know of honour?' a voice from behind her asked. 'What would a locust know of law or rule, or dignity?'

Eudokia turned slowly to gaze at this new participant. He looked much the same as they all did, beautiful and cruel. 'Whom exactly am I addressing?'

'You may call me the Lord of the Ebony Towers, should you find the need to speak to me directly, occasions that I trust will be rare as a double moon.'

Better known as the Shrike, according to her spies, an unprepossessing sobriquet had she ever heard one. 'Then tomorrow I shall light a joss stick to Enkedri, for seeing fit to bless me with such striking good fortune. In answer to your question then, my Lord of the Ebony Towers, the definition of honour is not always so easy a thing to provide, may show itself differently in different times and at different places. For instance; in Aeleria it is considered the very height of shame to treat a guest disrespectfully – though it appears this is an attitude which has not yet come to nest within the Roost.'

It took the Lord of the Ebony Towers a long time to realise that this was an insult. 'Be assured, you would not soon forget the welcome offered to you at the Ebony Towers.'

Eudokia tilted her head off-kilter. 'How strange a thing it is, but to my aged eyes, the construction surrounding us is rather more of a crimson colour than black.'

'Your eyes are not at fault,' the Aubade replied. 'We are within the walls of the Red Keep, the seat of my line since the Founding. And whatever may be the case in Aeleria or elsewhere in the city, those I have made welcome may rest comfortably in the full certainty of my hospitality, entitled to all the dignity due them.' It did not take a woman of Eudokia's subtlety to recognise to whom this last had been addressed.

Nor was the Lord of the Ebony Towers confused on the issue. 'And the Red Keep is within the Roost, and the Roost has been the home of the Eternal for a dozen generations before the coming of this . . . woman, and in none of them has the Prime ever lowered themselves to welcome a locust with such courtesy.'

'It is no surprise to me, sibling, that you demonstrate confusion as to the essential quality of magnanimity. The dictates of honour are not to be cast aside according to whim, nor is it a treasure to be reserved for the deserving – it is a kindness one does oneself, a reminder and a demonstration of one's own personal worth. That you have not yet grasped this fact I can only attribute to youthful folly.'

'Well spoken, my Lord Prime,' Eudokia said fondly. 'Epigrammatic, dare I say.'

'Does one offer hospitality to the rats in one's pantry? Or the lice on those rats?'

'Is that such a problem for my Lord of the Ebony Towers?' Eudokia asked. 'In Aeleria we use a certain sort of a poison; it's very effective against rodents of all sorts. Perhaps I might be so bold as to send my Lord a bottle?'

'In the Ebony Towers, we know well how to deal with pests. And I assure you none are so fortunate as to expire via poison. There are entire chambers within my house which are dedicated to nothing but the slow extermination of those creatures which I find unwanted.'

'It seems an awful lot of trouble to go through just to rid your pantries of vermin, but then the Lord of the Ebony Towers may arrange his eponymous domicile as he sees fit. Are there iron maidens for the cockroaches? Have you constructed very tiny racks for the mice?'

The Lord of the Ebony Towers loomed over her as an adult does a child, and his eyes were the colour of his home. His face was white as broken bone, and each of his four fingers would have run from Eudokia's wrist to her elbow. Jahan tensed ever so slightly beside her, though for once she did not suppose even the savage Parthan would be much help should the Shrike choose to give vent to his hate.

If Eudokia had not been Eudokia, she might even have been frightened.

She could hear the Aubade rise from behind her, feel him at her back like the noonday sun. He hissed something in their strange tongue, sounding more like the rustling of the leaves than human speech. The Lord of the Ebony Towers responded in kind, and in truth had she not been witness to the conversation prior, indeed if she had not directed it, then Eudokia would not have supposed them in the midst of dispute. But then, conflict is the universal constant, evident in all sentient creatures, many-branched stags bullying each other in the fields, alley cats in the trash heaps of the capital, and Eudokia knew it as well as anything that had ever lived. When it was over the Lord of the Ebony Towers had such hate in his eyes as would kindle a bonfire, but it was the sort of rage that would never pass beyond them.

He turned his loathing on Eudokia full-bore for a moment, then stomped away without farewell.

Eudokia turned slowly to the Prime, smiled her ineffable smile. 'Has the Lord of the Ebony Towers retired for the evening? Pity – I was so enjoying our conversation.'

7

There had been a time before the Roost – before the mountain was hollowed, before the first drop of water blessed the summit. Before the towers and citadels of the Eternal caressed the sun and scraped the full belly of the moon. Before the Source, before the canals. Before the slopes were graded into Rungs, before the walls were erected to separate them. Before the slurp. A time when Those Above roamed across the continent, unhindered, unfettered by home or the obligations of power. While humans in animal furs huddled round peat fires, fearing the night, the Eternal wandered the length of the coast and far beyond, as free as anything that had ever lived, bound only by sentience. And then the crime, the sin that could never be expunged, and the terrible punishment that followed – a culling without number, and those humans that survived scattering to the distant corners of the land, centuries before they would begin to eke out some semblance of civilisation, or marched to the coast to spend generations carving out the mountain and building the foundations of the Roost.

Or perhaps none of these things had ever happened. There were no Eternal alive who could remember it, and they had no books, no written records or documents. What was the difference between history and myth, Calla wondered? Both purported to explain the circumstances of the moment, but only the latter did so to any useful degree. Sentiment, theme, these are in the end more important than fact, because fact cannot be changed, fact can be only weathered. The punishment was reality, the punishment was fact, and thus the crime must have been true as well. A man will accept anything, if he is convinced he deserves it.

The Anamnesis was, regardless, the celebration of this punishment, the yoke that had fallen and now would forever lie on the humans of the continent. In the docks far below, the true balance of the slave nations' tribute had already been delivered – vast weight of ore, caravels filled with cotton and silk and silver, unfathomable quantities of foodstuffs, the raw materials with which the Roost operated. Across the First and the Second the Anamnesis was considered an occasion for great merriment, any concern about the origin of the holiday forgotten in frivolity. In the past it had been the same on the lower Rungs as well, though with the mood downslope so grim these days, Calla did not suppose there would be many bold enough to drink a toast to their continued subjugation.

Here in the Conclave the Source spilled sweet water high and bright into the open air. Waiting to be called in by the master of protocol were the representatives of the surrounding nations, ambassadors leading five pairs of slaves, males and females, the annual tithe of flesh to be paid as it had been paid for millennia. It was a motley if elegant assortment. Salucians in bright silk, high-collared, smooth-tongued and obsequious even by the standards of the slave states, though they could hardly afford to be otherwise with the Aelerians occupying half their kingdom. Their national enemies stood somewhat further back in line, the senator who had so nakedly stared at Calla's backside during the party at the Red Keep, and a number of curious-looking slaves who did not resemble him in physiognomy or dress. The Dycian contingent were all nearly as tall as the Well-born and dark as charred firewood, and they stared wide-eyed at the Source with undisguised wonder. Behind them stood the grandees of Vryngia and Gardariki, minor kingdoms far to the north, where rimefrost gripped the earth for nine months of the year, whale blubber was their chief source of sustenance and the Eternal were barely even myth. At the moment, pride of place belonged to the ambassador from the Baleferic Isles. A short man but well-formed, skin the colour of summer honey, and offering his pronouncement in the human speech of the Roost with an accent that was just scarcely detectable. He held a pomegranate branch, three fat fruits dangling from the end, and behind him were five paired couples, slaves hand-picked for their beauty and grace.

Across the First the Eternal prepared for the evening festivities, which were, even by the standards of the Roost, quite elaborate, and to receive this great parade of tribute there were only the Prime and the Lord of the Sidereal Citadel, seated a short distance above the dais, engaged in a not particularly quiet conversation, unrelated entirely to the proceedings. Protocol only demanded that the Prime be present during the submission of the Dayspans, not that he actually pay attention to it.

'The Sentinel says they receive reinforcements daily,' the Prime said. His robes were samite and sterling silver, the long stalks of his hair were pleated and particoloured, pavonine and glorious. The great diamond that was the sole evidence of his office shimmered and dazzled from its place in his headdress. 'That by spring they will have more than made up any losses they have suffered thus far during the campaign.'

The Lord of the Sidereal Citadel was known more widely among the humans of the Roost as the Wright, and esteemed for his brilliance as an inventor and craftsman. It was he who had been responsible for the aerocraft that had lately come to bloom in the skies above the Roost, as well as innumerable other wonders during the long centuries of his life. He was also the confidant and the closest friend of the Prime, though there were times when Calla was not certain this was a useful term to apply to Those Above. 'And?'

'It is a very large sword not to bother unsheathing.'

'The Dayspans kill one another,' the Wright explained. He held an empty flute, though after two quick tics of his second finger a house-slave came forward with a pitcher and then he held a full one. 'They have always, and ever will.'

'How strong will we allow Aeleria to grow without responding? Once they have added the great wealth of Salucia to the vast riches they have obtained from the Marches and Dycia? When they have used this wealth to further consolidate their supremacy?'

'Supremacy among the humans, you mean. Is not the Aelerian ambassador here today with his gifts? Have they not delivered their tithe? What concern is it whether one or the other flag waves over one or other city? We receive our due, as was ever the case.'

The Baleferic ambassador consummated his devotions by dropping to his knees and setting the branch at the foot of the Prime's seat. Moving past him with hurried dancer's steps came the slaves, naked to the waist, caramel-coloured, the women high-breasted, the men broad-shouldered and tight-muscled. Watching them, a flush gathered across Calla's cheeks.

'The Aelerians are late immigrants to the continent,' the Prime said, by all appearances unaware of the spectacle being performed in his honour. 'Scarcely half a millennium since their ancestors came to our shores, and only three centuries since we proscribed their king and his line.'

'I am not incognisant of recent history. What is your point, exactly?'

'They have never accepted their role, as have the other, older nations. They do not appreciate the blessings our rule provides. They are more than fractious, and their aims go beyond amassing the balance of power against their neighbors. They aim for dominance, supremacy. They would devour us, if they could.'

'So would the ants,' the Wright answered. 'It is not intent but capacity with which we ought to concern ourselves. By the Founders, surely you cannot have forgotten the last war. It was barely ten turns ago.'

The Baleferic ambassador struggled to keep himself level, an awkward pose and the strain growing on his face. His accompanying slaves remained still and silent, as is the way of slaves generally. Calla was about to make some small signal but it proved unnecessary, the Prime finally deigning to play his end of the charade. He stood in one swift motion, in the curious and abrupt fashion with which they moved, and announced in a sonorous version of human speech, 'Your crime was beyond forgiving, and law and honour enjoin us to proscribe you entire. But we are a merciful people, kinder than we are just, and your punishment shall be set back another year.'

The Prime sat back down again. The ambassador executed the final part of the ceremony, an elaborate bow of contrition, then departed. The master of protocol moved swiftly to gather up his leavings. The slaves would be parcelled off to one of the Eternal houses, more trouble than they were worth, in truth, beautiful but ignorant and unhelpful. Three years ago Calla had been stuck with a girl from Dycia, eyes rich as chocolate, heavy-breasted, not a word of Roost Speech to her and not much thought apart from that, so far as Calla had been able to discern. After three months as the worst seamstress Calla had ever encountered she had managed to marry the girl off to a cook from the Sidereal Citadel with more lust than sense. It had been long millennia since the Roost had required any further human labour, and the annual addition to the populace was simply one of those antiquated customs that could never be repealed.

'It was twenty years since the Aelerians last rose in rebellion,' the Prime corrected. 'Long enough for a generation to have been nursed on bitterness, and for those in charge of the Commonwealth to consider carefully their errors.'

'Bitterness, certainly, though what else could be expected of the locusts? As for the suggestion that their defeat has led to wisdom, there I'm afraid I cannot agree. Humans are, in my experience, little capable of assessing a situation and even less of affecting an alteration. Though of course, the point is moot – for how could a mouse learn to defeat a hawk? What are the tricks or stratagems by which the deer might hunt and chase and devour the wolf?'

'There were empty saddles when we returned to the Roost, sibling – the old Lord of the Ebony Towers, the Lady of the Aureate Seat—'

'Among how many who descended from the summit? What irrelevant fraction of the whole? I have never been known for my talents or interest in war, and your expertise is of course by far the greater. But I recall that morning, the locusts unable to stand the sight of us, panicking and breaking before even we reached them with our lances. It would not have mattered how many they brought that day. An additional ten thousand men, or twenty thousand, would have only meant more corpses, more food for the rats and the vultures.'

'That day,' the Prime conceded. 'Though that day was only that day, and not today, and certainly not tomorrow.'

The master of protocol called in the next ambassador, from Gardariki to the far north, some distant and miserable northern hellhole, thatch huts beside an icebound sea. The ambassador was fortunate to be spending the winter in the temperate climate of the Roost, and twice-lucky were the ten slaves who would never again need to concern themselves with the fierce chill of their homeland. Or at least this was what Calla told herself.

'You are wrong,' the Prime said, 'in thinking them beneath contempt. And if you are right now, you will not always be so. To keep the humans divided, to keep them weak, this was the policy of the Founders, nor has it diminished in wisdom in the ageless aeons since. Should Aeleria swallow Salucia, as it has Dycia and the border nations, there will be no further obstacles to their dominion. A few years with the wealth of Salucia and who knows what army it might amass?'

'The road to Hyrcania stretches past the Roost,' the Wright reminded him. 'Should the Aelerians suppose to violate our directives and attempt to conquer Salucia outright, there will be plenty of time to repay their foolishness.'

The ambassador from Gardariki held aloft a long stretch of ermine pelt, pure and unblemished white. His speech was rather less perfect, tumbling over the rote words in a thick and guttural accent. His slave couples were not, to Calla's way of thinking, quite so lovely as had been those from the Baleferic Isles. Too broad and too pale, skin so fair that she could make out the blue veins beneath, bright shocks of red hair.

'Time,' the Aubade repeated, as if it was a word that had never developed a consensus of meaning. After a long and uncomfortable silence, uncomfortable for the humans below the podium, at least, Calla did have to signal; the slightest clearing of her throat but he noticed it, standing swiftly and repeating his portion of the ceremony. 'Your crime was beyond forgiving, and law and honour enjoin us to proscribe you entire. But we are a merciful people, kinder than we are just, and your punishment shall be set back another year.'

The ambassador seemed pleased to hear it, bowing and leaving the stage swiftly. After a moment the Lord of the Sidereal Citadel did the same, excusing himself to prepare for the evening's merriment. The Prime alone was left – the Prime and Calla, and several dozen other human servants, and the representatives of the surrounding human nations, of slightly less account.

'How many are left?' the Prime asked, the first words he had directed at her and in the human speech.

'Twelve, my Lord.'

With one hand the Prime called for another glass of wine, and with the other he gestured at his slaves to continue their deference.

8

It was a nondescript building on the Fourth Rung, or at least Pyre so hoped, a red brick townhouse owned by one of their supporters, a man from the Second who had come to a meeting and been blessed by the truth, left desperate to give anything he could to the cause, his wealth and his goods and his children, the very blood in his veins. It was the sort of neighbourhood one walked past quickly, without paying attention to what one saw. The cafe across the street was the same as five others in the immediate vicinity and a thousand others on the Rung. The two men who sat at the outside table were nearly as unassuming, perhaps a bit larger than average, and a bit more serious, and if you were to hang around long enough you might notice that they did not make any serious effort to finish their pot of tea.

Pyre turned quickly into an inner courtyard and towards an exterior door. A very dark-skinned young man lounged in the dust beside it, one more downslope loser without anything to occupy his afternoons, sitting on a loose roll of aged fabric and swigging from a wine jug.

In the jug was water. In the bolt of cloth was a knife. 'You're late,' said Redemption, the First of His Line.

'I spent the last two hours criss-crossing the docks, making sure I didn't see any familiar faces in my wake.'

'You think the Cuckoos are clever enough to set a tail?'

'No. But in matters of such importance . . .'

'Of course.'

'All has been clear from your end?'

'Yes, Brother Pyre,' Redemption said quietly. 'Though he gets tired of being cooped up.'

'It's for his own good,' Pyre said.

'I know.'

'Where is he?'

'Where do you think? In the back.'

'How long are you keeping the boys at the cafe?'

'We rotate them through every few hours.'

'And the owner?'

'He doesn't know nothing.'

'People know more than they pretend,' Pyre said quietly, then nodded and headed further into the building.

Redemption let out a loud whistle, and the men with knives waiting behind the front door opened it and waved Pyre in, rather than murdering him and shoving his body into the slurp. Pyre passed through a long, dark passageway and then through a second door.

In the moment before Pyre stepped into the back garden his mind was filled, as it was almost all the time, by the responsibilities of his office; Tower's cell had been silent the last three days, long enough for worry to turn to grim certainty. No doubt at this very moment Tower was in a windowless room with a ferule ringing against his skull, one more victim of the demons, and may his blood hasten the age to come. There was a crate of blades at the docks that needed to make its way to the far corner of the Fourth, beneath the noses of the custodians who had grown in the last months to take their jobs with unforgiving seriousness. Across the Third they were at something like open warfare with the Brotherhood Below, two clashes the last night alone and neither had gone well. Back on the Fifth, one of their better lay preachers, spreading the truth to the lower Rungs, had gone missing the night before and no one was sure whether he'd been snatched up by the Cuckoos or if he was holed up with a girl or if he had fled the city or if he had fallen into the slurp.

A host of concerns, a concatenation of worries, but they went silent when he saw Edom. The smile that never wavered, eyes that promised forgiveness. Late autumn and the gardens were all but bare yet he tended to them anyway, with the same diligence and care with which he had nurtured the truth these long years. Edom turned from his work long enough to take Pyre's hand. The sun was bright and unseasonably warm, and fell pleasantly against the back of Pyre's neck.

'Pyre, the First of His Line.'

'Father.'

'You had said the hour of the Eagle.'

'The demons and their servants grow more clever. Not much more clever, but . . . I wanted to make sure I wasn't being followed. Your safety cannot be risked.'

'And your safety?'

'My value to the species lies only in so far as I am willing to risk it – your situation is a different one entirely. There are many who could be Pyre, but there is only one Edom.'

'Who would make so much of an old man, weak and enfeebled as I am?' Edom asked, work robes tight against his broad chest.

'Anyone who had ever met him. Anyone who ever heard the truth of that man.'

'Few are able to hear the truth, any more.'

Pyre sighed. 'There were spies in the last audience. There were spies of the Cuckoos and the demons themselves. They have grown to fear you, Father, they have that much wisdom in them at least. There are others who can give voice to the truth, not as well or as fully, but to a parched man a drop of water is better than none. I know it grieves you to sit idle. I know you loathe having others do work best done by yourself. But it is necessary, Father. You are too precious to risk.'

Edom shrugged the praise off his shoulders, knelt back down into the dirt. A crop of weeds had sprung up from soil, and he began to worry at their roots with his spade. 'I understand that your attack on the Slate Bank was successful.'

'There was such joy on the Fifth, Father, as I think has never been equalled. I am told the feeling upslope is rather reversed.'

'We do not celebrate their lamentation, Pyre.'

'No, Father.'

'They are slaves, as we were, as are all of those who have not yet heard the truth.'

'Of course.'

'Though one would need to be a saint not to feel some sense of satisfaction.'

'I am no saint.'

'Nor I.'

Pyre was not sure he agreed.

'And it was false wealth, it was chickenfeed and not gold. They are better off without such a yoke of sin weighing down their souls.'

'I suspect they would disagree.'

Edom laughed.

'Word has reached me from your benefactor,' Pyre said.

'And?'

'She has arrived in the city, and wishes a meeting. Somewhere upslope, near where the demons have her quartered.'

'Then you must arrange it.'

'Are you certain she can be trusted?'

'No,' Edom admitted, struggling with a particularly tenacious strand of green. 'I'm not certain of anything like that at all. But I can say with certainty that we need her.'

Pyre dropped down beside Edom, brushed his hands away gently. One firm pull and the thing was loosed from the soil.

'Thank you.'

Pyre smiled and set it on the pile.

'Our benefactor is not the only one who wishes to hold a meeting,' Edom said. 'The other members of the council grow concerned. It has been nearly three months since the last gathering.'

'Things are . . . difficult, right now, Father, and a meeting of the council is not so easily provided. It is one thing to sneak you safely to one of our locations, and another to do the same for a dozen men from every corner of the Roost.'

Edom handed the spade to Pyre, brushed loam up against the roots of a small fruit tree. 'Pyre is a very clever young man,' he announced, 'and I have faith in his abilities.'

'There are members of the council who may have the eyes of the Birds upon them unknowing. There are members of the council who may be the eyes of Birds themselves.'

'I will not hear this again.'

'Your safety is too important to be jeopardised stroking the egos of a handful of upslope financiers.' Pyre realised that his fist was tight round the handle of the spade.

Edom looked at him for a long time, then stood and led him over to a stone bench that bordered the nursery. For a few moments they observed the last of the late fall blooms, dahlias and purple salvia, Pyre taking Edom's lead in silence, as he did in many things.

'Did you sleep last night?' Edom asked.

'Yes.'

'For how long?'

'Long enough.'

'Five hours?'

Pyre smiled a little. He had not slept five hours in six months. He could recall a time in which he had spent the better part of the day lost in slumber, in which oblivion seemed the chief weapon by which he might combat life's miseries, but it seemed one long distant. 'Very nearly.'

Edom grunted sadly. 'I suppose the demons have committed worse sins than the theft of your youth. But I admit it is one for which I fear to answer the Self-Created.'

'For once, the demons need not be slandered, and you know your regrets are equally weightless. There are no children on the Fifth Rung. If I were still Thistle, I'd as like be dead, or worse, damned entirely. You saved my soul when you found me.'

'You heard the truth. Not all are willing to do so.'

'Thank you, Father.'

'But you are not the only one to have heard it.'

'I know that, Father.'

'The species did not come into being with Pyre, the First of His Line.'

'Of course not, Father.'

'There are men who suppose the enthusiasm with which you pursue our cause is more worrisome than laudatory. That behind your passion there is the budding seed of an usurper, who sees in the truth a path to power.'

'The nightmares of fools and ingrates are of no concern to me,' Pyre said, though the bile that rose up in his throat then belied his claim to indifference. 'So long as this is no fear of Edom's.'

Edom put his hand on Pyre's hand for a time, but said nothing.

'I apologise,' Pyre said after a moment.

'Then you will arrange the meeting?'

'Of course, Father,' Pyre said. 'Your will in all things.'

To judge by Edom's smile, this was a sentiment with which he could agree. 'The blessings of the Self-Created upon you, this morning. May you live to see the dawn.'

'So long as it comes, Father,' Pyre said, 'it does not matter if I am there to celebrate it.'

Edom returned to his tasks, knees down in the dirt as if he were no more than a common manservant. Pyre watched him from the doorway for longer than he should have, given everything that he had left to do that day, given his long slate of duties. He entered the house smiling but by the time he was again out front his face had returned to its usual hardness, black and hard as a lump of coal.

Redemption was where Pyre had left him, lounging languid

against a wall, ready for swift murder should the moment demand it.

'Purchase the cafe,' Pyre said.

'I'm not sure how amenable the owner is to selling.'

'I suspect you'll find a way to convince him.'

'I suspect.'

'And I'm sending you four more men.'

'Yes.'

'I would send you more if I had them.'

'I know that, Brother Pyre.'

'That man in there is the spark. That man in there is the most important thing in all of creation.'

'I know it, Brother Pyre,' Redemption said seriously. 'I know it.'

9

They called Oscan the Silver City, because its towers and buildings were quarried from the same stone as the slate mountains that rose up behind them, and because of the great wealth it had gained as the key trading post between the Commonwealth and Salucia. Even in the west, Bas had heard rumours of its markets, where steel and slaves and furs from the Marches met the silk and sugar traders coming down from Salucia. Twenty years since the demons had given it to Salucia in compensation for Aeleria's invasion, but they had done nothing to impoverish the city. What did the people of Oscan, far from the pretensions of Senate or Queen, far from the themas or the Eternal, care for the politicking of the great powers? There were always fortunes to be made by clever people who did not scruple to make a fetish of patriotism, who were more interested in trade than empire.

Until empire comes knocking.

The pillaging that had followed Oscan's capture had been no

more savage or brutal or cruel than usual, which was to say that by the end of it a native would have been hard pressed to recognise his home. The fires had begun the second day, the product of sabotage by a Salucian partisan, or brutality on the part of a hoplitai drunk on blood and liquor, or perhaps simply of an overturned candle, an errant spark that had found no one to extinguish it. When it had finished burning most of the west city was ash, more corpses by far than had been made in the city's capture. Plague came next, and was worse, as inevitable as the fires, men and women and children now homeless, ill-clothed, drinking fouled water, winter's approach in the air, and what food arrived in the city was commandeered swiftly by the themas. Belatedly, Konstantinos had attempted to restrict the evacuation of the citizens north towards the Salucian heartland, to make some effort to hold on to the human capital that had made Oscan a prize worth winning, but it saw no great success. Two months after its capture Oscan was no more a city than a skeleton is a man. Some pale fraction of the former population remained, picking through the debris, surviving as best they could, scavenging through the wasteland or accommodating the invaders.

As for those invaders? The three thema were not enough to fill the vastness of the dead metropolis. In the eastern portion of the city, where the army was garrisoned, there was some rough simulacrum of civilisation, small bazaars selling black-market goods, makeshift bars and whorehouses of course, always whorehouses. But in the hinterlands beyond it was still and quiet as a cenotaph. After the early days of plunder and rapine, the army had fallen into an unquiet and deleterious routine. They drank. They gambled. They fought each other and anyone else. They waited for the remaining themas to join them from the west, and they waited for whatever exactly it was they would do with those themas.

The smell of ale and of sawdust and of unwashed flesh. The rattle of dice against a hewn wooden table. A laugh, a shout. A woman's voice, sultry or trying to be so. A man's, cruel as men's often are.

'Let us see if the gods grant you luck,' Hamilcar said, 'having offered so little else by way of kindness.' Hamilcar was the leader of the Dycian contingent of the Aelerian forces, a few thousand men with recurved bows and long knives and a willingness to kill with either. They had been happy enough to turn those weapons on Aeleria, and they had been happy enough in the years since Dycia's fall to use those weapons in the service of their one-time enemies. Or at least they knew enough not to complain outright. He was of average height but somehow seemed taller, in part the product of his garish clothing, a disparate arrangement, borrowed from the dozen nations he had lived in or travelled through: heavy furs from the Marches, a bright silk scarf from his homeland, thick gold armbands, a jewelled necklace that he had not been wearing the day before Oscan's capture. But mostly it was because he talked constantly, incessantly, as if fearful of the silence, and because what he said was usually clever and always very loud.

'Your mother was a whore,' Isaac began in response. He was one of the ugliest men that Bas had ever seen, and the themas were not known as great showcases of physical beauty. Bas thought he would have been very ugly even if he hadn't had his ears cropped off some quarter-century earlier, partial payment for a crime of which Isaac had never spoken. The rest of his scars had come from the remainder of his restitution, the long years he had spent doing Aeleria's killing, working his way up from the ranks to become Bas's adjutant. He was tough as boiled leather and less mean than he might have been, given what he had done and seen. He was as competent as any man living, a better logistician than Bas, and if he feared death that fear was always far away when battle was joined. 'And your grandmother a temple whore, and your great-grandmother the biggest, blackest whore Dycia ever saw.'

'I take it you won't try and make the point?' Hamilcar asked. Bas had once seen Hamilcar cut two fingers off the hand of a man who had brushed past him disrespectfully while at table, but this sort of banter was so customary as to be barely noticeable.

'I didn't say that,' Isaac said, sitting back down and grabbing the cup from Hamilcar. He rattled the dice loudly and began again to curse, exhorting the gods or lamenting the certainty of cruel fate. In this case it proved the latter, and his pile of coins diminished appropriately.

'It's your roll, boy,' Hamilcar said, passing the cup to Theophilus. 'Or would it perhaps be easier simply to hand me your money now, and go find some other way to occupy your time?'

'I have memories of you, Hamilcar,' Theophilus said, setting his flagon down, blond beard wet with ale, 'in which you seem clever. Was that the folly of youth, or did you take a blow to the skull and not think to mention it?'

Isaac roared and beat his fist against the table. 'Wit will not make you the point, master of horse!' he said.

'It is obvious to anyone looking that Isaac is the beaten dog of Enkedri and his children,' Theophilus said, holding the dice cup in his hands for a moment. Hung round his neck was a chain of command, heavy gold linked with heavier iron, announcing to those who could decipher the customs of the themas that he was now head of horse for the Army of the East, reward in part for his good service in taking Oscan. 'And equally clear to anyone looking at me, at my face and carriage, that I am simply one of those fortunate few who the gods have always favoured.'

Though in that moment it seemed they decided to desert him, the dice coming up an unhappy pair of pips. Theophilus cursed bitterly and Isaac laughed loudly and Hamilcar passed the cup over to Bas.

In truth, Bas did not care to gamble, or at least he did not care to gamble with anything so frivolous as gold, and he made his roll with a bare flicker of interest. Isaac, having backed Bas on his bet, cheered lustily. Hamilcar winced and pushed a few coins across the table to merge with the rest of Bas's winnings, winnings he did not need and barely noticed.

Bas had seen the man from above the rim of his cup, standing near the counter and turning to look at their table every few moments, furtively, gathering up courage like a boy visiting his first whore. An Aelerian to guess by his colouring, though it didn't matter; Bas's celebrity had long since eclipsed national pride, in the past Salucians and Dycians and far-flung Chazars had approached him in the marketplace and the streets, asked for blessing as if he was a priest, or a lock of his hair as if he was a beauty.

'Excuse me sir—' the man began, crossing over to the their table.

'Yes, I'm the Caracal,' Hamilcar answered, puffing out his chest and adopting an expression of great importance. 'The greatest swordsman who ever lived, the strong right hand of the Commonwealth, slayer of demons, champion of humanity, a cock the size of child's arm. You can have my scrawl on a bit of parchment for two silver tertarum, or eighteen bronze nummu.'

Confusion, bewilderment. The world upended, right as wrong and up as down. 'But . . . you're black,' the man said.

Hamilcar looked surprised, then offended, then made an elaborate impression of surveying what portion of his skin was not covered with fur or cloth or gold. 'So it seems.'

'The Caracal isn't black,' the man averred, after a moment's consideration.

'Yes, I am,' Hamilcar said.

'Yes, he is,' Theophilus agreed.

'Black as night,' Isaac said. 'Black as sin.'

'Black as the winter moon,' Theophilus added, straight-faced in an ash-blond beard.

'But . . . the moon isn't black, either.'

'You're very clever,' Hamilcar said, emptying the dice cup and cursing at the result. 'And you're terrible luck. Go away now, you just lost me three silver. The Caracal is not pleased!' he announced to the bar in a voice loud and fierce enough to send the fool scurrying, 'bring more liquor!'

The last, at least, was a sentiment with which Bas could agree. The proprietor of the nameless bar in which they were whiling away the evening as they had whiled away the better part of the winter had been one of the innumerable camp-followers the army drew along in its wake, a double-dealer, a con man, a scavenger and a cheat, clever and fearless in pursuit of his fortune. He had moved into the place after the sack, its original inhabitants dead or fled or in any case, being in no position to dispute ownership. He came over with another jug of bad ale, set it down on the table with a heavy thud. In the days immediately after the conquest it had been possible to drink the finest Dycian wines for a handful of copper pennies, but the riotous orgy of waste had reached its inevitable end and the last few weeks there had been no decent liquor for silver nor gold, nothing but the strong and unappetising barley wine.

Bas drank it anyway.

'Do you ever wonder what it would be like to smile?' Hamilcar asked. 'Half my pot is now yours, and I've yet to see hint of a tooth.'

'Have you ever known the Legatus to be full of cheer?' Theophilus asked.

'There were times when I found him less overwhelmingly depressing.'

'I think he finds our accommodations insalubrious.'

'There are worse places to winter,' Isaac observed. 'You know how many years I shivered beneath a horsehide yurt, peat smoke and a half-breed my only hope for warmth? I, for one, am not so quick to forget the virtues of a stone wall.'

'It was cold,' Theophilus agreed, 'but at least it was clean. The rats grow large as dogs, and have begun to get ideas beyond their station. They say that in the far corners of the city they gather together in packs, pull down unwary children and devour them whole.'

'Then they are the only thing so flourishing,' Hamilcar observed. 'A girl offered me her daughter for a loaf of bread, last evening.'

'Hardly our fault,' Theophilus said, still young enough to

feel some semblance of patriotism, 'if the smallfolk would bring their goods to market, none would need starve. Our supply lines are stretched feeding our own people – we can't very well be expected to provide for three themas and the entirety of Oscan.'

'I thought the Oscans were your people,' Hamilcar observed. 'and we were here to liberate them from the oppressive yoke of Salucia.'

'But Hamilcar,' Isaac brought his cup down from yellowed teeth. 'We have liberated Oscan – can't you tell by the smoke?'

'We won't be here much longer,' Theophilus said. 'The Salucians will come to terms soon enough. A drop in their tariff rates, a bowed head, and we'll be back in Aeleria before the summer.'

'You think so?' Bas asked, his first words in a long hour, and he regretted them immediately.

His companions looked across at each other.

'The Caracal knows something we do not,' Hamilcar observed.

'No certainties. Only suspicions.'

'And what are those?'

'Three themas have been ordered to Oscan by the Senate. The Fifth, the Eighth, and the Thirteenth.' Isaac banged the table twice in recognition of their old thema, but Bas continued on above him. 'When they arrive in early spring we will have amassed the largest army in the history of the Commonwealth. Do you suppose we have collected them for leverage at the negotiating table?'

'And what does the Protostrator say of these things?'

'Konstantinos keeps his own council,' Bas said.

'And his stepmother?' Hamilcar asked.

Theophilus looked hard at Isaac, who looked hard at Hamilcar, who for once decided to shut his mouth further. Even among men well familiar with death, the Revered Mother's was not a name with which to joke.

'Are you the Caracal?' asked a man from behind him, the next in the steady line of well-wishers and sycophants drawn to Bas like flies to carrion.

Bas's shoulders slumped a bit but he didn't answer, or turn to look at the new arrival.

'Yes, he's the Caracal, you can tell by the fact that he's bigger than everyone else,' Hamilcar said flippantly, 'and he's trying to get drunk, which given his size is not so easy a task.'

'Piss, off,' Isaac added, blunter in all things and more protective of his leader.

Bas's cup was most of the way to his mouth and he had stopped paying much attention when something happened to Isaac's face, eyes starting to swell, and then Bas with that dim instinct for survival that lived in the hidden areas behind his conscious mind had flung himself sideways off the chair, shoulder banging against the hard wood of the floor. The man he had not bothered to turn and look at was standing over him then, a bright bit of steel in his hand, his eyes mad and wide and hateful.

'Murderer!' he screamed. 'Thief! Ravager! Killer of women and children, bastard son of a whore!'

'How could he have known that last one?' Bas wondered grimly.

Theophilus was nearest and moved to engage with this man whom Bas had never met before and who wished him dead as much as anything had ever wished for anything else, as much as parched earth wished for rain. Looking at him now as he had not a moment earlier, Bas could tell he was one of the Oscan upper crust, his clothes once fine but now faded, and also that he had no idea how to use his weapon, that he had probably not so much as held a fighting knife in the hours before his suicidal assault. But the curious thing about a knife is that it will cut as surely in the hands of an incompetent as in those of a master, and in the face of his unskilled but not ineffectual flailing Theophilus was unable to close.

'A city of bones, Caracal!' the man screamed, his blade whistling in the air, Theophilus dodging just out of reach, 'and you the cause! What hell awaits you, Caracal! What torment the gods have in store for your soul! Monster, demon, sower of discord and hate!'

Bas had not seen the blade in the moment before it landed,

was unsure even after where Hamilcar had hidden it, though unsurprised that it existed and even less at the unerring accuracy with which it was thrown. There was a flash in the torchlight and then a pommel jutted from just below the man's neck, and his eyes rolled back up into his head, and he tumbled backwards to join Bas on the ground.

Theophilus moved to help him to his feet, checking him over for wounds, saw there were none and remarked, 'Swift as ever, Caracal. Swift as ever.'

Isaac stood over the near-corpse, watched the last fluttering of his chest with the cool disinterest of a professional, as a cobbler might inspect a bolt of leather. 'A fine throw, seated as you were.'

'With my off hand at that,' Hamilcar said. He had come up from the table and dropped down beside the dying man, put one knee on the body, grunted and pulled the blade loose, being careful to dodge the spray of blood that escaped its release. 'Though in truth, I'd be ashamed to miss him at such a range.'

'Did you know him, Caracal?' Isaac asked.

'No.'

'War drives men mad,' Theophilus said.

Though thinking on it, then and later that evening, restless on the soft bed in his stolen quarters, Bas found he could not dispute any of the charges his would-be assassin had levelled.

10

On a cold, sunny day in winter they set Apple into the bay.

There were no graveyards in the Roost. The demons disposed of their dead by excarnation, leaving their bodies exposed on the cliffs at the top of the city to be picked dry by the birds. Those humans living upslope burned their corpses with little fanfare. In imitation of their masters they denied the existence of any divinity, supposed religion to be one of the many sorts of prejudices that they, alone among the species, were wise enough to be free of.

Of course it was an open secret that the inhabitants of the lower Rungs still clung to a slim belief in the pantheons of the surrounding lands, some choosing to offer their prayers and small sacrifices to Enkedri and his siblings, others to Mephet, Bull-headed god of Salucia, but most to a syncretic combination of the two. So it was not a general lack of piety that prescribed all but the barest rites for the corpses of the Fifth Rung; it was that there was nowhere to bury them, not with so many living cheek to jowl, and having abided in such a fashion for thousands and thousands of years. Most did not have six square feet to occupy when they had been alive, there was no possibility of finding such space for them after death. And anyway, below the ground were the pumps, and the sewers – a few shovel-fills and you started hitting pipe.

But still there was the sea. The canals were the exclusive province of the demons, but of the ocean itself even Those Above were not so mad as to think themselves owner. So it was that Mama and the three girls and Pyre and a handful of neighbours had taken Apple's body from their house, cleaned and wrapped in white cloth, and carried it downslope to the small quay set aside for this purpose, which had seen who knew how many of Pyre's ancestors sent out into the waves, an endless succession of flesh swallowed by the boundless sea. The craft they had purchased was waiting there for them, like a rowboat but smaller. They settled the body atop a bed of scrap wood and dry kindling, then set it adrift, Pyre himself throwing the torch. The smell of sea foam mixed with woodsmoke, and then with another smell, sweet and unpleasant, and then that was lost as well.

Mama did not weep. Of course she had been weeping all the previous evening, and the day before, when Apple had breathed his last, and the week before, when it had become clear how little time her youngest son had left. She had wept for a long time prior to that as well, a torrent falling fruitlessly to the earth, salt water with which to poison the ground. The girls cried to make up for it, though Pyre thought that only Thyme and Shrub, the two eldest, really understood what was going on.

Pyre did not cry either, though there was a moment, just before they put his little brother into the waters, his body so shrivelled and pale, when he very much wanted to. And this surprised him, because Pyre had rarely thought much of young Apple, now that it was too late to remedy the situation he could admit honestly that he had never been any sort of brother, not when he had been a boy, too caught up in misadventure and foolishness, and not now that he was a man. These last two years there had been barely a moment to dedicate to his family, and perhaps he had known also that there was nothing to be done, that Pyre had no more say in whom the gods chose to take than had Thistle.

He held his mother's hand on the short walk back to their tenement. The guests would arrive soon, adding plates of food to the feast that had already been prepared, and the people of the neighbourhood, who were decent despite what they had suffered, though sometimes Pyre had trouble remembering this, would do their meagre best to help a woman forget the death of something that had once lived inside her. It had been three months since Pyre had seen her, every waking minute since committed to the cause, to the mission, every waking moment and the better portion of his dreams, coming to fierce in the dead early hours of the morning, reaching for the knife hidden below his pillow in whatever safe house he was holed up in, realising it was not needed, not yet.

Pyre would not stay. It had been dangerous, perhaps even foolish, for him to have come this far. There were men in the Barrow who remembered Thistle, and who had heard of Pyre, and who were yet so foolish as to think to better their lot by doing him injury. Unbeknownst to his mother Pyre had stationed a pair of his people in one of the other rooms in her tenement; hopefully they would provide some warning if the Cuckoos ever managed to figure out who she was.

Pyre walked his mother to the doorway. She stood looking at him for a long time before she spoke. 'It was a good boat.'

'It was what we could offer, though less than he deserved.'

'He is with the gods now.'

'We all are.'

'You are safe?' she asked finally.

'As much as I can be.'

'And the work?' she asked. Pyre did not quite know what his mother thought he did for the Five-Fingered. Only that in those rare moments when he could afford to stop in and see her, when he felt it worth the risk, she looked at him in a way that she never had when he had been a layabout or a thug, and though she feared for his life, she had never asked him to stop.

'The truth is as the sun,' Pyre answered. 'Only a fool would seek to deny it, and with as much success.'

She nodded and held him tight and then went inside to mourn her youngest child.

Hammer was lounging in a caddy-corner alleyway, unobtrusive and unobserved. Against Pyre's orders he had shadowed them down to the jetty, as Pyre had known he would.

'Any trouble?' Pyre asked quietly, following the larger man through the narrow lane between his and the next strand of tenements. It had been an easy winter, and the withdrawing layer of rime had left behind broken spindles and stray bits of cloth, chicken bones and pig entrails, turds fresh and turds powdered.

'He was where you said he'd be,' Hammer answered. 'And he came along without any fuss.'

'Yes,' Pyre nodded. 'He was never much of a fighter.'

They came to the back door of a neighbourhood grocery, one of the dozens of safe houses that were scattered across the Fifth Rung and the Fourth and even some of the Third. A Dead Pigeon stood guard outside; Talon, tall, dark-skinned, very good with his fists. His father was a merchant of some renown and he had grown to manhood clad in soft silks, with personal tutors – all luxuries he had forsworn after hearing the truth. He nodded briskly and waved them down.

Through the back entrance was a small storage room, crates of empty liquor bottles and small sundries. Without saying anything Hammer moved a stack of these, revealing a small door behind it. He knocked twice, then paused, then knocked once, then paused and knocked again. The door swung open a moment later, another of Pyre's many comrades standing behind it and ushering them into the basement below.

Razor, the First of His Line, was tied to a chair, and he smiled a bit when he saw Pyre, muscle memory as much as anything else. They had been friends for as long as they'd been alive,

Barrow boys from back in the day. His name had been Felspar then, as Pyre's had been Thistle, according to the arbitrary nomenclature that ruled downslope, mothers naming their children after any passing thing that found their fancy. They had been close as brothers – or at least Pyre, not having known what that meant, had thought so. A passer-by seeing them together at five, at ten, at fifteen, would not have noticed much difference; the usual Fifth Rung runts, natty clothing and nasty eyes, making what trouble their inclinations suggested and their limited means allowed. Smash-and-grabs and cheap cons that went wrong as often as they went right, frantic dashes downslope to the docks or up to the Straits, looking for scrums and generally finding them.

But Pyre did not smile in answer. The two men standing on either side of Razor, the two men responsible for his captivity and, one could only assume, the line of bruises growing on Razor's face, did not smile either. Hammer very rarely smiled, did not start then. After a short moment, Razor's face shared a grim, even line with the rest of them.

'Hello, Felspar.'

'Hello, Pyre. I'm sorry about Apple.'

'Thank you.'

There was only the one chair, and it was clearly occupied. Unprompted, Hammer grabbed one of the heavy crates from the corner, pushed it in front of the captive. Pyre sat down on it but did not say anything, just watched Felspar with heavy eyes.

'I was scared to death the first time I had to do this,' Pyre said finally.

'I'm scared to death right now,' Felspar responded, and gave another weak smile.

'His name was Chalice, he was a tradesman on the Fourth Rung. We were not well acquainted, but he had known the truth for years, long before Edom's name had made its way down here. He was one of the men responsible for security, before that task was turned over in its entirety to me. It was an important position; it was also, potentially, a lucrative position, should the man holding it decide to make business with our misguided fellows, and the Four-Fingered monsters for whom they labour.'

Again Pyre went silent. Within the heavy stone walls the city sounds were obscured entirely; all that Felspar could hear was the slurp and his own beating heart, and to break free for a moment from the relentless rhythm of the latter, he asked, 'Can I have a cigarette?'

Pyre nodded to Hammer, who began to roll it. 'The organisation was growing; many were hungry for Edom's truth, already half-formed in their hearts, waiting only to be pronounced. Likewise, there were many who feared the word, who saw it for what it was; a blade sharpened, an arrow notched, a spark brought to tinder. The demons knew to fear it, and their human servants, still befogged, knew as well. Chalice had debts. Against them he set his integrity, the future of his children, the very soul of his species. The first time that one of our meetings in his section was raided, I thought it bad luck. The second time I grew suspicious. The third time I knew. I knew. But certainty is not proof; do you understand? You cannot kill a man because you dislike him, or even because you distrust him. That is not justice. I had Chalice brought to me – I determined, one way or another, that I would find the truth.'

Pyre held the pause for a moment, as a child with a ball or a god with the world.

'It was a room like this one. He was in a chair, as you are. I stood over him with a blade. He was older than me, a full-grown man while I was barely more than a cub. He began to speak; first angrily, demanding to know what was happening, why he had been taken, on what authority did I hold him prisoner? And when I did not answer he went quiet, and in the silence I could hear his guilt. I could hear it and so could he, as if the three of us, he and I and his sin, were sharing the room, as if it was seated between us. But even then, when I knew, knew for a certainty, knew the way I know the five fingers at the end of my hand, still I was frightened. For his crimes demanded only one sentence, one I had never before delivered, one I feared to pronounce.'

Hammer handed Pyre the cigarette he had rolled. Pyre lit it off a nearby candle, brought it tenderly to Felspar's lips.

'But from inside this fear there came truth, truth that swallowed and eclipsed my terror and Chalice's terror as well. Because it was not Pyre sitting in a room with Chalice, not Pyre who would be required to judge the truth of Chalice's words, to pass sentence, to carry it out. It was the future in combat with the past. The new age dawns, and we are driven on before it. And staring at the face of it, as I did in that moment with Chalice, as I am in this moment right now, one can understand the futility of falsehood, of anger or despair. The will of the gods is clear in all things, clear and immutable, and it is to us only to recognise that truth, to grow towards it as a plant does the sun. Chalice understood that, in the last, before we did to him what needed to be done. And I think you understand it now as well, Felspar. Behind me walks the spirit of a people who will be free. I am a slave to its destiny, as are you.' Pyre pulled the cigarette out from his old friend's lips. A bit of smoke escaped into the close air of the room. 'When did they approach you?'

'I was drinking in a bar on the Fourth Rung. The Borrowed Harp, I doubt you've ever been there. Maybe it was a set-up,' Feslpar said, then shrugged and shook his head back and forth. 'I don't know. I guess I might have mentioned a bit that I was in with you, to some girl or other. You know how . . . you know I run my mouth sometimes, don't mean to but there it is. When I woke up there were bruises on my knuckles and on my face, and there was a Cuckoo telling me that I'd gotten into a brawl, that they'd be taking me in front of a magistrate the next morning, that I'd be underground before noon. I couldn't go down there, Pyre. I wouldn't survive it. I knew I wouldn't survive it.'

To be forced to labour beneath the ground, performing upkeep and maintenance on the pumps, was the standard punishment for any petty crime a human might commit, unceasing effort without sight of the sun. 'And?'

'They told me that they knew I was an initiate. That they

wanted some background information, nothing that would ever come back to hurt anyone. I never told them anything important, I swear to Enkedri, I swear to Mephet, I swear to—'

'What did you tell them?'

'The location of some of the meetings,' he said, eyes on the stone floor and on the yellowed mortar between them.

'Which ones?'

'The big one – the one you figured they already knew about, in the weaver district by the Fourth Rung. I didn't think I was harming anyone.'

'Did you name me?'

'They know who you are,' Felspar said, the smile returning, then retreating. 'Everyone knows who you are.'

'And my family?'

'No! I swear, Pyre. I swear. I never told them anything like that. I never would.'

'You hadn't yet – but will you look me in the eyes and tell me that you wouldn't?'

'It was mumble or go in the sewers. You can't blame me for that. You can't blame me for not wanting to die beneath the ground.'

'But I can, boy they call Felspar. I can and I do hold you responsible for the choices you have made. That is what it means to claim yourself the first of your line; that the randomness of your birth, the misfortune of your life thus far, these are of no consequence. It was you and you alone who chose weakness over strength, the easy path over the just. In truth this is my fault more than yours; I shouldn't have let you join; you were not yet ready for your new name. But you took it, Felspar, you took it and you dishonoured it. For this, there must be reckoning.'

Felspar's face was wan, and his eyes could not meet Pyre's. 'What happened to Chalice?'

'Chalice's crime was worse than yours,' Pyre said. 'But he paid for it like a man, and I hope – I believe – that the Self-Created has forgiven him. And I hope that he will do the same for you, though your punishment will not be so terrible.' Pyre stood suddenly, turned to Hammer. 'Clip him,' he said.

Felspar's eyes went wide and bright with fear. 'Please, Pyre, by the gods, by the Founding, by the Time Below – I've known you since we were children, for Rat's sake, for the sake of—'

The mention of their dead confederate, slaughtered randomly by the hand of a slumming Eternal, brought a black flash to Pyre's face, calloused knuckles tightening. 'I ought to judge you twice so harsh because we were friends. I ought to slit your throat and dump you in the slurp.' His eyes were bright and furious, but he blinked past the rage and continued on. 'But I will not – vengeance is not justice, and you will be given no more than your due.'

From a satchel on his back Hammer removed a short wooden box of no particular distinction, slid open the top. Inside was a cloth lining, and a wide-bladed chopping knife. Pyre took it, inspected the edge. Talon abandoned his spot by the door, began to undo the binding round Felspar's hands.

'Scream and I'll gag you – struggle and I'll beat you down,' Talon said.

But he was beaten down enough already, and he neither spoke nor moved, unmanned by fear. It was more than the cut itself, though that was far from pleasant, for all that Pyre would make sure to do it quickly, two swift movements and then they would cauterise it and bandage it and take him back home. And in truth there was very little that a man with ten fingers can do that a man with eight cannot – juggling, perhaps, but then Felspar had never been a juggler.

No, the punishment was more than the injury, more than the loss of the digits; it was the humiliation that it entailed, incitement to all those friendly to the Five-Fingered. And there were many of them these days, on the Fifth and the Fourth and even on the Third, many who would look at Felspar's injured hands and scowl hard, refuse to serve him a drink or a slice of meat, maybe, if they were feeling antsy, take him out back and beat hell out of him for a while. To be clipped was to be known as an informer, as an enemy of the people. To leave them alive was to make manifest the consequences of betrayal, as well as to provide the faithful with a target, a reminder to be ever-vigilant, ever-righteous, that they were in the midst of battle, and the contest was not yet certain.

Pyre held the knife out over the flame of a nearby candle, watching it grow hot, watching Felspar watch the same. How similar they all looked in this moment – how little was left of a man once fear had taken residence in his soul. The same slack eyes, the same quivering jaw. Hammer brought over a cask of ale from the corner. Talon forced Felspar's hand down against it.

'It'll be quick,' Pyre promised, withdrawing the blade from the fire, coming to kneel down beside Felspar. 'And you know that I never flinch.'

II

From the entrance of the Red Keep Calla walked downslope, turning south at the Silver Orchard, its lines of apple and pear and quince gone barren for the winter, then west, running alongside the Abiding Redoubt, towering and grand and vacant for nearly twenty-five years, its former resident one of the few Eternal to be lost during the last war against Aeleria. Late morning but the streets were uncrowded, the few passers-by going about their business with languid grace, like the canals, like the Eternal against whom they patterned their lives. The custodian at the entrance to the Second, clad in blue robes and a wide smile, his ferule leaning listless against the wall, waved her through without comment.

The Second Rung was busier and louder, and it was only set against the wonders of the First that one might find complaint. Calla turned down a narrow but pleasant thoroughfare, footfalls ringing against cobblestone. She had arranged quarters for the Aelerians a short distance from the First, in a small corner of the Rung that specialised in the sale of books and parchment. Calla passed long rows of these shops, the walls and doors formed of intricately carved white oak, and hanging from the open shutters bits of bright paper, smiling strands of colour against the dark wood. In the doorway of one of these, a girl just on the merry cusp of adolescence and her younger sibling set a toy boat down into the gutters that ran, moatlike, on either side of the street, smiled and clapped as it continued bravely downslope and towards the sea.

Calla's message had suggested they order a palanquin, but the returning epistle had flatly rejected the suggestion, insisting that the Revered Mother wished to see the city by foot. As she came in sight of the two of them Calla supposed, as she generally did, that hers had been the right of it, for it was still no short walk to their destination, and Eudokia less than hale. Nearer to sixty than fifty, had Calla to guess, and leaning hard on her cane.

Leon stood beside her, smiling that smile of his, at once innocent and cynical. The resemblance between the two was clear: the piercing, light blue eyes, the high cheekbones and unshakable sense of self-regard. In the light of day he did not seem quite so handsome as he had during the reception at the Red Keep, but then, starlight gilds everything.

The third member of their triumvirate stood out distinctly in contrast, a squat, broad-shouldered, fat-faced Parthan to whom no one had yet bothered to introduce her. He wore unbecoming coloured robes, and had flat eyes that followed Calla without interest or scruple.

'Revered Mother,' Calla said, performing the Eternal greeting.

It was returned with equal grace, Eudokia folding her cane beneath one arm to allow for the full range of motion. 'Sensechal,' she said.

'Will your . . . colleague be joining us?'

'Senator Gratian, whom honesty bids me mention is only an associate and no colleague, is, lamentably, rather too busy with the many responsibilities of his position to have time for any of these excursions, however enlightening they may be. Needless to say, he sends his deepest regrets.'

'How unfortunate.'

'I must once again protest at the Prime's hospitality, which, like any virtue, can be taken to exaggeration. Surely someone with your slate of duties can find something better to do than squiring an old woman along familiar paths?'

'Graciousness can never be exaggerated, Revered Mother,' Calla said. 'You do yourself a disservice and me too great a kindness. Truly, it is an honour to be accompanying so esteemed a guest on a tour of some small fraction of the Roost's wonders, indeed, more of honour than I deserve.'

'I should have brought a book,' Leon said, smiling, 'to while away the pleasantries. Or perhaps there is a tavern nearby? You could come and find me once you're done?'

Eudokia smiled and Calla smiled as well, but neither of them looked at the boy. After a moment Calla led them onward, and despite her fears, Eudokia proved no hindrance to their movement, indeed seemed barely to need the ashwood cane she leaned on, as if it was affectation rather than aid. She halted for a moment when they came in sight of the Red Plum Canal, smiling her smile which might have meant anything. 'To spend a life always in sight of water! Magnificent. And yet I cannot help but observe that these aquatic thoroughfares receive little use.'

'The Canals are the exclusive province of Those Above,' Calla explained.

'And yet, there are no Eternal making use of them this morning. Thinking now, I cannot remember, in my admittedly short time here in the Roost, ever having seen one here on the Second Rung.'

'The Eternal infrequently find occasion to descend from the First,' Calla admitted.

'Curious, to guard so closely a privilege which is never invoked.'

'You must have, in your distant capital, a home of some size and expense? A keep or a mansion?'

'A modest domicile,' Eudokia admitted. 'Little more than a hovel, when compared against the splendours of the Eternal's estate.'

'Without question. And, in your absence, did you give permission for your servants to sleep in your bed? To fuss about in your closets, to feed themselves from your stores?'

Eudokia laughed. 'Well spoken, Calla of the Red Keep. Well spoken. Tell me, Calla. These waterways, they find their origin at the great fountain which is at the centre of your Conclave?'

'You refer to the Source,' Calla explained, certain somehow that Eudokia knew well its name, was pretending at ignorance. 'The origin of the canals and indeed, the essence of the Roost. Generations of humans laboured in its creation, a masterpiece of engineering undreamed of save by Those Above. The water is drawn up from the bay to the very peak of the mountain, then directed back to the oceans whence it sprung.'

'Magnificent,' Eudokia agreed, though she was looking at Calla and not at the object of her veneration, 'spectacular, unique in all the world. A wonder, I take it, which was bequeathed by previous generations, distant ancestors of the city's current inhabitants?'

'The Roost requires constant upkeep. The labour of dozens of Eternal and many thousands of humans ensures its maintenance.'

'Maintenance is not creation. I see no construction, no improvement, no alteration . . .'

'Why mar perfection?'

'Why do anything, dear?' Eudokia asked. 'Why get up in the morning?'

If Calla had an answer, she did not offer it, smiling the same false smile that Eudokia wore and leading them further west. Staring at Eudokia, Calla found, had begun to give her a headache, and her bodyguard offering no more pleasant a sight, she turned her attention to Leon. Too young for her, needless to say, but still she could admit to some sort of an attraction. Two years since Bulan returned to his homeland, fled the Roost in a moment that, she told herself, was one of unbecoming fear, and there had been no one serious since. Which was not, of course, the same as saying there had been no one at all – at thirty-one Calla had the same instincts as any creature of flesh and blood, and in the higher Rungs of the Roost, at least, there was no shame in indulging them. Cinnabar was an overseer for the Lady of the Azure Estate's vast collection of musical instruments, but he had lived far to the east and eventually the walk had proved more inconvenience than she felt the destination warranted. She had recently enjoyed a brief dalliance with the pastry chef for the Lord of the Stygian Freehold, but that had ended some weeks earlier, without rancour or animus or even much reason. Walking beside Leon, noticing the firm roundness of his biceps and posterior, Calla found the day growing ever so slightly warm.

The chancellor's office was towards the middle of the Second Rung, a far walk from where they had met, in one of the distant central sections that Calla very rarely visited. It was a massive, squat structure composed of white stone, large enough to contain the small army of custodians, bureaucrats, collectors and inspectors and functionaries who maintained order in the Roost. It could have fitted comfortably within one wing of the Red Keep, not that the Aubade would have ever allowed something so hideous to occupy space in his domicile.

'How very . . .' Leon scratched his head. 'Square?'

Eudokia made a sound which was not quite a snicker but conveyed essentially the same meaning. Their reception awaited them at the front gates, an honour guard of custodians standing at attention – blue robes freshly cleaned, hardwood cudgels well-buffed. From there they were taken into the bowels of the building, down long hallways and through unmarked doors, up several flights of stairs, coming finally to a broad office on the top floor, and a large desk made of mahogany, and a man who stood behind it.

In the moment after seeing the chancellor Calla had a strong and sudden recollection of breaking into her mother's chest of make-up one rainy afternoon as a child – the powders and paints that rested neatly inside, each in their proper compartments, and then those same powders and paints covering her flesh, thick-coating round the eyes and lips, and scattered about the bureau, and onto the floor. Her mother coming in that evening and gagging at the sick-sweet scent, looking at her daughter and not sure whether to laugh or find a strap.

Those lucky enough to serve the Eternal directly knew better than to try to imitate them in matters of dress or fashion. But among those residents of the Second Rung in particular, that curious stretch of territory between where the gods resided and where man held sway, it was customary to ape the aspect of Those Above. The chancellor wore robes of brightly patterned paisley, narrow-fitting and vile, and his cheeks and chin and forehead were obscured with white make-up, and he or more likely one of his servants had done something absolutely hideous with his eyes, swells of purple as if he had been struck hard in the face.

'Chancellor,' Calla said.

He offered the Eternal greeting comfortably, though, to Calla's practised eyes, with no particular grace. 'Seneschal,' he acknowledged as he stretched back upright, a few flecks of powder falling from his forehead. 'You esteem us with your presence.'

As indeed, she did – a visit from any representative of Those Above was an honour, let alone the seneschal of the Prime himself. 'You will allow me to introduce Eudokia Aurelia, the Revered Mother, and her nephew Leon of Aeleria.'

Eudokia offered the Eternal greeting with the poise and grace Calla had come to expect. Leon performed no less admirably, though neither attempt seemed to win much esteem from the chancellor, who returned the courtesy without enthusiasm and dropped back down into his seat. Calla joined him, and Eudokia, and Leon finally as well. The as yet unnamed Parthan, main-taining his implacable and absolute air of disinterest, remained standing.

'I am afraid I know little of the politics of the slave nations,' the chancellor said, in a tone of voice suggesting he did not strongly lament his ignorance. 'And thus fail to understand your particular function within the Commonwealth.'

'As I explained to the seneschal, there is no element of formality to my visit. An old woman, new to the customs and glories of the Roost, seeking only to learn everything she can about this extraordinary place before shuffling off into the night.'

The chancellor nodded and smiled a smile that didn't rise to his painted-purple eyes. Calla was happy to discover that, at the very least, this man largely responsible for the day-to-day running of the Roost was not so foolish as to believe anything the Revered Mother thought to tell him. 'And what role might I play in furtherance of this quest?'

'You might begin by explaining to me your role within the Roost.'

'The function of the chancellor is little different from that of the sensechal,' the chancellor answered smoothly. 'To oversee those duties which Those Above, in their wisdom, feel unworthy of their time.'

'Then I am to understand that the essential questions of governance in the Roost, of justice and of order, are supposed by the Eternal to be beneath their interest?'

The chancellor's lips pulled back into a sneer. His teeth were stained the colour of pistachio meat. 'I would not be so foolish as to presume to know the mind of an Eternal.'

'How modest,' Eudokia observed. 'And yet you feel bold enough to run their city?'

The chancellor composed himself for a long moment before speaking. 'The laws and customs of the Roost are immutable, absolute, have remained blessedly unchanged since the days of the Founders. To us falls little more than to execute orders long passed, whose specifics are clear as sunlight and whose wisdom has been proved by the tranquil harmony that the Roost has enjoyed for millennia uncounted. Like the Source itself, it is an ideal machine, needing only the most occasional tinkering.'

'Yes, it is this exactly which I find so marvellous. Since coming to the Roost, I have known wonders undreamed of. Vast castles and keeps, bridges of white and imposing mien, towers rising to the sky, the very oceans themselves tamed and made to work in the service of Those Above. And yet, who could deny that this placid amity of which you speak is a thousand times the more extraordinary? The smooth interaction of so vast a population, an uncountable horde interacting without rancour or dispute, is an accomplishment worth a thousand castles, though every one be as beautiful as the Red Keep itself.'

'The people of the Roost are an orderly bunch, content with their lot. They trust in the wisdom of the Founders, in the Eternal and the generations which proceeded them.'

'Marvellous,' Eudokia said again, the compliments falling so fast and free that one might almost have supposed them unmeant. 'Then these . . . rumours I have heard, of some cult which flourishes far downslope, near the docks – of secret meetings and whispered signs, of a vast and terrible tumult which goes on beneath us – these are stories, and nothing more?'

The false smile on the chancellor's false face dropped into a stern line, a dash of purple wax.

'The Revered Mother is well-informed,' Calla said quietly.

Eudokia waved away the compliment. 'The servants speak of nothing else,' she said. 'But then, you know the way of servants. Gossip is their daily bread, calumny their every motive. To hear them tell it, below the Third Rung the duly empowered representatives of the Eternal dare not even show their faces, and the docks themselves will any day be engulfed in flame.'

'Gossip and calumny, as you say,' the chancellor answered, after a long moment. 'Some small handful of madmen, smearing profanity on walls and intimidating the poorest denizens of the Roost. They are of no meaningful account.'

'Then this report of an attack on a financial centre on the Third Rung is entirely without merit?'

'It is true that there was . . . an assault on a bank on the Third Rung, one swiftly beaten off by the custodians.'

'A clever tactic, for madmen and fools.'

'A pinprick,' the chancellor said. 'The Roost takes no more notice of them than a bullock does a fly.'

'You seem very little concerned about the spread of disorder within your fiefdom.'

The chancellor took a moment to compose himself, drinking from a small glass of what Calla assumed, or at least hoped, was water, then running his pink tongue along green-inked teeth. 'As I said, Revered Mother, my job is a simple one. The Roost has held for time beyond measure, and in those vast ages we have learned how best to govern the population below. Among so vast a horde, there are, of course, some negligible few who fail to properly appreciate the blessings which are provided them as subjects of the Roost. It rarely proves difficult to enlighten them – with gold, or, if necessary, with steel. We have more than enough of both.'

'Not all men are motivated by avarice, Chancellor, nor fear.'

'Not all – but very nearly, very nearly. And if the man you are dealing with is one of those . . . zealous few who cannot see where his own interest dovetails with that of larger society, that in the end makes no difference. You only need to find the man below him, or the man below him. In the end, Revered Mother, it is not the threat of the custodians' cudgel that keeps the people in line – nor, I daresay, that of our masters above. It is awe of the thing they have built. These men, they do not truly desire to destroy what we have built, but rather to join it.'

'An ideal machine indeed,' Eudokia said, smiling. 'I cannot exaggerate the comfort it gives me to know that the duly appointed authorities of the Roost work with such wisdom, diligence and justice.'

'It pleases me to offer you succour,' the chancellor answered stiffly.

Their farewell was lengthy and eloquent and Calla worked hard to keep a smile on her face all the way through it. Before beginning their return upslope, Eudokia and her manservant disappeared to the lavatory, and for a few moments Calla and Leon were left to face the afternoon sun alone.

For once, Calla's fund of etiquette had dried away entirely, as had any enthusiasm she maintained for the errand. The sooner she had this foul old harridan back to her quarters, the happier she'd be. Some dim sense of guilt at the depth of her animus towards Eudokia bid Calla into awkward contact with her nephew. 'Are you enjoying your time in the Roost?'

'A singular experience, without dispute,' Leon admitted. 'There is nothing I have ever seen to match it.'

'Your aunt says the same.'

'And means it – do not suppose everything she says to be false, she is just as enamoured of your city as am I. I don't think I've ever seen her smile so often, nor so vigorously. Then again,' he observed, offering what Calla suspected was the first unfeigned grin to be exchanged that day, 'she loves a challenge.'

'Of course your aunt and I are not engaged in any sort of competition, though I am flattered at the suggestion.'

Now there was more pity in Leon's smile than levity. 'I had not been speaking of you.'

12

A palanquin left from the side exit of a small mansion on the Second just before the hour of the Owl, moved downslope along the Sterling Canal, the moon reflecting ripe and pale and pockmarked in the still water. It was an ugly and unobtrusive vehicle, of the kind used to carry furniture or heavy goods. Strange to see one out so late in the evening but not bizarre, not worth noticing. Though if one had made a point of noticing – as none of the passers-by on the Second that evening, clerks and bureaucrats coming home from the taverns and drinking houses or heading towards some or other late-night liaison, were doing – one might also have noticed that the four men carrying the burden looked less like porters and more like something else, particularly the heavyset Parthan, shorter than the rest but keeping up his corner seemingly without any effort.

They were halted briefly at the barrier to the Third Rung, but their marks were in order, and there was no reason to stop or even to pay particular attention to them, and the custodians in that portion of the Roost were not the sort of men inclined to prosecute their duties with any extraordinary effort. The guards at the Fourth Rung were even less predisposed, brushed them past without even a cursory glance at their brands. A few links downslope there was a young man of no particular distinction, save that he wore a strangely coloured ribbon in his long brown hair, and he nodded at the Parthan and slipped down a smaller side avenue, the palanquin following in train.

They ended their journey some time later, near the boundary to the Fifth. The warehouse was on a lonely side street, the distant suck of the pipes audible but not overwhelming. The boy with the ribbon in his hair banged on the main gate, a broken beat, two fast, pause, two slow, and after another moment the double door swung open, wide enough to allow the palanquin swift entry.

The interior was as the exterior suggested, a wide and unprepossessing space for the storing of goods. High-stacked bales of cotton took up most of the corners, but in the centre a space had been cleared of debris and merchandise, and a table set. Three men sat there silently, as if in a triptych for the stages of life: the first old but well-formed, white-haired and clean-shaven; the second middle-aged, well-dressed with nervous eyes; and the third in the very prime of youth, squat and hard and dark.

Once they were inside the men pretending to be porters set their burden down, and the Parthan reached inside to offer his hand, bringing Eudokia swiftly to the ground.

'Revered Mother,' said the white-haired man.

The palanquin had not been intended to transport humans, and the men who had been carrying it had never learned to walk in harness, mule-like, an art that by far the largest proportion of the men downslope mastered just after the onset of adolescence. More than two years since Eudokia had broken her ankle while escaping an assassination attempt, and she could get around easily enough with the use of her cane, but the awkward confines of the box had forced her into an uncomfortable position, and the ache in her leg was more than piquant. She dropped happily on the empty chair that awaited her. 'Edom, the First of His Line,' Eudokia observed, voice a friendly cipher. 'It has been far too long.'

A smile as boundless as the sea, though perhaps less deep.

Eudokia turned to greet the second man, handsome in a shrewish sort of way, looking nervous and perhaps for no weak reason. 'Steadfast, a pleasure.'

'Revered Mother,' he said.

And then a moment of silence as Eudokia inspected the third member of their group, cool eyes on the rough skin of his face, the unbecoming outfit, the thick shoulders beneath. What had Edom told him of her? What explanations were given for her presence? Had he any idea of the true nature of their arrangement? No, she did not think so. This one had more than the whiff of a fanatic, he had the very reek.

A long time she looked at him, but he did not look away. 'And you would be young Pyre, chief of the Dead Pigeons, whose name is spoken with equal fear and reverence the length and breadth of the Roost.'

'I would be Pyre. As to the rest? The people, yet ignorant, yet uncertain of themselves, not realising that it is their strength which will win themselves free – they need heroes, and will create them.'

'Well spoken, Pyre, the First of His Line, well spoken. And yet you can hardly blame the mob for settling upon you as the object of their adoration, if the tales I've heard have any truth to them.'

Edom smiled wider.

'Stories often grow large in the telling,' Pyre said.

'And the oak rises from a seed, though still it does not spread from nothing. Tell me, Pyre, the First of His Line, can you not claim responsibility for last month's attack on the financial infrastructure of the Roost? Are you not the reason that the bankers on the Second are gnashing their teeth and rending their

garments, and the men and women of the Fifth left correspond-
ingly drunk and happy?'

Pyre shrugged but she could see he liked hearing that. They
all did, it was one thing that you could rely on in men, and young
men in particular. 'It was.'

'One of our many efforts against the demons, and in service
of the age to come,' Edom said in his broad mahogany voice,
Eudokia and Pyre dutifully swinging their eyes back over to him.
'You can see that we have not been idle, Revered Mother.'

'That is abundantly clear.'

'Such vigour does not come without a price.'

'Nothing comes without a price, dear Edom,' Eudokia said,
though for the moment she gave no indication of being willing
to pay it. In the growing silence Steadfast began to scratch the
palms of his hands, but Edom remained imperturbable, and so
did the boy, heavy dark eyes hard on Eudokia's own.

Eudokia made a gesture, and from somewhere within the folds
of his overlapping robes Jahan removed a scroll, handed it to
Eudokia, who took it and pressed it against her breast for a
moment. 'A thousand gold eagles,' she said, 'ready to be distributed by the branch of Ioseph's Son's Bank on the Fifth Rung.
Take it with the blessings of Aeleria, and my own.'

Steadfast bowed his head and deposited the draft into his
robes.

'You are very kind, Revered Mother.' The boy had a smooth
voice, and he spoke softly but Eudokia found that she heard him
clearly – as did Steadfast and Edom.

'Justice is not kindness, young Pyre. What I do is no act of
charity, but the will of the Self-Created himself. All the world
knows of the evils done to the humans of the Roost, and wishes
to see it made right.'

'I think you do yourself a disservice,' Pyre said. 'All the world
knows of our misfortune, and yet you are the only foreigner who
sees fit to help us?'

'You are mistaken, my young friend – across the breadth of
Aeleria, from the Senate Hall and the capital to the furthest

flung settlement, your cousins know of your bondage, and yearn for your freedom. Indeed, this is to understate the case. Are not we Aelerians as much in bondage as you Roostborn? Does not Aeleria still, as all the nations of the continent, swear fealty to Those Above? Do we not send them our tithe, our grain, our ore and our slaves? I do not come as a simple citizen, but as the representative of that concern, for the nation and the species beyond, of the love and strength of the Aelerian people.'

'Did you know, Revered Mother, that I grew up along the docks?'

'I confess to being ignorant of the specifics of your biography, young Pyre.'

'A short distance,' he confirmed. 'Men of all nations visit the Roost, Chazars and Salucians and Parthans and Aelerians. Never were the last renowned for their sentimentality, or kindness of spirit.'

He had a rare self-possession, or perhaps he simply did not know enough to understand that, whatever he had faced in a life of violence both petty and grand, he had never met anyone as dangerous as the old woman from whom he sat across. 'Speak your mind, Pyre. Whatever you may suppose, you are among friends.' A lie in more ways than he yet suspected.

'What does Aeleria hope to gain from their generosity? And their representative? What does she gain?'

'Credit in the afterlife,' Eudokia said, offering the boy her first flicker of tooth. 'Kindness in the hopes that Enkedri might offer me the same. Of course, if my assistance – if our assistance, is unwelcome, if the people of the Roost imagine it an interference, I would certainly not think to force it upon them.'

'The boy talks nonsense, Revered Mother,' Steadfast interjected. 'Pyre has spent more time with knife unsheathed than he has in council.'

'It has been my experience that the knife speaks last, and so loudest,' Eudokia said. 'But in any case, Pyre is justified in his concern. Caution, wariness, for a man responsible for so precious a charge as the freedom of his people cannot be called anything but a virtue.' How could eyes so dark shine so brightly, Eudokia wondered? 'Tell me, Pyre, the First of His Line, what has my wealth bought for us, exactly? How has my largesse assisted the struggle for the freedom of our species?'

A scant few seconds while he determined, not whether to lie – this was a certainty – but how to lie, if he ought to diminish or exaggerate their strength. 'I can call with certainty upon the blades of five hundred hardened members, well-trained, certain of the righteousness of their cause, willing to die to advance it. When the cry goes up there will be many thousands more who answer, who will realise they have only been waiting to hear it.'

Exaggerate, then. 'Five hundred men,' Eudokia repeated, as if the sum was beyond her calculations. 'Truly, a vast number. And the custodians? How many of them walk the streets of the Roost?'

'Difficult to say,' Pyre admitted. 'Perhaps five thousand. Perhaps more. It is of no matter.'

'No? I would suppose the numbers of your enemies to be relevant to the outcome of a contest.'

'Not if they will not fight,' Pyre said. 'The Cuckoos are not an army, nor even a militia. They neither create order nor enforce it, and they are not even trusted with steel, have to make do with cudgels and noisemakers. They will be of little account, in the final reckoning.'

'And Those Above?' Eudokia asked. 'Have you forgotten them?'

'I never forget the demons, Revered Mother. They are the first thing on my mind when I wake, and the image to which I fall asleep.'

'Well spoken, Pyre, the First of His Line. Well spoken indeed. Your funds will be doubled. Two thousand golden eagles. I will make the proper arrangements'

'It is not gold we need, but steel,' Pyre said. 'With five hundred

Aelerian pikes we might build an army. We have men willing to fight, and we have men willing to train them, we lack only the weapons to place in their hands.'

'Have you such control over the docks as to make sure that such a shipment would find its way to your own people, rather than be picked up by the custodians as evidence of our treason?'

'I do.'

'How curious,' Eudokia admitted. 'For it was my under-standing that, for all the success you've had on the lower Rungs, the docks remain firmly in the control of Those Above. That what the custodians do not oversee is held tight in the grip of a criminal organisation which is their cat's paw.'

'Your information is outdated,' he said simply. 'The Brotherhood Below should be of no concern to you.'

'But they're of concern to you?'

'Not for very much longer,' Pyre said simply.

Eudokia stared at the boy a long time, then at Edom, then back at the boy. 'I find myself believing you, Pyre, the First of His Line,' she said finally. 'Pikes you shall have. Five hundred men you claim, but no doubt as word spreads of your deeds, your recruits will spread as well. I cannot imagine a thousand would long gather dust.'

'Half-pikes,' Pyre corrected. 'And short swords. Anything longer would be of no use to us.'

'I shall make a note of it.'

That was the end, apart from the final pleasantries, which were of no particular interest to anyone. In fact the entirety of the transaction could have taken place without her presence, without the long ride down from the Second Rung, or the long ride back. But Eudokia wanted to put eyes on her agents old and new, and to remind them of who it was, in the end, to whom they answered.

During the journey back upslope, a traverse that was no easier on Eudokia's leg than had been the descent, she slipped her head quietly out of the corner of her palanquin and whispered to Jahan, 'Well?'

Jahan continued along for a moment, steps even and rhythmic, as if the weight on his shoulder was inconsequential entirely. He spat yellow into the moonlit dust. 'The boy.'

'The boy indeed,' Eudokia answered. 'The boy indeed.'

13

In an empty lot near the eastern walls they had set up a small training ground, and on a patch of sand in the middle of it Theophilus sparred with one of his new adjutants, practice staves in hand, the clatter of wood against wood ringing loudly in a quiet afternoon. Hamilcar and Isaac sat on an adjoining bench, passing a flagon back and forth. Bas stood steely-eyed beside them.

'Up!' Hamilcar said. 'Keep your weapon up!'

'Down!' Isaac insisted, pulling the cork out of their shared jug and taking a long swig. 'You won't live to see the spring if you can't remember that much.'

The winter had been brutal by local standards, hoarfrost on the windows and the occasional dusting of snow, but for men used to the frigid misery of the Marches there had never been a day worthy of sincere complaint. That morning Bas had woken and thought he detected the scent of early spring, of new life, and though it disappeared after a moment Bas knew it would not be long before it returned in fuller force. It could scarcely come soon enough, so far as he was concerned. The winter hadn't been cold, but in every other regard it had to be held as unpleasant; dark and dull, nothing to do but drink and wait for the new themas to arrive, and to wonder what would happen once they did.

Theophilus's new adjutant was slim and dark and serious-looking, some distant aristocratic kinsman, one of the slate of patricians who had joined the army for the campaign against Salucia, the prospect of slaughter and plunder against their ancestral enemies more appealing than losing a toe from frostbite while garrisoning the Marches. He was competent enough with his practice stave, though not more than that, as Theophilus was making evident. Twenty minutes they'd been at it, and the boy had yet to score a touch. He thought he saw a chance for one just then, came forward incautiously and received a rap against his knuckles that echoed loudly and disarmed him.

'You will win few battles with your sword on the ground,' Hamilcar commented, the latest in a raft of useless criticisms.

'Again,' Theophilus said, pointing at the fallen stave, though the boy was slow to pick it up, sneering over at the Dycian. A second blow to the same hand brought his attention back to where it belonged.

'Why are you listening to him?' Theophilus asked.

'Because he's talking.'

'That's insufficient reason to offer a man your attention.'

Isaac laughed. 'It only took you three years to learn that?'

Though proving true to his lesson, Theophilus ignored this as well. 'A sword fight is not a Senate debate. The world will not quiet itself for your benefit. If you find the Dycian's speech distracting, you'd find his arrows more so. Now pick up your sword.'

The boy did so dutifully, set himself again in front of his adversary-cum-trainer. Another quick exchange of blows, wood struck against wood, and though the new boy came off the worst of it, off-balanced and in retreat, he at least remained unmarked.

'Not bad,' Theophilus remarked, 'not bad.'

They had set up their makeshift practice ground in a small park in what had once been, so far as Bas could tell, one of the wealthier quarters of the city. It was ringed by a number of small mansions, structures of white stone, the domiciles of the modestly wealthy, petty nobles and clever merchants. Once children had smiled out of the upper windows, and in the mornings the serv-ingwomen strayed from their tasks to gossip till their mistresses called them to account. The houses stared back now like ruined teeth in a broken smile, the walls destroyed by the fires that had raged in the first days; stone will not burn easily but the supports were wood and wood is not nearly so difficult to incinerate, roofs collapsing into ceilings, ceilings falling on floors, and what hadn't been destroyed with flame had been stolen by the rampaging Aelerian army or rotted during the winter. Bas watched a scraggly tomcat slink along a half-ruined roof in pursuit of a pigeon, or perhaps a dove, Bas was no expert nor his eyes so keen as they had once been. A pause, a leap, but the bird was too clever or too swift, scattering off into the sky, its pursuer left to hiss impotently.

When Bas turned back to the fray it was over, Theophilus's victim lying face-up on the ground, breathing hard.

'Why are you dead right now?' Theophilus asked the boy, pulling him upright with the hand that wasn't holding his stave.

'I was too aggressive.'

'There's no such thing as too aggressive,' Theophilus corrected, 'so long as it's done effectively. You were foolishly aggressive, and you neglected your own defence. Why else are you dead?'

'I stopped circling.'

'Why did you do that?'

The boy shrugged.

'Stop moving once, and you'll stop moving for ever,' Theophilus intoned. 'The Caracal taught me that.'

If Bas had, he could not remember it. But it didn't sound like him; too smooth, too well-formed, more like one of Hamilcar's epigrams than Bas's own halting speech. But it was essentially true, at least, which was just as well, since given the reputation Bas held within camp you could append his name to the most errant non-sense and still expect any average hoplitai to follow it unwavering. Spread the rumour that the Caracal preferred his meat raw and half the army would be vomiting up their insides by the morning.

'Also, you are the wrong sort of pretty,' Hamilcar called out from the sidelines. 'A good soldier should be either ugly as Isaac or beautiful as I am. The first may cause your opponent to flee in fear, and the second may distract him with lust.'

'I'm not ugly,' Isaac said, rubbing a hand along the ruined flesh where his ears had once been, 'I'm striking.'

'Enough,' Theophilus said. as much to the audience as to his student. 'If you fought like that on the Marches, your scalp would be decorating an outrider's spear, and your pretty steel sword swinging at his belt.'

'On the Marches, he said.' Hamilcar laughed loudly. 'The boy grows a wisp of blond on his chin and he thinks himself Jon the Sanguine!'

'Care to take a turn, Hamilcar?' Theophilus asked, though smiling.

Hamilcar knocked the long stem of his pipe against his boots, supple leather and well-worked. 'Would you ask a whore for a free throw? A professional does not demonstrate his craft without expectation of reward.'

'Practice makes perfect,' Isaac disputed, though he made no effort to rise.

'Hamilcar has no dream of perfection. Excellence, however, comes natural to him as breathing, and requires no rehearsal. Besides, you Aelerians are over-impressed with naked steel. If it came down to it, I'd feather you before you grew close enough to mark me.'

'The most arrogant man that ever fought in another nation's army, by the Sun God himself . . .'

'And you, Caracal?' Theophilus asked, turning towards him and smiling, knowing the answer even as he asked it. 'Will you try your hand?'

'Yes, God-Killer,' she asked suddenly from behind, 'why not bless the hatchlings with the benefit of your mastery?'

How had she managed to arrive so silently, he wondered, without alerting anyone? Foolish to travel through the city without her lifeguard, though she seemed to do it with more and more frequency these days. True, it would take half a dozen or a dozen men to kill her, but Oscan teemed with soldiers, and after a long winter of drink and rot some not inconsiderable percentage of them would have attempted it simply to break the monotony.

Bas found he was smiling. 'It would hardly do for a Legatus to busy himself with a melee.'

'That seemed of no concern to you outside the walls,' she observed. Bas's eyes were drawn to the single missing stalk of her hair, which had been removed and ritually burned when she had left the Roost to take up her post among men, a sign of sacrifice or shame. 'But then again, there seems to be very little flavour with these long sticks.'

'Do you not spar in the Roost, Sentinel?' Theophilus asked. Perhaps it was because he was twenty years too young to have fought in the last war against the Others, perhaps simply because etiquette had been bred deep down into his bones, but Theophilus, almost alone among the camp, seemed to have no hate for Einnes.

'In the Roost we practise with naked steel and full armour,' she said. 'It is the rare blow that will slip through.'

'I'm afraid we have none of your Roost-forged plate to make use of.'

'They would not fit you,' Einnes observed, slow to get the joke as always. 'Regardless, I am willing, in this at least, to abide by the customs of your land. Would you give me a match, Caracal?'

Pointless, foolish, nothing but risk and downside. Either he would lose and be humiliated or he would win and his name would grow louder, reinforcing that myth of invincibility that half the themas seemed to have fallen for. And he was old enough these days that he needed to pay for any serious physical activity;

when he had been twenty he could have fought a battle every morning for a straight week and woken up at the end ready to wage another. He was nearly as strong as he had been as a youth, and perhaps only somewhat slower, but the ability of his body to recuperate from exertion had degraded dramatically, a misstep sufficient now to make his knee swell for a week, and a morning worth of vigorous movement was repaid with a sleepless and miserable evening.

'As you like,' Bas said, tossing his fur onto the ground, stretching out his broad shoulders.

She did not smile, she never smiled, but still he could tell when she was happy, or thought he could. They each grabbed a stave from the barrel, made their way over to the practice ground that Theophilus and his adjutant had vacated.

'We can provide a shield,' Theophilus offered, 'should you wish one.'

'This will do well enough,' Einnes answered.

Bas grunted refusal, spent a moment getting a proper grasp on the stave. It was smaller than his own blade, the size of one of the cavalry swords, appropriate as Theophilus was now head of horse. He took a few aimless swings, got the weight of the thing in his hand, its reach. The practice ground was a matted circle of dead winter grass, and Einnes met him in the centre of it.

Theophilus took up a spot just outside its circumference. 'First to three touches,' he announced. 'Am I an acceptable arbiter, Sentinel?'

'As well as any of your kind,' Einnes said, little concerned. 'Are you feeling limber, Caracal?'

Bas grunted but didn't answer. Even in the best of circumstances, his tongue had never been clever, nor he the type of person who needed to steady himself with talk. He dropped unthinkingly into position, the tip of his false blade stretching between them. Einnes brought her own horizontal to her body, which in a human Bas would have supposed a sign of complete ignorance, but in an Eternal he presumed was simply some curiosity of style.

'Begin,' Theophilus said.

Bas gave a step immediately and still it was barely enough, Einnes's blunt stave just missing his chest. He had known she would be fast, but he could not have supposed – he simply had not remembered, it had been so long – how fast they were. He had never been so swift, not even in those distant days of youth, and certainly not with forty-five long years weighing down his body. But at least he had purchased something with those days and weeks and months, with torn tissue and scarred flesh and broken bone, something like wisdom or at least knowledge. She would wish to demonstrate her superiority quickly, and he played against that, circling right unceasingly, forcing her off balance. Thrice more she tried for a quick end and thrice more he avoided it, and after the last he feinted to her off side and came full-speed against her shoulder.

'Touch!' Theophilus said.

Isaac howled. Hamilcar laughed loudly and passed him a tertarum, seeming happy with the loss. Theophilus's adjutant whose name Bas had never learned or already forgotten watched the proceedings with slavish intensity, as if he had staked his life on the outcome. Nor was he the only one, the crowd swelling with passers-by, a half-dozen now though it would soon grow to more than that. He could hardly blame them – the God-Killer facing off against a god, a preliminary for the act to come.

Einnes retreated to their starting position. 'That would never have gotten through my armour.'

'Best not to let it get to that point.'

'Indeed,' she said, raising her weapon. 'It was a fine blow.'

This time when Theophilus gave the signal she remained as she was. Indeed there was a long moment when it seemed as if neither would make a move, and then she did and he was lost completely. She was fast, by the gods she was fast, faster than she had displayed during the first pass; between the reshuffling of her feet and the blow against his chest had been some half-fractured second, and he had barely seen the blow fall.

'Touch,' Theophilus announced unhappily, as if the spreading swell of pain across Bas's breast was not sufficient evidence.

'I think I grow used to the size of this,' Einnes declared.

Bas didn't answer. His breath was coming shallowly and he gave in to it, let his chest heave back and forth, wiped sweat away from his brow, scowled. Back to their starting positions and Theophilus opened his mouth to speak and Bas was off his back foot and full-force forward, Einnes unprepared and still managed to deflect the first blow and the second but not the third, her stave going spinning off into the dust, the gathered crowd giving a cheer.

'Very clever, Caracal,' she began, unconcerned with the reaction of the mob, indeed almost seeming to share it, 'here I had supposed this thing called age had finally gained a hold.'

He should not have smiled but he did, not at the cheering or at the enthusiasm of his soldiers, but at her response, at her eyes which were on his. And in fact just then he was feeling every one of his years, and also something else, some dim sense of gratitude for this last one, and indeed for this very moment.

Their fourth exchange was not as close as it looked, and though it lasted several long minutes, and though the onlookers held their breath and flinched every time wood rattled against wood, the contest was never in doubt. A slight error in judgement had set Bas behind at the outset, and from there on he was entirely on the defensive, working desperately to acquire equilibrium. To no avail – they locked staves for a moment and then she shifted and he went stumbling onward, with a blow against his back to speed him along.

Bas spent a long time catching his breath, Einnes retreating to her starting position without losing a moment, still and perfect as a statue, as if the previous four passes had not exhausted a single drop of her energy, as if she could so continue all evening and into the morning beyond. She was dressed in simple robes of deepest black, and the long tendrils of her hair, wrapped tight in silver cord, reached down past the backs of her knees. And below her hair those eyes, which were like purple perhaps, or darker than purple.

'We lose the light,' Theophilus announced, staring at the sun dimming itself beyond the mountains to the west. 'Will you call it a draw?'

'No,' Einnes said.

'No,' Bas agreed, nearly in the same instant.

Hamilcar laughed loudly from the sidelines, though to Bas's ears it had something fearful to it.

'Two and two, Caracal,' Einnes said, 'and the last to decide the matter.'

This did not require a response and Bas did not bother to offer one. He stretched his shoulders and twisted his neck back. He felt the sweat drip down off his forehead and the blood run fierce and free in his veins, he felt the last rays of the winter sun beat down on his face and his arms and his chest.

'Begin,' Theophilus said.

Her style was as dissimilar to his own as was every other thing about her, each strike a staccato movement, unrelated to the previous motion or the one that would succeed it. Their staves rapped an uneven tattoo. On the sidelines, noticed by neither warrior, the crowd had gone silent, tense with anticipation. Hamilcar was leaning forward on his stool, long pipe forgotten in the dust beside him, and Isaac was upright, leaning past the Dycian as if about to tumble over him. The crowd of pentarches and tourmarches and hoplitai that now surrounded the practice ground had grown to several dozen, though none made a sound, as if frightened to interrupt. They thought so much of him – even those who shouldn't, who knew better, who had spent years watching him in flesh and folly, seen Bas shit himself when sick with the flux, seen his bad decisions lead to the deaths of men in his charge, seen him sleep and dream and bleed; still they could never quite believe that he was a man, as they were men.

He planted his left foot, he shifted, he shifted back the other way, he saw her recognise his feint for what it was and decided in the instant before the final instant that it would not be a feint at all, and she saw the same and reacted, and the tips of their mock weapons fell against flesh, near simultaneous.

'Touch, Caracal,' Theophilus said, and the crowd erupted. Isaac raised his fists to the sky, bellowing, and rising with enthusiasm Hamilcar overturned his pipe, embers dying in the dust. The pentarches hooted, the tourmarches hollered, the hoplitai cheered, five-fingered hands gripped each other with happy enthusiasm.

Near enough for honest error, though Bas would not have supposed it such; rather that Theophilus, a long way from the guileless youth Bas had met on the Marches, was wiser than to announce anything else. And it had been close, after all. But Bas knew, and Einnes knew.

In the long moment afterward, as the spectators roared and beat their chests, the two locked eyes. 'You give good sport, God-Killer,' she said, tossing the stick to Theophilus and striding off. 'Too bad it was not more than that.'

'Too bad for you,' said a voice from the mob, some ignorant soldier believing what he wished to believe, Einnes ignoring him and Bas ignoring him also.

14

When Pyre walked into the whorehouse on the Second Rung late one evening in early spring, he looked neither to his right nor his left; not at the mahogany floors or the silver-plated water pipes, not at the walls, which were hardwood and draped with tapestry, not at the supple leather couches, not at the pale and rounded flesh of the courtesans who lounged on them, not at the silk that failed to cover that flesh. Behind him, as was generally now the case, Hammer loomed tall and broad and silent – another child of the Fifth, and equally disinterested in the view, a strangely passionate sort of dispassion.

The woman in the entrance was well practised in waiting for men. She offered the smile that she gave all of them, that she had been giving since she was too young to understand what it offered – though she had learned quickly enough, no woman can remain long in such ignorance. For once at least it failed to earn a response, Pyre and his follower as indifferent as eunuchs. She led them through a curtain, and then through another curtain, and then into a room that was not pretending to be anything but what it was, and four men doing the same. Pyre did not need to see the brands on their necks, stars and webs and geometric patterns of no clear purpose, to know them as members of the Brotherhood Below. He had never met any of them before but he knew them well all the same, knew the savagery that had been required to attain their position, knew the desperation that had driven them to that savagery, knew they would draw blood without regret or pity or enthusiasm, would draw blood because that was their purpose and they knew nothing else. Pyre pitied them, as he pitied the whores, though it was a distant sort of pity, one that would have no impact on the event to come.

The leader, or at least the man who then spoke, was bulky and pockmarked and heavily bearded. His robes were expensive, ugly and fashionable, and a long, curved blade rested outside them. 'Against the wall,' he said. Their guide had disappeared without a word, her purpose completed.

'We are unarmed,' Pyre said. 'As per the agreement.'

'This the first time you ever been patted down, Fifth Rung trash like you?' The man's sneer tore a hole through the sweat-matted fur of his face. 'Against the wall or into the ground, your choice.'

Pyre looked at Hammer for a moment, then shrugged and set his palms against the wall. Hammer did the same. The bearded man ran his hands swiftly down Pyre's legs and waist and hips, then did the same to Hammer. When it was over he led them down another hallway, out of sight of the rest of his guards. He paused at the last door, spent a long moment staring at Pyre before nodding and opening it.

The room was small and sparsely appointed. Two guards waited scowling beside the door, and one at the back did the same. At a wooden table sat four chairs and two men. The first was, Pyre knew, the head of the Brotherhood Below, the vast criminal organisation that had long been the effective power on the Fifth Rung and most of the Fourth. It smuggled goods up from the docks, it ran whores, it cribbed protection money, it left fathers dead and mothers weeping. It had done all of these things, at least, in the years before the Five-Fingers had come to power, had begun to push them steadily upslope. His name was Ink, and in his dress and composure he seemed little affected by the steady erosion of his base of power. He wore rich robes of coloured silk and a line of golden bracelets on arms not free of muscle. Ink could still count on the knives of some two hundred hardened killers, men who made a living from cruelty, whose daily bread was leavened with blood. He took in a thousand eagles a year, a sum that was quite literally inconceivable in the neighbourhood in which Pyre had been born, and in much of the Roost entire.

He did not matter a fig, he was irrelevant and extraneous to the moment at hand. One could see it even by the way Ink lounged in his chair – defiance that verged on petulance, like an upslope child. By contrast, the man sitting beside him was stiff and straight and almost regal. Probably past forty, though it was hard to tell, with his hair painted in two vibrant if unnatural colours, and with the heavy make-up that obscured most of his face, white powder extending mask-like down to the high cowl of his robes, black silk with threads of silver interwoven. The skin around his eyes had been painted amber, and the lids as well. He did not bother to introduce himself.

There were two open seats. Pyre took one and Hammer took the other. Then they all sat a moment in silence.

'Congratulations.' The chancellor's voice was high-pitched, unbecoming, like an untuned lute. 'You have succeeded in making yourself a nuisance.'

The bearded man who had escorted them inside smirked, rolled round the table to stand behind his masters. Pyre could sense Hammer quiver in the chair beside him. For his part, Pyre neither moved nor spoke.

'It is an accomplishment,' the chancellor acknowledged. 'It is a thing of which to be proud.'

The sounds of a zither came in from the adjoining comfort

rooms, muffled but recognisable, and the sounds that accompanied those sounds, soft moaning and occasional grunts, pleasure real and feigned. Pyre had the sensation – one he was long familiar with, as every child of the Fifth was familiar – of something small and foul running across his skin, lice or fleas or bedbugs.

'You've no response?' the chancellor asked.

'You've yet to ask a question.'

The chancellor's smile was as false as all the rest of him, as false as his coloured hair or his rouged cheeks. 'Fair enough. You are not the voice of your organisation, only the muscle. All to the good – a fool might pay his attentions to the puppet, but a wiser man directs his thoughts to the mummer.'

'You exaggerate my importance. I am merely a servant of the word.'

'Oh, I think otherwise – it is not to Edom that the Five-Fingers have replaced the Brotherhood as the chief source of order, all along the docks and even up as high as the Fourth Rung. Not to Edom that bullyboys leave slaughtered birds in the main intersections, not to Edom that there are few enough Cuckoos willing even to go out on patrol. We have been aware of the Five-Fingers since Edom first returned to the city. We allowed him to continue his activities, because you downslopers need something to occupy your minds – to the degree that you may be said to have any – and because we found it convenient to have the fulcrum of dissent so clearly in hand. Five years, I've been aware of him, but only in the last year and a half – since you've joined them, Pyre, the First of His Line – have they risen to their current level of importance.'

'Which would be?'

'A nuisance, as I said. An irritant. A headache, a minor misfortune, a blemish of the skin.'

'Hard to notice with all that make-up,' Hammer said.

'You watch your fucking tongue, boy, or I'll carve it out and toss it to a whore.' Ink sounded like Pyre had known he would sound, blunt-tongued and bitter. He was happy for the chance to say something, however petty or vicious, simply to remind himself that he was still in the room. This last explained, to Pyre's mind at least, the greater balance of human speech.

Without looking behind him, eyes still on the painted man, Pyre gestured Hammer into silence.

'As a rule, I think very little about the Fifth Rung,' the chancellor began, no more interested in his subordinate's outburst than was Pyre. 'And so long as you were willing to entertain yourself downslope, this dispute between Ink's organisation and your own was of no meaningful interest to me or mine. But this . . . expansion into the Third Rung, this attack on the bank last month; you overreach yourself, and you court disaster.'

'And I've been summoned tonight to hear a warning?'

'And in hopes of coming to some sort of mutually beneficial agreement. There are three ways that this situation might be dealt with. The first, and the easiest, is to tell me what you want, and for me to give it to you.'

'A simple enough thing, Chancellor, and one of which we've made no secret. I wish for this yoke which has laid across our backs for millennia uncounted to be lifted, and I wish for those who have held us enslaved to be brought to justice.'

The chancellor made a face as if Pyre had emitted some unexpected odour. 'And the sun to shine at the hour of the Owl, and the current in the bay to run backward? Perhaps I shall wave my hands and make you live for ever, or bring your dead grandmother back to life? Enough nonsense, boy, there's no point in holding up your facade any longer. I can offer you riches and wealth beyond anything you've yet dreamed – and power as well,' he added, 'real power, power over life and death in the borough where you reside, a king in your little kinglet. If, needless to say, one who still pays homage to an emperor above him.'

'You think me a hypocrite, then? To be bought off with coin or cheap favour?'

'Hypocrisy is a word that the weak use to bind the strong – to contain and corral them, to confuse and diminish them. It rarely works, of course, but then the weak have few enough weapons on which to rely. My time is not infinite, and I find the company insalubrious. You have thus far shown yourself to be a competent tactician—'

'Enough to make your dog run scared,' Hammer interrupted.

The eponymous dog snarled, cracked his fingers, then pointed one at Hammer. 'You just keep on thinking that, zealot,' Ink said. 'You just keep right on thinking that.'

The chancellor rolled his eyes, continued on as if the interruption had never taken place. '—and a man of some intellect. Surely you are not dense enough to believe the . . . pabulum you spread to the masses?'

'I have no need for gold,' Pyre said simply. 'If you had hoped to bribe me, you've wasted both of our time.'

'Drop the fucking act, boy,' Ink snarled. 'You done enough to get yourself a spot at the table, now claim your winnings and get back to your hole.'

The chancellor raised two fingers, the nails of which had been painted opposing colours, and Ink fell silent. 'You say you have no personal interest in the matter? You say you wish for the well-being of your people? Fine, I will take you at your word. If you were to fall in line, we could discuss . . . changes in the organisation of the lower Rungs. Those Above allow me wide leeway in that regard.'

'A better-fed slave is still a slave,' Pyre said simply. 'My people wish for freedom, and will accept no substitute.'

In the flickering candlelight the chancellor's lips were bright, and they left a stain of red on his teeth. 'Is that really what they wish? Do you honestly suppose that there would be any gain for anyone if the rabble that occupy the lower Rungs were suddenly to find themselves without our guiding hand? Think hard here, think honestly, do not simply mouth the platitudes that have been taught you. Given the opportunity, would they spontaneously assemble themselves in council? Would they draft laws, would they distribute offices and responsibilities? The Fifth would be an abattoir before the sun's rise tomorrow, the blood would rise about your knees.'

'At first, perhaps,' Pyre agreed. 'But the tide runs back out, doesn't it? And when it did we would be able to rebuild, as free men rather than slaves.'

'How many of the men on your Rung can read? How many can sum? How many can speak or act coherently, how many have thoughts beyond the end of the day's work, beyond the next drink, the next whore?'

'And whose fault is that?' Pyre asked quietly. 'They kill our leaders and any who might become so. They deprive us of every hope of growth and of advancement, they lock us in a cage as proof we cannot grow.'

'Perhaps you truly do think that,' the chancellor said. 'Perhaps you are so foolish.' He waved his hand across the table, palm down, as if scattering seed. 'No matter – the freedom you herald would destroy the Roost entirely, your people as much as mine. Happy for all of us that it will never come.'

'No?'

'No,' the chancellor echoed. 'I am trying to be forgiving. It is understandable, even appropriate for a man born in your circumstances. Likely you've never been in the presence of an Eternal. Likely you've never even seen one.'

False, though Pyre made no effort to correct him. The guard behind Ink, the bearded one, sucked at his crooked teeth.

'You see the custodians and you think, in your ignorance, in your vast and infinite stupidity, that it is they against whom you contend. You think, perhaps, that having had such success against their servants every victory will be so easy to attain. I tell you, Pyre, and if you have yet believed nothing I have said then believe this – you are fabulously wrong. You are wholeheartedly and, in every particular, mistaken. You have won nothing, you have not even begun the contest. You could slaughter every custodian in the Roost, build a fire with the bodies and toss the entirety of the Brotherhood Below atop it, and you would have come no closer to ensuring this victory of which you dream. I have dealt with Those Above my entire life, and tell you in simple language so there is no confusion – they are everything they imagine themselves to be. The names they have given themselves, the names we have given them, they are apt, they are entirely accurate. The Eternal are superior in every fashion that one creature might be to another. Every man and boy you could arm and train would be insufficient to defeat a handful in open combat. The mote of grime you scrub from your eye in the morning is of more concern to you than you and all your people are to them.'

'Then why have they not reached out with their four-fingered hands and . . .' Pyre made a motion with his own five digits, as if crushing something fragile.

'Because they are busy with their dreams. Do you think the ruckus you have made on the lower Rungs is loud enough to reach their ears? They, who have laid waste to armies since before time was time, since before there was such a thing even as man?'

'They think me important enough to treat with.'

'They have no idea I'm here,' he said. 'Any more than they are aware of the existence of the Brotherhood Below, or of our association with each other. So long as the water flows upward, and the goods and gifts with which they might play, the Eternal give no more thought to what goes on downslope than you might the tunnelling of the ants in the floorboards.'

'And you think this ignorance to be a virtue?'

'I think it reality, and one for which you ought to feel daily grateful. Should they ever concern themselves with what goes on beneath them, should you manage to one day prove sufficient distraction to draw their attention . . .' Imagining this cataclysm, he smiled, and this time it did not seem false. 'The blood would choke the fish in the bay, and be carried up through the pipes to the Source itself, and they would hold their conclave beside the crimson fountain and they would scarcely notice the stain. They are strong, yes, Those Above, they are stronger than you can possibly imagine – but they are even crueller than they are strong.'

'And yet, here you sit. With a child of the Fifth Rung, born within the sound of the slurp, a slum child.'

'I am not an Eternal,' though Pyre thought he was doing everything he could to obscure the fact, the absurd robes, the strange and unbecoming eye-paint. 'Do you need each particularity to be spelled out for you as a child? Fine. Those Above care nothing for what goes on beneath them. That is my job, and the job of those like me. To ensure that the Eternal may continue with their happy immortality, and that we beneath them might enjoy our limited span as much as possible.'

'And the Brotherhood Below is part of this control?'

'Everything is part of it,' the man said plainly. 'The Association of the Porters, the brands and the pass necklaces, each an interlocking piece of a system which was put in place thousands of years before your birth, Pyre, the First of His Line.' The last was said sneeringly – most of the rest as well but the last in particular.

The zither had stopped playing. Hammer sat unsmiling, fearless of death. The bearded man, still standing behind Ink and in front of one of the guards, shot Pyre a look that no one else was in a position to see.

'First came the bribe,' Pyre said, 'which I ignored. Next a threat, to which I gave as little credence. What follows?'

'Isn't it obvious?' the chancellor asked, gesturing at the two armed guards who stood behind Pyre and Hammer. 'If the promise of wealth does not sway you, if the certainty of retaliation from Those Above is not enough to enlighten you, then we will be forced to resort to other, more immediate options.'

'This is my fucking bar, kid,' Ink said, smiling for the first time now, back in his native element, a pig in loam, a maggot in rotted flesh. 'You think you'll ever leave it alive?'

'Indeed,' Pyre agreed, in response to the chancellor. 'It was extremely obvious.'

Ink was smiling when he died; he noticed the sudden flicker of movement behind him but did not bother to look, had been expecting it, had even signalled it, having no idea of where it was directed. The bearded man, his head of security, a hardened downslope thug who knew nothing but savagery and who, it was assumed, was capable of nothing more, pulled his curved knife from his waistband, and then there was a flicker-flash as the candelight shone against his steel, and then that self-same steel was buried down to the hilt through the hair and scalp and bone and brain of the last leader of the Brotherhood Below.

Ink's corpse collapsed face forward onto the table, flailing about like a fish removed from water, some dim biological instinct driving his fading body into a final spasm of motion. The chancellor screamed. The bearded man, whom Ink knew as Pebble but who had for two months answered in his heart only to Saviour, the First of His Line, turned his blade swiftly on the guard behind him, though Pyre had no time to watch the outcome.

The two by the door were quick but Hammer was quicker, the shiv he had bolted up his sleeve swift buried in a throat. Pyre was a step slower but fast enough, his chair spinning into a corner and then his own line of steel set loose, launching himself at the only unoccupied guard. He was tough, the guard, and he was mean, and he did well enough considering the sudden shift of circumstance. By the time it was over Pyre had a thin cut running up his shoulder, shallow but bloody, and Hammer was disposing of the guard who had managed to kill Saviour, a big man but badly wounded, a thrust beneath the armpit and then silence.

'The bar is yours?' Pyre asked, coming upright from the corpse he had made, chest heaving at the struggle, eyes bright against the darkness. 'The neighbourhood is mine. The Rung. The city. The world. Ours, had you cared enough to look, had you not been blinded by greed and cowardice into betraying your own species.'

Hammer cleaned his blade, put it back into its wrist sheath, then went to check on Saviour. After a moment he looked up from over the corpse, his one good eye fixing on Pyre, and he shook his head.

'May his blood soak the roots,' Pyre intoned, 'may it herald the new age.'

'For the dawn to come,' Hammer repeated, standing.

Ink's blood stained the powdered white make-up on the

chancellor's face, and added a third hue to his particoloured hair. He was too frightened to speak, not that there was much to say.

'Saviour heard the word, and was redeemed. Hè sits at the hand of Enkedri, and he watches over us as do all our fallen brothers. But there are some who cannot hear the truth though it be shouted in their ear,' Pyre said, scattering droplets of crimson into the corners, turning towards the chancellor to draw more. 'And there are some who hear the truth only too late.'

15

Moonlight fell soft against the windows of the Red Keep and the snow struck near as soft, curls of frost bright from the heavens, rime gathering transient against the panes. Outside there was the night and the cold and the sea far below, dark and wild and enticing. Inside braziers of damask and sterling silver spread light and warmth and the sweet smell of camphor, illuminated the Lord's study, the ebony walls, the mosaics of garnet and electrum, the patterns abstract and unknowable. The Prime sat bent-legged on a nest of silk. His robes, patterned in the house colours of crimson and aureate, lay half-open, his chest broad and smooth and hairless. His instrument was pear-shaped, rosewood inlaid with gold. He ran an ivory plectrum against the strings and recited a poem that had been ancient a thousand years before the Founding of the Roost, in a past. so distant as to be scarcely conceivable – before the crime, when the Eternal lived uncaged, free to wander the length of the continent. The words were archaic, a formal and all but forgotten dialect of the Eternal tongue, but the story was as it had always been. Of loss; of things that were and would not be again.

Calla stood quietly beside him, a soft smile on her face.

The words slowed, the music grew softer and then silenced entire. Calla closed her eyes and savoured the final strands of melody, and then savoured the memory of that sound.

'I have been thinking of death lately,' the Prime observed.

'Yes, my Lord.'

'I suppose it must be something you think of constantly, given how near you are to it.'

'I suppose.'

'Like a guest waiting just beyond the threshold. How can you stir yourself to anything else, anticipating such an arrival? How meddlesome, to think at any moment he might intrude on your business, render the entirety of your workings null.'

'We do not . . . conceive of things in exactly those terms, my Lord. Knowing nothing else, it seems no very terrible hardship.'

He continued as if he had not heard. 'I suppose it must be something of a kindness. The rot overtakes your kind so swiftly, aching knees and weakened limbs, a steady softening of the mind. Scarce ten years you have served me, and already I can see age's wither, in the lines around your mouth and towards the corners of your eyes.'

Calla would stare at herself in the mirror when she returned to her room, stare hard and long and perhaps not like what she saw. 'As you say, my Lord.'

'And what time does not take will be scavenged by accident or disease. Your father was very fond of your mother, though I confess I never quite saw the appeal. Still, he was distraught almost beyond reason when she died. It was months before he could manage his duties competently, and I daresay he never truly recovered from the blow.'

'He . . . loved her very much, my Lord.'

'Our kind thinks ourselves so different to yours, though the more I consider the less I am sure. Death is for ever, after all. And measured against eternity, what is time? I have known seven of your line, can recall the smile your father's mother's father's father's father offered when we left the Roost to take up our office abroad, can remember your father's mother's betrothal ceremony with perfect fidelity, could close my eyes and limn it on ricepaper without error. I might know seven more, or seven times seven, could shepherd your children and their children through future generations. But what is that against the void?' Staring down at her with his golden eyes unblinking, as if she might even have an answer! 'Against infinity, what is a hundred years? Or two, or three, or five? How is it possible to continue on, staring implacably at the full weight of that chasm? And why should it matter that this inevitability is further into the distance for some than others?'

'I . . . am not sure, my Lord.'

'Have you had occasion to visit my bestiaries this last week, Calla?'

Abrupt shifts in conversation were part of interacting with Those Above, but even so Calla found herself stymied for a moment. 'I check in on it every morning, my Lord.'

'Of course. Then you have seen this new species we have acquired?'

Seen it, by the Founders! Its cage alone, an aquatic enclosure the size of a Fifth Rung tenement, had cost twelve golden eagles, and twice that to capture the beasts and ship them to the top of the Roost. 'Yes, my Lord.'

'A peculiar thing – as strange an animal as I've ever encountered.'

'From Chazar, my Lord.'

'Far from lovely, in and of itself, to my thinking at least. Haired, four-legged. The females produce milk and, I am told, give birth to their young live.'

'This was what the broker explained.'

'And yet, it lives in the water, or mostly. They say it can even breathe it, as does a fish.'

'So they say, my Lord.'

'Life creates itself in the most curious and disparate fashion. Flesh bending and knitting and reforging itself to better suit its environment.'

'A wondrous thing, truly,' Calla said, because she had no idea of anything else to say.

'In fact I think the creatures rather hideous, though that is nothing more than a peculiarity of taste. Regardless, it has inspired me to develop a certain hypothesis. Is it not perhaps the case that selective blindness is a necessary adaptation for higher life to exist? That, just as this . . . otter, has developed lungs to swim beneath the surface, and fur to subsist against the cold, we Eternal and you Dayspan have likewise developed in such a fashion as to remain unconcerned of death? Perhaps there were other species, who walked upright and spoke as we speak and who were, at the same time, braver or less dishonest than we, unwilling to accept the limitations of sentience. Who ran steel along their wrists, who dashed their children against the rocks, who walked arm in arm into oblivion.'

'I . . . cannot say, my Lord.'

'None can,' said the Prime. They had no pupils, the Eternal, their eyes were like single facets of some great jewel. One could never tell what exactly it was at which they looked. 'She was very beautiful.'

She was the last Prime, the Lady of the House of the Second Moon, whom the Lord had loved quietly for who knew how many human lifetimes, whom he had killed in bloody single combat, her corpse set out on the Cliffs of Silence for the birds to pick, her great estate gone fallow.

'Marvellously so, my Lord.'

'I tried my best to convince her.'

'I know that, my Lord.'

'There are some among my siblings who suppose I challenged her because I hoped for power, or due to some personal quarrel, out of jealousy or pique.'

'I can hardly believe there are any Eternal so foolish as to believe such errant nonsense.'

'You think too highly of us,' the Prime said after a moment. 'Perhaps we do as well.'

'I know the truth, my Lord, whatever anyone may say,

Eternal or otherwise. What you have done was done for the Roost.'

'And what was the point of it? Assuming her position did nothing to bring my siblings to their senses. Still they bicker blindly, still they frolic amidst the growing inferno. Better to have played blind as well, and at least had the joy of her presence some short time longer. At least had her there beside me when the end comes.' The moonlight fell on his high forehead, and on his golden eyes, heavy and sad and seemingly far-seeing. The snow fell more fiercely, the hoarfrost growing thick along the window.

'Do you plan to attend the Lord of the Rose Hall's spring gathering?' Calla began, knowing the answer as she asked. 'I have heard from his sensechal that he has acquired a species of pachyderm which has never before been seen in the Roost.'

But the Aubade had already turned back towards the window, and the dark, and his thoughts. 'Thank you, Calla,' he said. 'But I think not. Please alert my sibling that I'll be unable to appreciate his kindness.'

'Of course, my Lord,' and for some reason she found herself blinking away tears. 'At your command.'

16

Sitting alone in an adjourning waiting room, Eudokia found herself missing Jahan's silent, heavy, reassuring presence, felt the least bit naked. Of course he had not been allowed into the Conclave; indeed they had not even allowed him to rise to the First Rung. So far as Those Above were concerned, Eudokia was a slave as any other, and there was no reason she needed to bring along one of her own. Just as well, really – today she was not the creature to whom half of Aeleria bowed and who the other secretly loathed, today she was not the Revered Mother, today she was an old woman far from home, weak and wavering and fearful. The costume reflected this sudden turn to modesty. Since coming to the city Eudokia had amassed a staggering array of clothing, curious Chazar headpieces, brightly coloured Roost-made robes that had no equal in Aeleria, a fact Eudokia could state with as much authority as anyone else alive. A hundred golden eagles' worth of silk and samite and careful thread, and all of them packed neatly away. Today she made do in a costume of mottled grey winter robes that trailed down to her narrow ankles, unadorned save for a necklace of prayer beads that she had snatched up in a last flash of inspiration.

She was playing with these loudly while sitting in a holding pen below the Conclave, agitating the master of protocol, a waspish, unpleasant-looking individual whose temper was not improved by the arrhythmic rattling. 'Will it be very long, do you think?' she asked.

'It will be as long as the Eternal deem necessary,' he said sternly.

Eudokia offered a meek smile, or what she supposed was a meek smile. Her glass beads continued their retort.

In fact a moment later a page entered and waved to the two of them, and Eudokia followed the pedant up a small staircase and through one of the side doors that buttressed the main room, and then onto a sort of witness stand. She took a seat, folded her hands on her lap, cast her eyes at the floor, tried to seem intimidated. This last was no very great task – the Conclave was, like every other piece of Eternal architecture she had seen, magnificent beyond all imagining. There was a rumour that the Senate Hall in Aeleria had been designed in imitation of it, and Eudokia could see at once that this was true and that in that task it was an abject failure, though one might at least applaud the audacity. Eudokia had by now grown some consideration for the vastness of the Eternal's creations, but still the scale was astonishing, the domed ceiling only distantly visible. And against the immensity every detail was perfect, the walls plated to the depth of a finger-joint in gold, the arms of the bench on which Eudokia sat formed into outstretched wings of some or other bird of prey.

Magnificent beyond words, and also mostly empty. The innermost rungs of benches were loosely occupied with Eternal and their servants, but the middle and outer reaches were barren entirely. Was it always this way, Eudokia wondered, or was her arrival among them simply not a matter of much interest? Not for the first time Eudokia felt the fear and the secret thrill of competing against opponents of whom she remained essentially ignorant, a rare pleasure after a lifetime spent dissecting human motivations with the callous efficiency of a butcher with a hog.

She set herself studiously then, as she had at every interval since arriving at the city and for that matter long before, to observation and deduction. The Prime was in the midst of an oration, the particulars of which Eudokia would have to remain ignorant of, her best attempts at comprehending the speech of the Eternal having thus far failed entirely. It was indecipherable, barely even identifiable as language. Blindfolded she might have assumed it some curious natural phenomenon, the rustle of the wind or the tide breaking against an uneven shoreline. But it was clear, at least, that her own personal ignorance was unshared or only partially shared by the other humans present. It was not difficult to make out the half-hidden signs of awareness, this or that body-servant leaning forward as the monologue developed, subtle but distinct indications of understanding. Calla sat beside the Prime, looking fetching as ever, and in the intensity of her attention she might as well have been listening to some rapturous chorus. It was only by the fortuitous obtuseness of Those Above that her renegade erudition was not sniffed out immediately.

Eudokia realised she was smiling, swallowed it back down between narrow lips. The Revered Mother was, she reminded herself, a meek and unprepossessing woman, forced into a situation at once terrifying and beyond her capacities. Good humour was entirely inappropriate.

The master of protocol, sitting stiffly at the end of the bench, looked over and gave her a swift wave. Then he stood and announced, in a loud voice that still did not extend very far into the vastness of the room, 'Eudokia Aurelia, of Aeleria, offers formal greetings to Those Above.'

Eudokia stood and did just that, so deeply that it strained her injured knee, performing the Eternal greeting with a rare display of awkwardness, her hands placed inexpertly and her posture less than perfect. She remained silent for a long moment afterward, as if too in awe to speak.

Without introduction or prologue, rising from the throne on

which he sat, the diadem of his office shining bright from his forehead, the Source sparkling behind him like some great crown of clear water, the Prime began to speak. 'Some time ago, the Aelerian embassy announced the Commonwealth's intention to go to war with the Kingdom of Salucia, offering as explanation violence done towards their ambassador, among a number of other grievances. We did not object, under the condition that said expedition not pass into the Salucian heartland itself – in short, that you made no effort, as you have in years past, to sack or conquer the Salucian capital. Two years and more have passed since we offered that agreement, and your armies have repaid whatever evils you claim the Salucians have done you. Your stated aims have been satisfied – Salucia has been chastened, your city regained. And yet we receive reports from the Sentinel of the Southern Reach that you have even now strengthened your forces, and plan an expedition towards the coast. What possible purpose is there in this continued belligerence?'

Eudokia stood silent for a long moment, eyes wide and quivering, then muttered something too softly to make out.

'She will speak louder,' a voice interrupted from the back. 'I cannot hear her.'

'There seems to be some sort of mistake,' Eudokia said, louder this time, though barely.

A Well-born seated towards the front, one of those who had been engaged in dialogue with the Prime, one of the few, Eudokia suspected, who ever saw fit to raise his voice in counsel, began to speak. 'In the past, when we have called Aeleria to account for their misbehaviour, a member of your Senate has been sent to answer, rather than some old female without any clear public function.'

'You are correct, of course, my Lord,' Eudokia said. 'And I know that the Senator Gratian was anxiously awaiting the opportunity to explain our policies to the Lords and Ladies of the Roost. I know only that the Prime commanded my presence at the Conclave this morning – I could hardly think of refusing.'

'The politics of the Dayspans is as opaque as they are inane,' the Prime explained, 'and the Sentinel assures me that the workings of the Senate do nothing more than obscure the direct involvement of this woman, to whom all true power has devolved.'

Eudokia would have been very good at many things. She would have been an excellent seamstress, a very skilled poet, a more than adequate torturer. She would have been the greatest mummer who ever put on a mask, who ever played a role, who ever feigned misfortune, misery, madness or love. She proved it just then, a quivering and confused facade dropping across her face. 'I have only very briefly met with the Sentinel,' she repeated, 'and cannot answer for her confusion. Please forgive me.'

Calla snorted unbecomingly, then looked down at her feet ashen-faced.

'I know the Sentinel well,' the Prime continued, after a long and not kind look at his subordinate. 'And I can assure you that she rarely makes mistakes of such an order. Is it not the case that you are behind the war faction of the Aelerian Senate? That you are their binding agent and animating force, this war with Salucia is the result of your plots and strategems?'

'I would not like to contradict the Prime,' Eudokia said, a bold try at diffidence, given the unfamiliar terrain.

'Speak, Dayspan,' said another. By his colours, a stark purple and grey, Eudokia knew him to be the Lord of the House of Kind Lament, though without this aid she would have been utterly lost. He looked the same as all of them, tall and unfathomably perfect and entirely bored. 'You need have no fear of offending us, so long as you give the truth.'

'You will receive it, Lords, I swear it, upon the Self-Created and all his children. Upon the Sun God, upon Tolb who keeps company with the low—'

'You need not labour your way through the entire pantheon.'

'Of course, my Lords, of course. Forgive me. In Aeleria it is not considered proper for a woman to speak in a public forum, and I find I have little talent for it,' Eudokia finished neatly, and in her second language.

'Indeed,' said the Lord of the House of Kind Lament, who

seemed to be the Prime's main adversary, at least among his own species. 'Is it not the case that those locusts unlucky enough to exist outside the reach of our example suppose the females of their species to be incapable of handling tasks of any complexity? That they hold no power or authority within their realm?'

'I have heard this to be true,' the Prime admitted. 'But it seems that the Revered Mother is a unique case.'

Eudokia willed a blush to her cheeks – no easy task, but then Eudokia had a very strong will. 'I am privileged to hold the position of Revered Mother, but this is a religious office, carrying some small weight of dignity but no political importance whatsoever. Perhaps this is confusing the Prime.'

'The Lord of the Red Keep is entirely clear on your role within the Aelerian Commonwealth,' he responded.

The Lord of the House of Kind Lament spoke to the Prime in their own tongue, and the Prime responded in kind. They were expressionless and imperturbable, but Calla possessed no such stock of reserve, and Eudokia could read from her face that the exchange was less than friendly.

'You will answer the Prime's questions in so far as it is commensurate with your own limitations,' said her new-found advocate. 'Nothing more will be required of you.'

'As you say, my Lords,' Eudokia acknowledged, dipping her head and then falling silent.

'Well?'

'Forgive me,' Eudokia said, blushing again, discovering that the habit could come when she needed it, 'I'm afraid I had forgotten the question.'

'Why do your armies march north towards Hyrcania?' the Prime asked. 'What is the continued purpose of your bellicosity?'

'Again, my Lords, I must protest that I am as ignorant of violence as a meadowlark,' except for a man she had once beaten to death with a heavy iron skillet, and the perhaps-less-than-occasional victim of the internecine machinations within the Commonwealth, and of course the virtually innumerable corpses whose misfortune was to find themselves at the wrong end of the growing empire of which she was leader. 'And hold no place within the war councils of my nation. Still, it seems clear enough – your orders were that we not enter into the Salucian heartland, and our armies have not done so. So far as I can understand, we have stuck well within the restrictions demanded by this august body.'

'True to the letter,' the Aubade admitted, 'not to the spirit. You make a wasteland of Salucia, pointlessly ravage their territory, destroy their industry and farms, to no end or purpose that we can identify. Is it vengeance alone that calls forth your armies? Is it nothing but your species's . . . petty love of cruelty?'

'Justice is not revenge, my lord, and the gods mete out what punishment they suppose fit.'

Those Above all looked much the same to her, but she recognised the Lord of the Ebony Towers when he rose to speak, from his beauty, which was somehow beyond that even of the other Eternal, so straight and so tall and so very fair; and also because she was Eudokia, and forgot neither insult or injury. 'Blessed are the dead, never to have seen this moment,' he affirmed in his flat monotone. 'Blessed are those who have yet to be born, that they have no share in this humiliation. A locust sits before you, unbowed and unchained, insults the Prime, lies without scruple or regard, as is the nature and essence of its species, while the Conclave allows her temerity to continue unchecked. This false and cloying insistence upon her own ignorance, which any of you not blind or drunk must see is nothing but a thin facade, cannot hide from me the naked arrogance and ambition which is the very heart of this creature, and of the nation of which she sits at the head. The Aelerians require, as does every other Low-born and not infrequently, a reminder that they exist due to the forbearance of their betters, ought be grateful for every day of life and crust of bread we allow them.'

'The Lord of the Ebony Towers overstates the case,' the Prime said quickly, 'but in certain regards he is correct. The might of Aeleria is worthy of consideration, and cannot be allowed to wax in such strength so near to our own borders. As I see it, the arrival of further reinforcements in the field can only be seen as an outright provocation, and warrants swift retaliation.'

'Surely the Prime does not suppose even the locusts mad enough to march upon the Roost?' said one of the Eternal in the audience. Eudokia could not see who but it did not matter; it might have been any of them, the consensus opinion, pronounced as if the sentence of the assemblage.

'I suppose nothing of the sort. But to allow Aeleria to violate with impunity the balance of power risks putting the very structure of our society at risk. The Salucians must continue to act as a distraction and counterweight for the Commonwealth, else within a few generations they will grow large enough to pose a true threat to our nation, one which might not so easily be countered.'

'The Conclave made clear their dictate, and even the Prime admits that we have not violated it,' Eudokia said. 'Hyrcania is untouched, our armies far from the interior of the nation. Is the law in the Roost such that it might be changed at the whim of one individual, however powerful?' Had any of the Eternal been thinking closely on the matter, they might have noticed that for a woman borne down by the sheer weight of awe, Eudokia had no problem presenting a compelling argument for her cause.

'What would a human know of law?' the Shrike asked. 'What would a rat know of poetry? The Dayspan forgets that her species is, always and for ever, deserving not only of reprisal but of extinction, that the punishment for the crime remains only in abeyance and not cancelled. Were we to ride out tomorrow and kill every single thing which walks on two legs and grasps desperately with five fingers, leaving alive only one mewling babe to weep for your misfortune, that would be just and more than just, that would be evidence of our too-tender heart.'

'Extermination,' one of the other Eternal quipped, 'how reasonable.'

'Retribution, at the very least. In the city below they murder our servants with impunity; is it any surprise that outside our walls the locusts breed and gather and roar, just as their name-sakes, and that they think to ignore our commands? What further provocations must we allow before answering?'

'The Lord of the Ebony Towers is conflating the particular with the general,' the Prime said. 'And the indiscretions of the Commonwealth need not be repaid upon the species entire, though they do need be repaid. It is the judgement of the Sentinel of the Southern Shores, one confirmed by the Prime, that the Commonwealth of Aeleria has violated our directives, and stands in breach of the covenant. It is, furthermore, the Prime's recommendation that this violation be repaid swiftly – that an order should be given to the Aelerian Senate demanding the immediate dispersal of their armies, and that this order be supported by the arming of our own forces, to answer with steel should our directive be ignored.'

'This again?' asked the Lord of the House of Kind Lament, or perhaps one of the others, all faceless to Eudokia in their perfection, interchangeable almost-divinities. 'Your answer to every development is war with Aeleria. Be it some skirmish in some distant province or rain on your garden party, the prescription is always and for ever war with Aeleria.'

'My sibling will forgive me if I suppose the stability of our city and empire to be a thing worth fighting to ensure.'

'No doubt my sibling will offer me the same courtesy if I do not suppose every minor feud which takes place among the locusts requires the full marshalling of our armies. Should Aeleria or Salucia or any other of the human nations be in possession of some or other city, what is that to the Prime? What is that to any of us? And despite the Lord of the Ebony Towers' perpetual ill-humour, in fact I find myself in agreement with this Dayspan. The Conclave forbade any attempt to invade the Salucian capital – they have made no such attempt. What, then, would be the purpose in our taking the field? Must the entirety of the Roost defile ourselves by descending to the ground simply that you might again have occasion to practise your bladework?'

'Thank you, my Lord,' Eudokia said, bowing deeply, 'it is good to find that there is still justice in the Roost, as there was in days of old.'

Again the Lord of the Ebony Towers rose, and again Eudokia was struck by his extraordinary and ethereal beauty, as well as the absolute implacability of his contempt. 'Hatchlings, ill-bred, head-struck, snake-bit, moon-maddened, false sons and untrue daughters. Inconceivable that ever an interruption was required of your endless amusements. You have grown so lazy that you allow this . . . thing to stand within sight of the Source itself, and to lie, to manoeuvre, to twist and to deceive. She runs her fingers across your strings and you sing just the note she wishes.' He turned his eyes and the full force of his hatred on Eudokia alone. 'Vermin, dogs and rats – worse than rats, for a rat at least has the sense to flee from the light of day and the footfalls of its betters, while you strut and preen and love the attention. Such mad and inconceivable vanity, such titanic and unfathomable self-delusion. We ought to drown you all in blood,' he averred, eyes bright and beautiful and impossibly enticing, and for a moment Eudokia could imagine that death might come not as a shrivelled skeleton, but as a man in the full blossom of youth, beautiful and naked, understood that thing that draws a moth towards a candle-flame, the glorious flicker-flash and then nothing. 'We ought to make a desert of your nation as a reminder to your fellows not to have thoughts above their station. And as for the thing in front of us, you ought to give her to me for a day, in punishment for her temerity and so that we might know the truth; that last I can promise you, there are rooms and chambers within my black walls which are for no other purpose but that.' Pronounced through a porcelain mask, his face unmarked with anger, his voice as even and steady as the beat of a drum.

For once Eudokia did not need to force a simulacrum of fear, her heart beating thrice-speed in her chest, the blood fleeing from her face into the far extremities of her body, her voice pitched high and broken. 'My safety was promised, my Lords,' Eudokia said, her attention on the Lord of the House of Kind

Lament, 'you swore it, my Lord, you swore it yourself—'

'You need not remind me,' he said, ignoring her entirely as being beneath notice and staring firmly at the Shrike instead, 'and whatever joys it might bring the Lord of the Ebony Towers, he will not have opportunity to practise his sadism at the expense of my honour. This Dayspan is beneath the protection of the Conclave, your predilections towards cruelty notwithstanding.'

'Thank you, my Lord, oh by the gods thank you. They hate us so, my Lord, they are mad with hatred, I know nothing of politics, my Lords, by all the gods and all their creatures—'

'Indeed – though the Lord of the Ebony Towers is well known for his obsessive contempt for the Dayspans, never did I suppose the Prime would fall victim to such error. Have you gone so mad with fear, sibling, that you see danger hiding behind every tree and branch, huddled beneath the cobblestones, slithering out of the pipes?'

'The Lord of the Ebony Towers does not speak for me,' the Prime said swiftly. 'Never have we sat in counsel together, and as regards the humans of the Roost, indeed we have ever been in fierce and open dispute, as any honest witness will admit. My recommendations carry no hint of cruelty, a luxury the Lord of the Red Keep has never allowed himself, but only of self-defence, the primary duty of all things living. Aeleria is a threat to the future of the Roost, I believe it and I have long believed it, and if we do not answer rapidly and with force then we may well lose the opportunity to do so effectively. The balance of power within the continent must be maintained, and for that the Aelerian army must be shattered. If left unchecked they will grow one day to devour us. This woman is the architect of this danger; it is her hand wielding the blade, her threat that we must answer today, here and now, at this very moment.'

But looking down from thrones of aureate and ivory, who would believe it? An old woman, enfeebled by the standards of a race that was so weak anyway as to be of no account, who died in the blink of an eye and who were replaced by some identical mass of flesh. Her voice quivered and she leaned hard on her cane, barely able to speak against the inevitable majesty of the Eternal; two species similar as the sun is to the moon, alike in rough shape but essentially and ultimately without comparison. Who would believe her a threat? Who could think such a thing possible?

17

In a province of no particular importance, lying roughly equidistant between Oscan, Hyrcania and the Roost, there was a valley. Nearby that valley there was a town called Actria, and afterward the battle would be named for it, but that was not actually the name of the valley. The valley did not have a name, not even to the people of Actria, who referred to it by compass bearing on those rare occasions when it needed to be mentioned. In the valley that did not have a name on that day in the early spring there were magnolia trees just starting to bloom, thin sprays of white and pink stretching out from the boughs. There were tanager and warbler returned from their winter quarters, beginning the laborious task of nesting, if they were female, or simply singing their joy to the sun, were they otherwise. There were evergreens still looking rich from winter, there were strands of catmint and lavender poking up from the dirt. There were voles in the grass, there were sparrows in the sky, there were ninety thousand men carrying sharpened steel, though by nightfall there would be a good number fewer.

It had not come as a surprise to Bas to find that the arrival of the three western themas, swelling as they had the ranks of what had already been the largest military force in Aelerian history, had not been sent back homeward. A month since they had left the ruined city of Oscan, scuttling east like a snail abandoning its shell, leaving in their wake the usual trail of burned townships and ravaged farms and weeping smallfolk. Unable to make peace, having failed to convince the Others to intervene, Salucia had scraped together the largest force it could field and sent it south to meet the invaders, and by divine providence or cruel fate or the random alignment of events, the two armies found themselves occupying opposite ends of a valley that had never before been important enough to receive a proper name, but which would afterward echo in the annals of human history, however brief a span that might be.

No, the coming battle was not a surprise to Bas – but it was an odd feeling indeed not to be in the middle of it. Outside a not over-modest command tent, positioned at the lip of the valley, Bas had a fine view of everything that would develop below, though no capacity to influence it. True, it was rare for a Legatus to be put in charge of a single thema, but there was nothing about this situation that could be considered normal. Konstantinos insisted he required Bas as a personal consultant, dealing with the strategic considerations of the campaign, though Bas was not exceptional in this regard and anyway his opinion had rarely been solicited. The sight of the men down below, his men, and their standard, his standard, the three-legged wolf snarling on a crimson background, had set the bottom half of Bas's jaw scratching against the top, and his hand curling round the hilt of his sword in unconscious sympathy for his comrades.

Protostrator Konstantinos watched the coming conflict like a man holding a pair of weighted dice. Battle orders had been signed out long hours earlier; there had been plenty of time to arrange the thema below to his satisfaction. Signalmen stood nearby, preparing their array of flags to transmit his orders, though Bas suspected it would require nothing more complicated than the simple black banner indicating forward movement. A clear day, cloudless, the sun descending on Konsantinos's broad smile as if by personal invitation. He wore a chain baldric and a sword that had never been bloodied. He had a sterling silver torc that was the just due of his rank, and he carried a short rod, ivory and gold-capped. He had not said anything for several minutes, though Bas could see that this happy interlude was about to come to an end.

'Hail, Caracal. May the gods look upon our work today with favour.'

Of this Bas had little doubt. It had been his experience over the course of near forty years of death and blood and slaughter that the gods preferred large numbers to small, and the Aelerians had that. Seven to five, had been the predictions of the spies and scouts and traitors, though looking at the army Salucia had assembled below Bas suspected it was closer to five to three. Not that it would matter, because that five or that three, however many there were exactly, were mostly not soldiers but only men holding weapons. At the other end of the valley men were praying loudly to their bull-god Mephet, and remembering the faces of their lovers or their sons or their mothers, soft contours they would never see again. The cream of the Salucian military – to the degree that such a thing could be spoken of in a race as silk-soft as the Salucians – had died at Bod's Wake and on the walls of Oscan. What was left were raw recruits, fresh levees impressed and forced to carry a spear, the unlucky sons of tenant farmers and the urban poor, fit only for dying.

'The contest would be more certain if I was in the vanguard,' Bas observed, though he didn't entirely believe it.

'No doubt,' Konstantinos said, smiling and gesturing with his rod to the men below. Not at anything in particular, more so that he could wave the thing around. 'But the Caracal's is too valuable a life to risk on so trivial an exercise. There will yet be time to show your claws.'

Which was true as far as it went, but which Bas secretly suspected was not the reason he had been withheld from the fray. Bas's heroics at Oscan had not gone unnoticed – nothing that Bas did went unnoticed, not since that day twenty-five years ago when he had battered the brains of an Eternal against the flat end of his warhammer and the mossy grass, his every cough and bowel movement fodder for some or other second-rate minstrel. Bas had heard the songs they'd written this last winter – that he had taken Oscan single-handed, that he had battered down the walls with his sword or with his voice or with his cock. That they were foolish beyond measure or meaning, that only a child and an idiot child at that would believe them, had done nothing to diminish their popularity. Perhaps it had grown wearisome to Konstantinos, that the larger share of legend due from the Salucian campaign had so far gathered about Bas's broad shoulders.

Bas excused himself and went to find Isaac. His adjutant stood a short walk downslope, staring at the armies below as a carpenter would an uneven table. 'They don't have enough men in their reserve line.'

'They don't have enough men, period.'

Isaac nodded, the ruined flesh of his cropped ears stuttering up and down. 'I'd have anchored the east end against that copse of trees,' he said. 'Rather than leave the seam open. If the Protostrator is any sort of clever, that'll be where he'll throw the cavalry.'

'He's clever enough,' Bas said grudgingly. 'Anyway, the boy's in charge of the horse. Theophilus will know to do it, even if he isn't told.'

The command had come after Oscan, just recognition for Theophilus's skill in handling the attack. An impressive ascent for a youth of his age, and for once a well-deserved one. His bloodline was enough to satisfy Konstantinos and the other aris- tocrats, and the years he had spent in tutelage to Bas and Isaac had left him competent and more than competent at the business of war.

'They never did have horse worth a damn,' Isaac said after a moment.

'They had the Marchers as auxiliaries, in the last go-round.'

Isaac grunted. He and Bas, as much as any two men alive, were the reason that the Salucians could no longer call upon the services of the March lords, having spent the better part of the last twenty years winnowing away at their territory and slaughtering any group of them that ever swelled large enough to dispute this loss.

'Any chance they can hold out till evening?' Isaac asked, sounding strangely hopeful. 'Organise some sort of retreat?'

'I suppose there's always a chance,' Bas said after a moment. 'I suppose.'

'You'd think they'd be wise enough to know when they're beaten.'

'They know,' Bas said. 'What can they do about it? Three embassies we had come to Oscan, and all turned away. That last was a prince of the blood, nephew of the Queen herself.'

'The one with the hat?'

'Aye.'

Isaac grunted. He removed a canteen from one of his pockets, unscrewed the cap with his worn, knotted hands, brought it to his lips. And why not? Neither would be doing anything but watching today, and a drunk witness would be no worse than a sober one. Isaac tilted the flask in Bas's direction but he pretended that he didn't see it, and after a moment Isaac put it away. 'What do we want with Salucia, exactly?'

'What did we want with the Marches?' Bas asked. 'Everything. Everyone wants everything.'

'I don't,' Isaac said after a moment.

'I don't either,' Bas admitted, then left Isaac to his drink.

Had Einnes been human, had she been possessed of that range of emotions that were common to Bas's kind, she would have been offended by the looks she received as she strutted towards the command tent – or perhaps insulted, wavering as they did between contemptuous and lewd. She was not human, of course, and the thoughts or feelings of the five-fingered beings among whom she resided were of no more interest to her than the cries of the kites overhead, or the chittering of squirrels. Bas was less sanguine about the matter, and when he noticed a tetrarch sneering – one of Konstantinos's, a well-formed youth who had risen to his office without unsheathing a sword – Bas returned the look with sort of blistering intensity that had sent killers off weeping, and the boy swallowed hard and disappeared.

Ignorant of his courtesy, Einnes took up a position on the cliff, glancing down at the fracas below. 'There aren't very many of them,' was the first thing she said.

'There aren't enough,' Bas agreed.

'They don't look very happy to be fighting, either,' Einnes said, squinting her eyes. 'Their leader is fat, and his eyes know fear. Also, I think those are wine stains on his jerkin.'

Could she really see such a distance? Bas wondered, but knew for a certainty that the answer was yes. As extraordinary as she was physically – her strength and speed, her hearing and her vision, a sense of smell to outdo a bloodhound – more exceptional in Bas's mind was the fact that she never lied, indeed seemed only distantly even to understand the concept. If Einnes said that the leader of the Salucian forces was working hard to drink away his fear, then she was right.

'And there will be no repetition of your performance at Oscan?' Einnes asked after a moment. 'No extraordinary heroics to tip the scale?'

'The scale seems well tipped.'

'It does that,' Einnes agreed. 'Still, a pity. I had quite enjoyed your last performance. I can't help but think that this little fracas will be rather less exciting altogether.'

'Exciting enough for the men fighting it,' Bas said.

Konstantinos broke away from his small band of advisers and approached at a saunter. 'Hail, Sentinel of the Southern Reach,' Konstantinos began, as polite as ever, decorousness second nature. 'You have come to bear witness to our victory?'

'Such are the demands of my position,' Einnes said flatly.

Whatever sympathy she enjoyed with Bas had not spread to the rest of the species, least of all to Konstantinos. 'To watch, and to remember.'

'You will have much to report to your superiors, come the evening.'

'The death of locusts is not a matter of broad interest to we Eternal, irrespective of quantity,' Einnes said, turning full to face him. 'And this morning's slaughter will have no bearing upon your situation, so far as I can tell. The Conclave did not follow my suggestion in demanding that your army disband, nor in meeting this force with an army of their own – you may thank the gods you claim to worship for this development. But do not think my threat empty when I assure you that whatever happens today your army will never set foot into Hyrcania, will go no further into the heartland of Salucia. Have you not yet received sufficient plunder to satisfy your greed? Always I had understood that your species is riven with divisions as arbitrary as they are trivial, that you hold these minor distinctions in colour and language to be worthy of savage violence, but I admit to finding your sheer willingness to commit slaughter . . . wasteful.'

'You will forgive me, Sentinel, if I do not suppose the long provocations of our enemies to be so casually forgotten. And our purpose in moving eastward is simple – so that in future years, when the Salucians in their mad arrogance think to again insult the might and honour of Aeleria, think to claim what they do not deserve, they will remember this day and grow cautious.'

'Violence is no remedy for foolishness, however often it's prescribed.'

It had been a long time since Bas had seen the Protostrator unsmiling. 'There is much which requires my attention,' he said, nodding to Einnes though not quite bowing, 'as I'm sure you will appreciate.' Konstantinos allowed himself to be drawn away by a neighbouring adjunct, no doubt hoping he would be more successful in the coming contest than he had been in this one.

Bas and Einnes stood silently for a time, though they seemed the only two people in camp who could claim this distinction, all the rest loud in their good humour, the scent of death inspiring to those who need not fear it. Two high-ranking officers, one fat, one thin, both loud, began to dispute loudly as to the proper placement of Hamilcar's archers, neither able to draw a bow but each confident verging on bellicose. Isaac had begun to talk to himself, or at least not to anyone else in particular, discussing the battle, comparing it to others he had fought in, drunk enough now to forget social convention – though it had to be said that the liquor was proving no impediment to his tactical sense, and his observations and suggestions were, to Bas's mind, entirely sound. Konstantinos was surrounded by a solid ring of adjutants and councillors, every one of them smiling or trying to hide a smile, every one a senator's son. At some point soon things would start to happen in the valley below, but in the interlude there was nothing to do but enjoy having been born on the right side of history.

'This has ceased to be of interest,' Einnes said simply.

'Yes.'

'I'll return to my tent,' she said, 'perhaps I can get a good ride in this morning. You'll let me know if anything develops?'

But what would? The outcome certain, the business grim and bloody. 'It seems unlikely that will be necessary.'

'Yes,' Einnes agreed, and retreated, and with her gone there was nothing to do but watch the battle.

Bas admitted, if grudgingly and only to himself, that Konstantinos had at least managed to form a competent plan of attack. The army was arranged in the standard Aelerian forma-tion with the broad mass of hoplitai split into three wings, cavalry filling in the gaps, Hamilcar and the other archers on the extreme ends. Nothing particularly clever or imaginative, but Bas had warred for long enough to know that even plain competence in a general is far from a guarantee.

And anyway, victory today would not demand genius. The arrival of the western legions had done more to steady the rest of the army than even their victories at Bod's Wake or Oscan. They were coolly competent, they were scarred, withered, bone-hard and brutal. They were squat and well-muscled, their calloused hands seemed to have been formed solely to hold pike and sword and knife. They cursed with every breath, they were tight-fisted and grasping, they stole anything not nailed to something else, they gambled constantly and usually lost and often refused to pay. They were generally drunk and always permanently scowling, their only smiles bitter ones, nasty jokes at the expense of others.

The Salucians had nothing with which to match them. Indeed, there was nothing human that could hope to stand against this vast engine Bas had helped to create, this rolling tumult of steel and fire and death, though looking at it Bas found himself with a curious lack of pride. There was a moment then when he thought hard about going back to his tent, drinking heavily and staring up at the cloth, at the line of sun running across the entranceway, watching it draw tight with the afternoon's arrival, waiting for evening's inevitable descent. Or perhaps finding Einnes, going for a long ride, away from the camp and out into the hinterlands, north along the river, riding until night began to fall, or perhaps a long time beyond that.

He didn't do either of these things, of course. There was one word written on Bas's heart, and that word was duty. He had no role in the day's events save as observer, and so this was the one he would play.

The horns were near deafening, even at this range, some curious auditory effect of the valley funnelling the noise back towards the Aelerian camp. Konstantinos stopped smiling at the sound, assumed an air of importance, of great and conscious dignity. He waved his rod to the chief signalman, who ran the great crimson battle flag up the pole, the gonfalon bright in the noon-time sun.

Battle was joined.

It was an awkward and ungainly means of combat, long rows of tightly packed men walking slowly into one another. Bas had been at the front of it often enough to remember the feeling, the growing sense of nausea, those moments before always the worst, thinking that perhaps this was the time that you broke and ran, wanting it to come, whatever it was, death itself better than uncertainty, or at least it might seem so before you met it. And the reek, the smell – that was something the minstrels never spoke of, the furious olfactory misery manifested by the press of thousands of men, their flesh and their sweat and their blood and their shit; shit comes with blood, as any soldier can tell you, after from death and before from fear. The ant-like ignorance of your own motions, the certain knowledge that your own victory or defeat will play no very significant role in the day's outcome, that your speed and strength and courage carry no more weight than the speed and strength and courage of the man beside you, and the man beside him, definitive evidence of the essential pointlessness of your existence.

'Magnificent,' Konstantinos said, as the hoplitai began to march forward in even ranks, the valley echoing with the rumbling of their feet. 'Magnificent,' he said again, savouring the moment.

Not so far below, a world away, men shoved metal into the flesh of other men, men screamed, men staunched their wounds and the wounds of their comrades, men suffered, men died. The Salucians had done their best to mimic the tactics of their enemies, long spears and leather armour, but neither their equipment nor the men carrying it were a match for the themas. It had taken a generation to create such a machine, tens of thousands of men working in admirable if imperfect concert towards the shared end of murder. The Thirteenth led the way in the centre, crossing the distance in unison, in rhythm that would have shamed a troupe of dancers, and seen from so far above it did seem beautiful, thrilling, even for those who ought to have known better. Bas felt his heart pump happily and Isaac let out a war-whoop when the Thirteenth struck against an equivalent mass of Salucians, equivalent in numbers though in no other fashion, the vast metal monster straining forward.

The day was at its zenith, sun blinding bright off the burnished steel of the hoplitai, as if the valley itself had been set alight. Bas wiped a blunt hand across his forehead, came away thick with sweat. Isaac took a long swig from his flask, and Bas waved him over for a sip, and then more than a sip. Konstantinos strutted up and down the line, making pronouncements and observations and exhortations, and his companions, aristocrats and half-nobleman, seasonal soldiers, cheered at everything, at his foolish hiccuped jokes and his predictions of victory, cheered the smell of blood, cheered the sound of their cheering.

The Salucians had determined to break the Aelerian centre, no very creative strategy but then there were no clearly superior alternatives. What few troops they had who could make any claim towards competence were fed into the middle, pike against pike, steel against steel. It would not have worked against any of the thema and it would certainly not work against the Thirteenth; even without Bas leading them they were still the fiercest array of men perhaps ever assembled, they were still more than any horde of lisping half-trained Salucians could hope to best.

Who knew how long it was building, a tremor of terror along the left flank? Who knew what had first started it: one weak link in a long chain, the cowardice of some or other farm boy, pressed into service for a cause he neither understood nor cared for. The collapse at Scarlet Fields had come when one hoplitai had pissed himself and an adjoining soldier had mocked him for it, the two both so mad with fear that they dropped their spears and assaulted each other, the terror spilling out like blood from an open wound, all with the Birds massing for an open charge. It was a part of that curiosity of mass combat by which an infinite number of tiny decisions, each irrelevant in and of itself, is somehow transmuted into victory or defeat. Some confusion along the wing, some unit refusing to go forward, and a seam began to open up between the Salucian centre and the Salucian left, a wide chink in the armour, an invitation to rout.

'They're splitting, by the gods they're splitting!' Konstantinos shouted, managed to get word to the signalman, who raised the flag for the cavalry charge, though Bas did not suppose Theophilus fool enough to miss the opportunity. And indeed the alacrity with which his band of cavalry set off suggested his old subordinate was living up to his new position. They struck against the hole in the Salucian line perfectly, and for the first time that day Bas did feel something like joy, for he could have done no better himself, no better than this boy he had taught to kill. Their cavalry plunged into the loose-packed mass of men, rode them down without mercy, long spears useless and less than useless in such a situation, an encumbrance and one that most of the Salucians dispensed with as swiftly as possible, along with their arms and armour and anything else that might slow them down, that might hinder their desperate escape, not a retreat but an outright collapse.

And above the valley the officers and nobles, hands uncalloused but steeped in blood, whooped and hollered, shouted joyfully, threw hats in the air, embraced each other fiercely, offered loud and fervent prayers to the god of war. Prayers well due him, an easy victory better even than a just one.

18

On a dark night half past the hour of the Nightjar, Pyre and Hammer slid down an alleyway on a distant corner of the Fifth. Above. A great width of pipe beat its steady tune, though as children of the slums they gave no more thought to the noise than they would the beating of their own hearts. On either side were bleak walls of faded red brick, tenement houses much like the one that Pyre had grown up in, finger-width walls separating small rooms into smaller ones, the smell of excreta and of cooked cabbage. At the back door of one of these hovels were two Dead Pigeons, nearly obscured by the shadow of the suck. Even back when the Cuckoos had been masters of the Fifth Rung, had strutted down the thoroughfares like capons ignorant of their deficit, they had rarely seen any point in visiting so impoverished and miserable a corner of their territory. These days, with Pyre's men leading lightning raids on unwary custodians, with Five-Fingered handprints up on every wall from the docks to the Perennial Exchange, there was no Cuckoo brave enough to show himself below the top of the Fourth, and many who would not attempt even that modest feat. There was, in all likelihood, not a single member of the civil guard within a dozen cables, and the only authority was wielded by Pyre himself.

But still he was wary approaching the back door, gave the parole with one hand on the hilt of his weapon. Caution had become second nature to Pyre; he did not walk into a room without thinking of how he would leave it, he did not meet a man without questioning how they might think to betray him, and what method he would find to return that evil.

'Brother Pyre,' said one of the guards quietly, a dark-skinned man, short and ugly as a swelling bruise.

'Brother Frost.' Pyre knew every man in the Dead Pigeons, every man or near to. Knew them and was known in turn. 'The rest are in attendance?'

'Yes, sir.'

'Make sure their escorts are ready to move before the hour of the Owl. This won't last as long as they think.'

'Of course, Brother Pyre,' Frost said, giving the salute, then holding it out in front of him, fingers open. 'Until the new age.'

'Until the dawn to come,' Pyre said, the words second nature if truly meant. Hammer came into the corridor but stayed outside the main room, as much to serve guard as because, like most of the Dead Pigeons, he preferred violence to parlay.

They had knocked down three dividing walls to make enough room for the table and the eleven men who sat round it. For most this was their first time so far downslope, and likely they found the accommodations insalubrious. This was not their fault, and Pyre had learned enough by then – Edom had taught him enough – that he did not hold it against them. They were his brothers, he reminded himself, his siblings, victims of the demons as he was, different in degree but not in kind. They huddled round the table, wearing heavy furs and shivering despite them. The walls of these buildings were weak enough to bend with a strong wind, and the cold seemed to leak right through, as Pyre had observed on innumerable nights as a child, sharing his small bed with his three sisters, chilled despite the tight, rank press of their bodies.

They all stared as he came in, a row of middle-aged men, smooth-skinned and unsmiling. Except for Edom, and that was enough, that smile that sanctified everything. Pyre returned it and moved to the one vacant seat, set next to their leader as was only appropriate. 'You will forgive my tardiness, brothers,' he said. 'It was the result of urgent business.'

'What sort of urgent business?' snapped Steadfast, ready as ever to give insult.

'It was a matter for the Dead Pigeons,' Pyre said

'Discussing the delay only exacerbates it,' Edom interrupted, 'and we have little enough time as it is.' Standing with customary grace he offered the Five-Fingered salute. 'Edom, the First of His Line, calls this meeting to order.'

'Steadfast, the First of His Line, bears witness.'

'Able, the First of His Line, bears witness.'

They went down the line one by one, introducing themselves unnecessarily, unwilling to dispense with formality despite their claims to haste. It had long since ceased to interest Pyre. Ritual had its purpose in indoctrinating and inspiring the faithful, but ritual was a distant second to action. And in truth this meeting was far from being the most important of Pyre's tasks that evening. At that very moment, some few cables to the east of them, Badger's cell was leading a raid on one of the last of the Brotherhood Below's safe houses. On the Third Rung, two members of Devotion's cell were getting set to snatch up a particularly recalcitrant merchant, one of the few in the quadrant who had maintained his misguided allegiance to Those Above, who refused the modest tithe required of all humans who wished to see themselves unfettered, which was to say all right-thinking men. In a few minutes there would be an attack on one of the Cuckoo nests up on the Fourth – nothing serious, nothing major, a bottle of alcohol and a lit rag tossed through a window, just enough to keep their enemies wary, frightened, off balance. When the meeting finally ended Pyre would hear the reports of the evening's activities, would plan the operations to come, would deal with the dozen other tasks yet required of him. Sleep that night would be a few stolen hours, no pleasure but a necessary oblivion, just enough to refresh his mind, just enough that when Hammer shook him awake the next morning he could go about the day with some semblance of reason.

'Pyre, the First of His Line, bears witness,' he answered when his time came.

'Let's break to the point of it,' Wolf said. He was one of their financiers, son of a docker, born on the far corner of the Fifth, one of those rare downslopers who had made good. He had earned a fortune selling cheap things to men and women foolish enough to buy them, and he had given some portion of those riches to the Five-Fingers. 'I object to the actions of Pyre, the First of His Line, actions that have brought us to the brink of open war, actions that were neither discussed nor agreed upon by the council.'

'We have always been at war,' Pyre said. 'Nothing has changed.'

'Nothing has changed? The entire Roost is up in arms. Our beclouded brethren on the higher Rungs walk fearfully, thinking the Five-Fingers their enemies. On the Third Rung, Cuckoos march in lockstep, and there are rumours that the demons themselves lead them.'

'It is time, and past time, that our siblings upslope came to recognise their fetters and their own role in maintaining them. If I had known all that was required to bring them to enlightenment was to slit the throat of an old man wearing heavy make-up, I'd have done it long ago.'

'Had you known,' Steadfast chimed in. 'Had you known? Last I had heard it was not Pyre who was in charge of setting policy for the revolution.'

'You overstep your bounds,' agreed Spectre, a grey-haired man wearing ill-cut robes. He had been a member of the Five-Fingered for long years before Pyre's own, was one of the first to have heard the truth. As far as Pyre was concerned, seniority was the only virtue he possessed, an ageing pedant who preferred speech to action. This fairly summed up, in his estimation, most of the rest of the council. 'It is one thing to assault a few guards on the Fourth, or to scrawl graffiti on a downslope wall, and quite another to assassinate the chief human political agent of the Birds.'

'I call for a vote of censure upon Pyre, the First of His Name,' said Wolf.

'Seconded,' Spectre said.

Edom cleared his throat softly, and the conversation stilled. 'It would be premature to take any such action before first hearing of Brother Pyre's explanation for the event itself.'

Though it took Pyre a solid twenty seconds before he felt calm enough to attempt one, willing his pulse to slow, shoving the rage back down into his chest, nor did he suppose the interim did anything particularly to help his cause. Pyre was many things but dissimulator was not one of them, and to judge by the faces of the other men at the table this fact was well appreciated.

When he finally spoke, his voice seemed calm. 'For the last six months, the Dead Pigeons have been working to infiltrate the upper ranks of the Brotherhood Below.'

'Why was the inner council not informed of any of this?' asked Wolf.

'It was felt that a matter of such delicacy was best to keep unknown to any parties not directly involved.'

'Who felt this?'

'Pyre felt this way. Pyre and Edom, the First of His Line.'

That shut them up quickly enough, by the gods. Though they might all maintain this happy facade of equality, there was no more real doubt in the mind of Wolf or Spectre or Steadfast who was truly in charge of the Five-Fingered.

'You knew of this, Edom?' Steadfast asked after a moment.

'I was aware that we had . . . stratagems in place. I had not been informed that they were so near to fruition.'

'There wasn't time to alert you,' Pyre said, for the first time feeling some slim sense of shame. 'Savior, the First of His Line, who brought the coming age closer with his own life's blood, informed me the very day of the meeting that he would be responsible for security. It was an opportunity which couldn't be overlooked. In truth, I fail to understand how this can be regarded as anything but a great victory, an accelerant for the fire to come. The Brotherhood Below, the hidden hand by which the lower Rungs have been kept in bondage for centuries, is broken and soon to be eradicated. Even now my men are working to extinguish this plague which has so long choked our people. As for the chancellor . . .' He shrugged. 'I cannot see why his death is of any great importance one way or the other. The demons will install a new man shortly enough, one likely to remember his predecessor's fate, one who will not perhaps be so swift to hinder the destiny of his species.'

'To reveal our strength before it's grown to fullness?' Steadfast asked contemptuously. 'Before we are equipped to bring it to bear? There are not yet so many of us as to afford retaliation.'

Pyre's lip dragged itself up over his teeth. 'A bared throat, a chink in the armour of our enemies – there was no time to bring the matter to the council. The chancellor had no intention of dealing with us honestly – he was no more capable of seeing the dawn than is the setting moon. He had arranged the meeting to bribe me, and if he could not bribe me to frighten me, and if he could not frighten me then to kill me. With his death, and the death of Ink, the Brotherhood Below has been thrown into chaos, and the custodians along with them. In the last two weeks alone our people have all but overrun the Fourth Rung, and made inroads into the Third. Where I was born, we consider the death of our enemies to be a thing worth celebrating.'

'Bask in your victory,' Wolf said, sneering, 'just until the demons come knocking at your door. We are not yet strong enough to make a stand. The chancellor himself, by the Founders—'

'By the gods,' Pyre corrected him harshly. 'And it was by the gods that I did it, that I felt his blood run down my hand and onto the floor, this enemy of his race, this – this – traitor to his species.' Pyre could tell they were looking at him and he fell silent, worked to contain his anger, chewed it back down, caged it within his broad chest.

'The chancellor's guilt is not the issue at hand, Pyre,' Edom said quietly, in that voice like a poultice on a seeping wound, like oil dropped over restless water. 'Your assault may provoke a response we are not yet prepared to deal with.'

Wolf chimed in again. 'The head of the Dead Pigeons is not the head of the Five-Fingers. I say that Pyre has overstepped the authority granted to him by the council. I once again request a vote of censure.'

'Seconded,' said Steadfast.

'Fine,' Pyre said. 'I serve the species at the pleasure of Edom,' he accentuated the last word firmly, 'and of the council. Should my behaviour as leader of the Dead Pigeons not meet with their approval, it goes without saying that I would be happy to occupy any role they see fit. Though I suggest you have a suitable replacement in hand before dismissing me. Is there one among you who feels themselves more capable? Brother Wolf? Perhaps you would choose to leave your house on the Second and come live down here in the slurp? Brother Steadfast, how is your knife hand? Swift? Sure? You will have need of it, of that much I can tell you for a certainty.'

'No doubt there are men within the Dead Pigeons who could perform your function adequately,' Wolf said.

'I'm afraid the members of the Dead Pigeons place a more substantial value on loyalty than the council. And whatever your feelings, among his own people Pyre is considered competent enough. I assure you, you will find no great thirst among the Dead Pigeons for new leadership – indeed, they might find the suggestion insulting.'

All was silent, for a time. Or not quite silent – there was the heavy and constant sound of water being pulled upslope, and there was Pyre's blood beating loudly in his veins. It was not the insult they had done him, an insult that stemmed as much from their own cowardice as from their contempt for him as a downslope thug, the demon's poison having worked its way into their minds, having polluted everything it touched, thinking him inferior despite Edom's words, despite Edom's promises of and demands for solidarity. This was annoying, this was unpleasant – but this was not what Pyre held against them. It was that they had wasted his time, and his time was not his time any longer, his time was the species', was humanity's, and every instant of it needed to be called to strict account. He would no more be removed from his position than he would sprout wings and fly up to the First, it was nothing but posturing, and this while battle was being joined, this while his own men were fighting and bleeding and dying in the gutters.

'Brothers,' Edom said finally, 'this is not the behaviour of those who would usher in the dawn. Pyre's service these last years has been . . . commendable, and more than commendable. His passion and skill have seen us go from strength to strength. If this enthusiasm has, perhaps in recent days, somewhat outstripped itself, well, passion in defence of the species is not so terrible a sin, and it is one that he will no doubt seek to curb in the coming days.'

Those blue eyes firm on him, and after a moment Pyre found his shoulders slumped. 'Forgive me, brothers. The day has been a very long one, and perhaps my patience is not what it ought to be. I will make sure to coordinate more closely with the council in the future.'

It made no one happy. Ten men left the room as distrustful of Pyre as when they had entered it, though it would be Pyre's soldiers who saw them safely back to their homes on the Second Rung and the Third. Pyre's soldiers who would die for them, if it came to that.

The eleventh was Edom, and for a moment, for a happy moment, it was only the two of them, Edom with his eyes that saw and understood and forgave. 'Were those the words of a man called Pyre?'

'They were not. They were the words of a boy named Thistle, and I regret them.'

'The council fears you, Pyre,' he said simply. 'They see the esteem in which the Dead Pigeons hold you, the Dead Pigeons and half the lower Rungs. They see Pyre's name scrawled on the walls beside our handprints, they hear Pyre's name spoken in tones of reverence or fear. They grow jealous, and they grow frightened.'

'Nonsense. All nonsense. I have no aims beyond the redemption of the species. The dawn and the dawn alone is my sole concern. If I thought it would bring it forward an hour or a moment or even a single instant, I would open a vein without hesitation.'

Edom's smile hung in place for a long time. It was a steady thing, that smile, it was a stone facade, or the still surface of an underground well. 'Of course,' Edom said, taking Pyre's hand and walking him towards the door. 'I know that, have no fear. Your presence within the organisation is invaluable, none could replace you. You must be careful, Pyre, the First of His Line. It would be a terrible thing if your talents were lost to us by virtue of your courage.'

'Martyr's blood is fine fertiliser,' Pyre said quietly.

'The best,' Edom agreed. 'The very best.'

19

Calla stood at the stone cusp of the Sidereal Citadel, a spring breeze caressing her bared shoulders. It was more than two years since the Wright's first attempt at directed flight had failed in fiery and spectacular fashion, a thousand clove of metal and wood and silk and steamwork tumbling from the sky, dozens dying in the ship itself, who knew how many more when the thing crashed amidst the busy thoroughfares of the Second Rung. It had not forestalled progress – the death of a few humans here and there was seen as small sacrifice to this sanguinary deity. In this, at least, the Roost was not so different from the rest of the world.

And in fairness, the Wright had perfected his marvellous creations swiftly enough. An expedition six months after the catastrophe had seen the Wright and those of his human coterie who had survived the destruction of the first aeroship spend a miraculous if brief period gliding cleanly through a late morning sky and, moreover, landing safely. In the fashion of the Eternal, whose passion for novelties and diversion of all kinds bordered on mania, this second, successful expedition had set off a panicked enthusiasm for flight among all the Lords and Ladies of the First Rung. Half of his species had come to ask for the schematic, the less skilled of the Eternal resorting to begging the Wright or some other of their brethren to manufacture one in their stead. The Prime had received his first, a miraculous-looking thing of crimson and gold that the Aubade had accepted with the most elaborate expressions of courtesy, and had occasionally even enjoyed the use of, though never in the company of his seneschal. After what she had seen, nothing short of a direct order could convince Calla to embark upon it, and the Prime was kind enough not to insist. There were few among the Four-Fingered who shared her reticence, and these days any clear afternoon saw a small swarm of aeroships floating high above the First Rung, bright spots of saffron and maroon and chartreuse against a blue sky.

Today would see the first test of a new iteration, some variant of the original the specifics of which Calla was less than clear on. A larger air sack, or a more effective means of manoeuvring. It was, like most of what the Eternal did, little more than an opportunity to celebrate their own existence, every occasion demanding a feast and a party.

Occupied with her thoughts, she was slow to notice him standing behind her, looking, as they all did, ageless and unknowable. 'Calla of the Red Keep,' the Wright began. 'I hope the sun finds you well this day.'

'My Lord of the Sidereal Citadel,' Calla said, the Eternal greeting offered second-nature. 'May the moon bless you with its touch.'

It was difficult and near impossible to determine the age of an Other, at least if one was not a member of the species. They reached their maturity nearly as swiftly as human children, remaining atop this sunlit peak for – who could say with certainty? The Eternal did not share the humans' conception of, or obsession with, time, thought in generations and epochs rather than weeks and seasons. But Calla knew the Wright to be among the elder generation of Eternal, old enough to have known the Prime's father, in some past so distant as to be scarcely imaginable. Regardless, he wore his centuries or millennia casually, his face unlined, the perfect brow, the chin as if carved from ore. 'I take it the Prime has not seen fit to accompany you?'

'Lamentably, the Lord of the Red Keep has other responsibilities that keep his attention occupied fully.'

'Then you are here to play shepherd to our Aelerian guests?'

'To accompany them, yes.'

'He rarely leaves his demesne, these days.'

'Except to visit the courses. He has kept up with his weapon training daily.'

This did not seem to comfort the Wright to any great degree. 'And his . . . mood?'

'There is much to weigh down the head of the Prime,' Calla remarked after a moment. 'Being responsible for the well-being of Those Above and Below.'

'It does no good to brood,' he answered. 'And eyes turned inward lead swiftly enough to blindness. You will come speak to me, Calla of the Red Keep, if there is any . . . depreciation in this condition, yes? You will not hesitate.'

'I'm not sure I take your meaning, my Lord,' Calla said, keeping the umbrage off her face.

'I think you understand entirely.'

And then one of the Wright's servants called him over for a last inspection of some part of the craft, and Calla was left alone, staring out at the skyline of the First.

Though not for long. 'That was our host?' Leon asked from behind her, and she suppressed a smile and turned to answer.

'That was the Lord of the Sidereal Citadel, the greatest genius and craftsman the Roost has produced in generations.'

'I wonder that you can tell one apart from the other,' he remarked.

'I've had long practice,' Calla admitted. 'But you're right – perfection allows for little by way of variety. Except in the eyes.'

Behind Leon, languid and unenthusiastic as ever, stood the

dark-eyed Parthan slave whose name she had forgotten if it had ever been offered. He was wrapped in loose overlaid robes of a fashion Calla had never seen before, and they gave full vent to his odour, which was less than fresh. The wonders of the First Rung, the towers stretching out for ever into the distant sky, the craft that bobbed along beside them in violation of all natural law, provoked no hint of interest from his heavy chocolate eyes. He masticated aimlessly over some forgotten piece of cud, and occasionally scratched his buttocks.

'Can he understand us?'

'Jahan? Oh, yes. Parthan, Aelerian, Roost Speech. Probably others, though it's hard to say with certainty.'

'Is he mute?'

'No, he just . . .' Leon shrugged. 'Holds speech in low regard.'

'How long has he served the Revered Mother?'

'How long have you served my aunt, Jahan?'.

His eyes, Calla noted, seemed always about to blink, though they never quite completed this intention. 'Years.' The syllables rumbled up his broad chest like bitter water from a deep well.

'See? Years. A regular orator, our Jahan.'

'He's a slave?'

'He does my aunt's bidding,' Leon admitted. 'But then, so does most of Aeleria. I would think it more accurate to say he is . . . a sort of a counsellor.'

'And what sort of counsel does he offer your aunt?'

'I can't say with certainty. My aunt keeps her secrets tight in hand, and Jahan, believe or disbelieve this at your discretion, is little given to intimacies.'

'I believe it,' Calla said.

'Yes, I supposed you might. But then again, I have never had occasion to ask him directly. Tell me, Jahan, what services do you render my aunt, apart from your obvious and indisputable value as a bodyguard?

A shrug of his bovine shoulders, a blink of his false-docile eyes.

Something about his blunt disinterest, or perhaps the conversation that she had just finished with the Wright, spurred her towards uncharacteristic rudeness. 'Strange, for I had thought that in Aeleria, women are held in low regard, and that it would be a source of shame for a man to serve one freely.'

It was an insult rather than a question, and Calla did not suppose to hear an answer. Jahan stared out at the city below and the sky above with his equanimous glower. 'The dog bows to the jackal, the jackal bows to wolf, the wolf bows to the tiger. To whom does the tiger bow?'

'A riddle beyond me,' Leon admitted.

'Bigger tigers,' Jahan said, and his mantle of silence again descended.

Eudokia returned then, as if on cue, smiled with dubious sincerity, executed the Eternal greeting with perfect competence. 'A pleasure to see you again, Calla of the Red Keep. I take it the Prime has chosen not to attend?'

'The Prime is very busy,' she said, not sure why she felt it necessary to defend him. 'There are many matters which require his attention.'

'Undoubtedly,' Eudokia said, turning to face the skyline arrayed before them. 'A magnificent view,' she said. 'A season here and I admit I haven't yet grown used to the city, it remains as wondrous and confusing as it was when I first arrived. What is that building?' she asked, pointing a long finger at one of the castles gracing the skyline.

'The House of Sweet Balm,' Calla explained. 'The Lady there is famed for the excellence of her gardens and orchards, and has incorporated her obsession into the very structure of her home. There are trees sprouting from her walls which were planted a thousand years before the Founding of Aeleria.'

'And that one?'

'The Prismatic Ziggurat,' Calla continued, enjoying the exercise. 'The stones were, so it is said at least, quarried from a mountain range in the very north of the continent, many weeks' journey from Hyrcania. Its rainbow hue is the result of some geological peculiarity.'

'And when was this?'

Calla laughed. 'Centuries. Millennia. Who can say?'

'And that one, Calla of the Red Keep?' Eudokia asked, pointing towards a distant peak, taller and perhaps a bit less grand than the others. 'What is that one called?'

'That is the Perpetual peak, one of the very oldest of the seats of the Eternal,' Calla explained. 'One of the few that can be traced back to the Founding. It reaches into the depths of the mountain, down even into the lower Rungs – or such at least is my understanding.

'And who lives there, Calla? What Lord or Lady is graced with so magnificent a seat?'

'None reside there any longer.'

'Such grandeur, allowed to go fallow?'

'One of the Unforgotten,' Calla explained. 'That is to say, a line which has fallen out of use.'

'By which you mean there are no longer any Eternal alive to claim it?'

'That's what I meant.'

'A curious thing, do you not suppose? Surely there must be some or other who could make use of it?'

'It would be . . . blasphemous for anyone not of the line to attempt it. In any case, there are more castles than there are Eternal to fill them.'

'Do you suppose that an auspicious augury for the species, Calla of the Red Keep?'

But Calla did not have the opportunity to answer. The craft was launched without fanfare, drifting slowly from where it was anchored out into the open sky. A few links into the ether and an array of pinions sprung outwards from within the substructure, fins of silk and light wood, wings draping streamers of cloth and silver, the whole vast apparatus resembling one of the creatures that could be found in the Lord's aquariums, something bright and beautiful swimming through the firmament. Some further artifice was then engaged, and the craft turned upward on a current of wind, listing gracefully. Leon laughed loudly, and Calla clapped her hands, as did most of the other humans present.

'What is the range of these aeroships?' Eudokia asked.

Calla shrugged. 'I have no idea. You would need to ask the Lord of the Sidereal Citadel, and I think it unlikely he would offer answer. The point is a moot one, of course. Those Above would no sooner leave the Roost by aeroship than they would walk.'

'Then it is used solely for recreation?'

'You might at least scruple to hide your contempt.'

'Have I caused insult?' Eudokia asked, one hand against her breast as if the suggestion had caused her some physical pain. 'Forgive me, though I hardly suppose your offence is warranted – is that not how they themselves imagine their existence? An endless dance, a continuous celebration of their own divinity?'

'Do the people of Aeleria paint the surface of the sky? Do the people of Aeleria drift amidst the clouds? You speak contemptuously of creations which are as far beyond your understanding as fire is to a dog. A thousand of your people working for a hundred years could build nothing of the like.'

'I would not think to dispute it,' Eudokia admitted. 'They are an extraordinarily clever species, Those Above, so clever and yet so blind. What a dream, to fly, and how pointlessly they waste their gifts!'

'What would you use them for?'

'For a thousand things! For transport and for communication, for surveillance, for exploration, for war. Imagine a fleet of these, carrying soldiers to the corners of the Commonwealth, putting down rebellions, appearing sudden and swift as a bolt of lightning from a clear sky.'

'You must forgive my aunt,' Leon interrupted, in a vain effort at peace. 'She has a tendency to slaver.'

'What need have the Eternal for transporting troops? What need have the Eternal for any of these alterations which you are so desperate to see made? For untold millennia the Roost has stood inviolate, has remained perfect and unchanging. The Eternal have followed the traditions of their forefathers for thousands of years before the Aelerians ever came to the continent, before your throne was emptied. They have no need of improvement, for the simple reason that they have already discovered perfection – they need only maintain their divine stasis.'

The Wright's distant bubble of colour diminished towards the horizon, flitting past the Red Plum House and the Castle of the Sun's Grace, moving further into the city, a flickering shadow running over the pedestrians of the Second Rung.

'Stasis!' Eudokia repeated. 'How happy they would be if existence offered them the same courtesy! But I'm afraid it does not, Calla of the Red Keep, I am afraid it does nothing like that at all. Autumn follows summer, and winter after autumn.'

'And spring comes next, and then we're back to winter.'

'True. But the leaves are not around to see it.'

20

When the priest of Eloha had finished offering the last blessing – the sentences intoned swiftly and without any excess of emotion, there being other men to bring the god's peace to that day, that day as every day – Bas folded Theophilus's hands across his chest, and made sure that his eyes were closed. He sat next to the body for a long time, however, listening to the moans from the other cots, the silhouettes of the dying tossed against the thin layer of cotton that surrounded the bed, which offered some semblance of privacy for the last moments of a man who had once breathed, and spoken, and walked above the ground.

It was not a surprise. Theophilus had been battling that thick, wet cough for the better part of a month, since a few days after the battle at Actria, though he never complained of it as he had never complained of anything in all the years since Bas had met him, a noble youth gone west to fight for the safety of the Commonwealth and the glory of the Empty Throne. Losing weight also, not the soft outer shell of a civilian but the gristle beneath it, the flesh draining off him until it had distorted his handsome, patrician face, made him look ten years older and hard as bruised flint.

It wasn't the cough that killed him, but it was the cough that weakened him enough for the flux to carry him off. First his eyes had gone red and then his hands had started to shake, though he did his best to hide it. Some of the hoplitai seemed to get better from it, but after Bas's first visit to the infirmary he had known that Theophilus would not be among them. Theophilus did not notice Bas for a long time, and when he did he had had nothing to say. The next time Bas had visited, just a few days later, he had thought Bas his father and not seemed pleased to see him, the unforgotten slights of childhood coming suddenly to the fore, Bas bearing witness to an unbecoming monologue of abuse, trauma made fresh from delirium. Bas had sat quietly until it was over, and afterward he had told Konstantinos they would need to find a new head of horse.

That had been yesterday – no, it had been two days ago, but here in the hinterlands of Salucia it was easy to lose track of time, the days crowding against each other, filled up with a routine that seemed purposeless as they had no enemy to fight any longer. It had taken the army two weeks after the battle of Actria to start moving again, unpardonable by any standard of warfare. You need work twice as hard after a victory as a defeat; Jon the Sanguine had always insisted upon that point, forcing his exhausted army onward, refusing a beaten enemy the chance to regroup. But the Salucians had been allowed to flee northward towards their capital, to take shelter within the boundaries imposed by the Roost's ultimatum. A week was spent following them, and then another week in camp, Konstantinos insisting that they were preparing to impose a new order over the conquered territories, Bas and every other man in the army without a serious head injury knowing this to be false. Would the Protostrator – or, it was whispered quietly, his stepmother – decide to call the Others' bluff and march into Salucia, or was it nothing but a great pantomime? An elaborate play that had claimed the life of Theophilus, an inglorious and pointless end, though Bas had seen enough death to know that they were all that way; whether from a gut wound or tainted water or the final dim victory of age, death is death is death, implacable, ferocious, banal.

Time passed. Bas left the infirmary and went back towards his tent.

Still early evening but the fires burned bright and high, as if to ward off more than the dark. Isaac and Hamilcar and some of the other boys sat around one of them, passing wineskins and talking, loudly and without any particular purpose, hoping to drown out thought with noise.

'I'd prefer an arrow,' Isaac said. 'That way you don't see it coming.'

'You ever listen to the sound a man makes with an arrow in his lung?' Hamilcar shook his head. 'Horrible, sucking thing. Goes on for a long time. Maybe if you're lucky and you get one in the eye, but if you are not being shot at by Hamilcar then you are unlikely to be so fortunate. Better off losing a sword fight, at least the man standing over you is usually kind enough to finish the job.'

Bas would need to write a letter to the boy's kin. He did not know at the moment what he would say, but he knew the words would come. They had always come before, letters crammed against one another, spelling dicey – it was never Bas's strong point – pointless sentences and false paragraphs. Bas had no truth to offer, no secrets, only that fact which everyone knew, that the answer to life's riddle is death, and we all discover it too quickly.

'Not always. Sometimes you're too busy to see the thing through fully, let a man drop and move on to the next.'

'You've got to make sure you give a good enough account of yourself so that whoever ends up doing you hates you enough to spare a moment.' Hamilcar added, raising his a flask to his lips. Wine ran eight times what it would have cost in the capital, and

Hamilcar never seemed to be without an extra flagon, though his famous luck at cards had run sour these last weeks and months, and Bas had heard unhappy rumblings that his debts were stretching from tawdry to perilous. And was it Bas's imagination or was the Dycian down one or two of his trinkets, the twist of gold that once hung from his beard or a few of those jewelled rings?

Whatever he had spent on it, he was not slow to share, nor Isaac slow to avail himself of his friend's generosity. 'The best any of us can do.'

'One less Aelerian,' Hamilcar said, after a moment. 'That's a thing worth toasting.'

Isaac rolled his eyes and spat into the dirt. 'With your wine.'

Deep in his cups and desperate for quarrel, Hamilcar refused to let up. 'I'll provide the drink,' he said. 'I'll set the table. A great feast in honour of our dead comrade! May all of the Commonwealth's children go the same way, and more swiftly.'

The other men at the fire, who knew Hamilcar less well than Isaac and Bas, and who liked him less than that, grew sullen and fierce-eyed. Even Isaac, used to Hamilcar's black moods and his bitter humour, felt it warranted a response. 'Who do you imagine this fools? You were as close to the boy as any of us, and will mourn as hard.'

'For whom would I mourn?' Hamilcar asked. 'An enemy of my people? Of all people who would rather remain free than become servants of the Commonwealth?'

'Of a friend – of a man who fought beside you, who carried himself without complaint, who held up his end of the line.'

When next Hamilcar spoke the skin sat empty in the dirt beside him. 'Oh, he was brave enough, our little noble. He did not bend before the Marchers' spears, nor the swords of the Salucians. Is that the only virtue? Can no thought be given to what a man ought to show bravery for, if that cause might be worth serving? How many brave men were needed, on the day of Dycia's fall? A thousand thousand just like him, brave boys and eldest sons and patriots, all willing to die, none ever wondering what they died for.'

'You were pirates,' Isaac said, more, it seemed to Bas, because someone needed to say something than because he really believed it.

'Every merchant is a pirate,' Hamilcar said. 'And everyone who lives on the sea is a merchant. We were the best at both, but we had no monopoly on either.' Hamilcar was slurring his words by then, rare for such a practised drunkard but there it was, consonants slanting against one another like a line of out-flanked hoplitai. 'When you decided our harbours were required to war against the Marchers, you summoned up a grievance to justify your need.'

It was just talk, it didn't mean anything, except that this war against the Salucians had dragged on too long, and the Others loomed clear behind them. And the boy was dead, in the ground and not coming back. They did not come back, that was something that Bas had learned long ago. Arcadius with his dark hair and his two children who he had never seen, would never see after a Marcher lance had put him down, four years prior. Valens who had taken an arrow in the side the day Dycia had burned, pulled the thing out and staunched the wound with a rag, led his men over the walls, fought for long hours, sat down quietly in the dust in the late evening after the thing had been decided, died quietly and without any preamble. Jon the Sanguine, dead on land he had conquered, dead by the smallest creature that lived on it, two holes in his ankle from a reed-snake. A woman's face, details blurred by youth and the time passed since youth, warm hands holding him, a song in a language he didn't know, her words interrupted by the hacking cough that had killed her.

'And what would have happened to you if we hadn't?' The voice was mean and quiet and after a moment Bas recognised it as his own. 'Would you have bought a farm, tilled the earth, grown cane and potatoes? Or perhaps you'd have taken up a trade, set aside your bow for a loom.'

'Hamilcar could have done many things,' Hamilcar informed them. 'If fate had not made him the slave of his enemies.'

'You'd be swinging from a gibbet, the kites feasting on your eyes. Your own people would have done it to you, and the children would play beneath your corpse and the old women spit on the ground when they passed. You can't be but what you are, Hamilcar, a man too lazy to build but strong enough to take. I didn't make you a killer, you were always a killer. I just gave you something to kill. You ought to be grateful.'

'Grateful? I was born on the docks, did you know that, Caracal? My home was one of those you burned in your great act of heroism, my people among those slaughtered in the hymns that collect around your name.'

'Was that the first time you saw a city burn? The first time you heard a woman scream? Or just the first you heard one scream in Dycian?'

'And how about your own chorus, Caracal? If they were to rise up with one voice, if they were to sing their song of despair, how loud would that be? How many men have you killed or caused to be killed? How many women? How many children?'

'I'm a soldier, nothing more. I go where I am pointed.'

'The world's last innocent! And with enough blood on his hands to water a rice field.'

The moon had risen low in the sky, a jagged little sliver of light, like a boot knife, offering little by way of illumination, serving only to contrast the intensity of the night. An owl hooted, and a dog barked in answer, one of that vast pack of scavengers that followed after the themas, nourished on offal and waste and blood-turned mud. Bas was standing and Hamilcar was also, close enough for an unfriendly touch.

'We took Dycia for the same reason that we took Oscan, for the same reason that we took the Marches, for the only reason that matters, that ever mattered – you weren't strong enough to hold it. And you talk too fucking much, Hamilcar.'

'It took you twelve years to say that,' Hamilcar said, his eyes bright in the firelight. Isaac looked back and forth between them, hand steadying on his weapon, considering if there was not some way to stop what seemed the certainty of violence, and if not, whether to kill Hamilcar himself or allow Bas the privilege. 'Twelve years.'

A spruce log burst in the fire. From far off, in some distant corner of the camp or beyond, carried to them on the wind, there was the sound of laughter. The killing moment passed, Bas and Hamilcar a hand's breadth from one another, blood slowing, heart returning to its normal beat, leaving the two tired and faintly ashamed, as after an awkward coupling.

'Go to bed, Hamilcar,' Bas said. 'There will be enough death to come. For both of us.'

21

Pyre was the first into Isle's bar that evening, Hammer holding the door for him. Pyre liked to come in first if he could, believing that the shock of his sudden arrival often did more to ensure the outcome of the conflict than even superior numbers. Of course he had those as well, four men, well-trained and specially chosen, Tallow from the Third Rung, dark as burned sugar and very slick with the Salucian-style blade he carried, thick-necked Asp, cruel-eyed Splinter, Harrier who had played in a band near the docks before he had heard the truth, who had sworn never to tune a string save he did it as a free man.

And Hammer of course, Hammer who had not left his side for more than a day since his initiation, Hammer who had once been known as Seed. Against the five of them there was only Spindle, sitting at a table near the bar, too big for his seat as he was for most of the things that surrounded him, a bushy beard covering a mouth that had been known sometimes to smile. He wasn't smiling now, of course; indeed at the sight of the Dead Pigeons his face seemed distinctly unfriendly.

'Isle's is closed,' Pyre said, loudly enough to wake the drunk dozing in the back of the room. The rest of the crowd didn't need the announcement, had already realised that Isle's was no longer a place they wanted to be just then, might have permanently lost that distinction. Half a minute later and there were only Pyre and the men he had brought and the dark-haired giant who obstructed their passage, upright and leaning against the bar.

'How you been, Spindle?' Pyre asked.

'All right before today.'

'No, in fact you've been living a life clouded by sin and foolishness, as I once was.'

'I'd heard you'd taken up with these fanatics. Couldn't quite believe it. Do they know what you used to do for us? Do they know what you were? What you are?'

'These are my brothers, Spindle. There is nothing which I would not share with them, no sin to which I would not admit, openly and with hope of forgiveness. You too might enjoy this camaraderie, were you to consider it. But now is not the time to speak of the truth, though I hope that time comes for us sometime soon. I need to see Rhythm.'

'You have an appointment?'

'I've had an open invitation for two years now, one I've too long delayed.'

'Rhythm never mentioned that to me,' Spindle said. There was a moment when Pyre thought things might turn nasty, because while the five of them could take Spindle in the end, he would not go easy; he was a deft hand with the dirk peeking up from his belt and those hands were large as a normal man's skull, and they led to arms and shoulders that were equally oversized. There would be a great deal of cutting before Spindle went cold.

But then something seemed to leave him, dribble out of his coin-sized nostrils and his mouth full of broken and yellowed teeth. 'What happens if I let you in?'

'It doesn't matter,' Pyre said, nodding at Hammer, 'because there isn't anything that you can do to stop us.'

Spindle spent a moment acknowledging the truth of this, and then his great shoulders stooped downslope and he tilted his head towards Rhythm's office.

Hammer came inside with him, because Hammer had taken to Pyre as Pyre had taken to Edom, as a righteous man would look after his firstborn son, someone whose existence was more important than his own, who needed to be guarded with more caution and more cruelty. The other three remained behind to watch Spindle, in case he had any untoward ideas.

Rhythm was an ugly man. Thick-necked, bald-crested, pock-marked. He had reached middle age, no small feat for a man in his profession, a business that was mostly about greasing palms but which had at its root, as did most things, the naked threat of violence. A little smile began when he saw Pyre, honest if bitter. He was sitting at one side of a not particularly well-made desk, and Pyre took the seat opposite. Hammer closed the door and stood in front of it, and Pyre knew without looking that he had one hand on the hilt of his weapon.

'Hello, Rhythm.'

'Good evening, Thistle. Been a while.'

'That's no longer my name.'

'Names are like trousers, you swap them if they get stained?'

'Thistle was a lie that I believed. Pyre is the name I have chosen.'

'A man can call himself an eagle,' Rhythm opined, 'that don't mean he can fly.'

In the Barrow, which was where Pyre was born and raised, the men were porters, slaves as all the humans of the Roost but the most pitiful, the most abject, the extent of their servitude written in their bent backs and bowed legs. Or they were bums, drunkards, wastrels so beaten and pathetic that they had ceased to perform that most basic and elementary task required of all living things, the care and nurture of their own seed. Pyre's father had been both: first a porter, and then a bum, and then one night when Pyre was around eight a corpse bobbing up in one of the canals. 'An accident', his mother had told him, too much to drink, though even as an eight-year-old Pyre had not really believed her, even as an eight-year-old Pyre had understood that a man might prefer death to life.

And in all the Barrow, from the straits upslope down to the broken pipe that signalled the boundaries of the docks, Rhythm had been the only figure thought worthy of emulation, the closest thing to a free man that the Fifth seemed to have. Didn't have to tote a pack, wasn't chained to the counter at some five-copper-a-day general store, didn't even have to dip his head to the Cuckoos. All he needed to do was hold a knife, and sometimes use it.

'Are you trying to get me angry?' Pyre asked.

'A little. Is it working?'

Pyre shook his head slowly.

'It would have two years ago.'

Pyre nodded.

'I've been waiting for you to show.'

'I've been busy.'

'Ain't you, though? I didn't believe it at first. All these stories cropping up about this fanatic from the Fifth, lightning raids on the Cuckoos, men who could out-savage even the Brotherhood Below. How'd you get to Ink, exactly? That was the nastiest son-of-a-bitch I ever had the misfortune of kicking up coin to.'

'The age to come will sweep away the demons and their servants. We are all slaves in its service.'

'All this talk about the age to come, and the tide of history, it's a bit too much for an old thug like me to follow. Way I see it, a man ought to be able to explain why he killed someone.'

'I killed Ink because he claimed the fruits of others men's labour, because he turned women into objects of play. Because he was a weight upon the back of his species, a traitor to his race, a leech upon our strength.'

'Were you any different?'

'No, indeed – and I would have continued in sin had I never heard Edom's truth. These divisions between us are the tools of the demons, the Cuckoos their right hand and the Brotherhood their left. But the second, at least, has been severed. The Brotherhood Below is ended. There is no longer any such thing as the Brotherhood Below. Your counterparts across the Rung and all the way up to the Third have closed up shop entirely or taken to dressing in homespun clothes, hoping to ingratiate themselves with the new order.'

'I never looked good in wool,' he said.

'I was not thinking of offering you a position, though should you wish, I can arrange for someone to speak the truth to you. Regardless – you're the last one, Rhythm, the last one of any account. After tonight there will no longer be anyone foolish enough to claim allegiance to the Brotherhood Below. For the sake of past history, I'd prefer to see you leave voluntarily. But because we share it, I don't really suppose you will.'

There was a decanter of something on the desk, likely not spring water, and Rhythm pulled the cork out and drank from it, savouring the taste as if suspecting he would not have another opportunity to do so. Then he set it back down on the table and began to laugh, a bellow that grew from his broad chest and escaped from his wide mouth and scattered to the far corners of the room. It went on a while, and when it was done Rhythm took another drink.

'Something funny?' Pyre asked softly.

'It's like your name – you think calling a thing something else changes what it is, but it doesn't. Pyre, Thistle, the Five-Fingers, the Brotherhood Below – one's the same as the other.'

'You can't be blamed for thinking that, I suppose. It took me a long time to realise that what the demons took from us, more than anything, is hope. Eternal, they call themselves, and if they are then so is everything else. Nothing can change, no point in trying.'

'That's a nice blade you've got there.'

'It serves a function.'

'You buy that yourself?'

'Every human is called upon to do their utmost towards the liberation of the race. My part sometimes requires a blade. Others, no less vital, no less honoured, do their part with their purse, contributing what their means allow.'

'What an interesting coincidence,' Rhythm said, leaning back in his chair and tapping the hilt of his own weapon with two fingers. 'I paid for mine with contributions as well. The dagger, my shirt, this bar, all the product of voluntary contributions from men satisfied with my service, happy to be labouring beneath the protection that I offer, happy to kick into the collective pot. It's astonishing how generous people get when you hold steel to their throats.'

'Your comparisons are surface-deep,' Pyre said, seeming very nearly calm. 'Every coin, every nummus and teratrum, goes to the species. It does not feed the coffers of slaves and whoremongers, silk-clad and sitting high on the Second Rung, gorging themselves on the misery of their own people.'

'And when it's all over, and the blood runs in the streets, and the seed-peckers have been cast down – when boys from the Barrow and porters from the Fifth nest in the castles of the Eternal – what happens then?'

Standing behind Pyre, Hammer let out an unhappy grunt. There were noises coming from the evening outside, though no one paid them any attention. 'There will be plenty of time to answer those questions after the redemption of the race.'

'Yeah, you make sure you don't start looking too far ahead, you might see something you don't like. But Edom thinks about it, I can assure you. He goes to bed worrying over it and he wakes up doing the same.'

There was a brief moment when Pyre could feel Thistle coming out, his left eye twitching, that bedrock core of anger, on which it sometimes seemed everything else about him rested, shuddering to the surface. 'Don't speak ill of Edom.'

'Why? 'Cause he's the boss? When I was the boss you didn't speak ill of me either. You ever get to thinking that maybe there ain't so much difference between the two of us as you'd like to pretend?'

'No,' Pyre said quickly. 'I don't.'

'You were always good at not thinking about the things you don't want to think about. They've made quite a weapon out of you, Pyre, a better job than I ever could have. A long blade, well-sharpened. Double-edged though, I hope Edom knows that much. Let me ask you something, Pyre, the First of His Line – what happens when there's no one else to cut?'

If Pyre had an answer, he was never able to give it. The tumult that had been growing outside the door, to which neither Pyre nor Rhythm, focused as they were on their conversation, had been paying much attention, reached a crescendo.

'Is that your people?' Pyre asked, knowing the answer.

'You know it isn't,' Rhythm said, already out of his chair.

The voice came from the street outside, through the exterior walls and the main room of the bar and into Rhythm's office, as loud as a hunting horn though each syllable distinct, coherent despite the strange accent. 'Will you die in the moonlight?'

'By the gods,' Hammer declared, and for the first time since he had taken on his new name Pyre thought he saw fear. 'There's a demon outside.'

'Will you die in the moonlight,' it continued, 'or in your little cage of stone? It is the last decision you'll ever make; perhaps you should take a moment and consider it.'

Though Rhythm gave no sign of doing so, overturning a dresser leaning against the back wall, then shoving aside a stretch of thin wood to reveal a hidden ladder leading down to the basement. He scampered down it without another word.

Pyre felt a hand against his back, not gentle, and Hammer shoved him onward. Hammer who had been Seed, Hammer who had decided already to die, Hammer who was smiling. 'I'll hold him as long as I can,' he said, performing the salute with rare vigour. 'Until the coming of the new age.'

Pyre's hand gripped the pommel of his knife so tight that he thought he might do himself injury, and his eye began to quiver, but after a long moment he released his grip and nodded. The cause and the cause and the cause were all that mattered; Pyre would have given his life for Edom in a heartbeat, not because he loved Edom – though he did – but because the cause demanded his survival, as the cause now demanded his own. 'The species redeemed entire,' Pyre answered, and decision made, he followed Rhythm through the false door and down the ladder.

The cellar was dank and lit only by the few stray strands of light leaking in from upstairs. He was following Rhythm towards a far door when the screaming began, individual voices indecipherable amidst the tumult, a cacophony that began and peaked and ended horribly inside of fifteen or at the very most twenty seconds. Above them Asp's thick neck was snapped in two, and Splinter's cruel eyes stared up blank and open and ignorant. Harrier would never again pick up his lute, and Spindle who had survived twenty years as bullyboy, who had an easy half-dozen kills to his credit, proved unable even to slow the demon's attack. The lock on the back door was stuck and after a half-second spent fiddling Rhythm cursed and planted a foot against the wood, another round of screaming, Hammer giving his life as he had promised, and with Rhythm's second blow the door broke and they sprinted through the broken frame, up a back staircase and into the street.

They were in a small alley that ran behind the bar, moonlight flat against the walls. 'How the hell did it find us?' Rhythm asked.

'I don't know.'

'Yeah you do,' Rhythm said, smiling hard and mean. 'You been treasoned, boy. You been sold down the canal.'

Which was impossible. No one but the Dead Pigeons knew about the night's raid, and none of them would have betrayed Pyre, he knew that, he was certain, he was entirely certain. And anyway this was not the time to think about it. 'We make for the sewers,' Pyre said. 'We might be able to lose him in the slurp.'

But Rhythm wasn't listening. He had a knife in his hands all of a sudden, one he might have stuck in Pyre had the evening gone different. 'This is my bar, and it's been my bar for fifteen years, and anyone thinking otherwise is going to have more trouble with me than they supposed, don't matter if they got five fingers or four. You run along now, boy, and you think about what I said. Not everyone's so honest as you are, and a man who stares at the horizon steps in a lot of puddles.'

Pyre didn't have anything to say to that, which was just as well because in that moment the thing rose up from the cellar like some chthonic god. Tall and perfectly formed even in the darkness, the moonlight reflecting off its single-faceted eyes and off its long white teeth.

'You ain't so tall as I'd figured you'd be,' Rhythm said, spitting thickly into the dust. His knife was double-edged, and he held it bent back down towards his forearm.

'A brave one,' it observed of Rhythm in its curious atonal accent. 'Unflinching despite the certainty of death. Then again, can it be called bravery? Are you capable of such a . . . complex emotion?'

'Your mother was a whore,' Rhythm said, almost cheerily. 'We used to gangfuck her for three silver a throw, and she used to beg us after for more.'

In the long pause that followed Pyre sprinted down the alleyway. 'What is gangfuck?' it asked, though it did not wait for an answer.

Rhythm lasted longer than Hammer, judging by the sound, Rhythm laughing, then cursing, then screaming, but the screams the loudest and the longest. If it had been anywhere else in the Roost Pyre would be dead, but this was the Fifth, this was the Barrow, Pyre knew every inch of this neighbourhood as he knew the rough backside of his hand, as he knew the inside of his own mind. Better than the last. Sprinting out of one alleyway and turning swiftly in to another, downslope towards the nearest pumphouse. The entrance to the sewers was half-covered with a rusted metal grate, and Pyre lost a strip of skin against the brick as he slid beneath it, barely noticing. Three rungs down the ladder and he let himself drop, the fall longer than he had supposed, a pain in his left ankle as he landed; but he ignored it and sprinted further into the suck.

As a child he had played in the sewers, all the Barrow kids had, though not when their mothers were around – even that indifferent breed were not so callous towards the well-being of their seed. Some of the day it was quiet and cool, some of the day it was flooded with raw sewage or baywater. A few children a year lost to it, unable to resist the temptation, drowning in a suddenly filled chamber or disappearing in the subterranean vastness, going mad with the dark and the fear.

If it hadn't bothered to take its time with Rhythm, if it had preferred efficiency over cruelty, Pyre would never have managed his partial escape, the thing would have ran him down without difficulty. But it had enjoyed ifself with Pyre's old employer; when it finally came down into the sewers there was blood on its hands and blood on its shirt, there was blood on its pale face and there was blood thick in the long tendrils of its hair, as if it had torn Rhythm limb from limb and then drizzled itself in the falling ichor.

'Who are you that so many would die in your defence?' it asked. 'Someone important, I gather? Or someone that people imagine to be important? The latter, most assuredly. The life of one of you matters no more than the life of a cockroach or an ant, though you call yourselves Prince or King or Emperor.'

It was too dark to see much but Pyre could tell by the tilt of the ground and the swift-moving sound of the water where it was he needed to go, sprinting forward, indifferent to the gloom and the heaving of his chest. Ahead a few flickers of moonlight escaped through the broken walls of the viaducts above, tinting the perfect black of the sewer a very very dark brown, the corridor opening onto one of the flood chambers that occasionally broke the monotony of the sewer passageways.

'Do you think to hide from me, locust?' The demon's words were clipped and abrupt and yet somehow entrancing. 'I can smell your stink through the shit, and it smells worse.'

Pyre stopped running some ways before he entered the chamber, turned back to face the thing coming for him. It was very quiet underground, the only sounds the water trickling back towards the bay and a quiet, growing rush from far above, and then the rustle of steel against leather as Pyre pulled loose his weapon.

'Another brave one,' it said, and Pyre got the sense that it could see clearly despite the dark. 'I like brave ones. They scream longer.'

Of course the demon knew nothing of the Fifth Rung, knew nothing of the slurp, knew nothing except for the majesty and grandeur in which it was born, the shimmering towers and the spires, this world that Pyre had imagined but never glimpsed. Why would the demon bother to learn about the extraordinary contraption that brought water to its home, that was the very lifeblood of the city? A bird nests in the boughs of the tree, they give no thought to the roots.

'Do you know the colour of your liver?' it asked, an unpractised smile, pale white against the grime-caked walls and the subterranean moss that grew over it. 'Do you know the scent? Do you know the taste?'

The sound louder now, though the demon did not notice it or did not pay attention, every fibre of its being caught up in the thrill of torment, relishing Pyre's fear, or the fear it imagined Pyre to be feeling. Pyre was backing away slowly, slowly, and his breath tightened in the instant when he passed beneath the gate, for it would be soon now, it would be very soon, Pyre could tell by the sound of the slurp. 'I fear no demon,' Pyre said loudly, discovering by the echo that this was even true, his voice even and unwavering. 'The gods themselves watch over me, and will shield me from evil.'

'There are no gods, you speck of dust and grime, you imbecilic and arbitrary arrangement of flesh. There is nothing waiting to judge or to redeem you, no hell for the sinner nor paradise for the faithful. There will be the pain I bring you, and then there will be nothing, an eternal blackness. Though perhaps it may seem paradise, after what comes before.'

'I am Pyre, the First of His Line,' he intoned, blade steady as Rhythm had taught him in that distant past when he had been Thistle, still backing away slowly, slowly, and the demon following after him as if they were two participants in a dance. 'And to me was promised the world.'

The demon saw the gate in the instant before it struck him, nearly enough time for it to make a dash – nearly but not quite, not even with its inhuman alacrity. Somewhere far upslope the locks had gone into effect, the flow of the water reversed, thousands of clove of stone dropping tight and seamless into its niche. It was enough weight to crush a boulder, enough weight to bend a bridge, though apparently not enough weight to kill the demon outright; half its torso and its long neck and one crippled arm and its perfect head and its beautiful eyes were left blinking at Pyre, still furious, still hateful, though dimming rapidly.

It was not until the demon was trapped that Pyre got a proper look at it, a look at it as more than a demon, more than the despised thief of Pyre's identity and future, more than as the implacable and absolute enemy of his race. And in that instant Pyre felt a profound sense of confidence wash over him; more than confidence, a sense of destiny, a certainty that most men, hopes taken up with thoughts of wealth or women, are never bold enough to dream. Because the demon that had been chasing him through the sewers, the demon that he had trapped beneath the falling gate, was the same demon that had killed Rat three years earlier, that had murdered Pyre's best friend out of pique or cruelty or sheer boredom, that had, as much as anything, set Thistle on the path to becoming Pyre. And what more proof could Pyre need that the demon had been wrong, its last words as false as everything else it had ever spoken? For not only did the gods exist but they smiled down upon Pyre, found favour in his actions, had made him an agent of providence, the herald and executor of divine justice, justice so long denied.

The demon was still not dead, an unbelievable truth but a truth all the same, a thousand clove of stone severing its spine, blood bubbling up through its mouth, a burnt maroon that was darker than the blood of a man. It did not scream and it did not quiver, not even in the instant when Pyre brought the point of his blade down through the back of its neck, severing its spine and killing it instantly, man or demon that was an injury from which no creature could survive.

The thing that emerged from the sewers was soaked red down to his shoulders, and carried in one hand an unbalanced sphere of pink, the spindly white of bone trailing below it. The road was empty so late in the evening, but it would be busy tomorrow, it would be filled with porters on their way to the docks, and then locals coming to see the impossibility made manifest, and shortly after the Cuckoos, wide-eyed, worthless, cleaning up and barring the way because they had no other idea what to do.

But then there was only Pyre, First of His Line, splattered with blood and shit, missing one boot from the struggle – and, by coincidence, a youth of the Fifth, come back from or on his way to some errand of petty foolishness or malfeasance. A child who might have been Thistle, who might one day even be Pyre.

'What are you?' the boy asked.

'The future,' Pyre informed him, then slipped back down into the slurp.

22

There was no way to avoid the escort that had been arranged for them, an officer and three custodians, large but soft. Indeed, they seemed very much like children to Eudokia, in their silly-looking robes, ill-fitting and ugly, with their ferules more like toys than weapons. Their leader had introduced himself with an obeisance better suited to an expensive courtesan than a master of arms. Jahan had stared at him for a long moment, heavy eyes dull as ever, then he had snorted and sucked at the end of his moustache and returned to being studiously indifferent to the world around him, declining to join Eudokia and Leon in the palanquin, shuffling along behind.

As a rule, new things did not happen in the Roost, and so the news of the Shrike's death had spread through the city like a tenement fire. A week since his body, or some part of it, had been left to rot on the Fifth, and still no one could speak of anything else. For three days there had been a curfew enforced across the

196

Roost; upslope there was nothing but shuttered windows and bolted doors and even the Perennial Exchange had been closed. As for what was going on downslope, no one seemed to be able to say with certainty. There were reports of massed groups of Cuckoos marching through the streets, stiffened with the occasional Eternal, searching for the Shrike's killer and not being particularly careful about whether they found him.

Leon leaned against the soft leather seats of the palanquin, holding the silk curtains with one hand, sunlight and a general aura of misfortune leaking in. They passed a group of Cuckoos, looking dirtier and meaner and rather more savage than those who were escorting them, had a line of youths faced up blindly against a wall. For half a minute as they progressed downslope Eudokia could make out strands of speech: 'wasn't me, wasn't us, don't know nothing, never heard of him, never heard of anyone,' the common refrain to be made out in any slum anywhere in the world.

'By Enkedri, they look so miserable.'

Eudokia shrugged and settled back into her cushions. 'They look poor, Leon. Do you imagine there are no slums in Aeleria? On our return to the capital you might take a stroll round the outskirts of the docks – though bring Jahan along, less you lose your life during this object lesson.'

'This is not my first encounter with poverty, Auntie,' Leon said, and to his credit he did not close the curtain. 'But I don't think I've ever seen despair quite like this.'

Eudokia took a sip of her watered-down wine and considered the matter. 'Perhaps. Our unfortunates can, at least, console themselves with thoughts of national destiny, or of religion at least, though a meal sanctioned with prayer is no more filling. But I think it more likely that the juxtaposition between the start and end of our journey exaggerates in your mind the extent of the depravity. Grime is grime, famine is famine, and despair the universal constant of the species, the single blessing which the gods distribute among the faithful and unbelieving alike.'

'The gods did not decree this squalor,' Leon said. 'The gods did not pack them into tenements or deprive them of any chance for improvement. This misery is attributable to four-fingered hands.'

'You think them unique in this? You suppose it is some curiosity of their species, unshared by ours? Surely I've taught you better than that. A second helping, a larger share. It is in our nature, nephew, to mistake our wants for needs and to suppose any good fortune well-earned. If the gods did not decree that the poor be miserable, then they decreed that humanity care more about their own desires than the well-being of a stranger, which is the same thing in practice.'

'Then there is no hope for them?'

'They might rise, I suppose. Tear down what the Eternal have built, nest in their homes. But that would only be to change the pilot, and not the ship's course.'

'You have no great excess of optimism in you, Auntie.'

'I'm not sure I agree. I have great faith in the happy outcomes of those plans put in motion by Eudokia. As for that far larger portion of human events, well,' she shrugged. 'A sure path to madness, despairing over things that cannot be changed. Another date?'

'Thank you,' Leon said, 'no.'

Eudokia took it instead, chewing through the sweet leathery pith, flinging the stone out the window.

'Why, exactly,' Leon asked, pulling shut the curtain and sitting back to face his aunt, 'are we doing this?'

'I need to meet a man.'

'At your age!'

Eudokia snorted.

'For what purpose?' Leon asked.

Though of course this did not receive an answer.

'Why exactly is my presence necessary for the resolution of this . . . as yet undefined liaison?' Leon asked.

'I had the vague though unpleasant suspicion that our escort might prove a hindrance to the free passage of information which is at the heart of all useful discussion.'

'And you imagined I might do something to help alleviate this situation?'

'Such had been my hope.'

'Then I'm to be the architect of a stratagem without appreciating its purpose?'

'Exactly,' Eudokia confirmed.

'And why would I be willing to help you?'

'Apart from maternal piety?'

Leon laughed.

'Because you'll enjoy yourself doing it. A simple thing, all told, just distract the captain and his men for ten minutes or so, when I give you the signal.'

'How do you suggest I perform such a feat?'

'I'm sure something will come to you in the moment.'

'You rely a great deal on my wit.'

The palanquin had come to a halt. A knock against the side and Jahan pulled loose the curtain. 'Of course,' Eudokia said before alighting, 'you are my nephew, after all.'

Eudokia was no sailor, had no particular interest in the docks as such, and indeed at first glance found little of fascination. Larger than Aeleria's, grander, busier, but the essential features of the thing – the stone quay, the porters alighting overladen from the bellies of the caravels and dhows, the fake beggars and the strutting whores and the foam-maddened sailors, they were not so very different from anywhere else in the world. 'Magnificent,' Eudokia lied neatly to the captain of the custodians, who stood stiffly beside her. 'As is everything in your fair city.'

Leon shuffled out of the palanquin a few moments later, looking as if he had spent the brief interim drinking a bottle of liquor in a rapid fashion. His shirt was half-tucked into his trousers and freshly stained with wine, and he blinked at the sun as if its presence was an unhappy surprise. 'What in the name of the Self-Created are we doing here, Auntie?' he asked, in a tone far from his usual patrician lilt.

'This, dear nephew,' Eudokia continued with a disheartened

look at the captain and his men, 'is the greatest port in the world. Ships from the length of the coast and from far beyond come here to trade, from Chazar and old Dycia, from—'

'Yes, yes, wood, sail, rope, hairy men. We have ships in Aeleria, and they look very much the same. I cannot possibly see what it is that required my attendance during this little escapade, and before noon at that.'

Eudokia could feel a smile spreading to the corners of her mouth, hid it with a grimace and turned to the captain. 'You'll have to forgive my nephew – he's . . . a bit—'

Leon burped loudly. 'Where can we find something to eat around here, Captain? My aunt sups on nothing but fruit, and after a long evening one wishes for something more substantial. Oil is a counterbalance to alcohol, once they've both reached the stomach. It's common knowledge.'

'I – had not heard that,' the captain admitted, brushing Leon's hand off his shoulder and turning back to Eudokia. 'Was there somewhere in particular you wished to see, Revered Mother?' His neat hair and his formal bearing were sufficient proof, so far as Eudokia was concerned, that he was spying for the Prime.

'Nothing in particular,' Eudokia admitted. 'The current is heading east – shall we follow it?'

A resolution to which the captain was perfectly pleased to agree. It did not occur to him until later that the current always went east at that time of the morning.

The docks were thick with people, as diverse an array of humans as could be found anywhere on the continent, a packed mass of nations, languages, ethnicities, colours and professions, all happy to make way before their escort of custodians, as the prow of a boat cuts through the water.

'Why don't they use the canals to move these goods upslope?' Leon asked. 'It seems like it would save everyone a lot of trouble.'

'The canals are the province of the Eternal alone, sir,' the captain informed them. 'We Low-born are forbidden to use them.'

'For anything?'

'Yes, sir.'

'What if I wanted to say, take an afternoon swim?'

'That would not be allowed, sir.'

'But Those Above never use the canals.'

'No, sir,' the captain admitted, gazing past and around Leon at the surrounding crowd, committed to the safety of his charges regardless of any personal feelings of enmity. 'Not often.'

'I've been here in the Roost for months, and I can't once remember seeing them use one.'

'Those Above rarely descend below the First, sir.'

'Exactly, they never descend below the First.'

'Rarely, sir.'

'Fine, fine, rarely. But still, so rare that really there could be no very good chance at all that one would be around to see me taking a swim.'

'That's not really the point, sir.'

'I don't see why I shouldn't be able to make use of them, if the Well-born don't feel like doing so. That's just selfish, that's all that is.'

'The canals are forbidden to we Dayspans,' the captain said, finally beginning to grow angry, 'as I've explained to you several times. It is a law of the Roost, inviolate and absolute, one extending back to the Founding, and I would no more allow it to be disobeyed than I would—'

'One moment,' Leon interrupted, a sudden smile on his face, breaking away from the crowd and towards a small food cart perched a precarious few links from the bay. A light-skinned Dycian stood behind a brazier frying bits of meat and red-fleshed pepper. Leon leaned in close and said something to the proprietor in his native tongue, and he smiled and shrugged and responded in kind.

'Captain, tell me,' Eudokia began, pointing off towards the bay 'Where is that ship from?'

The captain's eyes turned from Leon, following the direction of Eudokia's finger towards a caravel listing at a far quay. 'I . . . can't say, mistress. I am no seaman.'

'Chazar, do you suppose? Or is it Parthan?'

'As I said, mistress, I rarely descend below the Second.'

'Certainly not Salucian.'

'If you are certain.'

Leon returned then with the fruits of his expedition, two bags of brown paper reeking of cooked fat. 'One for me, and one for you, Captain – an insufficient reward for your service, but take it with my compliments all the same.'

'Thank you, sir,' the captain began, 'but we're not supposed to eat when on duty.'

Leon shrugged and threw away the now unneeded second bag. A porter, bent-backed, carrying a load of wool upslope, stepped in it, cursed, looked around at the Cuckoos and hurried on. By all outward evidence oblivious to the misfortune he had caused, Leon tossed a bit of fried liver into a fool's grin. 'Whatever you say, Captain. Now, back to my afternoon dip . . .'

They continued on to the disharmonious beat of Leon's rambling idiocy, staccato bursts of pointless questions and inane observations that left the captain exasperated and Eudokia holding back laughter. The great stone quay was interrupted by a finger of land jutting out into the bay, thickly crowded with administrative offices, merchant houses, branches of the great banks upslope. They were passing one of these buildings – handsome, well-built, indistinguishable from any of its neighbours – when Eudokia cleared her throat loudly. A few steps further and Leon went finally silent, halting mid-sentence, his pose of easy arrogance replaced by one of fervent concern. 'That – that little bastard! He stole my purse!' And indeed the purse was no longer there, his belt looking naked without it.

Eudokia had known it was coming, it or something like it, but even still she found herself half-believing the act, so frantic seemed her nephew in that moment, as if contained in his leather pouch were not a few bits of gold and silver, but the antidote to a poison he had recently ingested, or the secret names of the gods themselves.

'Calm down, sir,' the captain said,

'Calm down,' Leon said, face growing furious, piglike despite his high cheekbones and slender nose, 'calm down! Fifteen tertarum I had in there, and one of those bastard Dycians stole it!'

'Sir, I assure you—'

But Leon was gone, swearing furiously and tearing back off towards the quay, in desperate and, somehow Eudokia could not help but suspect, fruitless search of his lost purse. The Custodians looked at the captain, the captain looked at Leon's fleeing back.

Eudokia snapped her fingers loudly. 'Well? Go after him.'

'Forgive me, mistress, but my orders were to ensure your safety while you visited the Fifth Rung. Ensure your safety at every step of the way. They were very clear on that point.'

'Jahan is more than sufficient guardian, I assure you, no one will think to try and murder me in the public square. My . . . imbecile nephew, however, might well find himself in trouble while chasing after his purse, or, gods help us, if he actually manages to find the man who stole it.'

Which, upon brief consideration, the captain had to admit seemed true, though on the other hand, on the other hand . . .

'He may not have the wit of a beaten mule, Captain, but he is the only child of my only sister, and should anything happen to him she will make my life a misery, and should that happen, believe me, I will not endure such misfortune alone.'

The expanse of their robes hindered their movement rather less than Eudokia had been expecting. She waited until they were lost in the crowd before heading into the small stone building, above which a sign read, COBBLE AND CO., FACTORS.

There was a front room and a dowdy, unfriendly looking woman making sure that no one passed beyond it, but there was time for neither delay nor subtlety and before she could voice objection Eudokia made a gesture to Jahan, who made a different gesture at the woman, which convinced her to adopt a course of silence. The inner office was well appointed, a great walnut desk taking up most of the room, a back window open to allow the sea breeze to enter. Luxurious, but then Steadfast could be relied upon to line his pockets. So far as Eudokia was concerned, that was all about which he could be trusted. He was scrolling through a ledger when the door opened, and then he was staring up in wide-eyed consternation. He could not, of course, have been expecting Eudokia's arrival, but all the same she thought the depth of his shock was no very strong evidence of the stability of his nerves.

'Thank the gods,' Eudokia said, setting herself down neatly into the chair opposite Steadfast.

'What – what . . .' It would be a long few moments of hysteria, Eudokia knew, if she did not plough forward.

'It had been so long since I'd seen or heard from you, Steadfast, that I assumed the worst had happened. Our various avenues of communication blocked, your messengers failing to arrive as they should, and I left supposing some terrible and bloody misfortune had befallen you. Oh, what joy it brings my heart, to see you upright and healthy! And how deep does it grieve me, to think how perilous a situation you find yourself in, just how uncertain your well-being truly remains!'

Somehow, in that moment, Jahan seemed rather more present, though he did nothing in particular.

'The death of the demon has changed everything,' Steadfast said weakly. 'The Cuckoos press against us at every point. We were forced to pull our agents back downslope, for fear of losing them altogether.'

'We?'

'The Five-Fingered, of course.'

'Whoever was speaking of the Five-Fingered? I was speaking to you, Steadfast, and felt curious as to why our personal means of communication has been suspended. Surely you haven't forgotten our arrangement?'

'No,' Steadfast said, his head hung like a dog. 'Forgive me, Revered Mother.'

'Much better. Now, quickly and to the point—what happened to the demon?'

'Pyre killed it,' Steadfast muttered.

'Did he?'

'Killed it and left its head in the middle of the street. Not far from here, in fact.'

'He has a flair for the dramatic, that one. Where is he now?'

'Gone to ground, no one knows where, not even Edom. Only his own people.'

'The boy grows to wisdom,' Eudokia said to Jahan, who snickered but made no further answer. 'Tell Pyre to send men to investigate the Perpetual Spire, and in particular its roots on the lower Rungs. Do you understand?'

'Yes.'

'The Perpetual Spire,' Eudokia repeated, 'and the depth of its foundations.'

'I heard you,' Steadfast snapped, though after a long stare from Eudokia he dropped his eyes to the desk.

'I simply could not bear it, Steadfast, were our communication to once again be hindered. It would throw me into the sort of emotional dismay the results of which are unlikely to be beneficial to anyone.'

'Whatever we can do, Revered Mother,' Steadfast answered, the colour returning gradually to his face.

'Here's what you may do. Every evening at half past the Nightjar's hour, you will send a boy wearing a red cap to visit the Full Purse bar, on the Second Rung. Not the same boy every night – a different boy, with the same red cap.'

'This is not my first venture into the clandestine.'

'How happy I am to hear it. Should there be a plant there, he need do nothing. Should that plant ever be absent, he will know that I require a meeting with you and your master, to be arranged immediately.'

'Edom is not mine to command. I cannot snap my fingers and compel his attendance.'

'But I command you, Steadfast. Should I command it, you would get down on all fours and bark like a dog, you would pull something sharp down-side against your wrist, you would walk smilingly into a bonfire. And in that vein, you will bring Edom where I tell you to bring him, if that means binding him and carrying him upslope on your own two shoulders. When I give an order, Steadfast, it is not for you to determine reasons why it cannot be followed, but only to obey.'

'Yes, Revered Mother,' he said finally.

'I fear, Steadfast, that our long absence from one another, this time you've spent here in the Roost, has given you an inaccurate conception of your own position, may even have caused you some confusion as to the ultimate object of your loyalties.'

'No, Revered Mother,' a line of slaver over thin lips, 'no, nothing of the sort, I assure you.'

'What were you, before you met me, Steadfast?'

'No one, Revered Mother,' Steadfast said 'I was no one.'

'And who knows but that you might again return to such a station? You are mine, mine entirely. I own your right earlobe, and I own your left. I own your hair, your bone, your skin, your organs and viscera and genitals and toenails, every piece of flesh and every drop of blood. I own them entirely, free and unencumbered. This facade of obedience which you provide to Edom is that and that alone, and it would be excessively unwise if ever you were to forget it. Wouldn't it?'

He answered in the affirmative, though too quietly for Eudokia's tastes.'

'Wouldn't it?' she repeated.

This time when he spoke, it was loud enough to be heard from outside the open window.

'Well,' Eudokia began, standing without the aid of her cane. 'This was, as is every interaction with you, Steadfast, a source of almost ineffable joy. I will sup off its memories through boring afternoons and dismal evenings to come. One last question, before I leave you,' she continued, turning back from the open door, 'How exactly do you suppose the demons knew where the boy would be?'

Steadfast swallowed hard but did not answer.

When the captain came back a few minutes later, Leon in his train cursing with a fluent vulgarity that she had not supposed her nephew to possess, Eudokia sat on the low stone wall overlooking the bay. Jahan helped her to her feet, and she dashed forward with a speed surprising in a woman of her age and infirmities, cane rapping loudly against cobblestone.

'Oh, by the gods! Oh, by the gods, by every one of them!' Her high voice wavered between anger and tenderness, deciding finally on the latter, pulling her nephew down against her breast. Blue eyes peered over him at the captain, blue eyes heavy with gratitude. 'I can't thank you enough, Captain. I don't know what I'd ever do without him.'

23

Bas was an indifferent rider for all his time in the saddle, but even if he had sat a mount like a March lord he would have been no match for her, as his horse was no match for the writhing stallion that raced neatly below the fruiting orange trees, which seemed with all its essence to wish for nothing more than to gallop onward to the horizon and beyond, which was only restrained by her will and her hand. She pulled up short at the crest of the hill, the mount stilled by her silent command. When Bas joined her a moment later she had not moved, her focus occupied entirely with the view. The vista was of the flatlands of eastern Salucia, green and rich in this high summer, and the great river below, flat and blue and sweet-looking, curling its way towards the sea.

'A thing worth seeing,' Einnes admitted after a long time.

Her hair was bound tight, reaching upward and then cascading past her shoulders, like the sprouting top of some strange bush.

She wore dark blue robes of some fabric Bas had never seen before, thin as gossamer.

'Yes,' Bas agreed.

'How did you know of this place?'

'I scouted it last time I was here.'

Which had been a quarter-century past, two weeks before Scarlet Fields had seen slaughtered the cream of the Aelerian army, and six weeks before a lucky shot with a war-hammer at Ebs Wood had made Bas the most celebrated combatant in the Commonwealth and well beyond, the people happy for some hook upon which to hang their pride, some sliver of hope to take from the comprehensive defeat that was the outcome of the last war against the Others. Twenty years or twenty and one; Bas's exact age was a matter of mystery to him, the bastard son of a hoplitai whose name he had never learned and a Marcher half-breed whose name he pretended to have forgotten, both dead while he was still young. A childhood – to the degree that he could be said to have had one – spent in the company of men of the Thirteenth, viciousness with a veneer of sentimentality; they would come back from some savage punitive measure against a Marcher village, the smell of ash and blood still thick on them, and tussle his hair, sit him on their laps. When he was old enough to hold a pike they had shoved one in his hand and made him swear the oaths, to the Empty Throne, and the Senate, and most importantly to the Thirteenth itself, to the three-legged wolf that was their standard, ravaged and wounded but never beaten. Five years garrisoning the Marches, savage skirmishes that would never earn a line in a history book, warring against an entire nation of men for whom battle was the highest and finest and indeed only purpose of existence; and thank the Self-Created that they never learned how to forge steel, and that the only thing they loathed more than the Commonwealth was each other, every clan and every village against every other. And then the news that they would be heading east to make war against Salucia, and against their Eternal masters who Bas and most of the rest of the Thirteenth had largely supposed fictitious. Bas's first time amidst the great civilisations of the coast, cities one quarter of which held more people than resided across the entire vast length of the Marches, more wealth and more people and more despair than he had known in twenty years being raised with the legion, wonder and reek nestled so close atop one another that they often proved indistinguishable. He was not a ruminative man, little given to nostalgia, but still he remembered this distant period with fondness; before he had become the Caracal, when he was just a pentarche, no different or not much different from any of a thousand others, unappreciative of the anonymity that was soon to be lost.

'I had forgotten,' Einnes said, 'this is not the first time you've invaded Salucia.'

'It's something of a national pastime.'

'Is it all like this?'

'I've never been past Hyrcania,' Bas admitted, 'and even then only to burn it. But I believe most of the north is swampland.'

'Swampland?'

Near two years he had known her and still sometimes the sheer vastness of her ignorance overwhelmed him, particularly in contrast to the absolute certainty that she possessed in her own judgement. 'Where the earth is near level with the sea, and the two mix unevenly. Floods easily. They grow rice, I am told, and barley. But not much else.'

'I do not think I would like the swampland,' Einnes said after a moment's consideration.

'Nor I,' Bas admitted.

'Then again, I suppose there is little chance I will ever have to see it.'

'Not much, I would think.'

'Are the Marches like this?'

'Not really,' Bas said. 'They are flat, flat like the top of a table. From a hill like this you could see from the Pau River to the salt wastes. They are not beautiful, I suppose. At least they are not considered beautiful, not as the coast of Dycia or the Baleferic Isles. The winters are . . .' he shook his head, remembering, 'you have not known cold until you've spent an evening beneath horse-hide yurt, the wind travelling a thousand cables to strike against it. The summers are not much better, heat to kill a pack mule, grass brown and dying. The only time you see water is when the storms come, lightning bright enough to see for ever, and then the dark again . . .'

'And yet?'

'There is a month or two before summer comes, when there is no colour but green, a thousand different kinds of green mixing together, the grasses high enough to swallow a child, a man can sit in the silence and watch the breeze rustle through them. The Roost is beautiful, you say, and I do not doubt it – but you do not love the Roost because it is beautiful. You love the Roost because it is your home. It is a lie that we choose what we love, as if making a wager. The opposite is true. We love something and only discover afterward that it was the case, from the pain that comes with its absence. I grow windsome with age,' he said finally, abruptly, shut his mouth and turned his head away from her entire.

Einnes did not say anything for a long time, sitting quietly atop her steed, contemplating Bas's words. Bas was not sure if this thoughtfulness was peculiar to her or common to the others, but either way he wished it was more in appearance among his own species. 'I think you're right,' she said finally.

Bas dismounted and tethered his horse. After a moment Einnes did the same, with more grace, and once grounded she whispered a few words in her indecipherable tongue to her stallion, which whinnied and went still. Bas reached into his saddlebag and removed a cloth blanket and a small hamper. He spread the blanket out on the ground, overlooking the plateau, then sat down atop it.

She joined him after a moment, crossing the distance swiftly. Her scent was inhuman but not unpleasant, subtle and evocative. like a memory grown faint with age.

'Will you march on Hyrcania?' she asked, the question arriving, as usual, without preamble or warning.

Bas shrugged. It was the only question that anyone had been asking for the better part of a month, and he had no answer for it. With the victory at Actria, the heartland of Salucia was laid open before them; Thalia, which was the centre of the great banking houses, the silver mines of the Linnel Valley, the uncountable wealth of the capital itself. The whole vast treasurehouse of the northlands, and none to defend it – save the demons themselves.

'Probably.'

'Yes,' Einnes agreed. And then, switching course without preamble, 'My condolences on the death of the boy.'

'Thank you.'

'He seemed . . . I did not mind him.'

'I didn't mind him either,' Bas admitted. He thought of saying something else then, but did not. There was no need to say anything with Einnes. She understood, or at least she did not mind him keeping silent. From the hamper Bas began to pull out their packed meal. It was simple fare, cold chicken and some bread, a flagon of whatever wine Isaac had been able to get his hands on. Bas unwrapped it on the ground in front of them.

Einnes stared at it for a long moment, as if it was a species with which she was unfamiliar, searching to recognise it in her memory. 'The food of Dayspans is forbidden us,' she said. 'It is taboo.'

Bas shrugged, indifferent or seeming so. 'As suits you,' he said, taking a long pull from the wineskin. 'I don't suppose you'll die without lunch.'

Far below, the river continued on its lazy, circulatory, recurring journey to the sea. A pair of swallows chased each other just above it, skimming the surface or nearly, their duet twittering happily into the late afternoon. The redbud trees were in rich bloom, and the silverbell, their fruit bitter and inedible but fragrant and pleasing to view.

'But then . . . I suppose there is no one here to see it,' Einnes said.

'Only us,' Bas agreed. There was something in his throat but he managed to repeat it. 'Only us.'

After a moment Einnes reached out with her four-fingered hand to the corpse of the chicken, pulled off a bit of flesh, brought it to her mouth. She chewed it over for a moment, carefully, with great and sincere deliberation. 'It's not bad,' she said, running her tongue across her teeth.

Neither spoke again for a long time. The swallows had disappeared, song silenced, returned to their nest – or at least this was what Bas hoped. The sun passed slowly towards its home beyond the horizon, casting long shadows over the blossoming trees, and the river below, and over their horses, and over the two of them. And for a moment they might have been any pair of living things, a rose bush attended to by a summer bee, a trail of ivy choking an oak.

24

Amber's beard was white and his hair was white and his shoulders were broad and his hands were gnarled as the trees beneath which he had spent most of his life. The raptor perched on his arm was golden-brown and crownless, with flat, unsentimental eyes. The Prime was down on one knee, stretching the bird's wings with graceful consideration, so carefully as to draw no rebuke from her beak.

'You will see the spot just beside her alula, my Lord,' Amber said regretfully. 'I think it can only be the rot, but I thought it best to check before destroying her.'

The Prime allowed her wing to retract, then nuzzled the raptor for a long moment, grooming her feathers with his long second finger. 'Well that you did. It's not the rot. Feed her hibiscus root, and keep her out of the sun for a few days. She'll be healed before our next hunt.'

Amber nodded briskly, by all appearances neither surprised nor insulted to find his conclusion, one born of a human lifetime of experience, to be false. What, after all, was a human lifetime against the knowledge the Prime had acquired in his span? 'Forgive me, my Lord – the colour of the mottle, in particular—'

'You've given fine service, Amber, have no concern. There is no way you could be expected to have known. It is a peculiarity of her heritage, in fact, though I thought I'd bred it out of the line. Her grandsire twenty-three – twenty-four times removed suffered the same affliction. It mimics the effects of rot close enough for your mistake to be forgivable.'

The Lord's eyrie was in the far corner of the Red Keep, past the flower gardens and the fruit orchards, past the first terrestrial bestiary and the second terrestrial bestiary and the aquatic enclosure. In contrast to the rest of the estate, which was as carefully cultivated as a rose bush, the area around the eyrie had been allowed to grow unrestrained, resembling the virgin forests to be found in the distant human kingdoms beyond. Or such was Calla's understanding; of course she had never been outside the Roost, never seen the forests after which it was patterned. Certainly it seemed wild enough, towering groves of oak and cyprus, the boughs thick enough to blot out the sun. The eyrie itself was three storeys of dark wood built directly into the roots of the trees, the trunks weaving their way through the main room, the staircase wrapped round an elm. On the top two floors the Lord's collection of raptors enjoyed an existence that would be the envy of much of the Roost. On the bottom Amber and his two sons lived quietly, rustically even, taking their meals alone, rarely venturing into the rest of the Red Keep, let alone into the city beyond; rough-edged and lacking in etiquette, but they knew their craft as well as any other human living, if less so than an Eternal. Amber had been caretaker since Calla's father's day, and though the Aubade spoke occasionally of shifting some of his burdens onto the shoulders of one of his two sons, thus far the transition had not been necessary. It would be a sad day indeed when age forced him to vacate his post, his chief source of purpose and joy.

As they passed beyond the canopy of the trees bright strands of summer sunshine fell against them. In a few weeks or a month the heat would be oppressive, but just at that moment it was more caress than slap. In suffering weather, and perhaps that alone, are all sentient things equal – the rain falls on the rich and the poor alike, the sun offers its blessings to Four-Fingered and Five without consideration. For the first time in a long time, the Aubade seemed free from the duties of his office, free to concern himself with the joys on offer. Calla followed him back towards the Keep, along neatly pruned paths, the flowers rich and high beside them.

'Shall we attend to the summer gardens?' she asked.

'I had thought first to inspect the new creatures in the aquatic pavilion.'

'As you wish, my Lord,' Calla said, following him onward.

He was dressed very simply, long robes trailing behind him, his hair for once uncoloured, rough stalks of off-white tied tight and tumbling down near his ankles. 'How did you dispose of your free evening?'

'At a concert on the Second Rung, My Lord. With Leon of Aeleria. You had asked me to escort him to the Lord of the Sidereal Citadel's launch, you will recall.'

'With perfect clarity,' the Aubade confirmed. 'Though I made no similar claims on any future segment of your time.'

'True enough – that at least, was my own design. Does it meet with my Lord's disfavour?'

They did not lie or dissemble, the Eternal, not in love nor policy nor casual conversation. 'It does.'

Of course the raptors were the Lord's favourite, followed closely by the summer gardens in the far corner of the grounds, where resided the rest of the avians, singing sweetly or gambolling about on unsteady legs, looking kind and beautiful and pointless. But a near third was the aquatic pavilion, great tanks filled with bright-coloured carp and darting sequinned arowana, pits filled with greyish water in which slunk strangely shaped serpents, flat-headed and unfriendly. The Aubade spent a long moment inspecting his newest acquisition, a trio of hairy, friendly, big-eyed creatures enclosed in a small pavilion that was half sand and half water.

'You worry me, Calla,' the Lord said, reaching over the fence and stretching out his four-fingered hand.

'Yes, my Lord?'

'Thirty-one years. Not so young for one of your kind.'

'Not so old either, my Lord.'

'Old enough to have put aside the pleasures of childhood. Old enough to consider the responsibilities of the future. What will happen to you and Leon?'

'I was thinking of taking him to the Blossom Festival, my Lord. It's in a few weeks' time.'

'Was that a jest, Calla?'

'It was, my Lord.'

In the enclosure below the rodents were gathering up the courage to inspect this new arrival, coming towards the Prime's outstretched hand and then scattering back again with cautious joy. 'I did not enjoy it.'

'Forgive me, my Lord.'

'Seven generations your line has given me faithful service, Calla. It would grieve me were you to be the last.'

'. . . thank you, my Lord.'

'It is time, and past time, that you concern yourself with producing an heir.'

'I—'

'It is the ultimate obligation of every living thing, Calla,' the Lord said, 'to continue itself. No doubt the boy has some valuable qualities, or you would not allow him to pursue you. But surely you understand he can be no good match? He cannot provide your children with a father?'

'I admit your . . . concerns have rather outstripped my own, Lord. A date is not a proposal for binding, nor has there been any discussion of rearing his child.'

They were like animated rugs, Calla thought, nothing but thick golden fur and happy brown eyes, and it had not taken long for them to overcome their fear. They chittered happily against the glass walls of the enclosure, tumbling over one another as if in competition for the Prime's attention, which they had lost momentarily, the Lord of the Red Keep turning his eyes upon another one of his subjects. 'Do you understand, Calla, that there will be war between his nation and the Roost?'

'I know this to be a possibility.'

'Rather more of a certainty. Had the Conclave listened to reason, we would have struck already, the full force of the High-born, every Eternal who can wield a lance descending from the Source. Alas, my siblings are yet blind to the threat we face, but they will not always so remain. When next we meet, without that . . . woman, to distract them, and with this latest victory to report, I will be able to force an ultimatum against the Commonwealth to disperse their forces. They will do so, no doubt, rather than risk our direct ire – but their greed will not remain long in abeyance. In three years, in five at the very most, after Aeleria has had time to digest their new territories, they will again grow hungry, they will make eyes against Salucia or perhaps think to impact the Roost more directly. Eventually, my siblings will be forced to recognise that there can be no peace with Aeleria as it exists. And when that day arrives, Calla, there will be such slaughter of humanfolk as has not been seen since we removed their king from his throne, perhaps even since the Founding itself,' his eyes on hers, golden and opaque.

'The boy is not his aunt, my Lord.'

'He is the citizen of a nation which will be at war with your own, in not so very long a time. You ought not again see him.'

'Is this an order, my Lord?' Calla asked, feeling a sudden frantic flutter between her breasts, one that surprised her with its vehemence.

The Lord turned back to the enclosure; the jocund creatures within were doing everything possible to regain the Prime's attention. 'Do you know what the genius of the Founders was, Calla?'

'I wouldn't presume to say, my Lord.'

'There are those, even among my kind, who would say that

their brilliance lies in having created the laws by which the Roost abides. But they did not *make* the law, Calla, any more than I made the seeds that sprout in my garden, than I made the fish or the birds or the beasts that populate it. There is a law beyond the will of men or of Eternal, an ideal and a perfect order. It fell to the Founders to codify it. It falls to us only to correctly interpret it. The birds fly, Calla, and the fish swim. These things strut and dance and play. All beings act according to their innate purpose, find joy in its execution, confusion and misfortune if they fail to follow their natural course. A bird is no less than a fish because it does not swim, but nor would I think to submerge it in water. It is more than the duty of Those Above to rule, it is our nature. It is our nature, as it is the nature of the Dayspans to serve. But to reign over a thing is not to control it absolutely, and to command not the same as to be obeyed. The wise gardener allows for his flowers to sway towards the sun, and a skilled falconer gives his birds long leash. Your species is no less complex, and I would not think to convince you with too blunt an instrument.' He reached over the fence with sudden swiftness, grabbing the smallest of the blithesome creatures below, inspecting it at arm's length. 'As to the boy Leon, I give no orders. You may follow what course of action seems for you the wisest. Though it would please me were you to consider my counsel.'

Calla bowed her head in silence, insulted but not sure why. Did she not believe the same? Were not her life, and the lives of her father and ancestors beyond that, dedicated to this very truth? Was not her service to the Lord a source of great pride, indeed the chief source of her esteem?

'What is this festival, of which you spoke a moment ago?'

Though that moment seemed a long time past to Calla just then, she dragged her mind back across the run of conversation to find it in her memory. 'A tradition they hold to on the Second Rung, my Lord. There is a breed of tree that blossoms for a few days in summer. Their arrival is a source of celebration for those humans living beneath them. The children paint themselves and gorge on candy, the adults sing and dance and drink more than they should.'

The creature in the Prime's hands stretched forward, brushed a long pink tongue against his face. 'Particularly in the light of the Lord of the Ebony Tower's . . . misfortune, it is necessary to remind the people downslope that they play a crucial role in the Roost, a role that is not dismissed by Those Above. Inform whatever relevant authorities on the Second that I will attend this . . . Blossom day celebration.'

'Of course, my Lord,' Calla said, managing to smooth over her sudden second of shock, 'immediately.'

Allium was the name of the man responsible for overseeing the aquatic pavilion, and he stood at the side of the enclosure, pretending he had not heard their conversation, feigning ignorance being a speciality of all those humans blessed to serve Those Above. The Lord turned and handed the beast to him. 'The two larger ones grow nicely,' he said, 'though I scarcely suppose we need three of them. Have this one destroyed.'

25

Outside the streets were quiet and sweltering, the descent of evening doing little to lower the temperature. It was always hot in the summer on the Fifth, the closely packed tenements holding on to the day's warmth, the occasional breeze trickling in from the harbour the only source of relief – but it was not always quiet. Indeed, in normal times the people of the Fifth ameliorated the heat by flooding the few public spaces to be found, sitting on rooftops and lined up along the canals, hanging out of windows, passed out happily in the street.

These were not normal times. A month since Pyre had killed the Lord of the Ebony Tower, since he had left his skull on display in the centre of the Fifth, at once a threat to Those Above and a challenge to his own people, a reminder that, whatever else the Four-Fingered were, they were flesh as man is flesh. They had not caught him, obviously, but then the demons were less concerned with justice than they were with retribution, and one of Those Below was as good as the next, and any number of them had died in the weeks since he had made a corpse of the Shrike, broken and bleeding in the Cuckoo's cells, executed summarily by cudgel or four-fingered hand. Criminality of any sort was considered evidence of rebellion, every pickpocket and smuggler a dissident and a threat. Unused to fear, sensing on some dim level the coming age, they had reacted in the only way they knew how – as if a man might grapple with time, land a punch against the future! After more than a year of being frightened even to leave their headquarters, the Cuckoos had returned in force, buoyed by the occasional presence of some slumming Eternal, their ferules red-slicked and ready. And so the people of the Fifth stayed packed five to a room in their miserable apartments, sweated and fanned themselves, grew thick with their own reek, peeked outside their curtained windows with fear – or perhaps anticipation.

Inside, in the basement of an indistinct tenement, Pyre sat at the end of a slim wooden table, Edom and Steadfast opposite, the former explaining something in his quiet, easy, confident voice. The basement had the virtue of being comparatively cooler than the evening above, but that was as much as could be offered. After days used as a bedroom, study and toilet the air was foul, and below ground the sound of the slurp was loud and acutely unpleasant. There was a cot in the corner where Pyre lay at night, and sometimes even managed to sleep. There was the aforementioned table, big enough for Pyre though not really for the three of them. There was a thick wax candle, the single source of light, reflecting in the dark brown of Pyre's eyes.

'We are agreed, then?' Edom asked.

'On what?' Pyre asked after a long moment, turning his gaze back into the present.

Annoyance warred with fear on Steadfast's face, reached an uncomfortable armistice. 'On the need to pull back our operations.'

'For a time,' Edom added. 'Until things settle down.'

They must have been talking about it for a while, Pyre realised just then, wondered how much time had been lost staring at the little flicker of flame. 'To what purpose?'

'Cloistered as you've been these last weeks, perhaps you do not fully appreciate the situation above—'

'They hanged five men at the docks this morning,' Steadfast interrupted. 'On a gallows right above the thoroughfare, feet wriggling above the quay. Smuggling salted cod – these days apparently that is a hanging offence. Tomorrow there is to be a quartering, done the old-fashioned way, with heated iron and four horse – the leader of one of our cells, they say, caught with an apartment full of Aelerian steel.'

Pyre looked over at Grim, who had replaced Hammer as Pyre's bodyguard and counsellor. Indeed, with Pyre unable to so much as show his face above ground, Grim had become deputised to inform the other cells of Pyre's orders, to coordinate the activities of the Dead Pigeons – which, against the violence and the cruelty of the Cuckoos, had not slowed. 'None of ours,' he said.

'Of course he isn't,' Steadfast said, 'he's just some unfortunate, caught in the wrong place at the wrong time, a sop for the fear and the hatred of the Cuckoos upslope. And tomorrow he's to be tortured and murdered, in your name.'

Pyre scratched at the black bristle running in uneven patches down his chin. 'The cruelty of the demons is proverbial,' he agreed. 'As it has always been. As it will be until the dawn.'

'The Fifth never saw a demon until you started killing bureaucrats upslope.'

'If one must be a slave, be a beaten one,' Pyre said, quoting one of Edom's epigrams. 'An unmarked back will be a badge of shame in the age to come. And as for you, Steadfast, sympathy is a virtue in grandmothers, but it is not a luxury that can be afforded those of us who labour for the redemption of the species. You would have the Dead Pigeons curtail our activities in hopes that this would . . . satisfy the Cuckoos?' As if he had finished up a bit of arithmetic, but remained uncertain on the result. 'That it might curb the bloodshed of the demons?'

Daniel Polansky

Edom had not seen Pyre since that evening, months earlier, when they had met with the council. He had grown thinner in his captivity, naught but gristle and firm muscle. His shirt was cheap cloth, scratchy and undyed, and beneath his muscled shoulders there were unbecoming traces of yellow. His cheeks were thin and acne-speckled, and his eyes very wide.

Edom cleared his throat and added a faint hint of disappointment to his eyes, let his smile droop just ever so slightly. From deep within his broad chest he drew out the voice of a caring father, sympathetic, understanding, judgemental, overpowering in its self-certainty. 'It will do us no good, Pyre, the First of His Line, to greet the dawn with the entirety of the Roost slaughtered. We are the shepherds of the species, are we not?'

'Indeed we are, Father, and we cannot afford to be blinded by affection towards any particular member of our flock. Those who are lost, who are snatched and devoured by the demons, they are fuel for the fire, they are the horn signalling the age to come. Do you not understand, Father? We are no longer preparing for the moment. The moment is here. We are amidst it, encompassed by it. These men whom the Cuckoos arrest, whom they torture, whom they kill, they are blessed, fortunate above all other men, martyrs for the dawn to come. There could be no greater honour than to perish for the redemption of the species.'

'An honour they did not choose,' Edom said.

This point was lost on Pyre, or perhaps it simply failed to sway him. 'In the struggle for the future, there are no neutral parties. These men will be remembered in the hymns of the coming age, their names will echo down through history, their service to the cause never forgotten. Nor has their blood been shed in vain – every cruelty distributed upon us by the Four-Fingered is a burr, a seed; and the crop they raise will be bloody retribution for the demons, and redemption for their slaves.'

'Till the morning of the new age,' Grim said from behind him, eyes rapturous.

Pyre nodded firmly. 'No, Father, this is not the time to be holding back our forces – indeed, quite the opposite. We must torment and brutalise the enemy at every turn, we must be unceasing in our aggression, we must make clear, to free men and slaves alike, that we have not been cowed by the demons, that our blades are sharp and our souls on friendly terms with death. Now is the time for the lordlings upslope, and the demons above them, to know what it is to fear – to discover that there is no portion of the Roost to which they can justly lay claim, that they can never be safe from the righteous hand of the Five-Fingered, not surrounded by their castles and their towers, not however high they build their walls.'

Sweat beaded down off Edom's long nose, caught itself in the mask of his white beard. 'What are you suggesting, exactly?'

Pyre did not answer. He had started to nod along as he spoke, and he continued to nod, an even rhythm, carried along by his own internal harmony. 'Forgive me for saying so, Father, but you have misread the situation. And despite whatever the demons may imagine, despite what they suppose in their mad and bloody ignorance, this last month has been no victory for them. If I had planned it out in consultation with the demon king himself, it could have worked no better. They fear us, Father, do you not see that? Every bruise on every human shouts it to the sky, and every bit of cruelty from the Cuckoos brings the day of reckoning that much nearer. For the first time in centuries and millennia, the demons walk the streets of the city, and they do so armed and fearful. They know, they understand, they intuit, what you yourself have not yet come to realise. The war has not begun – the war is over. There is no war. There is only our species coming to realise its own strength, as a boy grown to manhood. How many men live in this city? How many women? How many are there to stand against us, how many demons in their castles of stone? It is not their strength that has kept us in thrall to them these last centuries, it is our cowardice, our indifference The remedy to that indifference is blood; ours or theirs, it will make no difference. Now is the time to steel ourselves, Father, to be merciless, to turn a blind eye to the suffering of our people. What is the death of a man, or ten, or a thousand, or a hundred thousand, what is any of it set against the future of the species? What is any of it set against destiny, fate, against the will of the gods?'

Grim stared up at where the sky would have been, if it hadn't been blocked by a ceiling and four storeys above that. Steadfast looked pale, and sickly. Edom was not smiling, though Pyre had turned his gaze back to the candle, and on the future, and did not notice.

26

Calla led Eudokia upward into the Red Keep, down hallways of burnished brass and thousand-thread carpet, up ebony-oak staircases, hanging braziers steaming sweet smoke.

'Will there be some sort of public funeral in recognition of the tragic loss of the Lord of the Ebony Tower?' Eudokia asked. 'Where I might tender the proper respect?'

'There already was. His corpse was taken to the Cliffs of Silence at the north of the Rung,' Calla said. 'His flesh was given to the birds. His bones were returned to his castle. No humans were present.'

'Though the same apparently cannot be said of his death.'

Calla whipped her head back round, stared hard at Eudokia, at her flat eyes and her imperturbable good humour. 'So it is reported.'

'And what will be the Prime's response, against this unimagined act of violence? Surely the Eternal have mustered some response.'

'A question better asked of the Prime himself.'

'No doubt. But you can guess easily enough, can't you? A clever girl like you. I am told that your Prime's pet project has been taken up in the conclave, that even now squads of Eternal filter through the lower Rungs, searching for signs of rebellion and meting out appropriate punishment. For the first time in decades, perhaps centuries, Those Above have seen fit to descend to the depths of their own city. Do you think it is a happy time to be a resident of the Fifth Rung?'

'I'm not sure it was ever a happy time to be a resident of the Fifth Rung,' Calla admitted quietly.

'Clever girl,' Eudokia repeated. 'Leon asked me to bid you greeting,' she went on, as if just remembering it. 'And also that he will understand if, given the new developments, you think it better to cancel your meeting next week.'

'What new developments?'

But Eudokia didn't answer, only nodded slightly and entered the drawing room.

The Aubade sat silently in the shallow of a great bay window, long tendrils of summer rain spiralling past to the bay far below. The glass panes were sprawled open, and for a long time he seemed not to notice Eudokia's arrival, though of course this was choice and not ignorance. He had heard the door open, he had heard the footfalls up the stairs. His pose of ignorance was either an outright insult or simply one more manifestation of the comprehensive disregard that Those Above seemed to possess for everything that was not themselves. Somehow, Eudokia suspected the latter.

'Lord Prime,' Eudokia began, bowing in the Eternal greeting.

'Revered Mother,' he responded after a moment in his curiously clipped tongue.

'Might it be possible to shut the window?' Eudokia asked. 'At my age skin grows thin as parchment, and these old bones take chill easily.'

After a long moment the Prime slid two of his four fingers upwards against the heavy glass, closing the aperture firmly.

'My thanks.'

'I admit to some confusion, Revered Mother – after your passionate protestations of innocence in the Conclave, it hardly seems appropriate for you to be meeting, in any sort of political capacity, with the head of the Roost's government. Should I not be having this conversation with Senator Gratian, as official representative of your nation?'

'Indeed you should – regrettably, though, Senator Gratian has just this morning come down with an unexpected but rather vicious bout of intestinal distress. He sends his most sincere apologies.' In fact, the sudden eruption of his illness – a diagnosis that had, needless to say, been provided by Eudokia – had proved a source of what could only be called jubilation for her long-time pawn. Short of being savaged by wild dogs, or dropped from a very great height, there were few things Gratian would enjoy less than facing the Prime with the Senate's news.

He need not have worried. Eudokia had long ago come to appreciate the necessity as well as the wisdom of obscuring her direct involvement in the political machine, of working through stalking horses and hidden agents. But still, but still – the better part of her life spent in bringing about the moment, the endless machinations and subterfuge – who but Eudokia deserved to make that final cast?

'It is with heavy heart that I come to you this morning,' she said.

'Strange,' the Aubade said after a moment. 'You scarcely seem bent with despair.'

'One must maintain appearances.'

'Indeed.'

'The Senate has considered the ultimatum put forth by the Conclave, that the Aelerian army return immediately to the capital and to their garrisons further west.'

'Have they? Was there great debate, in your Senate House? Did the grandees and the wise men of your nation discuss the matter in vigorous counsel?'

'How could I know, my Lord, not having been there to witness it?'

'I would suppose your servants sufficiently trained not to require direct oversight. Regardless, continue.'

Though she did not, not for a long moment at least; she savoured each detail: the sound of the warm rain that beat against the windows, the smell of camphor emanating from the braziers hanging in the corner of the room, and the smell of the Prime himself, clean and sweet and not at all unpleasant. 'By order of the Senate, in response to the continued aggression of the Salucians, aggression that has been exacerbated and allowed by the Roost and Those Above, Aeleria does hereby declare ourselves independent, autonomous, owing fealty to no nation nor overlord. All past duties are extinguished, any future claim of fealty repudiated altogether. The Sentinel of the Southern Reach is no longer welcome in Aeleria, or in any land to which Aeleria holds claim. Whatever peace is to be made with the Salucians will be determined without the assistance or input of Those Above. The Roost is yours, and the plantations which surround it. Should the other human nations wish to continue in their servitude, that is their business as well. But never again will an Eternal think to claim Aeleria among their inheritance. Never again will Aeleria send tithe, nor obey the orders of the Conclave. The Commonwealth is sovereign, absolute and recognises no master.'

The Eternal did not laugh – or at least, Eudokia, who had been watching them closely and for the better part of nine months, had never seen one laugh, not a chuckle, not the upturned corner of a lip. But some ineffable sense of levity overcame the Prime just then, limbs easing of tension, as if a weight had been removed from his shoulders. 'I hardly need to take this to the Conclave. Your terms are entirely unacceptable. There is no such thing as Aeleria; it is a fiction which you have been allowed to maintain because we did not care to disabuse you. You own nothing, not the land that you stand upon, not the water you drink or the air that you breathe. All are received in trust from us, who came first, who were masters of the very earth while your kind were little better than dogs.'

'So be it,' Eudokia said. 'Then there is only war left between us.'

'That would seem to be the case,' the Prime agreed. 'Shall I speak freely with you, Revered Mother?'

'There seems, at this point at least, little need for obfuscation.'

'Indeed. The last three years have been the most difficult of my life, though they represent some bare fraction of my span. I have long been filled with the most abiding sense of . . . dread, I suppose, as if I was standing atop the Cliffs of Silence, staring down at the bay below. Desperately I have worked to convince the Eternal of the seriousness of the situation, of the need to marshal our forces against your Commonwealth. Continuously, my hopes have been disappointed. I do not mind saying, now that there is no longer any need for masks, that my people often seem to me foolish, frivolous, undeserving of their role and position. They are unified only in their pursuit of pleasure, in their unwavering desire to follow their own urges irrespective of the outcome. No warning I gave them was sufficient to convince them of the seriousness of the situation, no call to action loud enough to be heard above the sounds of their own merriment.' The Prime opened the window again, two long fingers pushing against the clean pane, and the rich odour of summer entered the room, the ripening orange trees, the roses and the tulips and the dahlias. 'Almost nothing, at least. What a gift you have given me in your foolishness, Eudokia of Aeleria. The madness of you locusts, to think yourself fit not only to subvert our wishes but outright to reject them! This will galvanise my people as no other thing might, this will, finally and fully, allow me to release the strength of Those Above against you who seek to stand against it.'

'How happy a moment this must be for you then, my Lord.'

'In fact, I find myself of two minds on the subject. On the one hand, there is this inescapable and abiding sense of relief. Of . . . joy, I suppose, though I am not altogether sure that this is an emotion which I possess, and if not whether we are incapable of it as a species or if its lack is a peculiarity of my own person. On the other, the dawning awareness, the continual and uncomfortable realisation, that perhaps of all these things that are said of me – that I am moribund, or war-loving, or so obsessed with my own person as to seek to create crisis I might then resolve, criticisms I have dismissed – are, in the light of this new information, revealed perhaps to be more valid than I had thought, or would wish.'

'I'm afraid I'm having some difficulty following the complexity of your logic, my Lord. A natural enough position, given the innate inferiority of my species.'

'You mock, and yet I think never, in a lifetime which exceeds yours as yours does an insect, have I ever thought that to be more certainly the case. Eudokia Aurelia, the wisest and most clever of the Five-Fingered. Who rules Aeleria from the shadows, whose whispered words have destroyed mighty kingdoms. And till this moment, I confess, I nearly believed it. There is something about you, some strange quality which seems almost to make you an equal of one of my kind. Or at least, I was fool enough to suppose. Such madness,' he said, as if the thing itself was impossible to believe. 'Truly, I must reconsider my judgement on your species. Perhaps it is as my siblings have said, and an excess of empathy has led to error.'

'Such is often the case, my Lord Prime – though I confess it is not a problem I have found in abundance here among your people.'

'True, that at least is a personal peculiarity – as a species we are quite thoroughly brutal. And so I shudder to think of the cruelties it will mean for your own race, your nation, your hearth and your home.' The Aubade paused for a moment, turned to look out the window at the rain cascading down towards the water below. 'We can be very cruel. I am afraid that after we finish with the army you send against us, I will not be able to stop my siblings from marching on your capital, as we did in ages past. The . . . Lamentation, I believe it is called in the Commonwealth? When we brought fire and sword to your people, when we slaughtered your king and his line and anyone else who might hope to claim distant kinship? I wonder what name your grandchildren will give to the horrors that will soon befall you? I wonder if there will be any left alive still capable of such sentiment, or if the thoroughfares and avenues of your city will be emptied entirely, with none remaining to recall your name or the misfortune you caused. Such foolishness. Such madness. And all of it will lie at your feet, Revered Mother. The blood that will come, the torrent and the river, the rotting flesh and the weeping children, are on your head. There is nothing I can do now to halt the tide, not even if I wished to, not even if I thought it was undeserved. When mongrel dogs rut in your castles and sparrows nest in your temples, when your people weep and moan and subsist on stonecrop and goutweed and on the flesh of their own children, when the spines and viscera of your senators and generals and noblefolk are left drying on the broken walls of your city, know well that it will be due to the foolishness of Eudokia, Revered Mother.'

'Whatever comes of this,' Eudokia said, and for once the false humility that was her habitual garment was cast aside, and the bare audacity laid naked beneath, 'It will indeed be by my hand.'

27

The brewing summer storm whipped her travelling coat east, towards the Roost, towards what was to come. She held the reins in a four-fingered hand, and the great beast at the other end pawed the ground furiously, snorted at the gale and the damp and the still-hateful smell of man. They were on the outskirts of camp, within the distant site of the last pickets.

'Is it wise to travel alone?' Bas asked. Einnes had dismissed the lifeguard of mercenary Parthans that had been her occasional companions since he had met her years earlier. 'There are many cables between here and your home, and the roads far from safe.' Which was to put it mildly. Once word spread of Aeleria's invasion – and word would spread, in all likelihood it already had – what little was left of civil authority in the territory they were marching through would collapse completely, the usual spread of banditry and chaos, one of the lesser misfortunes of war. 'You might do better to travel with an escort.'

'There are not so many cables,' Einnes responded, a warning or a threat or a promise. 'I shall be there in ten days, travelling alone. Mounted on what passes among your kind for horses, it would take them twice as long, perhaps longer. And as for the dangers of the road—' the hilt of a long blade jutted above her shoulder, and a glance over at her stallion revealed any number of other weapons, a curved hatchet, a lance with three sharpened prongs, '—it will be good practice for what is to come.'

Bas nodded.

'Did you know?' she asked.

'That the Senate would vote for war?'

'That war was coming.'

The wind shifted then, for a moment, carrying the sounds of camp towards them. The mobile forges, metal struck against metal, instruments of death being born. And the men who would carry them, laughing, swaggering, cursing, fearful, violent, uncertain. All the potential of a vast and disparate nation, focused and sharpened towards one single end. What was the point of making such a thing, if not to use it?

'We both knew,' Bas said finally.

'Yes,' she agreed. 'It was to be expected. Your lives are so short, so madly brief. It would be impossible to learn anything in time to put it into practice, and so each generation is left to recreate the idiocy of their forebears, to leap nimbly over the same cliffs'

'Perhaps,' Bas said simply. 'I think we are more dangerous than you suppose. Take care, Einnes.'

'I don't suppose I'll ever hear that name again,' she observed, though with the flat and affectless way she said everything, Bas could not tell how she felt about it.

'Probably.'

'What possessed you to give it to me? Some old friend? Some old lover?'

Bas had never had a woman for whom he had not paid, and none of them stood out in his memory particularly. 'Not a lover.'

'Then what?'

Though when no answer proved forthcoming she paced back over to her steed. The flanks of her horse came up near to the top of Bas's head, but Einnes mounted without assistance or difficulty; one hand on the pommel and she vaulted into the saddle.

He made sure to look at her then, to look and remember, the stalks of trailing hair, that strange jut of a nose that altered the entire cast of her face, the cheekbones high and cruel, those eyes like, like, like—

'On the last day, you will find me at the front vanguard,' she said. 'Beneath the sigil of the white heron.'

'I'll find you,' Bas promised in a low voice that nonetheless reached her. 'I'll find you.'

Her horse, ever hateful, ever furious, tore eastward at a thunderous pace, as if it had always been waiting to do so, as indeed perhaps it had. She did not look backwards, though Bas watched until he could make her out only as a black dot against the flat landscape, wishing in vain that he had told her what her name meant.

A brave man, Bas. All of the songs said so.

28

Dusk descended on the Second, on boughs of trees thick with white blossoms, on scenes of joy, of frivolity, of ribaldry. Of men blushing and women laughing and lovers embracing passionately, in dark corners of warm bars and wedged tight on public benches and in the midst of crowded thoroughfares, the obstructed traffic accepting their misfortune with good humour, a small price to pay for being above ground, and that ground, the Roost! Liquor poured like the water from the Source, kegs of light ale and casks of dark, bowls of rum punch, flutes of pink cordial, snifters of buttery brown booze, and wasn't this the time to break out that vintage Salucian red, and if not now, then when? And now it was. Every cafe, barroom, tavern, hostelry and restaurant had its own band, a complementary cacophony that somehow never devolved into bedlam, the competing strands united in the singular purpose of merriment. And if, among all this amusement, there was some distant scent of danger as of smoke, there was a vague glimmer of the violence that had engulfed the lower Rungs, there was perhaps even some slim cognisance that it might spread – was this not, in the end, only reason to embrace the evening more fully?

Leon waited beside a sparkling stone fountain, watching the proceedings with a wide and reasonable grin, looking tall and handsome, dressed in the Aelerian style but with a touch of grace to him all the same. Or at least some of the other denizens of the Second seemed to think, a buxom brunette breaking away from her giggling and identical coterie, throwing a necklace of flowers over his shoulders and planting a kiss just off his mouth, a smudge of bright purple lip-paint, and then she laughed and sprinted off into the mob.

'Come, Leon of Aeleria,' Calla said, arriving a moment after, hoping her smile hid any distant tick of jealousy. 'Let us escape, before the women of the Roost devour you whole.'

He said something in response but it was too loud for her to hear it, as it was too dark to see his blush. The street lights by common consent were dimmed during the Blossom Festival, to offer a better view of the budding efflorescence and the moon above, and the fireworks that would crown the public spectacle, and finally also to allow for any private entertainment that might be best preserved beneath the cover of darkness. Calla took his hand, because it was so busy, of course, because there was otherwise a chance of him getting lost, and then she led him to a just slightly less crowded side street and into a bustling tavern. The main floor was packed, but the proprietor was an old friend and had kept a table waiting for the Prime's seneschal.

Not just a table but the best table, in fact, a little alcove just above the street. Calla ordered a flagon of red but promised herself she would only drink some of it.

'Captivity seems to suit you,' she said.

'It is true; for a citizen of a nation with which the Roost is technically at war, I have found my privileges little curtailed. We are forbidden from leaving the city, and my aunt has had some people posted to watch her. That seems to be roughly the limits of the Roost's interest. And where, may I ask, is the architect of these policies? Has the Prime changed his mind regarding the evening's excursion?'

'The Prime's word, once given, is as certain as the rising sun or the coming of the new moon, is as certain as anything you can imagine.'

'Unfortunate,' Leon said with a smile that showed teeth. 'I had hoped to have you alone for the whole evening.'

Calla laughed, feigned wide-eyed surprise. 'And where would you have me, Leon of Aeleria?'

And now the light was good enough to make out the blush clear, though to Calla's eyes it made him no less fetching. The server came back then with their wine, and Leon thanked her with a courtesy that was just the proper side of elaborate.

'You've an impressive grasp of our language.'

'Auntie insisted. Roost, Salucian, Dycian, a smattering of Chazar, though I've never used it outside of my study. I admit that at one point my . . . facility with languages was a source of pride, though no longer.'

'No?'

'Relatively little difference between them, all things considered, flowerings of the same essential root. Having no comparison to the complexity of the Eternal's tongue, and the truly mammoth task that would be required to comprehend it.'

'More than mammoth – impossible.'

'Truly?'

Calla looked around sharply, but it would have required more than a casual aside to interrupt the evening's revelry. 'A curious attempt at humour,' she said finally. 'No human is capable of grasping the nuances of the Eternal's speech, not to the faintest or vaguest degree. Even the suggestion of such is a blasphemy of the most . . . profound and hideous kind, of the sort which perhaps no foreigner could fully appreciate.'

'Then you ought to be rather more careful about how you display your erudition,' he said.

Calla looked down into her cup. She should have been fearful or at least concerned, but in fact in that moment what she felt was pride and the sly good humour of a disobedient child. 'When did you notice?'

'That first night I met you,' he said. 'Those Above do not look at us when they speak, a happy bit of discourtesy, in your case at least. If ever they thought you worth their attention, I fear your deception would not last an evening.'

'And you, Leon?'

'I find it hard to place my eyes elsewhere,' he admitted.

Outside, a soft summer wind trailed the blossomed limb of a cherry tree against their window, the soft white bud, the moonlight beyond. Inside, Calla's heart fluttered.

She told him of the Book. Passed down from her grandsire six times removed, a secret compendium of the High Tongue, of its fluid consonants and ethereal vowels, of its esoteric grammar, syllables shifting based upon the time of day and the placement of the moon and the seasons and whether you were standing up- or downslope of your interlocutor. Of the assiduous observations made over the course of a century and a half, a bequest of knowledge stretching back through the generations. Endless hours spent behind barred doors, sifting through its secrets, adding to them when she was certain of her conclusions. Words muttered with curtains drawn on moonless nights, endless practice after long days of work, falling asleep exhausted and numbed, having dreams in which she and the Aubade conversed casually in her secret tongue. She told him of her facility, which was near to fluency, an accomplishment that was her chief pride, that was unequalled in the human history of the Roost; which on point of death need always remain a secret.

She had never spoken of it before, not so fully at least, not to anyone. He did not answer for a long time afterward, considering the matter with the serious interest that she found one of his most attractive qualities. 'No one else knows of your expertise?'

'The Prime suspects. But we've never spoken of it outright.' A sudden and belated hiccup of fear, and Calla added, 'No one must ever know of this, do you understand? Not even your aunt.'

'My aunt has, I'm sure, come to the same conclusion as I have, though you need not worry she'll say anything to anyone. And I understand better than you do, I think. Our minds are as some great edifice, a mansion or a castle. A room might be rearranged, a wing perhaps renovated, some minor alteration to the exterior or the facade. But the bedrock core of it remains the same, yes? The pillars and the foundations. Were they ever to shake loose, the entire thing would crumble. You would need – it would be a requirement – to do anything you had to to defend against that possibility. A man will believe whatever lies he must.'

'Is not honesty preferable to falsehood?'

'We are a febrile species, and prefer our truth diluted.'

'The Eternal are rather more resilient.'

'Are they?' Leon asked quietly. 'I am not so certain this is the case.'

There was a tapping on the window then, and Calla looked down to discover a pretty girl, dressed garishly, pressing her face against the glass, and behind her a youth strumming on a lute. Calla swung the pane open and called for a song. The girl's voice was thin and wavering, but she was enjoying herself immensely, and the boy who accompanied her was not altogether incompetent. The song itself was a bit of doggerel about the war to come, and the ease with which the Aelerians would be defeated, and how afterward everyone would be happy as they always were, and the vocalist leaned forward and stroked her hand against the top of Leon's boot as she sang the more vulgar verses. At the end of it Calla gave them three drahms, and then, laughing, three more. Leon feigned offence at first, crossed his arms and turned his head away, but after a moment he laughed and dropped a solidus into the hands of the girl, who winked and smiled and pranced onward.

The prelude to the Nightjar's hour chimed happy and loud across the Rung, and Calla called for their bill. They were to meet the Prime downslope a ways, at one of the innumerable small harbours that had been built along the canals, in some distant age when the Eternal had been more likely to descend from the First. From there they were to escort him to a nearby public garden, a far cry from the splendours of the Red Keep but it seemed enough for the people of the Second, who would be attending the festivities in great numbers, greater even than normal, as the news of the Prime's participation had managed to increase enthusiasm for what was already one of the most beloved evenings of the year.

The flagon of wine was near empty and she delivered the killing blow before standing and setting off on feet that were, if not wobbly, perhaps not entirely sure. Leon rose as well, and seeing her unsteadiness or, perhaps, for some other reason, offered his arm. They walked with more joy than hurry, and more hurry than grace, travelling downslope on a bed of fallen flower petals, a bright white carpet for their steps. They passed children in garish face-paint, devouring sticky-sweet buns and brightly frosted butter cakes. They passed a thick-shouldered man in a travelling coat too heavy for the season. They passed a circle of dancers, citizens of all ages swaying back and forth in happy if arrhythmic fashion, a fiddler and a girl with a drum in the centre trying their able best to keep everyone on the beat. The fresh scent of the blossoms mingled with Leon's own musk and Calla found herself unsure which she preferred. Just off the path a pair of lovers huddled beneath a large blanket, and what exactly they were engaged in none took the time to see. Two men, tall and unsmiling, in something like porter's clothes, skirted past a laughing band of youths trying without success to scale one of the blossoming trees. The surface of the canal was covered with a merry line of white flowers, the current like pale cream. A short, squat, very dark young man sat on the edge of the quay, arms and shoulders naked to the night. In the distance Calla could make out the Lord's pleasure craft gliding silently through the evening, silvery sails reflecting the moonlight, the Aubade himself standing on the prow, Roostborn watching from the banks with wonder.

'He has no brand,' Calla said suddenly, as much a surprise to her as it was to Leon, and to the seated boy himself, who looked up with sudden unmasked hatred. 'He has no brand!' Calla shouted again, the full meaning and weight of that only now becoming clear to her then, a sudden spurt of fear accompanying the repetition.

The boy was up from where he sat faster than she could have thought, and he had something in his hand that Calla could not make out clearly but feared all the same. He was fast but Leon was faster, intercepted him before he could reach Calla, the two grappling, then Leon twisting and the boy going sideways into the canal. Calla was still screaming and then the surrounding mass of people was screaming likewise, the shift from jubilation to terror surprisingly swift; at the first sight of steel the dancers and the climbing youths, the lovers holding hands, the children eating sweets, broke and ran. Left to struggle against this current of flesh were the broad-shouldered man beneath the too-heavy travelling cloak, and the two false porters who had not been smiling, and the boy who was pulling himself out of the water and not smiling either.

'Stupid fucking slave-bitch,' he said, eyes so thick with loathing that they might well have been open wounds. 'Ruined the whole damn thing.'

Leon stepped in front of her, a noble if pointless effort because there was nowhere to run, no escape from the long knives that shone bright in the moonlight. A twist of steel, a jet of red blood on the white blossoms, Leon screaming and collapsing, Calla screaming also but staying upright, wanting to offer him comfort but feeling some strange injunction against dying on her knees, a pitiful sort of rebellion but it seemed better than nothing. And perhaps this was the reason also that she ceased to scream, though the boy with furious eyes and a bloody knife drew closer, Calla a poor substitute for their target but, it seemed, she would do.

And then suddenly he was behind them, looming, silent. He must have leaped from the ship and come sprinting along the banks of the canal, too far a distance to have possibly crossed in so short a time surely but what was impossible for a god?

There was an instant, distinct in Calla's memory forever after, the dawning realisation of his presence on the part of her assailants, an interruption of the bloody savagery that had prefaced it, and the bloodier savagery to come. That moment was vivid, but not the tumult that followed, the dim light and the frantic motion and the terror that had surrounded Calla's conscious mind all conspiring to render it opaque. Four of them and well-practised in violence, but they were as nothing before the Aubade, who edged out of the way of their blades with seeming unconcern, without a sound of exclamation, and then a motion that was too swift for Calla to follow and one of the men was dead, and then a second motion that was too swift for Calla to follow and so was another. This left the third, the largest, squaring up against him, and then the Aubade made a motion as if clapping his hands, though the sound was muffled, and then what was left of the man was on the ground and Calla did not dare to look at him directly, nor at the Aubade himself, who was covered in something slick and pink and foul.

And then there was just the one who had injured Leon and perhaps killed him, backing away, the red on his knife slick in the moonlight, and his eyes brighter still. 'The blood of the martyrs will fuel the fire to come,' he said, and his smile was, to Calla's eyes at least, an honest one.

The Prime did not expect it either, Calla did not think, or he would have tried to stop the boy. He committed to death neatly and without wavering, the blade outstretched and then through his throat and jutting out of the back of his neck, Calla turning away too late.

Leon had stopped screaming. His face was very pale, and his eyes were unfocused.

The Aubade, at least, had no moment of confusion, but moved swiftly and with purpose as ever. 'Are you safe?' he asked, and then louder and a second time, 'Are you safe?'

'Yes,' she managed finally.

'I'll send help,' the Aubade said. 'In the meantime, it would be a misfortune were the boy to die within the Roost.'

And before she could answer he had lifted Leon's weight as easily and carefully as a mother would a newborn, turned and sprinted upslope, disappearing into the darkness, leaving Calla behind with the bodies of the men who had tried to kill her, growing raw in the moonlight, blossoms falling softly on carrion.

29

The door swung open, hardwood slapping against the wall, hinges squeaking in futile protest. The man behind it was wide and dark and scowling, and no one paid him attention, entranced as they were by the elderly woman walking swiftly in his train, blue-eyed and well-dressed and furious as a sudden storm. Her cane rapped loud against the floorboards, an arrhythmic gait, her thick-shouldered bodyguard struggling to keep up with his own awkward crablike sidle.

The bar was on a distant corner of the Third, where the riches and luxury of the upper Rungs gave way to the dilapidation and despair of the lower. Under normal circumstances the arrival of some upslope wench in these rough and rude environs would have been enough to elicit commentary of the insulting or lewd variety. But the countertop wits and the half-soused porters took one look at Jahan and found themselves looking in other directions. The bartender was a man ill-suited to his profession, taciturn and unpleasant. His father had owned the tavern, and his father before him, and on and on down into the distant roots of the past, and if he had ever had any option other than becoming a bartender he had not been aware of it. He disliked casual conversation and found the smell of ale nauseating, and between the two he had lost enough money to require taking on a five-eagle loan, which without collateral was little different from taking on a partner. 'Can I help you, Lady?' the publican asked.

'And what sort of help do you suppose I need?' Eudokia snapped. 'What would possibly compel a person such as myself out of her bed and into a palanquin and to descend into the depths of this absurd, endless, monstrosity of a city, and then into a random and unhandsome establishment, and then up to a fat man with what appears to be chicken grease on his lapel? Do I want some of the beer you've watered? A turn with whatever hand-me-down whore works the evening shift? I'm here to see the man in the back, you waste of blood and bone.'

'He's waiting,' said a man at the other end of the counter, quietly but loud enough to be heard. He was big, dressed unassuming, and if you had looked carefully you might have seen that the tankard in front of him was full to the brim, as if he had ordered it with no intention of drinking.

Eudokia snapped her attention over to this speaker. 'How subtle. I'd never have given you such credit, after this recent rash of foolishness.'

The man muttered something unintelligible, made a head-feint towards a back door. Eudokia paid him no more attention, save to follow the direction he had indicated. But Jahan stopped a moment in front of the man, weighing him silently. He lifted the tankard from off the counter and brought it to slug-like lips, thick neck straining, brown eyes steady, without blink or shudder. Then he put it back down empty and scurried to catch up with his mistress.

Through the small back corridor in a small room at a small table, Edom and Steadfast and a man Eudokia did not know sat silently, with an air of unpleasant anticipation. Eudokia took the single empty seat, allowing Jahan to remain standing. Had Eudokia never seen Edom before, she might have supposed him calm, so skilled was he at dissimulation, but past experience allowed her to note the occasional flutter of his blue eyes, the small signs of tension and concern. By contrast, Steadfast was half-frantic, swallowing hard when she entered and looking down at the wood of the table. Only the third man, as yet unnamed, seemed without fear, though objectively one would have to admit this was more a sign of foolishness than of bravery.

'I have come directly from the Red Keep,' Eudokia announced, settling her hands firmly on her lap, as if it was only her preternatural self-control that was keeping them from violence. 'From the bedside of my now one-handed nephew, administrated tenderly to by the seneschal of the Prime himself, who, along with her master, is extremely alive. Alive in every particular, uninjured, not wounded at all. He is sleeping at the moment, my nephew, deep in soporific slumber, but I am told his injuries were the result of defending himself from a group of assassins, members of the Five-Fingers, fanatics, zealots, madmen attempting to break the peace of the Roost. Which I admit to finding immensely curious, as I am of course the chief patron of those same fanatics, zealots and madmen, a fact I had imagined would be sufficient to keep them from injuring my own flesh and blood.'

No one seemed in any very great hurry to answer her. Steadfast found something on the far wall that required the seeming entirety of his attention. There was a brief moment when Edom was not even smiling. 'Revered Mother,' he began slowly, and then his teeth were once again on offer, friendly and reassuring. 'Word has just a few moments ago reached me of this . . . tragic misfortune, one which we regret entirely, it goes without saying. But are you sure our meeting like this is wise? You yourself said the demons and their servants are watching you closely.'

'The day Eduokia cannot outwit a handful of custodians is the day she draws a warm bath and presses steel against her wrist. The three men who were posted to follow me are following three sets of palanquins, which have dispersed to different points around the city. But you're right, this is unwise. What is happening right now, Edom, the First of His Line, is not an example of the proverbial cleverness of the Revered Mother. Instead, you are about to bear witness to one of her rarely seen though no less storied qualities – an astonishingly savage capacity for vengeance. Not quite yet, but soon, very soon indeed if I do not start to receive answers, rather than prevarications.'

Throughout the course of Eudokia's monologue the boy's face had gotten redder and redder, and at the end it burst like a boil. 'Perhaps your ire might better be directed at your nephew, spending his time with the demons and the whore-slaves who serve them.'

Eudokia responded in a tone of voice sweet enough to draw a swarm of hornets. 'To whom am I speaking?'

'Grim, the First of His Line.'

'Have you any hopes of there being a second, you will vacate your seat and the room as well. This conversation will be conducted in your absence or over your corpse.'

'You are very bold with your threats, Revered Mother,' Grim responded after a moment.

'I don't make threats,' Eudokia said. 'Threats are for savages, for thugs, backroom criminals. I am a woman of stature, of class and refinement. I prognosticate – I predict, I augur and foretell. I read the future in the bloody entrails of the world, and I am very, very rarely wrong. And so when I tell you that you sit right now on the very knife's edge, a breath of wind, a shudder, a false word or blink or thought from oblivion, you would do well not to take that as the empty words of a woman wronged, but as a firm certainty, as the sun rising tomorrow, as the very oath of Enkedri himself.'

Jahan's eyes, as he stood beside her, were their usual flat imperturbable brown, the colour of mud or of shit dried in the sun, but his swollen lips were bared up over unwhite teeth and those teeth were drawn into a smile. Apart from that he had made no movement to prepare himself for the conflict threatening to arrive, except in so far as he was always, in every waking moment as well as casual slumber, so ready.

'It's fine, Brother Grim,' Edom said. 'The Revered Mother is concerned about her nephew, as she has every right to be. And of course we are old friends, Eudokia and I, friends and more than friends.'

'Yes, Father,' Grim said, rising after a long moment, though he stared hard at Eudokia and even harder at Jahan after. It was not lost on Eudokia that it was not her warnings that drove the boy from the room, but Edom's command. In fact it gave her a little burst of confidence for the thing to come. Five hundred of such fanatics, all chasing after death as frantically as a pack of mutts might a bitch in heat.

'There was a misunderstanding,' Edom said finally.

'A misunderstanding?' Eudokia repeated, as if the concept was alien but pleasant-sounding. 'Yes, a misunderstanding – that was exactly what this was. Do continue.'

'It was, of course, never our intention to injure your nephew,' Edom said. His smile remained unchecked. A run of sweat had accumulated over his brow. 'Our spies on the Second Rung informed us that the Prime was making a rare visit to the Second. It was thought . . . we had thought . . . it was determined that this was an opportunity which could not be missed.'

'An opportunity to what, exactly? Have your men slaughtered? What is the life of one or other Eternal, in the balance?'

'Not just one Eternal, the King.'

'Gods.' Eudokia shook her head vigorously. 'An entire life lived at their feet, and you do not understand them in the slightest. The Prime no more commands Those Above than he does the evening tide.'

'After our recent losses, it was thought wise to remind the demons and our yet-enslaved brethren that we have not been broken, that the flame of rebellion burns bright as ever, that our species, so long held in bondage, has not yet—'

Eudokia cut him off. 'I am not one of your followers, Edom, and I find your passion for pomposity more windsome than enthralling. They've been killing your people and so you want to kill some of theirs, yes? Fine, an understandable reaction. Although it seems rather trivial, given the slaughter to come. In the meantime, not only have you injured my nephew, but you will have rendered our communication immeasurably more difficult. What do you suppose the response from the Eternal will be, at your assassination attempt? Foolish to attempt it, and foolish twice over to fail! This demonstrates very little of the caution which I have come to expect from you. Indeed, it seems much more the thinking of your sometime subordinate, slayer of demons, who I take it is too busy to attend in person?'

'Pyre is not the head of the Five-Fingered,' Edom snapped. 'He is my servant, whatever confusion there sometimes seems to be on the matter. The Roostborn rise to freedom, and they do so under the guidance of Edom, the First of His Line.'

'Freedom which will be bought with Aelerian gold, fought with Aelerian steel, and most of all, won with an Aelerian army, one which will be at the foot of the Roost in a short period of time and, with the gods' assistance, inside it only a little while after. By the end of the season, my hoplitai will march upslope along the canals, or the Birds will have made corpses of us all.'

'And how will they know where to attack? And who will distract the demons while you launch it? I am not the same man you met in Aeleria, all those long years ago, Revered Mother. Edom has grown to his full strength, and is not one to be casually dismissed. You need me as much as I need you.'

Inside her head Eudokia did the bloody tally. Jahan would be across the table before she had finished giving the command. Of course he could not carry his sword within the Roost but his hands were more than sufficient for the task; a twist and Edom's neck would be snapped like dry wood, though Steadfast might have a moment to scream before he reached the same end. Two that she knew about for certain, the one who had been waiting in the main room and Grim who had gone to join him, probably more, probably not enough to cause a problem for Jahan but then what? Try to blame it on the demons, but for that to be convincing she'd need make a slaughter of everyone in the bar, sanguinary even by Eudokia's standards and probably impossible – some might already have left. Eudokia's pride was a bonfire, though it dulled beside her sense of purpose, and Edom was right – she needed him.

For the moment. 'Perhaps I spoke too harshly,' she said. 'You must forgive an old woman for an excess of passion in defence of her family.'

'More than forgive,' Edom declared, 'applaud. It is the same principle which is at the heart of the Five-Fingered, extended onto the species entire. Are we not all one vast family in opposition against the demons?'

'We are that exactly,' Eudokia confirmed. 'United for a single end.'

Mirrored smiles from opposite each other, wide and bright. Unnoticed beside them, Steadfast shivered.

30

Far above, the hour of the Nightjar chimed from the public clocks, and bright street lamps held back the dark, but down on the Fifth there was only the sound of the suck and the heavy dark of a moonless evening. Four men travelled upslope, moving swiftly but off the main roads, up narrow passages, through warrens of alleyways, along the shadowed banks of unused canals. The gate was one of dozens interrupting the great barriers that obstructed passage to the Fourth, unique only in that the Cuckoo stationed there had woken up one morning an odd year earlier to discover a slaughtered avian on his doorstep, and decided henceforth that while Those Above might be terrible they were terrible a very long way upslope, while whatever the Dead Pigeons might have lacked in sheer horror they made up for with unhappy proximity. He made it very clear that he did not notice any of them when they passed, staring at the basalt walls as if trying to decipher some hidden secret.

Pyre had been thinking about how to kill the Roost for a very long time, for longer even than perhaps he realised, since before joining the Five-Fingered, since he was a boy on the top of his tenement, spending the summers in a cleaned-out bird hutch, surrounded by the pipes with their odious slurp, gazing upslope with hatred proportional to his ignorance. Its size and its wealth and its unfathomable age gave an impression of invincibility, but this was false, this was mummers' paint and sawdust. Its size made it too large to defend, its wealth had enfeebled the demons and their human slaves, its age left it moribund and incapable of reaction. It was like some great beast rotting from the inside, wounded and maddened by its wounds, reaching out for death blindly and unknowing.

The sounds of the suck faded soon after they reached the Fourth, but the dark remained, just as well given their mission. Glory and Vigour were both from Grim's old cell, had been his top soldiers before Pyre had promoted Grim to his second-in-command. They were big men, bigger than Pyre and bigger even than Grim, broad-shouldered and handsome. They kept a few paces ahead of him and Grim kept a few paces behind, for Pyre was more than Pyre now, more even than the leader of the Dead Pigeons; he was a symbol, he was an idea. The demon's blood had sanctified him, had redeemed him, as it soon would redeem the species entire. Glory signalled a halt once they had come within sight of the walls of the Third, a swift downward hand gesture and Pyre and Grim took shelter against the dark of the alley, the other two hurrying on to the nearest gate. On the upper reaches of the Fourth the Cuckoos were less inclined towards amiability, and with Pyre's description handed out across the Roost, subterfuge was too dangerous to attempt. A few moments of silence and then Glory returned to lead them onward to the next Rung, looking unwinded, looking not at all the worse for wear, the only evidence of a scuffle being the two blue-robed bodies lying still in the moonlight.

The revolution would start in the late afternoon, half past

the hour of the Kite. There were two main headquarters for the Cuckoos on the Fifth Rung and two on the Fourth, and as the guard returned at the end of their shifts a picked squad of Dead Pigeons would descend for the slaughter. Two months of oppression had done little or nothing to affect the fighting capability of Pyre's men; the Cuckoos and their demon masters raged about but they did so blindly, their sweeps rarely succeeding in catching anyone of value, their indiscriminate slaughter serving only to further enrage the populace. When the day came Pyre would be able to count on nearly four hundred oath-sworn brothers, a small army but an army nonetheless and moreover an army who had heard the word, who knew themselves to be at the great vanguard of the age to come. Before the last rays of daylight the Cuckoos would have learned, as they had learned many times over the last years, that one free man dying for his species was worth five still enchained, and the bottom third of the Roost would be, to all intents and purposes, the possession of the Five-Fingered.

Grim took the lead once they got to the Third, the only one among them who could claim personal familiarity with the terrain, bastard son of some banker on the Second, his mother a servant to whom he'd taken a passing fantasy, seduced or raped and bought off with a back chamber in a downslope apartment. Pyre and the other two followed blindly, faithfully, for every man of the Dead Pigeons trusted every other man as the right hand trusted the left; that was one of Edom's sayings but it was true all the same. Nor did Pyre's faith prove mistaken, for after twenty-five minutes of swift movement they had come to one of the Third's few pumphouses, an entrance to the sewers within the mountain. A short way inside they found a great oak door bound in brass. Glory pulled a half-maul off his back, and after a few swings of his corded shoulders it burst like a ripe pimple. Inside was a long-disused staircase, narrow and circular, leading further up into the mountain. Glory and Vigour hesitated a moment, staring into the unfathomable darkness above, but Pyre plunged past them without any further word.

The news of the rebellion would ascend like an unwanted burden, each sub-commander and bureaucrat faltering before passing it higher, fearful that the loss of the city would somehow be attributed to them personally. The last months Those Above had taken, on occasion, to accompanying squads of custodians downslope, as on that fateful night with Rhythm, but they did so informally, without order, as if setting off on a hunting expedition. Creatures of pleasure and sin, they would spend the evening whoring and feasting in their castles far above; it was unlikely any would be about to make trouble. And if there happened to be one or two attending to the bottom half of the Roost, well then, they would discover that they had chosen to pursue a more dangerous prey than they had supposed. The Eternal were falsely named – had not Pyre, of all men, proved that?

Upward and upward and after a few minutes Pyre told the other three to extinguish their torches. They had replacements of course but still, caution is always better than its opposite, and so it was only Pyre's dim flicker that illuminated their ascent, twisting and turning, surrounded by the unfathomable vastness of the mountain.

The utility of a wall, of course, is determined by who is standing atop it. After the slaughter of the Cuckoos, Pyre's men would spread out to the major entrance points on the Fourth and the Fifth, tearing up cobblestones for barricades, blockading the gates between the Rungs, shutting down entirely the normal progress of the city. Pyre's men and not Pyre's men alone; they would be assisted in their struggle by the great ravenous mob who anticipated unknowingly the age to come, who would rise with the first hint of rebellion. Porters and clerks, thugs and inebriates and wild-eyed youths, they would see the Five-Fingered banners flying from the walls and they would stream into the streets with brickbat or hammer or their own bare hands, an army numerous beyond counting and vengeful beyond measure.

In time the suck of the slurp grew quieter, and then they came finally to another door, barred once again by brass and cobweb. She had said it was empty, she had said it was long forgotten, but who was she, really, and why could she be trusted? Perhaps there was an entire family of demons waiting for them, a family of demons and an army of servants beyond. A reasonable concern, but not one that checked them for long. Pyre had grown to learn – Pyre had known since becoming Pyre, but he had known for certain since slaying the demon – that his life and future were in the hands of the gods, of bloody-handed Terjunta, of Enkedri whose throne sat above all things, and that there was no more purpose in struggling against fate than in raging at the sun for coming east in the morning. In the narrow staircase Glory struggled to make good use of his maul, and it was a long few moments before the thing was burst on its hinges, every blow echoing loudly, and no sooner was it broken than Pyre had rushed inside.

Those Above would gather a force to respond eventually, Cuckoos leavened with a firm core of demons, and they would descend from the top of the Roost in retaliation at the audacity of the Five-Fingered in supposing themselves free men. The Dead Pigeons would hold out on the walls as long as they could, tumbling rocks and hot oil and anything else that they could find, but they would not hold out for ever, nor try to. They would leave a token force on the walls to distract attention, volunteers happy to die if dying brought forward the age to come, and then they would scatter back into the city, burning what could be burned, killing anything that needed to be killed. The demons would need to go house by house and street by street, and every cable and every link bought thick with the crimson blood of humans and the darker ichor of their tormentors.

Pyre's boots fell on soft carpet, and his eyes on luxury beyond imagining, things of gold and silver, things of silk and rich soft fur, riches that had been left to decay for decades, perhaps for centuries. The hidden entrance came up into a narrow hallway, moth-eaten tapestries on the walls, the images they had once depicted rendered hallucinatory and fragmented. Glory and Vigour were left to hold their avenue of escape, and together

Grim and Pyre scuttled onward through the castle, a vast menagerie of rotting wonders, beautiful and silent as a cenotaph.

'How long has this lain empty?' Grim asked.

Pyre ran a finger along a heavy ebony side table, breaking a smooth blanket of dust. 'Generations.'

'You could fit a dozen families in here,' Grim said, with more wonder than fury. 'You could fit a hundred.'

Pyre hocked and spat loudly, phlegm falling against a crushed velvet carpet. 'The demons are profligate beyond measure.'

'Indeed,' Grim said, reminding himself of his hate and following Pyre further into the darkness.

By the evening the docks and the Barrow and the Straits, and a hundred other similar neighbourhoods on the Fifth Rung, and a hundred other neighbourhoods on the Fourth, would be scenes of frantic battle, the demons and their deluded followers struggling to hold back the new age. A grand and bloody sideshow, the feint that would obscure the killing blow.

Through a final door and out into the summer evening, scented sweetly by aster and lilac and dianthus. While they had been below ground the moon had shed her veil of clouds and now streamed bright and full on the city below. They stood on a balcony that hung, girdle-like, a few floors over the street, and above them the tower seemed to climb up for ever, seemed to rise as far into the sky as it had descended into the mountain, the peak lost from view. It was a quiet spot on the First Rung, all but empty so late in the evening, and the only sounds to be heard were the chirrup of grasshoppers and the rustle of the canals and the slightly more distant sounds of a stringed instrument that Pyre had never before heard.

Grim's jaw was slack. His eyes were wide.

'We can fortify it during the evenings,' Pyre said, pacing over to the edge of the balcony. 'Most of the material can be scavenged from the keep itself, and anything else we can bring up from the staircase. The gods know we have enough porters.' A series of concentric walls formed of the same material as the tower itself radiated out from the spire, more for aesthetic purposes than for defence, though they would serve well enough for that last. 'Funnel them down through the main entrance. Numbers don't mean anything if they can't bring them to bear.'

One of the castles in the skyline looked to Grim more like the boughs of some infinitely large tree, twisting and turning as a willow over a canal bank. One of the towers was formed of some composite of stone that was so dark it seemed to swallow whole the night; he could only make it out by the penumbra that surrounded it. Another, by contrast, seemed composed all of silver, reflected the light so brightly that for an instant Grim found himself thinking that perhaps the moon had a hidden sister, one that shone for the demons alone.

He turned away from the blow, not a particularly hard one, meant only to draw his attention. 'Forgive me, Brother Pyre,' Grim said. 'I was distracted.'

'Keep your focus,' Pyre said, snarling. 'We have the future to plan.'

'Of course, Brother Pyre,' Grim said, turning back to the matter at hand. 'Of course.'

31

A new moon's night in high summer, and with the fire settling dimly the stars were bright and clear. A week's march from the Roost, at the outskirts of what was properly considered the Birds' territory, and there was little that resembled the rich human kingdoms of the coast, no towns nor even any villages, only huge tracts of farmland, millet and rye and oat, the basic foodstuffs on which the vast population of the Roost subsisted. For days now they had been marching through fields of grain interrupted occasionally by squat, ugly barracks, where small colonies of Roostborn had been housed like worker ants, all abandoned shortly before the arrival of the Aelerians.

They ate better than any army of which Bas had ever been a part, but for once full stomachs had not led to high morale. A war with Salucia was one thing – the Commonwealth had been engaged in those for the better part of a half-century, nibbling away at the border states, growing strong from trade dictated at the point of a pike. Sometimes they had overplayed their hand, or the Others had been bored or vicious enough to descend from their mountain fastness and give battle, but these had been the unintended consequences of imperial overreach. What they were about to attempt was a different thing altogether, was a species of madness. Never before, not since the Lamentation itself, had a human nation thought to lead an assault on the Roost. The day before Konstantinos had strung up a half-dozen hoplitai who had tried to desert, marched the entire army past them as an object lesson, their legs quivering and the strong smell of shit, not from the Thirteenth thank the gods but still . . .

'Why didn't they burn them, do you suppose?' asked Nikephoros. He had become the new head of the Thirteenth in the reshuffling of positions that had occurred after Theophilus had died. A steady enough man according to what was said about him, though Bas as a rule did not believe the things that were said about anyone.

'Because they expect to come back,' Isaac said. 'No point in destroying a whole summer's worth of crop when the Birds will ride down and devour us whole.'

'And why haven't they done that?'

'Why would they bother? We're coming to them.'

'Pay no attention to Isaac,' Hamilcar said. 'The thought of having to spend a few days without me has made him morose.'

This verged closely on treason, though it was a half-open secret that there was to be some sort of secret attack on the Roost, by the time Konstantinos had bothered to give the order Bas had known for half a week. And why not? There were no Eternal spies within the camp; indeed so far as he could determine from Einnes they had no intelligence service to speak of, would have thought it beneath them. Bas discovered that his wineskin was empty, called to one of the slaves for another. It was the first he had spoken since dusk.

'Fear not, Isaac – I'll bring you back a fine trophy. Roost-forged steel, like the Caracal has – a battleaxe, perhaps. Or maybe one of those great-helms to cover your ears.' But it was a bad bluff at good humour. Hamilcar had sulked for a day and a half when he found out Isaac would not be accompanying them, nor was Bas thrilled about the matter himself. Whatever hope this mad plan had of success, it would be improved with Isaac's assistance. But Nikephoros could not yet be trusted with the Thirteenth, not to Bas's satisfaction, and they could not be left to the half-competency of Konstantinos and his nobles. A short argument with the Protostrator had been enough to confirm Isaac as second-in-command of the thema. Bas was no speaker, but once his word was behind a thing it was all but impossible to shift it, and in the end Konstantinos had the wit to bend gracefully. At least Nikephoros would have the benefit of Isaac's experience when he faced the heavy cavalry of the Roost.

And perhaps, also, Bas had some dim idea that he was not likely to come back from this mission. Perhaps he did not want to. Perhaps the thought of his best friend living on past him was not entirely an unpleasant one.

'What are they like?' Nikephoros asked.

'You saw the Caracal's, didn't you?' Hamilcar asked, smirking, never knowing to leave well enough alone.

But Bas was in no mood to speak that night, it would have required more than a snide remark to draw him out of silence – a naked blade, perhaps, or a sudden earthquake.

'Only from a distance.'

'Big,' said one of the other men, a tagmatarch who had been present that day when the two of them had sparred. 'As tall as the Strategos, though not as broad. Not that it did any good – the Caracal made short work of her, didn't you?'

Bas drank more.

'I've heard it was close,' said one of the other men seated round the fire. Bas did not bother to look, the dark and the liquor conspiring to render them faceless and indistinct, and what was the point of looking at them anyhow? One soldier was as good as another, so long as he would carry steel and go where he was told. 'And that only a female – what must their boys be like?'

'They say their men are the same size as their women.'

'Imagine one of those riding down on you, heavy plate thick as your hand, all of that strange metal they use?'

'No horse could carry that much weight,'

'Their horses aren't like our horses. Twice as big they say, with claws instead of hooves and hooked teeth. Say they eat nothing but flesh. Say before battle they slaughter a child and feed it to them, one for every horse. Say the Birds take part as well.'

'They say they can shit lightning,' Hamilcar interrupted, 'and piss blue flame. You boys will believe damn near anything.'

'You know an awful lot, for a man that's never been within a hundred cables of the Roost.'

'I was born knowing more than you,' Hamilcar answered. 'Came out of my mother twice as bright and half as strong again.'

'I never knew a Dycian who didn't talk,' said the tagmatarch. 'And I never knew one to speak anything worth hearing. The cleverest, strongest, bravest set of people ever found themselves the slaves of the Aelerian Commonwealth.'

'Numbers,' Hamilcar said. 'Sheer numbers, and nothing else. Get enough of anything together they'll manage to prove half-lethal. Ten years I've had to listen to you talk about the bird men that broke your line, watched you piss yourselves from the memory, been woken up in the night by your screams. Now I finally get to have a look at these creatures that turned your livers to jelly.' The Dycian was talking to talk, talking because that was what he did when he didn't want to think, the same way Isaac drank. 'Every man who ever lost a fight lost it to the toughest son-of-a-bitch that ever walked on two feet. You Aelerians are unused to defeat, and so any victorious foe must be tougher than stone and fiercer than a one-eyed whore.'

Isaac was seated on a squat travelling stool, though only barely. The conversation had seen him slide continually further into inebriation; indeed many evenings seemed to find him in such a state, and though Bas knew that he ought to have made an issue of his adjutant's drink, he had not yet done so, nor had he any immediate plans. Far from the only one these days, after all. 'You talk so much shit, Dycian, it's a wonder you can tell your mouth from your arsehole.' Isaac's eyes were red-rimmed against the firelight, and he spoke in a dull monotone that belied the words, the bitter evenness of a frequent drunk.

'Is it now?' Hamilcar asked, his voice deceptively soft.

Isaac shoved the top of the bottle into his sneer, popped the cork out between crooked teeth, spat it onto the ground and took a long, hard swallow. 'You want to know about Those Above? I can tell you. I'm the man to ask. Me or the Caracal, and you know he won't speak on it. From a distance you might not see a difference, two legs and two arms and a head that won't take well to an arrow or a knife blade, not so different from a man. And how many of those have I killed, going back to that first one that took me here?' Isaac seemed to lose himself for a moment then, in the memory or from the drink, but he started up again. 'Then they come riding down on you and they get bigger and bigger and bigger, giants every one of them, bigger than the Caracal, bigger than any man you've ever seen, armour as heavy as an anvil, sun blinding bright off of it. The horses they ride – you call them horses but do you call a boy a man? Thirty links at the shoulder, I watched them measure the corpse of one, had to make a corpse of it because you couldn't ride them, couldn't even get close, not without losing enough flesh to turn a man a cripple. Nasty beasts, horrible things. And when their masters ride down on you the sound they make is the same as thunder on the Marches, the lightning about to come, making the night sky bright as noon. Oh you can kill them, the Dycian is right, all it takes is three spears in their chest and a sword-blow to the face. I'll tell you something else, and though it may sound mad every man who faced them will tell you the same. They feel no pain, or they do not show it – they hold their hatred until the very last beat of their heart, straining to take you with them, to carry you down along into hell.'

Isaac fell silent finally, and for a long time no one spoke.

'But the Legatus killed one, didn't he?' asked a soldier soon to die.

'Aye, killed him dead, three strikes with a war-hammer hard enough to turn iron into pith. Rode straight out to meet the man, answered a challenge in single combat, bold as you please, fearless. But the question to ask yourself now, boy, is this – are you the Caracal?' He swivelled his head across the assemblage, one by one, eyes cold in the firelight. 'Are any of you?' When no one answered he tossed his empty bottle into the darkness, nodded. 'Nor I. There is only one God-Killer, but there are many thousands of gods.'

32

Eudokia descended from her palanquin, Jahan forming a pair of steps with his hands and lowering her to the ground with a grace that belied his brutish form. It was obvious Calla hoped for a second passenger, obvious from her dress, which fit snugly and presumed much of the sun, as well as the cast her face took when the curtain was shuttered and Leon had not descended from it.

'How kind of you to take the time out of your hectic schedule to accompany me on this little expedition. Between you and the custodians, I confess to feeling nearly drowned in compassion,' Eudokia said, nodding to the four Cuckoos who had accompanied her down from the Second Rung.

'They are for your safety,' Calla answered. 'Given the . . . state of affairs at the moment, the Lord has thought it best to make sure that no . . . overly enthusiastic Roostborn seek to do you injury.'

Around them the Perennial Exchange hummed with its customary intensity, stalls and stands and storefronts extending out in every direction, a metropolis of commerce, a city within a city. Two men – Chazars, Eudokia thought, though she had not met enough to be certain – exchanged abuse with one another in their guttural tongue, poked fingers, shouted, came to some arrangement or reconciliation and hugged each other close and without shame. An old woman stirred a thick iron pot of stew that smelled of cinnamon and pork. Next to her, a whip-thin youth with a stand full of housewares attempted to make up for the deficiencies of his stock with exaggerated demonstrations of friendliness, calling to Eudokia in terms of uncomfortable intimacy. Boys in dirty robes and hemp slippers carried tea services through the packed commercial thoroughfares, glassware piled on silver trays.

'Indeed,' Eudokia observed, 'the mood seems very tense.'

'Was there anything in particular you hoped to see, Revered Mother?' asked the captain, the same officer who had escorted them to the docks long months past. Leon's dearest friend, though Calla might have disputed the point.

'I am told that the tailors in the Perennial Exchange are second to none in the world.'

'Unquestionably the truth,' he said, smiling white teeth. 'The silkman's strip, along the north-western quadrant, is where the finest goods are sold. They have been known even to sometimes take the commission of the Well-born.'

'Then that is where you must bring us, Captain,' Eudokia said, fluttering a smile and waving him onward.

The Perennial Exchange had thus far lived up to its name. Whatever tension or violence was present within the city, whatever fears might be felt downslope and even in the surrounding neighbourhoods, they seemed to have no effect on that vast engine of commerce. If anything, in fact, these last weeks had seen a flurry of activity, vast sums gained and lost, wagers even madder and more wasteful than might usually be seen, as if it was hoped that sheer vigour would be sufficient to maintain the happy position they had long enjoyed, that excessive optimism would prove a self-fulfilling prophecy.

They promenaded through the corner of the market dedicated to fine clothing, to silk and linen, furs of sable and silver fox and black squirrel, long rolls of Dycian dyed cloth and of the curiously patterned Parthan robes. Here in the wealthier section of the exchange the stalls were wide canvas tents, and Eudokia stopped into one of these that caught her fancy, Calla accompanying her while the custodians remained outside. The proprietress was a handsome woman halfway between the two of them in age, and she performed the Eternal greeting and offered them tea. Eudokia returned the first and declined the second, then made her way through the collection of robes and dresses, shawls and silk gloves and, in a back corner, an elaborate selection of lacy undergarments.

'The stitchwork is fabulous,' Eudokia said, holding for a long moment a skimpy black half-dress. 'Though these days I can't imagine they would receive much use. Perhaps Calla might have some interest?'

Though Calla did not, and so they moved on to the rest of the shop.

'I had not supposed you a seamstress, Revered Mother,' Calla said.

'Busy hands are happy hands. I spent the winter knitting socks for our themas. Salucia can get quite chilly, so I'm told.'

'You'd think it would be best left to the Salucians.'

Eudokia laughed. 'Your wit gets buried so deep beneath that facade of yours that sometimes I forget to see it.' She pulled at a stretch of fabric and turned abruptly to the proprietress. 'These are marvellous.'

'The Revered Mother is too kind,' the woman said. 'Though I admit that we have the use of some extraordinarily skilled workers. We have even been known to do pieces for the Well-born – small things, of course, no Eternal would think to wear anything sewn by a human, but still. The Lord of the Sidereal Citadel commanded our assistance in providing tablecloths, and we have a steady patronage in the finer bladders of the aeroships.'

'An admirable accomplishment,' Eudokia said, inspecting a

robe between her thumb and forefinger. 'The craftsmanship is singularly impressive, though I confess I find ochre an unutterably unattractive hue. Perhaps something in blue or green?'

The proprietress bowed deeply, and with grace. 'Allow me a moment to check my stock,' she said, disappearing towards the back. Eudokia continued on with her perusal, the captain waiting by the door looking some long way from fascinated.

'You might think to visit him,' Eudokia said

'Who?'

Eudokia rolled her eyes.

'How is he?'

'As well as can be expected. His wound is a source of pain and embarrassment. The former can be assuaged with narcotics, though the latter remains piquant.'

'I was unsure whether my attentions would be appreciated.'

'In my day, a man's willingness to sacrifice life and limb in your service was taken as ample evidence of interest.'

'I had not meant with Leon.'

'Surely you don't suppose I have any objection to your union?'

'Have we not reached the point that we might dispense with this pretence that you are a simple tourist, taking in the splendours of the Roost? With your army marching on my home, and all your long plans come finally to false flower?'

'Reached and passed it. Fate has rendered me the implacable and perhaps even the fatal enemy of the Eternal. But whatever does that have to do with you or my nephew?'

'How long can you trace your line, Eudokia Aurelia?' The girl had a magnificent figure for pontification, Eudokia had to admit, and she used it to its full effect just then, stiff-chinned, high-necked. 'Mine have served the Prime for seven generations, and his line for five centuries previous. I can name them, should you wish – it was the first task my father set me as a child, before I could sum or even read. Before your ancestors first reached the southern shores, when your Empty Throne yet held a king, my family resided on the First Rung and owed our fealty to the Red Keep. An enemy of the Prime is my enemy as well.'

'There is a woman back in Aeleria who has changed my chamber pot for fifty years without word of complaint. She is quite the most loyal thing that ever existed, but I would not ask her to wield a sword in my defence. This curious pride you have taken in the length of your subjugation notwithstanding, you have no role to play in what is to come. You are an observer, a privileged one perhaps, but nothing more, and I certainly cannot see any reason why my strategems should be any barrier towards your paying a visit to my nephew's bedside, nor, for that matter, slipping beneath the covers. You are clever enough, and of course your beauty is without dispute. Admittedly, you share that curious sort of naivety that is a hallmark also of my nephew, though I can only suppose that is part of the attraction. All in all, I think the two of you a fine match,' Eudokia confessed. 'I daresay, as a side note, should you ever wish your relationship to extend beyond the purely amiable you would do well to grasp the reins. He is younger than he sometimes seems.'

The proprietress came back then, carrying a pair of dresses that matched Eudokia's specifications, meriting an elaborate series of compliments and, after a friendly but spirited dispute, eight solidus and three tertarum, to be paid upon delivery to Eudokia's home on the Second.

Calla managed to stay silent through it all only through a fierce act of will that could be read across her scowling face, and as soon as they were outside she snapped back. 'You cannot know your nephew's feelings, and less so my own.'

'For the sake of the gods, girl,' Eudokia said, pushing onward through the bazaar, 'am I really expected to believe that you've exposed half your breasts to sunlight in hopes of a tan?'

The captain had, in a demonstration of wisdom, chosen to walk far enough away from their conversation as to at least feign ignorance of its subject, the rest of his men doing the same. Jahan laboured along behind Eudokia, though as usual he gave no indication that the ongoing conversation was of any interest to him, nor indeed for that matter, anything else that was going on around them. That portion of the Perennial Exchange which focused on garments gave way to one selling jewellery and metal-work, precious stones, objects of art and foreign relics. At one of these, looking to Calla or the custodians no different from a dozen others along the same stretch, Eudokia pronounced herself interested and made to enter, the captain swift to open the door, displaying his characteristic gallantry.

There was much to be said about the grace and merit of the Eternal, but as regards their capacity for dissimulation they were rank amateurs, Eudokia thought, and their human agents little better. The labyrinthine subtleties of the Salucian court, the endless buried plotting that was the chief preoccupation of the Aelerian Senate, these were utterly alien to Those Above. Perhaps this was to be expected – they were, after all, a species with no conception of dishonesty, or perhaps whose conception of dishonesty was so subtle and so all-consuming that they had long ago ceased even to realise they were practising it. Adding to this difficulty was the general sense that nothing a human could do was seriously worthy of consideration, a belief that, perversely, had spread to their five-fingered subjects as well. To the best that Eudokia was able to determine, they had no intel-ligence service as such, and their attempts to constrain her own operations consisted of little more than posting custodians outside of Eudokia's house, and ensuring that they followed her wherever she went. The basic tricks of spycraft – dead drops and false fronts and the like – seemed quite utterly beyond their ken. With the exception of the brief period after the death of the Shrike, there had never been a period during Eudokia's stay in the Roost when she had not been more or less entirely capable of running her network of spies and agents without meaningful hindrance of any kind.

Indeed, as was so often the case, it was not the wiles of her enemies that Eudokia needed most to fear, but rather the incompetence of her allies. She would never learn why Steadfast was in the stall that day – perhaps he was confused on the timing, perhaps there was some problem with his agent that demanded his presence. Whatever it was, as Eudokia and her entourage were entering he was just about to make egress, and there was a discomfiting moment when they nearly bumped into one another. Of course, Eudokia gave no inkling of recognition, no hint or suggestion, just smiling the wax smile she gave to everyone, stepping aside to allow him passage. Steadfast, equally true to his nature, went pale, mumbled some distracted greeting, looked as conspicuous as a bruise on a stepson.

The shop sold jewellery and curious bits of steamwork, minor creations of Those Above, little more than toys but worth more than a bolt of silk or a flawless diamond. Calla followed in after Eudokia but turned back to stare at Steadfast, eyes narrowing. Near the entrance a knee-height vase of fine porcelain held a number of fresh-cut roses, or at least did in the moment before the tip of Eudokia's cane overturned the inoffensive flowerpot, shattering it loudly. Calla turned towards the noise, and Steadfast, in a rare and happy moment of competence, took the opportunity to make his retreat. By the time Calla thought to turn back he was gone.

Eudokia's display of lamentation regarding the destruction of the vase was, even to her own ears, rather exaggerated, but the proprietor matched her in melodrama.

'It was quite the ugliest piece I ever owned,' he assured Eudokia without evident irony. 'I was planning on breaking it myself, after the end of the business day, so really you've done nothing but save me the trouble.'

Calla's attention, Eudokia was displeased to discover, was back on the door, or perhaps the individual she had just seen leaving it. Had Steadfast so botched her play as to give the girls some warning of her plan? Surely not. There was no way, after all, that Eudokia could have known who Steadfast was, apart from an awkward and ill-behaved stranger. And indeed, as Eudokia made her way further into the shop, Calla attended her without any further evidence of concern. Eudokia spent some time modelling a large golden brooch, though in the end she dismissed it as being too heavy a burden, both of weight and ostentation. She was more pleased with a silver and sapphire torc from far-flung Chazar, held it up to the light, inspected the craftsmanship.

'Would it go with his eyes, do you suppose?' Eudokia asked.

Calla spent some time considering, and behind her Jahan shook loose a line of paper from somewhere within the folds of his robes, set it beneath the base of a heavy statue on a table nearby. The statue was an eagle, wings cast wide, eyes cruel. The parchment detailed the expected movements of the Aelerian forces then marching on the city, and the pass signs by which they would know their Roostborn liaisons, and a number of other details of the plot to come.

'I think it would,' Calla said, handing it back to Eudokia.

Eudokia smiled widely, at the affirmation or perhaps at something else, and in purchasing the necklace she did not haggle quite so vigorously as might have been expected.

Back outside the hour of the Kite was turning towards the hour of the Woodcock, though the market showed no lessening of its freneticism. 'You were honest, Captain, when you spoke so exultantly of the wonders of the Exchange,' Eudokia said.

'It pleased me to hear that you think so, Revered Mother,' he said, almost blushing. 'Is there somewhere else we might escort you?'

'Perhaps only back home,' Eudokia said, revealing a tired smile. 'I'm afraid all the excitement is almost too much for me.'

The captain sketched a bow and led them back in the direction they had come.

'Such expressions of enthusiasm,' Calla said, 'for a place you would as soon see in cinders.'

'Not at all,' Eudokia said, smiling toothily, 'I'd prefer to see it mine.'

'Aeleria's, you mean.'

'Yes, of course.'

'And what sort of city would it be, beneath Aeleria's possession? Beneath your laws and tithes?'

'Better for some. Worse for others. There is no wind which blows only ill, and no good fortune which is not diluted with misery.'

'Miserable, for instance, for Calla of the Red Keep? Or the proprietress of the clothing store you so enjoyed? I am told that in Aeleria, despite your sterling example, women are allowed no public role. Cannot conduct business, or hold political office, or even formally own property.'

'A slight simplification,' Eudokia observed, 'though broadly true.'

'One struggles to understand why you would allow such a situation to continue, given your role within the Commonwealth.'

'Why encourage the competition?'

'Your wit is sharp as ever, though it does nothing to change the fact that were you ever to reign in the Roost, as impossible and absurd a suggestion as that is, that woman would never again be allowed to operate her shop, nor Calla to oversee the Red Keep.'

'You claim kinship from our shared aperture? Ought I to feel the same sentimentality for anyone else with the same arrangement, any halfwit or whore, because she might give milk or bear seed? Do you suppose men think the same, call each other brother for the nubbin of flesh between their legs? You'll forgive me when I admit the similarities do not seem so distinct as you make them out to be. When the gods created Eudokia, child, they broke the mould.'

They had come again to the outskirts of the market, and the captain hurried off to find their palanquin, quartered with a number of others in a lot nearby. In the square across from them two children tottered uncertainly towards a nearby flight of pigeons, laughing, scattering the birds at peck.

'You have a peculiar notion of your self-worth,' Calla said.

'Quite the opposite in fact – it is one I hold in common with every other human being who yet resides above the ground, present company not at all excluded. Whatever lies you may tell yourself, your actions belie the truth. You love yourself and those few close to you, and you feel indifference to that vast multitude failing to enjoy so privileged a position. Such a perspective is an essential necessity for any sentient being. The death of a thousand strangers in a land you will never visit is of less consequence than a cut to your finger too small to require a bandage.'

'I have sometimes noticed this tendency, in those lacking in basic scruple, to universalise their immorality, as if hoping to ameliorate guilt by spreading it more broadly.'

'Tell me then, Calla of the Red Keep – you weep for the benighted and oppressed females of Aeleria, labouring in backward ignorance? Do you reserve any of that torrent of sympathy for the multitude of women held daily in despair as a consequence of your own country?'

'In the lower Rungs as well, there is no legal distinction between the sexes. A woman on the Fifth Rung is free as a woman on the First.'

'Free to do what, exactly? Free to squabble over bread? Free to watch her children die impoverished? What comfort do you suppose it is to the females of the Fifth that they are no more miserable than their husbands? You judge the health and prosperity of your society by your own privileged position – an understandable bit of blindness, and one which further proves my point. When you say that the people of the Roost are free and happy, in fact what you mean is "I am free. I am happy". Indeed, this is all anyone means when they say such a thing. There is no universal – there is only the particular.'

'Even you do not really believe what you are saying,' Calla retorted. 'This mad self-regard, this titanic narcissism. I was there when you attended on Leon the night he was injured, and did not suppose your consideration feigned.'

'It was nothing of the sort. Leon is my nephew – I would sacrifice bodily for him, I would steal and maim and kill in defence of his interests. But I do not suppose that my affection for his person is common to the species, nor do I extend that sympathy to every other nephew of every other woman who ever lived. We look after our own, Calla of the Red Keep. That is the very best thing that can ever be said of us.'

The palanquin made its way down the boulevard. Eudokia offered the captain an elaborate series of thanks by the end of which even she felt winded, then passed to the entrance of her vehicle. Jahan squatted and offered his hands as platform, then raised Eudokia up into the coach. Before pulling shut the curtain she crooked a finger and gestured Calla forward.

'For the feeling I bear him,' Eudokia said softly, 'and for the feeling he bears you, I will do my best to save you when the time comes. But be careful, Calla of the Red Keep – Eudokia is far from omnipotent. And what is to come will be terrible beyond all reckoning.'

33

Leon was staring up at the ceiling, but when Calla came in he bolted upright and pulled his mutilated hand back below the covers. Weeks in bed had not done anything good for his complexion, which was sallow, or for his tone, which was slack. She would discover what it had done to his mind soon enough.

'Welcome, Seneschal,' Leon said. 'You will forgive me if I do not rise.'

'I can overlook it.' Next to Leon's bed there was a stool and a table and a small *shass* set, the game far advanced.

'You and your aunt?'

'Yes.'

'White is losing,' Calla said after a moment.

'True.'

'And who is white?'

'Who do you suppose?'

'The Prime asked me to express his deepest and most sincere apologies. If there is anything else that you desire, know that you would be treated with great attention in the Red Keep.'

'The Prime has done more than enough for me already,' Leon observed, 'and if my quarters are not quite what might be expected on the First Rung, I have no complaints about my treatment.' His smile was forced, and false, and sad. 'The solitude has allowed me to return to my studies.'

'Do not suppose my absence indicative of a lack of concern.'

'What should I suppose?'

'Things have grown . . . tense, within the Roost. The attempted assassination of the Prime, the movement of your armies – I was not sure it was wise for us to be seen together, wise for either of us.'

'You might well have been right,' Leon admitted. 'And while I confess myself happy that you've broken your self-imposed exile, I can't help but wonder what it was that changed your mind?'

Calla explained the matter neatly, simply. Sixty seconds at the most, and then the spreading silence, Leon's eyes tightening. A final slow nod. 'Could you get some water from the pitcher on the table? The one on the table has been diluted with a narcotic.'

Calla rose, poured a cup and brought it over to him. He took it while sitting up in bed, but it remained in his good hand unconsidered for a long time before he spoke. 'You are certain that this man you saw at the Exchange was the same Steadfast who spoke at the meeting of the Five-Fingered?'

'Confident enough that I came to you,' she said. 'Confident enough that we are having this conversation.'

Leon stared out the window for a long time without speaking. His room offered no particularly prepossessing view, just a small courtyard in which some of the servant children were playing rat-in-a-hole, and above them the gabled rooftops of the Second Rung, and above that the sky and the sun and the gods. 'It would be entirely characteristic for my aunt to be in touch with whatever dissident forces within the Roost exist. It would be even more like her to have created them, to have sown in some distant past the seeds of your current misfortune. It would not take very much, not so very much at all. Down on the lower Rungs they have been left to rot for so long as to grow mad with hate, indeed it seems in retrospect surprising rebellion has taken so long to develop. There is more than enough discontent to tap within this paradise you have created.'

'True enough.'

'Though not immediately relevant. Let us assess the situation further. Eudokia is in touch with the Five-Fingered. To what end? Simple enough. One hardly needs to be in my privileged position to see that the Revered Mother has been working to bring about war against the Empire for the better part of five years. Far more than that, in fact, but the last five years it was obvious to anyone who thought to pay attention. Indeed, I have often found myself wondering, given the naked-ness of her provocations, why the Roost did not think it fit to retaliate.'

'They are lazy,' Calla said quietly. 'They have grown so used to their strength that they cannot imagine it would ever be challenged. And they do not suppose you a threat.'

'Their arrogance may yet be justified,' Leon admitted. 'Though my aunt is scarce familiar with defeat. Regardless. The Aelerian army is on the march. I have no head for military affairs but it is said to be quite the largest force ever assembled, twice the size of what was brought to bear against the Roost in the last war. In a few days, or perhaps a week, they will arrive at the walls of the Roost. When they grow close enough for Those Above to concern themselves, they will assemble en masse, and ride down from the Source, and slaughter my coun-trymen like scythed wheat in autumn. A certain massacre, you say, as do the Prime and the rest of the Eternal, as does every wag in every bar and cafe and bazaar from the top of the Roost to the middle. Murdered to a man, and then Those Above will march into Aeleria and make of it a wasteland. It would be a curious fact indeed if, alone among the creatures of the Roost, Four-Fingered and Five, Eudokia Aurelia alone did not see what was coming.'

'Perhaps she has more faith in your armies than the Eternal. Everything that has happened these last months, and still it is impossible for them to imagine that you present a threat.'

'They are the most madly arrogant things that were ever bred, but that is neither here nor there. And besides, my aunt prefers her contests more certain. I do not suppose that she is willing to risk everything on a simple clash of steel. No, she has another card to play, one that your stroke of memory seems to have laid bare. Something involving the Five-Fingered, but what exactly? My understanding is that apart from their recent provocations they are everywhere on the run, the Eternal and their patrols on the lower Rungs proving effective in battering them into submission. Indeed, from this perspective their naked attack on the Prime can be seen as a last desperate attempt by forces nearly defeated. Or it could be seen as an unpleasant augury of things to come.' He was not smiling but there was good colour in his cheeks, and he sat fully upright, rubbing the palm of his good hand against his forehead, as if to tease out some excess strand of thought. 'There are too many vari-ables,' he said finally. 'The broad outline of the thing is clear, but the specifics remain unknowable. The only option remaining is to find this Steadfast.'

'Easier said than done – I know his assumed name, and could pick him out of a crowd, but I've no idea where he lives, and I don't suppose he calls himself Steadfast in mixed company.'

'To set that question aside for a moment, in favour of two of my own.'

'Which are?'

'First, why have you not already brought this matter to the Aubade?'

'What would I tell him? That I suspect the Revered Mother

of malfeasance? I more than suspect it, I am certain of it. But suspicion is not proof.'

'He would trust you.'

'He would trust me,' Calla agreed. 'And he would listen to what I tell him. And he might, perhaps, kill your aunt, and he might kill you, but regardless that would do nothing to stop whatever machinations have already been put in place.'

'It would be quite pointless,' Leon admitted. 'As well as being personally unpleasant. Though speaking of such consequences, I am forced now to ask my second question – why would I be interested in helping you, Calla of the Red Keep? Whatever else Eudokia is, she is my aunt, and Aeleria my country.'

Calla said nothing for a long moment. Then she reached out and stripped the covers off him. He flinched but made no move to return them. His pointer and long finger were severed roughly down near the knuckle, and the first joint of his ring finger jutted out awkwardly.

'Far from lovely,' Leon admitted, affecting a sneer. 'But I've had a few weeks to grow used to it.'

'A spare month was sufficient for you to forgive the men who savaged you?'

Leon laughed bitterly. 'I admit the end is rather fuzzy, but my impression is that they were well paid for any injury they did me.'

'And their masters who sent them? Do you not suppose their actions warrant a response?'

'Yes, what a glorious thing revenge is. How wise and how fruitful!' He drank most of the water in his glass, wiped his chin with his savaged hand. 'Do you know that I killed a man, Calla of the Red Keep?'

'I did not.'

'I shoved a sword into his back, while his attention was otherwise occupied. No very admirable or heroic a feat, I admit. I don't imagine it will ever be immortalised in song, though it has found firm purchase in my memory.' He blinked twice. 'You sit at the bedside of a murderer. Oh, I had my reasons, of course. He had been in the process of attacking my aunt.

And no doubt he had, or thought he had, sufficient reason for trying to attack her. And no doubt she had sufficient reason for doing whatever it was that caused her to be attacked. And so on and so on, endless and pointless as one of your Eternal. Searching, one does not struggle to find a pretext for violence.'

'It's not simply a question of justice,' Calla said softly. 'War is coming. Do you wish to see your people made corpses? Or mine? All the wonders of the Roost destroyed, the Eternal expunged entire? Or the reverse, your countrymen slaughtered, your capital ravaged and broken? If we knew what your aunt was planning, perhaps we might find some way to avert it. Perhaps there is still some hope. Perhaps there is still time to stop it.'

'I fear you are over-sanguine on the matter. What have you ever seen of my people, Calla, that made you think them irenic? What have you ever seen of anyone?'

The clocks chimed across the Second, announcing the evening and the hour of the Woodcock. Calla was seated on the edge of the bed, and she moved closer then, engaged him with her eyes. It was not a ploy, or if it was it was one so natural, so instinctive, that it could barely warrant criticism. 'Then do it for me,' she said. 'Because I will not sit idly while my home burns, and I will not throw myself at the feet of the Revered Mother and beg for shelter. However slim the chances, I will venture them. With you, there is some hope of success. Without, I will surely die. Help me because I need you, and because I am asking.'

Below her Leon swallowed hard, gathering up his courage, managing finally, intertwining with arm and hand and tongue. It was not until she was beneath the covers that Calla realised Leon was a virgin, from the way his flesh quivered when she brushed against him. Impossible to imagine a boy of the First Rung reaching twenty-and-two without having taken a woman to bed – she had supposed it uncommon even in Aeleria – but it was indisputable, he betrayed his innocence in his excitement and his joy, in his hardness that pressed against her, in the thinness of his breath. Or perhaps it was more than that, for Calla, who had been no stranger to the sex act since her sixteenth year, found herself near as excited, each laboured touch sending frissons along her tanned skin and up her spine. His good hand fumbled with the back clasp of her robes, and then with her ripe breasts, unsure of himself. But what he lacked in expertise he made up for in passion, in sheer joy, shuddering at every brush of skin against skin, eyes wide and warm and kind. She lifted his ruined hand to her lips and kissed the wound tenderly, and he blushed and he moaned, for is that not the last and the kindest gift a lover gives? To forgive what is flawed and broken, more than forgive, to cherish?

Downslope the city moved swiftly towards conflagration, fanatics sharpening their knives and laying their plans for slaughter. Upslope the custodians and bureaucrats cracked down on any faint hint of insurrection, dispensing violence with an open hand. Higher still their Eternal protectors continued unceasingly their games and their dances, ignorant of what was coming if not innocent of its arrival. Everywhere, there was injustice, there was avarice and bigotry, there was fear and soon after fear, cruelty. But in the small room on the Second Rung, in a soft bed with silk sheets, there were only the two of them, and the world seemed still a place worth saving.

It had gone quickly – he was new to the thing, after all, one could hardly hope for expertise in a novice. But he had been tender, and that was the most important thing, that was the only thing that could not be taught or learned. In the kind light of the early evening they held each other close, and Calla knew only his scent, and the beat of his heart, and even forgot for a time the original purpose of her visit.

Though reality inevitably intervenes. 'I fear now that I have thrown away my virtue too cheaply,' Calla said mockingly, 'for while I have given you good answer to your question, you have done nothing to answer mine. This Steadfast of your aunt, who you say is the critical piece to the whole thing – how in the name of your gods do we find him?'

'Actually that part's rather simple,' Leon admitted, running his fingers through her hair. 'He goes by Cobble, and he has a trading house on the Fifth Rung.'

34

At the far end of the docks there was a neighbourhood called Three Forks, consisting mostly of a complex of warehouses, out of use for much of the year. Vast structures, decaying, lightless except where the occasional spot of sunshine slipped through a broken windowpane. During the Anamnesis they were used to store the excess tithes that came in from the Commonwealth, salted cod and smoked ham, foodstuffs stacked to the rafters. Nine months later it contained another product of Aeleria's abundance – five hundred hardened soldiers, killers to a man.

Nominally Aelerians, at least, though half were undiluted Dycian, darker even than Pyre, lean and wiry and rarely out of arm's reach of their curved bows. The Aelerians themselves were paler, and broader, and they rarely smiled. The two groups were identical, so far as Pyre could tell, in their vulgarity and general meanness, as well as their love of gambling and drink – for three days they had done nothing but roll dice and swill sour wine, were most of the way through the provisions that Pyre had squirrelled away for them, heavy kegs that ought to have lasted a month.

Courage, the First of His Line, had been left behind as their liaison, and he was growing close to the end of his tether. 'These are our allies in the struggle against the demons? These are the men who will bring about the age to come? Sots and murderers?'

There was much required of Pyre these days, the last of the old era, many tasks required if the dawn was to come. Across the lower half of the Roost the Dead Pigeons had gradually taken up their positions, waiting only for the word that would send them into battle, waiting only for the standard to be raised beneath which they would die. Pyre was needed everywhere, at every point of attack, to plan out each route and designate each target. For the first time in two frantic years of civil strife Pyre was approaching the end of his reserves. The night before, hidden in an alleyway across from one of the headquarters of the Cuckoos, he had fallen asleep standing up, a blissful moment of darkness and then sharply awake as his knee struck the stone wall. That had been ten hours earlier, hours he had filled with labour. He would need to find a spare moment for slumber soon, or be no good to anyone.

'It won't be much longer,' Pyre said, rubbing the heel of his hand hard against his eyes.

'They are without honour,' Courage said disapprovingly. 'Nothing but mercenaries. They deserve no share of the dawn.'

'Edom knows his business,' Pyre snapped, exhaustion as much as filial loyalty fuelling his anger. 'And it is obedience required of you at the moment, not commentary.'

'Of course, Brother Pyre,' Courage said, eyes belying his name, 'forgive me.'

As little concern as the demons gave to the lower Rungs, they were comprehensively more ignorant of the farms that extended out from the Roost, of the vast numbers of near-slaves who laboured there. Edom's words had spread quickly amidst this ocean of grain and black-seeded cotton, men huddled around cookfires and in the great communal barracks in which they slept during those scant hours when they were not labouring. To bring the contingent of soldiers through them quietly, without giving notice to any of the demons' few human agents, had required no very great excess of skill. The detachment from the main army had been met by one of Pyre's scouts, shuttled through those plantations that he knew to be theirs entirely. Midnight three days prior had seen five hundred men appearing at one of the less-used gates on the far side of the Fifth Rung, then moved swiftly to their secret quarters nearby. In any human city it would have been absolutely impossible for so large a movement of armed men to enter undetected, but even with an army only a few days from the city, the demons still could not grasp the full extent of their danger. When the Aelerians arrived, they would destroy them, as they always had, as they had every band of men who had ever been sent against them. There was no need for strategy beyond that.

'We must make use of the tools available to us,' Pyre said, after a moment, in modest apology. 'And by all accounts they have done well enough against the Salucians.'

Courage shrugged. What went on in the outside world was of no more interest to him than it was to Those Above, and like most of the rest of the Dead Pigeons he had only the most casual knowledge of the war that had been raging across the continent these last years. 'The Salucians aren't the demons.'

'If it isn't the young king himself,' said a voice from behind Pyre. Courage's eyes narrowed nastily. Pyre turned away from him.

The speaker was Hamilcar, the leader of the Dycians, tall and thin and darkly handsome. Standing next to him, not smiling, for he never smiled or at least Pyre had not yet seen it, was a hulking brute, dull-eyed, the most famous man alive or close to it. In the Roost as well they spoke of Bas Alyates, perhaps especially in the Roost, for even those who laboured beneath the demons' lash, and even those who thought that lash a kindness, still there was some part of them that breathed for freedom, that revelled in the knowledge that the demons were flesh. Pyre could remember nights as a child on the roof of his building spent in blissful fantasy of slaughter, fighting back to back with the legendary Caracal.

Perhaps no reality could have matched the legend, but Pyre could not help but feel that he might have approached nearer to it. A big man, but old, his face like a cracked pane of glass, withered and well-lined. Still, his eyes were flat and hard and gave away nothing, and among a group of men who were remarkably savage even by Pyre's standards, when he said a word that word was taken as if had been passed down from the foot of Enkedri's great throne.

'It is well to see you still alive, Pyre,' said the Dycian, in the pidgin travellers' tongue that was an amalgamation of all of the languages of the Tullus coast, mostly gutter Roost Speech with a few loanwords from the Salucians.

'Blessings of the gods upon you this day. May the light of the coming dawn illuminate your path.' Courage had taken this opportunity to find somewhere else to be, happy to let Pyre take the lead.

'I sometimes get the sense,' continued Hamilcar, who, in contrast to his superior, always seemed to be grinning, 'that your man is not so fond of us as we are of him.'

'He says you drink too much.'

'What else is there to do but drink?'

'Alcohol is a tool the demons use to weaken us. The Five-Fingered abstain from it.'

Hamilcar laughed and wiggled his digits. 'And yet these held a skin of wine scarce five minutes past.'

If the Caracal followed any of this, he gave no indication. With each interaction Pyre tried his best to determine whether he was playing dumb or was the real thing, and he had yet to arrive at a conclusion. He muttered a few words into his subordinate's ear, but his eyes didn't leave Pyre.

'He wants to know when we will move,' Hamilcar translated. 'He says the longer we stay here, the more likely we are to be discovered.'

'The neighbourhood is ours,' Pyre said simply. 'The people here are proud followers of the word – there are none who would think to inform. And we have our own forces ready to intercept anyone who would try.'

Hamilcar – presumably – translated this into Aelerian for the Caracal's benefit. He said a few sharp words in response.

'The Caracal wants to know how you can be certain?'

'My followers are utterly reliable, they can be—'

But Hamilcar cut him off. 'The Caracal was not asking a question – he is saying you can't be certain, not about that, or about anything. Every second spent here is a second which might potentially lead to disaster.'

'He is right, of course,' Pyre admitted. 'But there is nothing else for it. Your army has been slower to approach than I had anticipated, but our people are in contact with them daily. We will move when they are ready.'

Hamilcar translated this. Bas nodded, but his eyes were on Pyre's own. He spoke again.

'The Caracal wishes to know something.'

Pyre shrugged.

'They say you killed an Other.'

'A demon?'

'That's what they say.'

'It's true.'

Hamilcar said something in Aelerian to Bas, who chewed over it like salted jerky, then spat something back.

'He wants to know how you did it. Was it just you, or did you have help? Did you trap the thing, or surprise it?'

'It was the will of the gods,' Pyre said simply. 'Whom Enkedri chooses, that man is invincible, though he be unarmed, though he carry nothing but a stone, he will be victorious against whatever stands against him.'

Hamilcar looked at Pyre a long time before translating this, and even in the dim light Pyre could detect contempt in his rich brown eyes.

'The Caracal says that he has seen battle from the far Marches to old Dycia to Salucia itself,' Hamilcar said after a moment. 'And in none of them can he remember having seen Enkedri taking the field.'

'Perhaps the Caracal knows less of war than he supposes.'

'I will do you a favour,' Hamilcar said, smiling suddenly, teeth white against the dark of the warehouse, 'and not translate that.'

Bas looked at Pyre for one moment longer, then nodded and headed back towards the rest of his men. Pyre was about to make for the exit when Hamilcar reached out and grabbed him with one calloused hand.

'Did you want something else?'

'Do you wonder why there are two hundred men of my country, interspersed among the throng?'

Pyre shrugged. He could feel the need for sleep building heavy against his eyes. 'You are auxiliary forces of the Commonwealth.'

'And do you know how we became so?'

'I don't,' Pyre said flatly, in a way that suggested he was not strongly interested in the answer.

'It was penance,' Hamilcar explained. 'For our temerity in opposing the Aelerians' desire to swallow our homeland. They are clever people, the Aelerians, they make use of what they find. Why kill us when we might kill for them? A slave is better than a corpse.'

'I have more to do today than sit around in the dark, swilling wine. Is there a point to this story?'

'The Aelerians sacked my city as well, but I didn't help them do it.'

'The Roost is not my city – the Roost is the city of the demons, the Roost is a festering sore on the earth, the Roost is a cage in which I and my people are bound. The Aelerians are helping only to free us from it.'

'And then they will march home, leaving all of this behind? You presume a great deal on the magnanimity of your new comrades.'

'They will rid themselves of the tithe they have so long been forced to provide,' Pyre said. 'And of the humiliation of being beneath the heel of the Eternal. Are not the Aelerians human, as I am human, as are you? Are not we all united in this struggle?'

A long pause, during which Pyre could hear the rattle of dice in the dark, and the loud cursing of the Aelerians, and of course the slurp, the slurp, always the slurp. And then Hamilcar began to laugh, loud enough to drown out the rest of the noise, loud enough to draw the attention of onlookers, of Courage and of the nearby Aelerians, and then he shook his head and went off to join the Caracal.

An hour later, on a cot in the basement of a safe house, exhausted beyond measure and yet unable to sleep, Pyre stared up at the ceiling and thought about the laugh.

35

Leon began to put on his face as they passed through the gate to the Fifth. From the cool, keen-eyed composure that was his normal look he scratched away prudence and good humour, and to it he added terror and a dash of foolhardiness. By the time they alighted from the palanquin he was fully inhabiting this new role, flinging a handful of coins at their bearers and then sprinting towards the quay, pulling her behind him in train. The harbour was as busy that day as on any other, nor was there any shortage of miserable men, so their passage caused no particular stir.

By the time he came rushing into the entrance Leon could add honest fatigue to feigned desperation. There was a waiting area and a woman seated inside it but Leon ignored her, shouting something incoherently and bursting into the next room. It was the modest office of a mid-level clerk, a few shelves, windows through which the bright afternoon sun and the salt air of the bay entered freely, a squat desk. Sitting behind this last was the man that Calla had seen all those long months ago, when the Aubade had first detailed her to spy on the Five-Fingered. The year sat heavy on him, or perhaps the day had already proved particularly trying. Turning to settle her in one of the chairs, Calla offered Leon the slightest nod of confirmation.

'Steadfast, thank the gods,' Leon said, turning back to face their quarry. 'Thank all the gods that you're here.'

'Who – who are you?'

'She always said that if things fell apart, then Steadfast was the man to go to. That no one else would be trusted but Steadfast. She always said that. Very often, at least.'

'Who?'

'My aunt, of course.'

'Your aunt? What the hell does your aunt have to do with this? Who are you and what are you doing in my office? Speak swiftly, before I call the Cuckoos.'

'The Cuckoos!' Leon's laugh had something manic in it, something despondent. 'I fear they'll be here swifter than either of us would like! Indeed I fear they may very well be on their way! I am Leon of the line of Aurelia, nephew of the Revered Mother,' the smile melting his face, eyes wide and mournful, and he dropped into the remaining chair. 'May the gods grant her rest on the other side.'

There was a ceramic flagon on the desk, probably not water although Calla would never learn for certain, as Steadfast poured himself a cup but did not offer anything to his guests. 'They . . . have her?'

'She would never have allowed that,' Leon said, somewhere between pride and despair. 'That was why she carried essence of toadbane round her neck.'

'A prudent woman, even to the end,' Steadfast said, and between the drink and the news he seemed to have calmed down slightly. 'Who is this?' he asked, turning suddenly to Calla.

'I couldn't leave her,' Leon half-explained. 'She's carrying my seed.'

Calla allowed the blush to spread across her face, thinking it would play to the role.

'How quickly can you call it off?' Leon continued. 'What are the passwords? Where are your messengers? There might still be time to save something.'

Steadfast took a long time to answer, working through this unexpected development. 'Why would we call it off? Your aunt's . . . noble sacrifice has surely—'

Leon's pose of desperation was alloyed with sudden, blistering contempt. 'Are you mad? If they knew of Eudokia's hand in it then they know of everything else! You've traitors in your organisation, that's the only possible explanation.'

Whatever had been in the flagon, there was a good deal less of it when Steadfast next responded, having forgone the glass entirely. 'Perhaps . . . perhaps it was bad luck, or inattention, or—'

'Bad luck?' Leon repeated, shouting this time. 'Inattention! From the Revered Mother herself? Are you daft or just drunk? If they knew enough to get her then they know everything, and the plan can't very well succeed under those circumstances. There's nothing to do but regroup, try to save some part of our forces.'

The day had already been, so far as Steadfast was concerned, quite the most stressful he had ever survived. Leon's arrival had pushed him from anxiety towards outright terror, and just then the fingernail's grip on composure that he had maintained collapsed. 'There's nothing to save!' he shouted. 'We gambled everything on this mad plan of your aunt's! There's no going back now!'

'Anything is to be preferred to seeing our forces slaughtered in ambush! You need to call off the attack.'

'And how in the hell do you suggest I do that? It's after the hour of the Kite, Pyre and his forces are already in position! Even if I could get him a message he wouldn't listen to it, pigheaded fanatic! And by now your countrymen have already reached the Perpetual Spire; there is no force on earth that can call them off. Your aunt's mad arrogance has doomed us all! Doomed us all!'

Leon had so far proved himself every bit the scion of Eudokia, maintained his facade impeccably. But this revelation was so sudden and extraordinary that for a few fractured seconds his mask fell away. 'Then there's no other choice,' Leon said, trying to cover for his indiscretion. 'We must flee the city, try and take shelter with the army beyond the walls.'

Steadfast didn't say anything for a moment, but he narrowed his eyes. 'When did they take your aunt?'

'An hour ago, perhaps two.'

'How did you get down here so quickly? Who let you use a palanquin?'

'We slipped out the back while they were busy with her, and flagged one down on the second,' Leon lied, neatly but too late. 'Why does any of this matter now?'

'By the gods,' Steadfast said, rising suddenly, 'I'm a fool.'

It was the product of instinct and of need, not of conscious forethought. Calla was sitting in her chair and then she was standing, and then the fractured top half of the ceramic flagon was powdered across Steadfast's skull. She was altogether shocked at the audacity of her own behaviour, though presumably not quite so shocked as Steadfast himself, who had collapsed backwards over his chair and now lay supine, groaning piteously.

Leon was the only one of the three who seemed unsurprised by the development, already out of his seat and moving quickly round to the other side of the desk. 'It was neatly struck, Calla,' he said, unwinding the bandage from his injured hand and gagging Steadfast tightly with it. 'Now if you would be so kind as to bring me the sash from that window curtain.'

But Calla stared down at her victim for a long time before answering. 'What for?' she said finally.

'At this point we need either to bind or kill him, and there should be enough blood for all of us come the evening.'

When they walked out of his office a few minutes later they did so hand in hand, moving upslope at a swift clip. 'Not so fast, not so fast,' Leon reminded her, 'we are two lovers out for an afternoon stroll, there is nothing that concerns us, no need for such haste.'

'Did you not hear what he said? The attack is about to begin, we've no time to waste!'

'I heard him very clearly,' Leon said through a false smile, wrapping her arm round his neatly. 'There is little enough we can do about it regardless – certainly getting murdered on our way upslope will not assist in the furtherance of our cause.'

And seeing the wisdom of this Calla managed to fall into his rhythm, though every moment she was certain there would be alarm, some cry of warning and then the entire Rung would descend upon them, the bent porters and the mean-eyed youths, though by the time they were out of sight of the docks Calla began to feel a slow ebbing of her terror.

It returned in force with the thick scent of smoke that struck her as she came within sight of the Fourth Rung, the scent of smoke and the distant sound of battle. Calla had no idea who Pyre was, but the hour of the Kite was long past, and whatever he had set in motion, it seemed, had already begun. On the Third the smoke was thinner, but still an occasional scream reached them on the wind. On the Second there were Cuckoos everywhere, it seemed, posted at the intersections of every major thoroughfare, though their presence did little to reassure Calla, indeed quite the opposite – because looking at them in their shapeless blue robes and their cudgels, readying them-selves for war, swinish faces, pink hands, looking well-fed and nervous, Calla felt certain that if these men were responsible for the safety of the Roost then things were very bad, things were very bad indeed.

By the time they had made it to Leon's quarters evening had fallen, Calla's legs ached and her throat was dry and she was too exhausted to feel fear. Leon closed the door firmly behind her and locked it, a flimsy defence but it was as much as they had. He poured a glass of wine and handed it to her absently. 'An attack on the First itself, by the gods,' Leon said, and he seemed, in a strange sort of way, almost happy. 'She dares anything, my aunt. Anything.'

'Madness,' Calla said, very much wanting to believe it. 'What force of men would be large enough to capture the First Rung?'

'Not ten thousand men,' Leon admitted, 'but they don't need to capture it, they need only distract Those Above long enough for our army to reach the gates below.'

'Will it work?'

'Eudokia thinks it can, clearly. And she is not wrong often enough to make it wise to bet against her. The more relevant question is, what can we do about it?'

'We go to the Prime,' Calla said. 'Your actions in defence of the Roost will outweigh your aunt's guilt, I'm certain.'

'And tell him what? He will learn of the attack soon enough, Calla, it may already have happened, he may already know. As for my aunt's involvement, I cannot imagine he will be in any ignorance of that either.' Leon took Calla's empty glass, refilled it, did the same for his own cup, though another few seconds more and it was once again empty. 'I am sorry, Calla,' he said, wine dampening his pale beard, all trace of his elation gone entirely. 'She was only a day ahead of us, but a day in such matters is a mile in a footrace. There is nothing left to be done but watch it all play out.'

Calla turned to stare out the window at the city below. Outside the window the Second Rung continued as it always had, unaware that their world was ending, and ending soon. People decent, or as decent as they could be, kind to their families and their acquaintances, most of them. They lived atop the bones of the less fortunate, but in this at least, Eudokia had not been wrong – everyone does, in some fashion or another, and the struggle is ultimately to extend their happiness further and further downslope, not to upend it entirely, not to see the world consumed in flames.

'There is still a chance,' Calla said quietly, saying it as if she believed it though she was not sure she did. 'Your aunt has never understood the Roost. She thinks, they all think, that it is only the Eternal. But it is not. There are those in the Roost who would struggle to destroy it, and perhaps they are not fools to try, perhaps what they have suffered justifies and even demands it. But there are those as well who would fight to save it, there are many of us, I am not alone. The Roost is not the hell that the Five-Fingered suppose it to be. There is suffering and injustice here, but there is beauty, and decency, too, and it would be better to salvage what can be saved than see the entire thing made ruin. We Roostborn are not so weak as the Revered Mother supposes. We would give aid, if called upon – a citizens' militia, one to match that which has been raised downslope. Properly armed, it might allow us to check your aunt's machinations, at least long enough for Those Above to defend against the army at our gates.'

'And who would give you the chance?'

'If the attack comes tonight, then tomorrow morning the Prime will call a meeting of the Conclave, to organise a response. I will broach the subject myself – according to their custom, and in their own tongue. Staring at annihilation, they will see the necessity of change. They will have to see,' she said. 'I will make them see.'

36

The enemy looked more like mummers than soldiers, blue summer robes that would offer no protection against blade or arrow, carrying a length of timber with a ratchet attached to the end, whirring it furiously and impotently, the buzzing grating but far from mortal. The first had been drawn a few moments after Bas had unfurled the great flag that now towered over the Spire; two of them in fact, the Empty Throne of Aeleria and below it a stretch of black canvas with a five-fingered imprint. Curiosity turned swiftly to horror, but they stalled there, failing to move on to action, precious time being lost as they tried to comprehend what had happened, as they reached out to the Others to explain it, as the system, not meant for speed under the best of circumstances, strained to operate. By the hour of the Woodcock dusk was beginning to fall across the city and there were a few hundred of these Cuckoos milling about, trying to work up the courage for a suicidal frontal assault against the Spire.

Hamilcar ran his hand up along the wall of the keep. 'By the gods, have you ever seen anything like this?'

Bas grunted.

'It's smooth as sea glass. I've been looking for an hour and I can't find the seam. It can't possibly all be one piece, can it?'

Bas was less impressed with the aesthetics of the Perpetual Spire than he was its defensibility. The only entrance was through a long, roofless gatehouse, the pathway now festooned with caltrops and traps. It opened up on a small courtyard, now barricaded, and three hundred-odd hoplitai. The tower itself jutted up seemingly for ever; looking at the steeple Bas felt himself grow dizzy. Impossible to imagine the entire thing going fallow, the whole vast edifice left to rot, floor upon floor without even a caretaker, but there it was. Without intending to the demons had allowed them a foothold in the very heart of their city. 'Is that the only thing you have to think about right now?' Bas asked gruffly.

They stood on a sort of balcony, which circled fully around the third storey of the tower. It offered a good view of the Roost below, and it offered Hamilcar and his men an ideal line of fire for anyone trying to retake it. No, Bas had to admit, it was an eminently defensible spot, you could scarce have dreamed up a better. Without siege engines it would take an army of ten thousand men to force it, and even then the contest would be uncertain. Ten thousand men or how many demons?

'We'll know they're coming when they stop whirling those damn noisemakers,' Hamilcar grumbled. 'You are sure they have no bows?'

'They have no bows.'

'Why?'

'The Others do not kill from afar. They think it beneath them.'

'And the humans?'

'Are not allowed weapons.'

'What sort of a place is this?'

Bas did not have an answer. His new adjutant returned

from the front barricades, queried Bas on a number of minor issues, then saluted and went back downstairs. Staurakios, his name was, a competent man of the Thirteenth, though Bas found himself wishing that he had Isaac there to rely upon. Twenty years had made for a shorthand between them that was near to telepathy, and this was not the moment for miscue or error.

'What's that?' Hamilcar asked, pointing towards a distant portion of the skyline.

Squinting, Bas could make it out, a sphere of white and gold that caught the last rays of the afternoon sun and threw them back twice as bright, but his ignorance allowed for no answer. 'I have no idea.'

But Hamilcar would not be put off. 'Like some . . . gigantic fountain.' His bow was ashwood, with silver rattan, and it hung limply at his side. 'Have you ever seen anything like it?'

'You know I haven't.'

'Can you imagine how long it must have taken to build any of this?'

'Now's hardly the time for playing tourist. They're mustering to charge.'

And indeed they were. The noisemakers had finally gone silent, as if doing so would obscure their intentions. It was not the guards' sole sign of incompetence; indeed it was matched by every other aspect of the attack, which went forward only by the loud haranguing of their leader. Bas did not know the language but he could guess the thrust of it, something about home and country, and beneath that the presumed certainty that the demons would look with disfavour on cowardice. It proved sufficient to send a rough hundred men sprinting down the narrow entranceway, but it was fitful, desultory, it was an assault by men prepared altogether to see their efforts end in failure. Hamilcar waited until a mass of them clogged the narrow corridor and then he gave the signal, the first volley finding purchase in tight-packed flesh, the guards screaming, bleeding, dying, fleeing – those who could flee at least. The hoplitai below shouted their contempt, and waited for a few minutes to see if another charge would be forthcoming, though Bas knew that it would not.

And now to the other sounds of the evening, to the beat of the noisemakers and the crickets, were added the ragged screams of the wounded. To Bas's mind there was nothing that more thoroughly proved the uselessness of the city guard than that the survivors made no effort to save their wounded comrades, the more lightly wounded limping or crawling back to safety, the rest loudly lamenting the bitterness of their fate.

Bas did not care for cities, though he had seen more of them than any man who wasn't a sailor or a diplomat; seen the great cathedrals and mansions of Aeleria, the wide streets and the wretched and miserable poor that lived on them. Had seen Dycia, though only after he had helped to burn and loot it, the great temple aflame, stained windows bursting from the heat, endless wealth spilled out into the streets like blood from punctured flesh. But Bas had never seen anything like this. Bas had never dreamed that there were such things as this. Of course Bas was not a dreamer, in fact he had come to realise over the years that he was quite the least imaginative man in existence, as if the gods had decreed its lack in compensation for the many qualities that he possessed to a super- or near superhuman degree. But even if he had been a poet or a minstrel, Bas did not think he could have imagined such beauty. Trying to describe it, even to himself, Bas found he could only compare it to other, unrelated things – a woman dancing, rich autumn foliage shaken loose in a crisp breeze, the crackle of a warm fire, the distant and half-recalled touch of his mother.

At the Nightjar's hour an Eternal finally arrived; Bas could read it in the complexion of the troop of city guard as if on the face of a second-rate cardplayer. They did not cheer but they stood up straighter, putting up a front. He caught a glimpse of her and his heart beat so rapid in his chest that for a moment he thought it would burst, and then he blinked and squinted and it returned gradually to normal.

'She looks a great deal like yours,' Hamilcar observed.

'They all look the same,' Bas said, though it wasn't true.

The Eternal who was not the Sentinel of the Southern Reach, a neighbour perhaps, or just someone who happened to be passing by, stood for a long time before the entrance to the Spire, at the extreme edge of bow range. When she came forward it was without warning and with preternatural speed, as fast as a galloping horse or very nearly, the first volley of arrows mistimed, finding only her footprints. She was unarmoured and barely armed, nothing but a borrowed truncheon with which to assault the array of hoplitai before her, but they did not know fear, the demons, or at least they did not show it. She made it to the top of the barricade with one leap, as a child might stone-step across a stream, looking down at the mass of men below with vague disdain. Sprinting down the length of the parapet, graceful steps along the narrows, the club falling and rising and rising and falling, skulls shattering, teeth scattered into the dust, hoplitai screaming. A thrust half-pike was grabbed just below the tip, ripped from the hand of its wielder, brought in a wide scattering arch against Bas's soldiers, drawing blood and snapping from the force of the blow. The feather that appeared suddenly in her shoulder proved no impediment to her movement; indeed she seemed not even to notice it, her cudgel breaking against the skull of a hoplitai, the cudgel and the skull as well, but she noticed the second arrow, tearing through the soft flesh of her cheek and out against the back of her jaw, barbed arrowhead pinning her head against her shoulder, distracting her just long enough for a pike to enter the flesh below her knee. Collapsing forward into the scrum, not screaming because they never screamed but still fighting, one four-fingered hand grabbing the head of a hoplitai on the way down, crushing it as an egg, and then the unavoidable press of men, the downward fall of a short blade, a hand severed, the corpse lost in the mass.

With the death of the first Eternal the hoplitai let loose a roar of triumph, blood-soaked and savage, and after not so long a moment the head appeared atop a half-pike, eyes of uniform cerulean staring back at the city she had once owned. Bas was used to the cruelty of men and paid no attention, occupied by other tasks, doing the grim maths in his head: eight men, maybe ten it had taken to bring her down, and she neither armed nor armoured. What happened when they came with their Roost-forged steel, with their many-headed lances, with their swords so long and so sharp?

Hamilcar's face was ashen black and unsmiling. 'She was faster than your Sentinel.'

'She was faster than the Sentinel let us think,' Bas said, wiping sweat off his face, an absurd moment of vainglory for a creature who hoped to see him dead.

'I have never seen anything move so fast. How many of them are there?'

'Thousands.'

'Thousands?'

Bas did not repeat himself.

And yet they did not come. They did not come! The sun passed away entirely, evening taking full grip of the cityscape, the hoplitai reinforcing the barricades higher and ever higher, the Cuckoos milling about uncertainly like eunuchs outside a whorehouse. Against the damp ochre light of the street lamps was mixed a faint but growing crimson, as the promised bands of partisans in the city continued their brutal business, raids on the custodians and the other forces of order, anarchy blooming swiftly across the metropolis.

'They burn their own city?' Hamilcar asked.

'It seems so.'

'These are lovely allies we've acquired. They reek of madness like an outhouse reeks of shit.'

'They've done a competent job so far.'

'Fanatics fight well,' Hamilcar admitted, 'and die better. That is the sum extent of their ability.'

'Do we need them to do more than that?'

'We don't. Though if I were a citizen of the Roost, I might

find myself wondering about what sort of city they're likely to be living in come the morrow.'

'You aren't a citizen of the Roost,' Bas said, the two of them leaning over the edge of the balcony and none else within earshot, 'nor it is likely you'll live to see the morrow.'

'It doesn't look promising, does it?'

Bas spat over the side in answer. The night was clear, the views of the constellations unobscured by cloud, the cluster of lights reflecting from the city below, which seemed the mirror and the obverse of the sky's naked glory.

'Have you ever seen anything like it?' Hamilcar asked quietly.

'No,' Bas admitted.

And still hours passed, and still nothing happened, still the Eternal failed to respond in force, still the city guard dithered. The Owl's hour chimed out across the cityscape, towering chronological edifices echoing across the Rung. Hearing them and wondering at their construction, Bas could understand why rumour and myth had turned the Birds into something that resembled gods, had credited them with the ability to fly or spit fire. Because here was the product of a race so utterly alien as to defy measure with the works of man, as one would not think to compare a rat's nest to the Senate Hall.

They arrived finally, deep into the evening, though Bas could make them out clearly in the bright light of the torches and the basked fires that lit the Rung. It was not a concerted effort, so far as he could tell, only the independent reaction of the immediate neighbours, a half-dozen Eternal assuming themselves sufficient to put to flight whatever quantity of men had taken up residence uninvited within their homes. Five were clad in full plate, intricate as a costume mask, leering heads for pauldrons, space in the comb through which their tendril-like stalks of hair escaped. The sixth wore a set of loose silk robes, and had a sword the length of a spear in a scabbard on his back.

'Finally,' Hamilcar said, though you might almost have thought he'd have been willing to wait longer. His archers were arraigned in three tiers along the balcony, and he gave the order to make ready, though there was not a member of that grim company who had failed to note the presence of the demons, nor questioned how best to receive their arrival.

The Eternal stood in a line and conversed for a short few moments in their mad foreign tongue. The unarmoured one faded back into the crowd of Cuckoos and then the evening-clad city, leaving his five fellows alone to spearhead a frontal assault.

'Where is he going?' Hamilcar asked.

'That's a good question.'

'There is no back passage?'

'Did you see one?'

'No, but that doesn't mean there isn't one.'

'There isn't one.'

'Does he mean to scale the tower?'

'Smooth as sea glass, you said it yourself. And I saw no climbing gear. Did you?'

'No. Then what's he doing?'

There proved to be no further time for discussion. They had given no war cry at the battle of Scarlet Fields and they gave no war cry now either, but the themas offered one in counter, a bellow and a curse, the battle finally joined. Full plate but they were fast as a sprinting man and footsure despite the dark, darting through and around and above the caltrops and traps that had been prepared for them, and the bodies of the dead and dying Cuckoos. The wave of arrows broke uselessly against the bright chrome of their armour, save one lucky shot that fell through the thin visor of a great-helm, the demon beneath collapsing like a puppet with its wires snipped. But the rest made it to the barricades without revealing any serious injury. The first, a behemoth in blue and argent, leaped clean over the barricade, landing in heavy-shod boots amidst the mass of hoplitai – though it paid for its temerity, for its boldness, soldiers collapsing round him, dying and screaming but fighting furiously all the same.

That left only three, and three was not enough, not even for them; they were mad with pride, they were arrogant as strutting roosters but still they could not have imagined that five of them alone would be sufficient to cause a breach in the defences.

What, then, did they think?

Bas turned his back from the battle and gave a shout of warning, sprinting towards the far corner of the porch, his blade coming out of its sheath but too late, too late. Between the ground and the balcony were three storeys, an easy sixty links, but there was a *thud* and a hand on the ledge and then the thing atop entire, looking larger than even it really was, and it was terribly large – it towered over the Dycian archers as a man above a child, robes billowing, torchlight reflecting back eyes of bright sterling, the falling cascade of its hair like the mane of a lion. Before even loosing its blade it had killed a man, tossed him from the battlements one-handed, the loud scream audible though not the sound of impact, and then its sword was free and upright, stretching forever into the evening, the curled end mirroring the sliver of the new moon high above, then sweeping down into the flesh below, blood and bone and flesh scattered like grass cuttings.

Brave men, the Dycians, veterans of combat across the breadth of the continent. They ran screaming, ran screaming or died swiftly, all thoughts of defence lost entire to fear, none willing to contend with the monster, as if to stand against a flood or a wildfire. Bas shoved his way through the stream until he was in front of it, taller and thicker and more terrible than Einnes, blade about to dispatch another archer to whatever grim fate awaited him. Bas caught the strike with his own sword and he flung his shoulder against the giant and he came back again as if from a stone wall, dazed as much from the blow as from the discovery that here for perhaps the first time in his long life he had finally met something stronger than himself. The demon advanced fearlessly and without pause, the implied contempt nearly proving justified in the next instant, Bas deflecting the great sweep of the thing's sword but only barely and then giving ground, rapid and incautious, turning his foot against something and struggling to keep upright. He'd have been a corpse had not two hoplitai found the courage to assault the demon, from the back of course, for who was brave or mad enough to think to best one of them in honest combat? An admirable effort, though futile; the demon heard or sensed or intuited their presence and turned from Bas just long enough to deliver two swift blows, the whistling of its blade clear to Bas despite the sounds of battle that echoed through the evening, the screams of men and the clatter of steel but mainly the screams of men.

Their deaths bought Bas the half-moment he needed to reassert himself, and when the demon turned back round to deliver the killing stroke it was Bas who took the offensive, Bas whose Roost-forged blade gleamed bright against the moon and the torchlight, the demon parrying and twisting out of range. Stronger and faster, but its sword was prettier than it was useful, too long to wield effectively in defence, fashion at the expense of utility, and it had to keep giving ground until they were back near the parapets, out of view of the battle that was raging at the front gate. Not that Bas had any attention to spare regardless, every bit of focus and energy reserved exclusively towards the demon's end, an end that was coming soon now, the thing too sure of itself, the thing not having known that Bas was just as swift and terrible as ever. The Caracal surged forward in the next exchange and the other came off the worst, pushed back further, to the edge of the balcony, and Bas roaring and the point of his blade searching for the demon's flesh, pirouetting out of the way neatly, the opening a feint, Bas moving forward recklessly and soon to pay for it. Bas not the only one who knew something of combat, and how many decades had the demon practised that last move, how many centuries? It wasn't really fair, but fair or not Bas would be dead in a moment, pivoting to try to face the thing but not fast enough, he would die in the moonlight, and not so terrible a thing – it came to everyone, and not all of them in the moonlight either.

Hamilcar's arrow – Bas did not see him shoot it but he

knew it was Hamilcar's, could have been no one else's – jutted
out from the demon's breast, fletching tight against flesh. And
still it came forward, Bas barely managing to deflect the next
blow. The demon dodged the second arrow somehow, a whistling but no *thump* to accompany it, an impossible feat accomplished neatly, though still it required the thing to contort
itself and Bas responded, took the offered opening, a wide
scattering of blood against the clear walls of the Spire. With
torso half-severed it now showed signs of injury, shifting backwards on unsteady legs, and their insides were at least the
same, the pink of intestine in the torchlight, the pure white
of bone. Still it caught Bas's next blow with the edge of its
sword, and the one it offered in return was no half-hearted
attempt at violence, would have taken the top off Bas's head
if Bas had not been as swift as Bas always was. Hamilcar's
next arrow settled the matter; a spot of dark against the dark
and then the point past teeth and tongue and through its
throat and breaking against the demon's spine, death swallowed whole as it collapsed down on one knee. And still the
demon's eyes were fluttering, and still with some dim sentience
it struggled forward, until Bas's next stroke removed its head
from its shoulders.

It died silently, it died in magnificent and glorious futility,
like all of them. The battle for the front gate was over by then,
Bas knew without looking, its only purpose having been to offer
a distraction for this attack. The Spire would hold, Bas knew
that as well, Those Above would not respond with sufficient
swiftness, not before the full mass of the Aelerian army arrived
at the walls the next morning. Whatever their strength, they
could not bring it to bear, too old and stagnant to react to
events as they were unfolding. And the city that spread out
below them, a city exquisite and wondrous beyond imagination,
a city the sort of which Bas had not thought existed, which had
been not even a dream to him before he had seen it, that city
would burn, that city would sunder, that city would drown in
the blood of its inhabitants. That city would die just as surely

as the demon had died, just as bravely and with no more purpose.

'Damn you, Caracal,' Hamilcar said, coming to stand above the corpse he had made. 'Damn you to hell.'

37

When Eudokia awoke the next morning she stared out of her open window, looking for evidence of her machinations in the skyline, some hint of the bloodshed that was, one way or the other, sure to come. As yet she saw no evidence of its arrival, but she did not suppose that would long remain the case. There was a steam shower attached to her bedroom, part of the slate of luxuries that were ubiquitous upslope but which had no corollary anywhere else in the world of men, and she spent a long time luxuriating in it. If things went according to plan, it would be a long time before she'd have the opportunity for another. If things went badly, it would be her last altogether. Then she dressed and went down to breakfast, finding Jahan outside her door as always.

Leon was waiting for her in the small garden in the centre of the complex, sitting at the wooden table where she took her breakfast most mornings. Whatever was going on in the rest of the city, if her grim strategems had blossomed or failed entirely, it had not affected the good service of her house-slaves, and a tray of bread and fruit and clear water awaited her.

He seemed to have slept little. His face was pale and drawn, but he rose and offered a swift bow as she sat. 'Revered Mother.'

'Nephew,' she said. 'Have you eaten?'

'I'm not hungry.'

Eudokia curled a tab of butter onto a chunk of bread, drizzled it with honey and handed it over.

'I've no appetite,' he said again.

'Surely you can manage a few bites?'

And indeed after a moment of staring at her he consumed it swiftly, and washed it down with most of the flagon of water that had been left her. 'I have spent the morning wondering what I was to hope for from today's events.'

'Did you reach any conclusions?'

'The one hand holds the death of tens of thousands of my countrymen, perhaps the destruction of the nation. The other would see the end of a species entire, the world they have built, and the death of countless innocents under their sway. They seem neither rosy options.'

'You've pieced it together, then?'

'The essential points. You supplied a revolutionary group within the walls of the Roost, you pointed them towards acts of violence meant to provoke a similar response. You baited them and led them to the slaughter, provocation provoking provocation, till all hope of reconciliation became impossible.'

'It was Steadfast you turned?'

'Tricked, more like. He was a fool.'

'We make use of the pawns available to us.'

'Was that all this was? A game? Something to occupy your own genius? Surely you do not expect me to believe that all this is revenge for your poor Phocas, a man dead a quarter-century of whom I've never heard you speak?'

'Don't suppose you know every secret that lies in the heart of the Revered Mother,' Eudokia said, eyes clouding over. 'Not a day has passed that I have not mourned for my husband, and of what we might have done together. But it's true, what comes today has little of revenge, nor can I claim honest hatred of Those Above. In fact, apart from some ultimately superficial dissimilarities, they seem virtually identical to our own species. One would think that their longer span might make them wiser, or at least more prudent, given that they have to deal with the ramifications of their own foolishness, rather than passing the injury on to the unborn. But in fact the opposite seems true. They float along on the surface of the moment like children, with no more reason or purpose.'

'Then it was simply mad ambition? You saw so immense a prize within reach, and could not but try and grasp it? So much death in service of your own grandeur! So much death!'

Eudokia looked at him for a long time, longer than the normal give-and-take of a conversation ought to allow, long enough that Leon, even having steeled himself for conflict, grew uncomfortable. Then she brought the back of her hand up to his face, laid it against his cheek. Leon, more surprised than had she struck him, flinched at the unexpected moment of kindness. 'I find myself saying this very rarely – but you overrate me.'

'Do I?' Leon asked, brushing her hand away. 'Ten years at least you've been planning this, since Dycia fell, and then the long campaigns out west. A masterful stratagem, Auntie, I confess freely there was never in all the world a thing more clever than you. I hope you find the ocean of blood to come sufficient reward for your genius.'

'There was no death before Eudokia? There was no hatred, there was no savagery or avarice? No man ever looked at his neighbour and felt the edge of his hatchet with his thumb? No man ever dreamed of a life without labour, of a life lived upon the toil of others? It was Eudokia and Eudokia alone who brought evil into this world? A wise captain trims his sails with the wind – do you imagine that there is anyone so clever, so powerful, as to force upon the infinite chaos of the world a pattern that is unnatural to it? What happens today was certain to happen. Perhaps I sped it up a few decades, perhaps not even that. The

Eternal . . . an inapt name I'm afraid. That which is green will grow black. Like bubbles of soap, we expand and burst and leave nothing more behind.'

'There is nothing else? No ethic, no purpose? By the gods, what a bleak portrait you paint.'

'The gods?' Eudokia gave a mocking little laugh. 'Listen close, child, I will tell you of the gods, of the single commandment they have written clear across all creation. Are you ready? The strong devour the weak. It is the way of all living things, of every creature that flies, walks, crawls, slithers or swims. The weed strangles the flower, the ant eats the cricket, the wolf the stag. And we? We humans? We eat everything. The Others were strong once, and in their strength they made slaves of us. They are weak now, old and trembling, and what they have built but cannot hold will become ours. In time, no doubt, Aeleria will falter as well, decaying from its own richness, and some fiercer, crueller peoples will usurp our position. But at least I won't be around to see it.'

'You're wrong,' Leon said, standing suddenly. 'There is more to life than this endless savagery. And you count your victory too swiftly. Calla and I have deciphered your stratagems, broken your spy. Even now she is at their Conclave, revealing your betrayal. There is still time to stop this, to halt the conflict to come. Still time for reconciliation between the peoples of the Roost, still time to save it from destruction.'

And now for the first time Eudokia could hear the first hint of her bloody yield, a distant scream; somewhere nearby something terrible was happening to someone – but then, is this not always the case? Does not every passing moment bear witness to cruelty, barbarity, brutality?

'War is not the wind, boy,' Eudokia said, shaking her head sadly, 'it does not change its course at a moment's notice. You have doomed her with your innocence. I had hoped to save her, as much because I liked her as because of your . . . obvious affection. But your intransigence has made that impossible. That brave, foolish child. That foolish, foolish child. Raise the city?

The Eternal to redeem their bondsmen? The rivers to run backwards, the mountains to collapse. The hawk does not share meat with men, and I fear you have seen the last of Calla of the Red Keep.'

Leon swallowed hard and turned his face to a sneer, as if contempt would be protection against the misfortune his aunt had predicted. But he did not wear it long, indeed it began to quiver almost as soon as it had formed, his eyes wide and wet, and then he turned and sprinted out of the garden.

Eudokia would wish ever after that she had done something to stop him.

38

The Conclave was full for the first time in human memory. The white marble benches were crammed with the flesh of the Eternal, so busy that the lesser servants were forced to take up space outside, clustered tightly around the entrance. Never before in her lifetime, perhaps not since the last war against Aeleria, perhaps not even then, had so many Eternal been present in one place at one time.

There were so few of them – by the Founders, there were so few. Enough to choke the Conclave, but not enough to fill a corner of a corner of the Second Rung. There were neighbourhoods downslope that Calla did not know the name of, which held within their boundaries five or ten times their number. The Aelerian host, resting outside of the city and, terrifyingly, having taken up residence inside as well, were surely many times as large.

They did not look fearful, though whether that was because they did not yet appreciate the danger, or that they were bold enough to face it without flinching, Calla could not say. Given that he had been predicting this event or something similar for the better part of the last five years, given that he was now enjoying the rare honour of having his madness confirmed as truth, the Prime seemed very little pleased. He began the meeting swiftly and with a minimum of ceremony, and when he rose to speak he turned directly to the heart of the matter.

'Siblings,' he began. 'The Lady of the House of Rose and Sorrow avers the Aelerians are less than five cables from the Roost. If not checked their riders will be at the foot of the Roost in hours, and their infantry by the morning. I am informed by the chancellor that downslope is in rebellion from the docks to the Third Rung, and that every available custodian is required to stop it from spreading any further. Likewise, the rumours you have heard are true. By some or other stratagem, the Dayspans have fortified the Perpetual Spire, and a force of unknown size now rests within walls of the First Rung. The custodians spent the night trying to retake it, without success. A number of our siblings have fallen in the same attempt.'

'By the Founders,' said the Lord of the House of Kind Lament, 'we ought have done as the Lord of the Ebony Towers bid us, and drowned the locusts in their own blood.'

'We ought have done many things differently,' the Prime said imperiously. 'But there is no time to discuss guilt or past foolishness.'

'The external threat must be dealt with first.' Having been wrong in every past prediction did not prevent the Lord of the House of Kind Lament from further augury. They were not so different from humans as they liked to believe, Calla thought then, though she was unsure to take comfort or warning in this fact. 'We scatter the locusts below, then we return to deal with their counterparts on the First.'

'The forces inside the Roost are surely waiting for just such an attempt,' answered the Prime. 'Would you leave our hatchlings to the mercy of the Aelerians? We cannot rely on the custodians alone to defend the Rung.'

'Then we divide our forces. We keep a body here to ensure that the Spire is quarantined, and the rest of us ride down to dispose of the Dayspans.'

The Sentinel of the Southern Reach rose to speak then, the missing stalk of her hair seeming very distinct. 'Fifty thousand Aelerians march on us this day. They have spent two years supping on the corpse of Salucia, and they come well-nourished but unsated. Whatever my siblings may have convinced themselves of in this long autumn of foolishness, they will not break at the sight of our forces, nor at the first charge. We will need every lance if we hope for victory.'

'The Lady of the Ivory Towers has spent such time among the locusts as to confuse herself with their champion. However large the army they have amassed below, it is yet an army of humans, no more concern than an army of rats.'

'The Sentinel,' she corrected. 'And the Lord of the House of Kind Lament is every drop as foolish and blind as I ever remembered. Should we see tomorrow's sun, I will settle his insult at the courses.'

'Enough,' the Prime said. 'This is no moment to waste on strife. It is unthinkable to allow the Rung to remain unprotected. A contingent must remain to hold the First, and another must be offered to the custodians to try and put down the rebellion which is taking place below. What is left will ride out to confront the army at our gates.'

'That will not be enough,' the Sentinel answered.

'It is the only option available to us.'

'If you will forgive me, my Lords and Ladies, that is an alternative yet to be examined.'

It was Calla's voice, though she only realised it when they all at once turned upon her, row upon row of unblinking, single-faceted eyes, terror as though a yawning sinkhole had opened up below her. Since waking up that morning with Leon's head upon her shoulder, since long before, she had been planning this speech, choosing her words, but in the moment itself she found her mind blank. It was the language itself that inspired her beyond this first exquisite moment of fear. A quarter-century of practice but Calla had never dared enunciate above a whisper, and she discovered then that it was not meant to be spoken at all in fact but to be shouted, to be sung. It was not language but a prayer, a poem, a love-ode. The words came all of their own, somehow, the Eternal's language but in her own voice, her own dialect, as much her own creation as a newborn child.

'I am Calla of the Red Keep, whose family has faithfully served the Prime for seven generations. The Roost is the only home I have ever known, the only home I have ever wished. I have always imagined that in time an eighth member of my line would one day assume the role of seneschal, would perform the duties and obligations of the office as had their mother and grandfather and their ancestors before them. That our rituals and traditions, hallowed by age, would remain inviolate and unchanging.'

In her brief pause Calla could hear the scattered droplets of the Source falling against its basin, the attendant humans quiet by custom and made doubly so by fear, the Eternal watching her with pregnant and unknowable silence.

'That was an error, one that we have all been operating beneath. Today we see that the Roost was a far more fragile thing than we had ever supposed. The humans downslope – ignored, oppressed, abused – have taken shelter in the false promises of the Aelerians, and the result is as you have seen. The enemies of the Roost swarm towards our gates, and will soon be inside. As humans were the cause, so they will be the remedy. You say that you have not the numbers to assault the Aelerian armies below and to protect the upper Rungs simultaneously, but all the while you hold your hand upon an unsheathed blade, a vast army upon which you might call. The subjects of the Roost are more than fearfully passive, or made monstrous with misfortune. There are many like me who would fight for their homes, who would die to stop it from becoming a satellite of some foreign power. Equipped with weapons from your armouries, they could maintain the quarantine here on the First Rung, they might even be strong enough to halt the spread of violence below. They would rise to meet our mutual foes, they would fight to protect what is theirs – if their service was recognised, if they were called upon. With a militia drawn from the First and Second Rungs, you would not need to split your forces. You could meet the enemies of the Roost with the full might of your army, rather than piecemeal. No doubt there are many among you who imagine such a thing impossible, but if today has taught us nothing else, it is that humans are capable of more than you suppose.

'An audacious proposal, my Lords and Ladies, as is my presenting it. But crisis demands audacity and there can be no question but that we are at that moment. Our sole certainty is that by tomorrow morning the Roost will be changed irrevocably. Either it will be consumed in fire and blood, the homes of the Eternal become the abode of the Aelerians, millennia of history undone entire – or it will be transformed, reborn into a city all of whose members are called upon to serve it to their fullest, and to demand an equal share in their labour. A city in which Those Above and Below strive in concert towards the betterment of both species. We will set out on this journey together, or we will die alone.'

And as she came to the last word she found that she could almost see this future unfolding below her, a syncretic fusion of the two species, a city undivided, without rancour, where the hideous misery of the lower Rungs was ameliorated by the vast wealth that resided above it, in which the superiority of Those Above was tempered with justice and even mercy, in which the splendours of the Roost were accented with freedom, a jewel more priceless even than that which graced the Prime's diadem.

It was a beautiful dream – Calla was privileged to die staring at it.

She did not feel the blow, or only for a short, shattered instant, her neck snapping like a dry twig. And it was well for her that she died so quickly, because what was done to her person after by the nearby Eternal, and even those somewhat more distant, was cruel beyond measure, ripping and tearing with their strength that was so much greater than that of a man. And also because, with the darkness falling so swiftly, she never knew that the first strike had come from the Prime, hoping, perhaps, to end quickly the suffering that Calla's temerity was certain to cause, or simply as savage and blood-mad as the rest of his species, his and not his alone.

39

J ust after the hour of the Eagle, with the sun high and hot in the sky, a snaking line of metal and flesh descended from the Source to the main gates on the Fifth Rung, a sudden pulse passing down through the metropolis, rattling crockery off the walls of Second Rung mansions and shuddering the foundations of slum tenements, riding straight through the barricades, even the fiercest Dead Pigeon not so mad as to try and obstruct its passage. Twenty years since Those Above had gone to war, the kaleidoscopic fluttering gonfalons, the horses monstrous and spiteful, lances couched and cruel-looking, thousands of riders in synchronous and perfect union. The fate of the city, the fate of the nation, the fate of much of the world, would be decided in the coming few hours – it would be seen whether this army of heavy cavalry would be sufficient to break the Aelerian line, and forestall in blood the future that was to come.

Some short time later Pyre and a handful of Dead Pigeons marched upslope from their base at the top of the Fourth. The

Roost had been in open rebellion since the night before, and thus far everything had gone according to Pyre's plan, everything had followed within the clear rut of destiny. The custodians were weak and undisciplined and represented no serious threat to Pyre and his men. Here and there in the savage skirmishes that had taken place across the Rung an Eternal had made their presence known, in the blood and brain and bone of humans, but they had been carried down by the sheer mass of men against which they contended. Their casualties had been terrible, Courage and Mace, Badger and Grim lost when they retreated from the walls, Frost and his entire cell slaughtered by a single Eternal. But they had martyred themselves gloriously, and their losses had been made good ten times over by the army that had arisen, as Pyre knew it would, from the cobblestones and the slurp itself, men ignorant of the word but willing to die in its service.

Upslope the city was a certain sort of quiet, a silence that was more than the absence of sound, which seemed almost its own active presence, a great beast lurking over the spires. There were no guards on the gates to the Third Rung, the Cuckoos posted there and across most of the rest of the lower portion of the Roost fled. There were two Cuckoos manning the gate to the Second, though they bolted at the sight of Pyre and his bodyguard. He gave no thought to pursuing. It was far too late to be concerning himself with any individual traitor; indeed now that the contest seemed over or nearly, it was time to turn attention from vengeance and towards forgiveness. Without Those Above to torment and beguile them, the people of the Roost would be able to live in harmony with one another.

Though there was little suggestion of pardon in the pose, face and tone of Eudokia, Revered Mother, when they met in the antechamber of her mansion high up on the Second. At her side was the Parthan, chubby-cheeked, eyes brown as chocolate, breasts like a whore, hands that might have wrapped comfortably round an aged oak. At his side hung a curved cutting sword, the make of it unfamiliar to Pyre but the purpose clear enough, of the blade and the man who carried it. A killer, Pyre

knew from a glance, and wondered why his presence was needed
if Eudokia was so suitably protected, his presence or the presence of the four men he had brought along.

Pyre had arranged for a safe house nearby, on a further corner
of the Second Rung. It was a reasonable precaution. It was
possible that the Eternal or their misguided human chattel might
seize on Eudokia as some reasonable proxy for the forces outside
their gates and, regardless of the violence that was to come, it
would do well to keep the Revered Mother protected.

'I was told there would be a third,' Pyre began. 'A young man?'

Eudokia's eyes were stones, and her mouth was a line, and
neither revealed anything of what she thought. 'It is only the two
of us.'

Pyre nodded and led them out of the gate and onto the main
road. He set two of his men half a block ahead and put two half
a block behind, and between them he supposed himself safe from
attack.

A reasonable supposition, though it would soon become
clear that he feared danger from the wrong point of origin.
'I take it by that last caterwaul that our tormentors have
evacuated the city?' Eudokia asked, as if the matter was of
only casual import.

'Such was our assumption.'

'And the Spire?'

'It holds, Revered Mother, at least it held according to our last
report.'

'Excellent, excellent. All moot of course, if my stepson can't
manage his end of it outside the walls. But then again, if the
thing was certain there would be no point in doing it.'

The street down which they walked was narrow and formed
of perfectly fitted slate. On either side of the thoroughfare a
clear, thin trickle of water had been diverted to act as moat or
adornment for the buttressing houses, things of hardwood and
polished stone, lovely and unassuming. Here and there were bright
little spots of colour flaring out against the afternoon sun, purple
silk awnings, flags and streamers fluttering in the wind. The

windows were shut tight, the doors barred. The smell of smoke in the air was strong but not yet overwhelming.

'It does not quite seem so terrible, does it Pyre, the First of His Line?' Eudokia asked. 'It does not seem, at first glance, like a thing which needs to be destroyed.'

'A cage is no less confining for being made of gold.'

'Return in a week and knock at the door of one of these cages, and ask the women and children cringing inside if they preferred servitude beneath the Birds to their new-found freedom.'

Pyre was clever with his hands, and he was more than clever as a tactician and as a leader of men, but words had never been his strength, and after nearly a straight day of labour he would have preferred to remain silent. 'Good fortune borne on the backs of their species and their kin,' he snapped. 'For every one of these happy householders there are a hundred families on the Fifth Rung starving and dying and rotting in misery.'

'Correct, exactly,' Eudokia agreed, seeming pleased. 'They've enjoyed themselves long enough. It's your turn now.'

'In the age to come humanity will know of no distinction,' Pyre said, again quoting from the prophet, 'a happy family, without division or rancour.'

Eudokia paused for a moment, staring at him 'I think that was quite the most foolish thing I've ever heard anyone say.'

But Pyre did not respond to this provocatio, and Eudokia continued hobbling onward. 'And where is Edom, on this glorious occasion? Where is Edom, at the moment his long dream has finally come to fruition?'

'Safe,' Pyre answered confidently. 'His is too valuable a presence to risk until the outcome is certain. Should the demons rally and break our line, he will be needed to renew again the struggle.'

'And you will not?'

'There are others who can do as I do. The word is what matters, and the word speaks most honestly from Edom.'

'Truth is to be preferred over even modesty, in my experience, Pyre, the First of His Line, and you will find that there is no virtue which cannot become a vice if taken beyond its proper boundaries.

Take loyalty, for instance – an admirable quality, necessary for the stability and the progress of civilisation, frequently and easily carried beyond all objective reason.'

'Therein we disagree, Revered Mother,' Pyre said. He more stalked than strolled, and his eyes flashed round for signs of threat as happy distraction from the conversation. 'Loyalty is the essence of the Five-Fingered. Loyalty to our species, loyalty to our descendants, loyalty to one another.'

'The essence, you say? The very essence? This continued fidelity towards a man who sought to kill you is more masochistic than admirable.'

Half of the escort were twenty paces ahead of him, and half were twenty paces behind, and none seemed to hear this blasphemy. Pyre bit down against his fury, felt his tongue give way between his teeth, took his hand off the hilt of his sword. 'That was a foolish joke.'

'Levity is one of the pleasures which make existence bearable, and Eudokia has been known on occasion to let a jest slip into the wild. But that was not one of them.'

'If my men heard you speak in such a fashion,' Pyre said, still quietly, 'I am not at all sure that I could stop them from hurting you.'

'I suspect Jahan would have better fortune,' Eudokia said, 'though it seems best not to discover either way, which is why this discussion does not include them. Oh, come, boy, so far you've been nothing but clever, and perhaps even a bit more than that. A decade now I've dribbled money into Edom's accounts, wondering all the time if I was not pissing away silver. I had anticipated it would take another five years to build to this moment, but you and your little army have brought my timeline forward half a decade. Best for all of us.' Eudokia halted for a moment, rubbing at her knee for relief – or effect. 'I'm scarce sure I'd have been capable of running things by then. Age is implacable, Pyre, the First of His Line.' She began moving again, and returned to her monologue. 'As for this false modesty, it is a delusion which you and you alone labour beneath. Your confederates look to you, rightly, as the source of their success. The people praise your name as a slayer of demons and a leader of men. I assure you Edom is entirely cognisant of your qualities, indeed I suppose he thought of little else in the days before arranging to have you murdered. Curious, perhaps even fitting, that it proved to be this attempt on your life that would ensure your pre-eminence among your people. But then, if I am to confess bluntly, I have never considered Edom to be worthy of this reputation you and the rest seem to have granted him. He has a very square jaw, and his hair is distinct-looking. He has some modest talent with epigram. There are less clever men, certainly, though this hardly qualifies someone for leadership. But then again, one must never underrate the willingness of fate to thrust an individual beyond their proper station. Mark my words, you will live long enough to see Edom's name used in blessing, to see him named prophet and called saint. In thirty years children living in the city will struggle to fall asleep the night before the festival of Edom's name day, will wake the next morning to toys and sweet treats, will watch the mummers perform a pageant in his honour. Though, if you act wisely in the next few hours, that signal honour will pale beside the praise heaped upon your own name. How many sons will be named Pyre in the generation to come! Babes across the great length of the Roost!' Eudokia had a light, sharp laugh, like the point of a stiletto, and Pyre did not realise his hand was back on the hilt of his weapon until he noticed the Parthan doing the same, his curved blade already a few finger-widths out from its sheath, his eyes effortless and uncaring and dark as night.

'I would again advise you to do nothing which would worry Jahan,' Eudokia said, a small dash of concern in her voice, 'it would set my plans back terribly if you had to be killed. He's very protective of me, dear Jahan,' she continued, setting a hand on the giant's shoulder that served to return the weapon back to its sheath. 'Where were we? Yes, Edom, the First of His Line. When I met him he was calling himself Samite, though I very much doubt that was ever his real name. A runaway from the plantations, according to the men I sent to look in on the matter, slipped off with a passing merchant, preferred a life on the roads to one in the fields. By the time he reached Aeleria he'd morphed into one of those countless street-corner visionaries one finds wriggling round the Senate Hall, hoping to trade future prospects for coin in the moment. He was immodest and pushy, but he spoke well, and he gave the strong impression of believing what he said. There was some hint of promise. I cleaned him up, I gave him a stipend and helped him return to the Roost to peddle his dreams. In truth he's achieved far more for himself than I'd ever thought him capable of. Had you told me ten years ago that this clipped-copper hustler would have been instrumental in the overthrow of the Eternal, the dream of hungry-eyed man for the better part of for ever . . .' She smiled, shrugged. 'I admit freely, that was beyond the range of my vision. But that's what it is, you see. You set a hundred plots within motion in the vague hopes that two or five of them might take hold. Like scattering seed in the dust.'

Pyre's body continued in its rhythm, moving forward by momentum and reflex, feet rising and falling without any conscious intent, which was good because in that moment Pyre found that he could not hold within his mind even the simplest of thoughts, and they walked another hundred steps before he managed to respond. 'Madness,' he said, convincing no one. 'You would suggest you developed the creed of the Five-Fingered? That it was your hand that has brought about the dawn?'

'Not everything,' Eudokia admitted, 'only the wiser bits. I was not, for instance, made aware of Edom's decision to have you killed until the deed had already been attempted. Though of course that proved fortuitous enough in the end. More proof, as if it was needed, that to be wise is not to be omniscient, that we all follow along in the tread of history.'

Pyre had been awake for perhaps seventy of the last seventy-two hours. He had raised the standard of rebellion in the very heart of the Roost, and defended that standard with such vigour as to have stalemated the demons themselves. He had come to or near to the final culmination of his dreams. He could no longer think with very much clarity. 'What are you talking about?'

'You are careful, yes boy? You are clever? You move through the city as a fish through the rivers? Did you not think to ask how the custodians knew of your location? To be certain enough as to bring in the assistance of an Eternal?'

'The Birds have spies everywhere.'

'Everywhere, yes, everywhere, exactly. They have spies in your bedroom and your chamber pot, they have spies within the inner council itself. One member of the inner council in particular, who heard your name on every man's lips, scarred by strangers on alley walls. Every revolution needs its martyrs, and who better than Pyre, the First of His Line? Cut down in the prime of his strength, and the city needing to avenge him? Pyre, the First of His Line, brave and strong and above all, loyal?'

The truth slid slowly, comfortably, neatly into place. He thought now that perhaps he had already known, known and refused to consider it.

'The Five-Fingers,' Eudokia said, interrupting his thoughts. 'And what will you call yourselves now?'

'What?'

'The Five-Fingers, to contrast with those less generously endowed. What happens when there is nothing here in the Roost, nothing across the breadth and length of the world, that can walk and speak and hate as men except for man himself? It is a concept given definition by its opposite, without whom it will wither and collapse.'

'I hadn't thought of it.'

'Edom has, I assure you. Why be a prophet when you can be a king? Someone has to be in charge, of course; or did you suppose the death of the Eternal would usher in a new age of enlightenment, that without its ancient enemy mankind would have no need for line or law or leader? The Eternal did not teach us to kill, Pyre, the First of His Line. Nor to desire, not to lust, nor to hate. Their annihilation will save no man from the sins which haunt him. There must be someone who can

Daniel Polansky

stand above the fray, who can keep his evil in check.' She
shrugged. 'Perhaps too great a task. Who can focus it, at least.
Edom, needless to say, would be that someone. It was that which
he was thinking of when he revealed your location to the
Cuckoos, the night you killed the Lord of the Ebony Towers.
He was thinking of your name, and how to murder it before it
grew too large.'

'Why would you tell me this?'

'Really, child, isn't it obvious? Because Edom is too slippery a
character to build atop, and I'd rather be dealing with you than
I would with him. And because now that your eyes have been
opened, now that you understand who it is that you've sworn
obedience towards, this man who has sought your death, you
will be sure to do the same of his – though, I suspect, with more
success.'

'You're lying,' he said, though it might have been a question.

'A pointless affectation, dishonesty. For the weak and less
than clever, a vice we sowers of discord have little reason to
indulge. Quite the opposite, in fact. Do you wish to see the
towers torn asunder, to see blood run in the streets? Give every
man true knowledge of his neighbour. The world would become
an abattoir within the hour.'

A band of hooligans, downslope thugs making their first excursion above their home Rung in search of plunder and rapine,
came out from one of the alleyways, saw Eudokia in her finery
and laughed nastily. One of them carried a rug over one shoulder,
woven of silk and threaded gold, one of them carried a large urn
that seemed made of pure silver, one of them held a stout length
of wood and the two others bits of sharpened metal. Flush with
the day's violence and the coming certainty of more, they did
not seem to notice Pyre standing beside her.

'What have we here?' asked the one holding the club, a few
years younger than Pyre, taller but thinner. A recent discovery
of the simple efficacy of violence had made him very bold, but
his eyes went wide at Pyre's snarl, and the following blow sent
him halfway to his knees, and before he had reached them Pyre's

blade was out from its sheath and its point perilously close to the downed child.

'I am Pyre, the First of His Line, and this woman is under my protection, and by Enkedri the next thing out of your mouth will be an apology or what follows will be your life's blood.'

Damp red appeared on his lips, fear in the corners of his eyes. He swallowed hard, and held his hands up before him, the club forgotten in the mud of the thoroughfare. 'Forgive me, mistress,' he said, standing and backing down the way he'd come, his friends quick to follow him.

'You grow to it already,' Eudokia said, smiling.

40

The battle that Bas had missed while storming the Roost would go down in history as the Salvation. In fact history is the wrong word – it skipped swiftly past history and moved directly into legend, bards' songs and mummers' tales and the games of children. For generations and centuries to come boys would relive it with sticks as swords and broom handles as spears, argue over who would play the demons, who would play Konstantinos, the Gentleman Lion, who would play the Caracal, his red-handed subordinate. It could be compared to no other human conflict—for a corollary one needed to reach towards religion, to the great conflict that Enkedri and his siblings had fought before the beginning of time, against the chthonic forces that had hoped to dethrone him. This battle that had already, in the hours since it had been fought, attained an almost mythical status, that had firmly established Konstantinos – so far as popular opinion was concerned, and is there anything else that matters? – as the foremost captain of the age, that would once again confirm Bas as the Empire's greatest champion, even though he had not actually fought in it, that a thousand thousand braggarts and liars and fools from across the continent would claim to have participated in, this epic triumph, this signal victory, had lost the Aelerians five soldiers for every Other that was killed, the blood of fifteen thousand men watering the summer fields.

And among this innumerable dead – perhaps not innumerable; you could count them, if for some reason such a task appealed to you, and you had a few dozen hours to spend looking over the corpses – was Isaac, Bas's oldest friend.

Bas could get no clear information about what had happened to him. A pentarche said that he had seen him ridden down in the first charge of the demons, another insisted that this was not possible, that the adjutant had rallied them after the third, when things looked all but lost, had led them surging forward into the heart of the Other front. Mostly the men of the Thireenth just shrugged and shook their heads sadly. How could anyone be expected to keep track of a single corpse, among such a vast assemblage? You might as well ask follow the passage of a drop of water through a river, through a bay, through the ocean.

Konstantinos had evacuated his tent, every spread of canvas being needed to tend to the wounded, and still there was not enough and not nearly enough, long rows of the injured waiting to be treated, limbs stacked upon each other like firewood, left unveiled against the sun, which was, kindly and according to its fashion, dimming beneath the horizon. Bas found the Protostrator standing beneath a peach tree, a short way out from what had been his sleeping quarters and was now a silk-lined cenotaph. The greatest victory in the history of Aeleria seemed to have done the man very little good. He looked exhausted – he looked more than exhausted, he looked close to collapse. He did not bother to rise when he saw Bas, made do with a vague wave of his hand.

'Hail, God-Killer,' he said, and he dropped his arm back down, as if even this much had been too much effort. 'I'm afraid that sobriquet is no longer so rare as it once was.'

'Congratulations,' Bas said, not really meaning it.

'Yes,' Konstantinos said, not really meaning it either. 'I take it the fact that we faced four thousand Birds instead of six was your doing?'

'It was,' Bas said. 'The Roost is in open rebellion. There are none on the lower Rungs who dare show for the Eternal. Our allies there have performed as promised.'

'And the tower?'

'Will hold,' Bas said confidently. If there had been any chance otherwise Bas would not have left, for in the end there was nothing to him but duty, or perhaps that had been his defining feature for so long that he could not imagine himself doing anything else. Regardless, he had only descended from the Spire after the first wave of reinforcements had arrived from below, when it bristled with victorious hoplitai and the fractured remnants of the Eternal had returned to their homes at the top of the Roost for what was certain to be the last time. 'The force I led into the city has now been supplemented by two more contingents of soldiers, as per the plan. There are a thousand hoplitai on the First Rung, and there will be two thousand before morning. Soon there will be enough to make a raid on the surrounding castles. Not that I suppose it'll matter by then.'

'No,' Konstantinos agreed. 'It'll end tomorrow. Who's in charge?'

'Hamilcar, the Dycian.'

'And why are you not with them?'

Bas shrugged. 'Someone needed to report. And I suppose I wished to be there at the end.'

Neither said anything for a while; they stood quietly, listening to the screaming coming from the tents, the sawbones with their hacksaws heating in the fire, the stray dogs collecting outside, lapping up the blood, carrying away loose cuts of man meat.

'How many survived, do you suppose?' Bas asked.

Konstantinos shrugged. 'A thousand, perhaps more. When it was clear the day was lost, the Prime managed to cut his way out and flee back to the Roost.'

Was one of those Einnes, Bas wondered? Was she at the peak

of the city just now, engaged in whatever desperate debate occupied the remnants of Those Above, searching for some dim means of escape, or accepting their bloody fate? Or was her corpse even now rotting amidst the vast ocean of dead, a crow pecking at her eyes?

'I'd have thought they'd have died on the battlefield,' Konstantinos said. 'Rather than flee. Is there any chance they will try and make terms? Or take up position in the city, fortify the approach and make us starve them out?'

'They won't make terms, even if they thought we might accept them, which we wouldn't. They'll die tomorrow, outside the walls,' Bas said, somehow confident. 'They're just figuring out how to do it.'

'Yes.'

'I'd like to take charge of the Thirteenth.'

'Only fitting,' Konstantinos said after a moment. 'Tell Nikephoros I gave the order.'

Bas nodded. Another long pause.

'What was it like inside?' Konstantinos asked.

'Beautiful,' Bas said finally.

'I thought it would be,' Konstantinos said, gazing distantly at the Roost. 'I thought it would have to be. I'm sorry about your adjutant,' he added, as an afterthought.

'Yes.'

'He had lots of company.'

'No. We all go alone, at the end.'

41

That night the Roost ran red.

Blood gathered in little pools on cobblestone streets and leached into the rich black soil of the public gardens. Blood ran in trickles down alleyways and in torrents down the main thoroughfares. Blood soaked through silk bedsheets and plush carpets, blood dripped off the faces of screaming men and weeping women, blood clotted and dried and grew cold beside a thousand thousand bodies, dockers, tradesmen, porters, merchants, custodians, milliners, carpenters, cooks and maids and servants, brute thugs and crime lords, wealthy merchants and civic leaders. Rich crimson blood, and blood a shade darker, though blood all the same.

Blood leaked out the nose and mouth and punctured stomach of a tradesman on the Fifth Rung— no supporter of the Birds, either open or covert, at least any more than virtually everyone had been in the day before the world was upended. But he had been wealthier, and was not that wealth evidence of complicity with the demons? Certainly the men laughing and standing atop his shattered corpse seemed to think so, though they were unlettered porters who had heard no word of the truth. On the Fourth Rung a custodian barricaded himself inside his house, he and his wife and his three children and the suckling that still nursed at her breast, propping every item of furniture he owned against the door frame, holding his ferule should anyone manage to break through. In the end it did no good though, the mob outside firing the house, the custodian and his wife and his three children and the suckling that still nursed at her breast. In the Perennial Exchange on the Third a woman sat amidst the ruins of the shop she had spent a lifetime building, dresses and shawls trampled in the dust, the mob that had passed through not bothering even to steal them, destruction itself a joy, and thinking on it for some time she went to search for a pair of scissors, deciding she had no taste for what was to come. On the Second Rung were such seeds of depravity, of rapine and cruelty and foulness as to make the Self-Created blush, as to make him turn away, as to make him wonder in what moment of foolishness he had seen fit to decree that base matter ought ever to organise itself into thinking creatures, irrespective of the number of their digits.

And on the First? On the First?

In between dropping Eudokia off at her safe house and finding himself at the Third, the afternoon had turned to early evening had turned firmly and fully to night. How had Pyre spent those hours? He could not say, not then nor at any point after. They were stripped from his memory in their entirety, never to return, a spot of history obliterated, only faint impressions of crimson, and of children crying, and of corpses left to rot in the moonlight. Downslope the battle raged onward, Pyre's minions continuing on despite the absence of their leader, the victory clear within sight. They had succeeded, they had succeeded beyond their wildest dreams, had tapped deep into that simmering vein of rage of which Pyre himself had always been the truest and most vivid example. There were not a thousand official members of the Five-Fingered, and only four hundred of them able to wield a blade – four hundred two days earlier, of course; who could say what remnant of that now remained? A tiny drop of passion in a vast sea of indifference, or seeming indifference. And yet at a word, at the slightest suggestion, at the first glimmer of resistance, the city had risen up against the demons, giving vent to long-simmering hatred. Surely this could only be taken as evidence of the justice of the cause, that the truth was written, faded but legible, on the heart of all men – that freedom was theirs by right, that they need only be strong enough to take it.

Or was it otherwise? Was it simply that most men are constrained by routine more than by any sense of morality, and that should these basic covenants ever break down, should it occur to them that they might not go to work in the morning, that they might not pay homage to their superiors and to the civil authority set over them, should this revelation ever strike, then blood and massacre and death are certain to follow?

Pyre could not say, Pyre did not know. Pyre stalked through the city as if through the body of some ancient dying god, its viscera and intestines and sweetmeats on display, the raw rich red flesh rendered skinless and visible. He had one hand on his short sword and his eyes were wounded pinpricks of open hate, and the thugs and petty bandits gave him a wide berth.

Pyre had been in front of Edom's safe house for a long time before he realised that was where he was standing. A building on the Third, nothing important about it except what it held, part of the elaborate shell game that Pyre had been playing for the better part of two years, since being made responsible for the security of the Five-Fingered, since being made responsible for the security of Edom, the First of His Line.

Two hard knocks, two soft knocks, one final blow with his full fist, the door shuddering in response. It opened swiftly to reveal an expectant Redemption, who smiled when he saw Pyre, smiled and offered the salute, though Pyre did not return it.

'Brother Pyre,' he said, 'We've had no news – how is the war downslope? Have you heard anything of our brothers outside the walls? Or on the First?'

Pyre brushed inside. Only meant to be used for a few days during the rebellion, the house was mostly unfurnished, and the large parlour that Pyre had entered was empty except for a rough wooden table, occupied by three members of the Dead Pigeons, brothers to Pyre in all but name, trusted implicitly and implicitly trusting. 'Victorious on all fronts,' he said in a curiously neutral monotone, and before this announcement gave way to general jubilation he asked, 'Where is Edom?'

'On the top floor, with Steadfast,' Redemption answered. 'He is unable to sleep.'

'Grim is gathering men,' Pyre said quietly. 'Gather your weapons and join him at his headquarters on the Fourth.'

'Where on the fourth?'

'At the Hallowed Gate, near the Sweetwater canal. Do you know it?'

'Yes.' Redemption had been Dormouse, a lanky youth from the Straights, and Pyre had sworn him in to the Five-Fingered, Pyre had made the cut and said the words, Pyre had cheered loudest when he had taken on his new name. For two years he had followed Pyre's orders with obedient joy, and he struggled to turn against custom. 'This was not part of the plan.'

'Who makes the plan?'

'You do, Brother Pyre,' Redemption said, the moment of uncertainty past. A good soldier Redemption, as Pyre had been. 'Until the age to come.'

To come, to come, always to come. Edom's guards left swiftly, pursuing their phantom errand downslope, and the door had not shut before Pyre was ascending the back staircase.

Steadfast stood outside the entrance to Edom's cell, a swelling bruise on his temple, and now that he could finally admit it to himself Pyre hated him as much as he had ever hated anyone, near as much as he had hated the Four-Fingered or the custodians, simpering and obsequious and without purpose, a parasite. You could speak of the unity of the species, but cannot a man hate his brother? Steadfast opened his mouth to say something, something cowardly most likely, superior and condescending, and Pyre's blade slipped free of his sheath and then across a throat, one swift motion as Rhythm had taught Thistle in those years long ago. Steadfast died quickly. Steadfast died easily. Steadfast died as men die. Pyre barely noticed, the corpse sliding to his feet. He did not bother even to clean his blade, stepping over the body and opening the door.

A small room in the high corner of the building, a not particularly lovely view of the Third Rung beyond. Edom sat beside the window, looking down at what he had caused – he and Pyre, now that it was perhaps not a question of pride but of guilt Pyre could admit to that, could recognise his part in the thing, though it was a small one, though it had never been more than as a puppet or perhaps a hunting hound, duty done and then back in the kennels.

'My son,' Edom said, in that same rich voice which had instructed and explained, which had forgiven, which had offered purpose and meaning to lives which had never known either. 'I give you greeting on the first day of the new epoch, at the beginning of the future you have fought so hard to see.'

'Not the beginning,' Pyre said, the sword in his right hand weeping blood onto Edom's floor, Edom unaware of or uninterested by the threat, or at least giving no sign of it. 'The end.'

'Every beginning is an end. Today will be the beginning of an age undreamed of by your fathers, who knew only slavery and subjugation. And today will be the end of the demons, and of the perversion they have created.'

'Not the demons only,' Pyre said 'Not the demons alone.'

From the open window could be heard a distant scream, like the trilling of a summer lark, evidence of some minor and unnoticed atrocity, one of the countless infinity that were playing out across the Roost.

'You've been listening to the lies of that Aelerian whore,'

Edom said, the profanity unexpected and out of character, the first evidence of concern. 'I had thought you cleverer than that.'

'The truth comes to those who will hear it,' Pyre said quietly.

'And what is the truth, Pyre so wise? Do inform me, please.'

'That you are no prophet,' Pyre said, 'and I only chief among fools. The word, the Five-Fingered, all of it nothing but a ploy to bring the Roost beneath the sway of the Aelerians. The Dead Pigeons nothing but deluded foot soldiers of the Commonwealth, dying to expand their empire.'

A second scream, and the smile that had slipped off Edom's face returned. 'It would be a simpler thing if that was the case, and you always did prefer simplicity. But it is not, Pyre. My word filled the empty stomachs of thousands, my word gave meaning and purpose to men who had none. Without my word you'd be a downslope thug, no different than any other, a thief and a murderer.'

'And what am I now, Edom? If I had spent a lifetime as a criminal I could not have dreamed of such savagery as I have seen this night.'

'What do you imagine a newborn looks like? Powdered and perfumed, burbling in joyous contentment? In blood it comes, choking and gasping for air, its first sensation pain, its first instinct fear. And yet that babe will grow to manhood, that babe will do things of greatness and of value. As will this new age, Pyre, the First of His Line. As will this new age.'

So far Pyre's voice had been low and unsteady, and his sword hung limp at his side, but at this last line it flew up suddenly, scattering Steadfast's blood to the far corner of the room. 'Lies!' he screamed. 'You would say anything for another few seconds of life. There is nothing to you but falsehood!'

'Still a child, after everything you've done, black and white, and nothing in between.' Edom shook his head and leaned for a moment towards the window. 'From where I stand just now, Pyre, I can see an alleyway, and the back of a building, and the teasing first light of dawn. If I stood somewhere else, I'd see something different. There is not truth, Pyre, there are only truths, particular rather than universal.'

'Yes, the particular and nothing but – Edom and Edom alone the only thing of importance. You would have me dead,' Pyre said, hating the quiver in his voice and continuing over it roughly. 'You sold me to the demons because you thought I might threaten to overtake you as first slave to the Aelerians! Such slaughter, such blood, and it will change nothing! Nothing!' Pyre was screaming every word though Edom accepted it unflinching, his smile like a Roost-forged shield. 'We've traded one yoke for another!'

'What did you suppose? That the new age would be a golden one, bereft of misfortune, of inequality, of pain or of suffering? That you could murder your way into paradise?' Edom shook his great leonine head, the smile stretching to fill it. 'The new world will be the same as the old. The weak and the foolish and the ill-fortuned will suffer, the strong and the cruel will flourish. Those Above will die, and Those Below, or some portion of them, will take their place, will rise to the first Rung and rule with no greater kindness than their predecessors. Paradise for some, a hell for others. As it was, as it will be. The Roost will be the greatest city in Aeleria, and you will be chancellor, or mayor or whatever they decide to call you. Wealth undreamed of, an entire castle for you, and an army of slaves, sleeping where the demons slept, eating where they—'

He was speaking as the steel entered his flesh and even continued on for an instant thereafter, though the words were garbled and indistinct. And who could blame him? This man whom life had taught that if he could only talk long enough he might convince anyone of anything, might convince the canals to run upward, the mountain to crumble, the blood not to seep through his wound.

This last at least was false. When the light went finally from Edom's eyes he was close enough for Pyre to taste his dying breath, the misery and the fear. Through the window, sanguine and bright, spilled the first morning of the new age, indistinct from that which had preceded it.

42

The last sun Bas would ever see rose high and clear in the sky, flooded the valley with light, rendering each detail fine and clear, neither cloud cover nor illusion left to obscure his vision. From atop his mount at the of the vanguard he could make out the ranks of cavalry, the packed force of the Eternal, the final charge of Those Above. Could see the strange and exotic curves of their armour, like holiday masks or the drawings of a lunatic. Could see their lances, many-pronged and each the length of a short sword but far sharper. Behind them the Roost rose in the distance, riches unknowable and vast, an array of wealth that Bas would never hold and would not have known what to do with had he grasped it.

'They look magnificent,' Nikephoros said. 'They know they're dying.' The interim head of the Thirteenth had made no difficulties over Bas's reassuming his title. It was only appropriate that the Caracal would be here for the end – it was part of the gathering magnificence of the moment, one of which every member of the Aelerian army, from Protostrator on down, was cognisant.

Looking at him Bas thought of Isaac, rotting somewhere nearby, unburied though not unmourned. Of Isaac's rough eyes and savaged ears, of his heart that was – not decent, none of them could claim that, but no worse than he had to be, no worse than life had made him. But Bas didn't think about him for very long. There wasn't any point in thinking about the dead. It didn't do them any good, and it did you less.

Had Bas been the leader of the forces opposite, they would be tearing up cobblestone for barricades, setting fire to the houses by the entrance, sending any humans within fleeing for cover. And then he would have taken up place behind it, daring the hoplitai to come forward. The Aelerian pikemen were more dangerous in defence than attack, and their numbers would count for less within the confines of the city, funnelled down alleyways and narrow side streets. True, the partisans would be active, but it beat any of the alternatives. It would not have worked for ever – the Eternal needed food, as did every other thing of flesh, and they would not get it with their lands in uproar, with Konstantinos sending outriders to pillage the slave plantations that had kept the city fed. But it would work for a time.

A moot point, as of course there was no sign of fortification, and the Eternal would do as they had done the day before, as they had done in every day of battle back and back and back down to the roots of time, back to the dawn of the world, back to the beginnings. The valley would shudder and pulse with the beat of their great cavalry charge, and then that charge would bend and flatten and break against the rows of pikes, and then the life's blood of a species would water the high grass of late summer. When the moon rose it would shine down upon the corpses of ten thousand humans and upon the final remnant of the species that had, two days earlier, credible claim on the ownership of the world.

Bas took a long sip from his waterskin. In the distance he could make out the Prime's sigil fluttering from the centre of the host, as high as a full-grown elm, a thing of sterling silver and peacock plumage, the same as had flown above Red Fields twenty years earlier, and the Lamentation three centuries before that, which would be scattered in the mud before the sunset. And beneath it a sea of personal standards, a fluttering breeze of red lions and silver foxes and great, twisting, verdant dragons, and perhaps – though it was impossible to say for sure from such a distance – a white heron.

Bas took another sip, swirled the water around in his mouth, spat it into the ground. It would be the last time water would touch his lips. Many things now were happening to him for the last time, and since waking up that morning he had become peculiarly cognisant of each one – his last piss, his last morsel of food.

The wind blew and the Eternal came with it, the only sound to be heard – though this was loud enough, this was almost deafening – was of the thundering hooves of their horses, the valley bright with their streamers and their pennants and their flags. Hamilcar and the better portion of his archers were still in the Roost, but even had the army had their full complement it would not have much mattered; the Eternal came too swift for a decent volley, and their armour was sufficient protection against any but the luckiest shot.

The hoplitai gave way; they could not but otherwise, there was nothing that could have withstood such a charge, not had the Eternal thought to punch their way through the side of a mountain. Lances bit into human flesh, warhorses crushed the skulls of men beneath their heels, men screamed and horses screamed, uncanny counterpoint to the silence of their killers. The charge cut deep into the the Aelerian line, through the first packed ranks, surging further, further, further, then slowing, and then stopping altogether, horses faltering atop writhing human flesh, skewered by pike tip, demons punctured by spear and cut down by short sword. They had never learned to war, Bas could

see that now, as individuals they were marvellously skilled but
of tactics and strategy they had no real conception. One good
charge, that was all they were capable of, that was all they had
ever needed to offer. And though none of the demons would go
down easily, still they would go down, for the thema had the
taste of blood in their mouths, the fresh-faced innocents Bas
had led out of the capital three years prior replaced by savage-
eyed iron-capped butchers, every one of them. And the most
powerful element in the demons' arsenal, their mystique, their
seeming invincibility, was shattered now, shattered beyond repair.
They weren't gods any more, only things of flesh and of blood,
their strength and their endurance more of a reason to bring
one down, and what a thing to tell your children, that you were
there when a species died! That you took part in the end of a
world!

Their enemies' battle plan being so simple, the Aelerians'
own needed to be no more advanced – the central mass of
pikemen having broken the Others' great charge, Bas and the
cavalry would strike from the wings, a vast enfilading manoeuvre
against which there could be no defence. Bas waited until the
demons' vanguard had shuddered to a halt, their comrades
behind slowing, and then he bellowed and surged forward,
forgetting his duties as an officer, caught up entirely in the
sublime rush of death. He saw rising above the centre of
the Eternal host the Prime's great standard, and he made for
it with all the haste his beast was capable of, stamping the
pointed narrow of his boots against horseflesh, goading it
onward, for Bas would not live through the day and neither
would his beast, by the gods and not the beast alone. Two
thousand men following close behind him, and another two would
come in from the opposing flank, the others swamped beneath
an ocean of men.

Bas had been the first off the mark but he was no great
horseman and by the time he reached his first opponent, a
giant clad in armour of cinnabar and cerulean, the demon was
already surrounded by three Aelerian cavalry, one hoping to

distract its attention while the other two circled round, but the demon was too swift, its blade whirling from one to the other. Fools! Fools, for there could be no contending with the Eternal in speed or strength or technique but only savagery, and Bas roared and spurred his beast harder, through a brief gap and past his countrymen and towards the demon and then still roaring into the demon and the both of them tumbling through the air and then the impact of the ground and then, for a time, nothing.

When Bas came awake the sun was bright against his eyes, and the Eternal was dead, and both horses were dead, and there was blood matting his long hair down against his face. Standing, his vision dipped and pitched for an instant before settling into equilibrium, and his ankle was not moving as it generally did, and Bas barely noticed either, pulled his sword from off the corpse of his mount. With nowhere to ride, with the vast weight of the Aelerians closing round them, unhorsed and unused to defence, the final flower of the Eternal made a desperate last stand beneath the gonfalon of their leader, and Bas sprinted towards it as a bee to flower, or a moth to flame.

An Eternal blocked his path, its suit of armour pale blue and bright argent, and overlaying its face was the Roost-forged steel of some hideous chimera. In one hand it carried an ungainly looking single-edged broadsword and in the other it carried its twin; one would be the feint and one would deliver the killing blow, and Bas knew that he had no hope of defending against both and did not attempt it. A toss of the dice, a gambler's luck, the left was the feint and the right the true attack, and Bas deflecting it and the counterstroke ate away at a gap in the Eternal's armour and at the gold skin and pale bone beneath it. It did not scream, they never screamed, but it gave a step and then it gave another, and when it thought to give a third it slipped or nearly slipped on a corpse, human or Eternal Bas could not say for certain, there being little enough difference between dead flesh. But Bas was not slow to take advantage of the error, the first strike ringing off the demon's guard but the second catching it just above the breastbone and the next severing its throat, blood spattering briskly onto Bas's blade and onto his chain hauberk and against his face, blood rich on his jaw and his tongue.

Beneath the Prime's standard he could see a fluttering pennant of white, and he sprinted towards it, and he roared greeting though it was lost amidst the tumult, amidst the screams and the steel that rang against steel. The battle had devolved into the final mad melee, which would go on for long hours, no longer any attempt at strategy, just groups of hoplitai surrounding and savaging and then slaughtering their betters, like hounds bringing down a wolf. Amidst it he ran to her as he had promised he would, hoping she saw him, hoping she was doing the same.

Another blocked his way then, small by the standards of the Eternal, just slightly taller than Bas. Squaring up against it Bas saw or thought he saw that old familiar glint in its eye, that glint that Bas had thought no Other could possess, that fear that Bas had seen in a hundred men across a dozen different lands. He – or perhaps she, Bas could not see through the helmet – could only see the eyes through the visor, oblong slots of yellow, and through them at the terror beneath – moved backwards, playing for time, time that Bas would never allow, coming forward swiftly, swiftly, swiftly. And if they could feel fear, might they feel love also, might that not be possible? And still pondering this question in the dim recesses of his mind Bas feinted low and then reared back and thrust the narrow point of his sword through the visor and those eyes that had felt fear and perhaps love and now, as a certainty, nothing at all.

Bas stumbled suddenly, faltering first and only then feeling the sensation of pain, howling and going down on one knee. Above him stood an Eternal carrying a crescented hand axe slick with Bas's blood, and he turned then to deal with another hoplitai, thinking surely and not unreasonably that he must have killed Bas, that no human could have survived so savage a blow, paying for this miscalculation with his life, Bas's ruptured side straining in agony but he was upright almost as soon as he had gone down, and he planted his sword into the demon's back and shoved halfway to the hilt. Spine severed, puking blood, still it tried to grab Bas with a backward hand, flailing aimlessly and as if of its own volition, Bas managing to hold the thing off until it gasped finally, dead as all things die, and slid down the length of Bas's sword and into the mud, and Bas continued onward without a pause though his wounds no longer allowed him to run.

She was close now, he could see her on her great horse, strangely bent blade turning swift and terrible, and how beautiful she was, like a bolt of lightning on the Marches, like a newborn shrieking, like something ephemeral and transitory, like something that was not long for life! The first blow fell against her back and her shoulder, bit deep but did nothing to slow her. She turned and disposed of the cavalryman who had attacked her, a movement of her blade severing his neck from his shoulders, the skull itself tumbling and spraying blood on Einnes and Einnes's horse and the ground below, and Bas realised he was cheering.

In between them two human soldiers were fighting an Eternal and he shouldered them aside unthinking, bearing down on the demon they had been facing like a force of nature rather than a living thing, like a rain-swelled river overspilling its banks. The demon was short and squat by the standards of its race, which was to say that it was as tall as one Bas and as wide as two, the sun reflecting so bright off its plate that Bas could not make out the colour, and wielding in two hands a great mace that must have weighed the same as an anvil, richly flanged and flecked with bits of bone and brain. There was no time for subtlety nor strategy, Bas would be gone in a moment and she would not last much longer either, and Bas hurled himself, feinting low and then twisting the great blade of his sword. But the Eternal anticipated it, shifted out of the way of Bas's assault and returned it with a speed that no human could match, not even Bas, and it was only by the barest thread that he managed to deflect it, the flanged head of the mace striking against Bas's blade, the Roost-forged steel that he had thought unbreakable cracking at the midpoint. Brought down on one knee from the force of the blow, holding a hilt and an arm's length of blade beyond it, bleeding and dying but not dead, no, not dead yet; only one was deserving of that signal honour, and as the Other raised its mace to deliver the final killing blow Bas roared one final time and came upright, moving as if the lifeblood that was dribbling and pouring out from his wound had served only to slow him, and free of it now he could move faster, and that half of his sword that Bas still held disappeared again and again into the chest of the Other, three times, five, and then Bas was stumbling over the corpse and rushing forward to meet her, shouldering aside hoplitai like jackals closing in on the kill, bellowing like a wounded bull, ignorant of the blood that was filling his boots, uncognisant of the torn muscle and of the jagged length of bone, his bone, sticking through flesh, his flesh.

Bas did not see what brought her horse down, that magnificent and terrible creature, streaks of red along its flanks and then one last horrific scream and then it stumbled. And she so swift and so graceful, so perfect, that she managed somehow to disentangle herself from it and land standing, her weapon still in her hand, turning it on the mass of men surging around her, the blade rising and descending and rising and descending and then she was lost in the press.

Bas screamed and surged forward but there were too many, of his kind and of hers, and both serving to separate them. Something struck him in the side, he lashed out at whoever had delivered it, not knowing whether it was man or Other, not caring, flesh being flesh being flesh. So close, just inside the next ring, and if he could only make it to her, if he could only die at her hand, or she at his, or they together.

But he never made it. On his knees again, the light dimming around him, and it didn't hurt so much any more and he knew he was breathing his last. 'Einnes,' he said, the name of his mother, and the half of the sword he still held, and the only thing that he had ever loved. 'Einnes,' he said again, the blood coming swiftly now, swiftly and unstaunched. 'Einnes.'

43

It was whim, it was folly, it was a mad and uncharacteristic ambition that took Eudokia Aurelia from the sanctuary the Five-Fingers had offered her and into the chaos of the First Rung that final day. For once there was no purpose in her movement; for once, for the first time in years and decades, she gave free rein to a moment's passion, rather than meticulously executing a task that she had previously planned. The men Pyre had left to guard her protested her decision, though unsuccessfully and not for very long – it was a rare circumstance indeed in which Eudokia did not ultimately attain what she wanted; the day itself was firm and finest evidence of this.

Ascending upslope, Eudokia's robes and jewellery and age caught the attention of a group of men coming out of a ransacked building, holding bits of metal and brickbats, eyes locking on to her and seeing prey, mouths opening, though before insult could be offered Jahan's blade was out and the lead man – boy, really – was handless and screaming, his confederates staring at his stump and considering revenge, though not seriously and not for very long. After that Jahan did not bother to return his talwar to its sheath, blood leaking down to the hilt and onto his hands and onto the cobblestones, and they had no further trouble.

The violence, the anarchy, the immolation; none of it came as any surprise. Eudokia was a woman who had long lost any illusions about what might be expected of a person when they suppose they will never be called to account for their actions. And it was more than greed, lust, the simple basic cruelty of all living things. The mass that was ascending and would continue to build, a great river of flesh and steel and hate flowing upslope in violation of the natural law, they had legitimate grievance, their loathing was well-earned. There is an understandable if sadly specious notion that suffering breeds wisdom or at least restraint, that having felt the bite of the lash one is slower to distribute it. Alas. In Eudokia's experience, pain only leads to pain, and a kicked dog is first to bite.

Lost somewhere amidst the rising slaughter was her nephew, absent since the morning prior when he had walked weeping out of her garden. Eudokia had ordered a number of the Dead Pigeons stationed at her old quarters in case he chose to return, though even while doing so she had known it was pointless. Indeed, with that grim-eyed certainty that had allowed her to rise to the summit not only of her own nation but of the world, that perceptive pessimism, that willingness to stare full-bore at cruel reality without blinking, Eudokia knew that she would not see Leon again. He was dead, one of the tens of thousands or hundreds of thousands of corpses caused by the extraordinary explosion of force that Eudokia had conspired to release. Or he was taking part in the violence himself, vicious recompense for the savagery done to his paramour, his innocence lost in the futile melee below. Eudokia did not think this last was the case but you could never tell, we are all capable of more evil than we dream possible. Regardless, he would never return to her – if he lived, he would flee the city on his own terms, he would lose himself in the vast army of exiles or he would take ship to some distant land, to mourn one woman and curse another until the end of his days. Stepping lightly beneath the cover of the budding dogwoods, Eudokia suffered a memory of the boy as he was when he first come to her, not yet ten, so blond as to be nearly translucent, trying his very best to be brave.

There were no guards on the gate to the First Rung, the custodians, or the Cuckoos; in this last moment it was clear that they deserved the pejorative, had fled, more desperate to escape the coming violence than even their fellow citizens. Apart from that, there was little immediate evidence of the end of the world. In curious contrast to the state of anarchic violence that existed throughout the rest of the Roost, the First Rung was quiet. If you had not known better, if you had not come through the slaughterhouse that had been made of paradise, if you were somehow unable to recognise the scent of fire on the wind, of burned wood and charred flesh, you might have supposed the place calm. The Eternal had descended en masse to the gates of the city, where they had already ridden or were soon to ride to their deaths, and their human servants were barricading themselves in their castles, or stuffing their most expensive belongings in the pockets of their cheapest clothes and fleeing downslope, hoping to lose themselves in the mob below. A false hope, Eudokia suspected – the reckoning to come would be thorough, and bloody, and brutal.

And it would come soon. By nightfall the first contingent of the great Aelerian army would be at the gates, and with the instincts of veteran campaigners, which was to say scavengers, thieves, rapists, they would make swiftly for the First Rung. The estates and castles of the Eternal would be picked clean as a corpse staked over an anthill, fortunes beyond imagining devolving to those hoplitai who had been fortunate or skilled enough to survive the slaughter. In ages hence, in fifty years or a hundred, there would be great fortunes sprung from this act of robbery, merchant houses and bankers and industrialists who could trace the roots of their wealth to a chunk of gold lifted off the facade of one of the Eternal's homes, to some or other work of art broken down to its constituent ore. Eudokia would, needless to say, be first among them, had already marked out the Red Keep as her own personal preserve. In a few moments she and Jahan would stake their claim to it, and none could suggest that she had not earned her share of the spoils.

But it seemed that in the interim the larger portion of the Roost had not yet screwed up the courage to approach the seat of their fallen gods. Eudokia continued her walk through the First, a warm afternoon turning to a pleasant evening, and for long moments the only sounds to be heard were the fall of her cane on the cobblestone. Midway through her perambulation Eudokia noticed that the canals were less full than they had been, by a third or perhaps more. Had she made her way to the Conclave she felt sure that she would discover the Source had gone dry, the apparatus that had kept the water flowing for millennia beyond recorded time stuttering to a halt. Perhaps Those Above had decided to destroy it rather than see it used by their freed slaves, or perhaps it was sabotage on the part of the Five-Fingered – or perhaps it was simply that some necessary bit of upkeep had not been performed, that without the integration of the two species working in harmony or at least concert, the Source and all the wondrous workings of the Roost would swiftly decay.

Eudokia did not go towards the Conclave. She had seen it already, in its full splendour, had no particular desire to visit a second time. In fact there was only one portion of the Roost with which Eudokia remained meaningfully unacquainted, that sliver which was set aside exclusively and without reservation for the sacred use of Those Above. What was it that turned her steps northward, towards the Cliffs of Silence? Did she have some inkling of what she would find there? Or was it simply that, having made conquest her lodestar and defining point, having burned incense and slaughtered men at its altar, she could not leave even this last remnant unconsumed? Forty minutes of walking took her to the far corner of the First, saw them prom-enading along a broad expanse of stone.

The cliffs were perhaps the only portion of the Roost that

the Eternal had not fundamentally altered, reshaped to suit their particular aesthetic, had left untouched as memory or memorial to a distant past when they had still wandered free about the world. A wild stretch of mountain peak that jutted out over the bay below, weathered by the storms and the wind, open to the sky. It might have been any length of high coastline along the coast – save for the collection of creatures that crowded the edge.

There were few of them, these last remnants of a species that had once owned the planet, these things which were near enough to gods to sometimes confuse the two. All who could shoulder weapons, the vast majority, were dead or dying at the foot of the mountain. Here at the summit were, so far as Eudokia could tell, only those unfit for combat, made so by youth or age or illness. Strange-looking children, the height of adolescents but with the same ageless eyes as their parents, hobbled elders assisted by or assisting them, here and there the swelled belly of a pregnant female. A line of them but not a long one, a hundred or perhaps a few more, their attention fixed exclusive and entire on the sea below. Extinction, like every other event in the long but not eternal lives of Those Above, was an artistic act – even from a distance Eudokia could see their costumes were elaborate and colourful, flowing prismatic robes, trailing silk and peacock feathers.

How long had they stood like that, Eudokia wondered? Greeting the sun one final time, bidding goodbye to existence? And then without any signal, verbal or visible, with that same curious synchronisation of which humans were incapable, like a skein of geese wheeling in flight, they began to move. Eudokia could not tell the sex of the creature or determine much detail, could only make it out as a member of its species, as a silhouette against the sun. It spread its arms, as if to engulf the enormity before and below, or as a baby bird takes a running start before throwing itself out into infinity, before its wings catch the wind and carry them off into the blue expanse ahead.

It did not fly. Male or female, child or elder, it did not fly.

The next came a moment behind, and the next just after, an unbroken chain of flesh, each dropping in an even rhythm, and then far below, too far for Eudokia to hear, the crash of bone against stone, blood diluting the seawater, a slick sheen of crimson atop the blue and white crash of foam. Though not for long, the sea taking everything, in the end.

Eudokia did not speak, but she watched, she kept her eyes open at the ongoing tragedy – or triumph. They were owed that much, these beings who she had driven to slaughter, this sacrifice to the new world she had built. She would bear witness to this thing she had caused.

And then it was over, the last pitching itself into oblivion as smoothly as the first, without a stutter of hesitation, one last bright spray of colour and then the void. A lifetime spent in service of this moment, endless laboured machinations, nations raised up and brought low, an unknowable quantity of corpses, all put towards this end. There were none alive now who could dispute it – she was triumphant, supreme, matchless. A barren mother on an empty throne.

ACKNOWLEDGEMENTS

When the first book came out, I was all like, 'man, acknowledgments, awesome! I get to mention all of my friends and acquaintances and the girl I'm dating and make cute in-jokes that only they get, *hahaha*.' But from there on out it was like, 'right, acknowledgments, make sure you don't leave anyone out or they'll get offended.' Anyway, here goes. Business wise; thanks to Chris Kepner, Oliver Johnson, Anne Perry, everyone at Hodder who keeps believing in me. Family wise, Mom, Dad, Dave/Alissa/Julian, Marisa, Mike, my grandmother, my aunts and uncles on both sides, my first cousins, my second cousin Jacob who gets a special shout out because he's adorable and loves my tattoo. Thanks to Sam and Elliot. Thanks to Will, John and Alex; you guys will get the next one. Thanks to Lisa for being the best British sister anyone ever had. Shout out to Will for marrying her. Andy Keogh for being an odd-looking Englishman. I've learned by this point not to thank any particular girl because by the time the book comes out you usually aren't talking anymore. Thanks to everyone who bought this and bothered to read it, not expecting their name to be here at the end. Cheers.

WANT MORE?

If you enjoyed this and would like to find out about similar books we publish, we'd love you to join our online SF, Fantasy and Horror community, Hodderscape.

Visit our blog site
www.hodderscape.co.uk

Follow us on Twitter
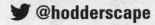 **@hodderscape**

Like our Facebook page
Hodderscape

You'll find exclusive content from our authors, news, competitions and general musings, so feel free to comment, contribute or just keep an eye on what we are up to. See you there!

Do you wish this wasn't the end?

Join us at www.hodder.co.uk, or follow us on
Twitter @hodderbooks to be a part of our community
of people who love the very best in books and reading.

Whether you want to discover more about a book
or an author, watch trailers and interviews, have the
chance to win early limited editions, or simply browse
our expert readers' selection of the very best books,
we think you'll find what you're looking for.

And if you don't,
that's the place to tell us what's missing.

We love what we do, and we'd love you to be part of it.

www.hodder.co.uk

@hodderbooks

HodderBooks

HodderBooks